MINE AFTER DARK

GANSETT ISLAND BOOK SERIES, BOOK 19

MARIE FORCE

Mine After Dark
Gansett Island Series, Book 19

By: Marie Force
Published by HTJB, Inc.
Copyright 2018. HTJB, Inc.
Cover Design: Diane Luger
Print Layout: Isabel Sullivan
E-book Formatting Fairies
ISBN: 978-1946136534

marieforce.com

View the McCarthy Family Tree here. marieforce.com/gansett/familytree/

View the list of Who's Who on Gansett Island here. marieforce.com/whoswhogansett/

View a map of Gansett Island. marieforce.com/mapofgansett/

The Gansett Island Series

Book 1: Maid for Love (*Mac & Maddie*)
Book 2: Fool for Love (*Joe & Janey*)
Book 3: Ready for Love (*Luke & Sydney*)
Book 4: Falling for Love (*Grant & Stephanie*)
Book 5: Hoping for Love (*Evan & Grace*)
Book 6: Season for Love (*Owen & Laura*)
Book 7: Longing for Love (*Blaine & Tiffany*)
Book 8: Waiting for Love (*Adam & Abby*)
Book 9: Time for Love (*David & Daisy*)
Book 10: Meant for Love (*Jenny & Alex*)
Book 10.5: Chance for Love, *A Gansett Island Novella* (*Jared & Lizzie*)
Book 11: Gansett After Dark (*Owen & Laura*)
Book 12: Kisses After Dark (*Shane & Katie*)
Book 13: Love After Dark (*Paul & Hope*)
Book 14: Celebration After Dark (*Big Mac & Linda*)
Book 15: Desire After Dark (*Slim & Erin*)
Book 16: Light After Dark (*Mallory & Quinn*)
Book 17: Victoria & Shannon (Episode 1)
Book 18: Kevin & Chelsea (Episode 2)
A Gansett Island Christmas Novella
Book 19: Mine After Dark (*Riley & Nikki*)
Book 20: Yours After Dark (*Finn McCarthy*)
Book 21: Trouble After Dark (*Deacon & Julia*) (*Coming Soon*)

More new books are alway in the works. For the most up-to-date list of what's available from the Gansett Island Series as well as series extras, go to marieforce.com/gansett.

CHAPTER 1

*R*iley McCarthy aligned the hydraulic nail gun with the
sheet of drywall held in place by his brother, Finn, and
nailed it to the wooden frame. *Bam, bam, bam.* Down one side, across
the top, down the other side, along the bottom. With that sheet
finished, they started on the next, positioning and securing it before
starting again. The rote nature of the work suited Riley's glum mood
as he listened to the January wind howl outside the new home of
McCarthy's Wayfarer, Gansett Island's shore dinner hall, event facility, beachfront bar and hotel.

The entire McCarthy family had come together to fund the
purchase of the run-down facility that occupied prime real estate
adjacent to the ferry landing. His cousin Mac's construction company
was handling the renovations, which would take most of the time they
had left in the off-season to get it ready for the summer. Riley and
Finn had come to Gansett for their cousin Laura's wedding fifteen
months ago and were still there, working for Mac as one project
rolled into another.

With the winter deep freeze keeping everyone in hibernation
mode lately, Riley had too much time to think about the direction of
his life, his career, his living situation, his love life—or lack thereof—

and whether he should move back to the mainland to shake things up. Not that he was unhappy on Gansett Island living with his brother, near their father, uncles, cousins and friends. He wasn't unhappy, but he was... out of sorts.

For more than a year, Riley had been content on the island. But in the last few months, something had changed for him, and he couldn't decide when the island had become less appealing or when the restlessness had set in that had him questioning everything.

"Riley," Finn said.

Riley looked up. "What?"

"Are you listening to me?"

"Sorry. What'd you say?"

"I asked where you were, and when you didn't answer, you confirmed you're not here."

"What? I'm right here."

"Maybe so, but your head is somewhere else entirely, which makes me nervous when you're pointing a nail gun at my hands. What's up with you anyway? You're zoned out more often than not, and you never want to go out or party or do anything."

"It's freezing."

"That's never stopped you before." Finn held up another sheet of drywall and waited for Riley to nail it into place.

Riley could dodge a lot of people. The brother who knew him better than anyone wasn't one of them. "I don't know why I don't feel like going out. I just don't."

"I know why," Finn said with a smug smile.

"Can't wait to hear this."

"It's because of Nikki, the roof girl."

Riley took his eyes off what he was doing just long enough to nearly run a nail through his own hand. "What're you talking about?"

"This funk of yours started when she left without saying goodbye."

"What *funk*? And so what if she left without saying goodbye? I barely knew her."

"But you *liked* her. Admit it."

Riley shrugged, hoping he appeared far more nonchalant than he felt. "She seemed like a nice enough person."

Finn snorted with laughter, and Riley seriously considered aiming the nail gun at his brother's head. But only for a second. Most of the time, he liked the brother who was also his closest friend. This was not one of those times.

"She 'seemed like a nice enough person,'" Finn said mockingly. "Is that your story and you're sticking to it?"

Riley put down the nail gun and walked away.

"Riley!" Finn called after him. "Come on. I'm just messing with you. What the hell? Where're you going?"

"Hey, Riley," Mac called out to him from atop a ladder. "What's up?"

He didn't stop or reply to them on his way through the double doors that led to the beach, where it was about ten degrees with a wind chill of negative two hundred, or so it seemed. The wind whipped the sand into mini cyclones as huge waves pounded against the shore. Seagulls flew above the surf, seeming oblivious to the fact that it was too cold for any living thing to be outside.

Riley zipped up the heavy coat he wore to work in the building that was still heat-challenged, even with the new HVAC system fully installed and nearly operational. No one wanted to spend the money to heat the vast space, so they bundled up and spent their days freezing their asses off. He tugged work gloves from his pockets, put them on and pulled his ever-present wool hat down over his ears. He'd rather be out here than inside listening to Finn psychoanalyze him. They got enough of that bullshit from their father, the shrink.

Riley wished he smoked, so he'd have something to do besides shiver uncontrollably on this unscheduled break. Anything to give him something to do or think about besides the truth of what Finn had said, a truth that Riley hadn't allowed himself to entertain before his brother had knocked him over the head with it.

How could he *miss* someone he barely knew?

And he did barely know Nikki Stokes, granddaughter of Mrs. Hopper, one of the island's longest-standing summer residents. Nikki had arrived last fall with her identical twin sister, Jordan, to stay at the family's island home. Jordan, a reality TV star, had been hiding from the media after her malicious on-again-off-again husband released a sex tape that prominently featured her. The roof at the Hopper house had been leaking in a rainstorm. Mac had sent him over to fix it. He'd talked to Nikki a couple of times.

That was the extent of his so-called relationship with Nikki.

Had he been bummed when he showed up to work one day and the sisters were gone? Sure, but that was months ago, and what did any of it have to do with him? He'd taken a casual look online but hadn't seen any news about Jordan in the months since they'd suddenly left. He hoped wherever they were that Nikki was taking care of herself and not devoting all her energy to her troubled sister.

Beyond that, what did it matter to him where she was?

The icy wind beat against his face, almost like it was trying to get his attention, to make him see that *freaking Finn was right*. His gloom-and-doom phase *had* started around the time Nikki had suddenly left the island. Fucking hell.

Riley could've done without the realization that forced him to consider why he cared and why her departure had put him into a months-long bad mood. He'd gone out of his way to avoid the kind of entanglements that had other men making fools of themselves over women. It wasn't at all like him to let a woman get to him this way. And *how*, exactly, had she managed to "get to him" in the span of a couple of conversations about a leaking roof? It made no sense whatsoever.

The double doors swung open, and his cousin Shane came out, zipping his coat against the blast of frigid air. "What the hell are you doing out here?" Shane had to shout to be heard over the relentless wind.

"Taking a break."

"In what might be the coldest place on earth?"

"Why not?"

"Riley, what's going on?"

"Nothing. I just wanted a break. That's allowed, right?"

"You know it is, but anyone can see you're not yourself lately. If something's wrong, we can help, but not if we don't know what it is."

Oh, for fuck's sake, Riley wanted to say but didn't. Shane was a good guy, and his offer of help was sincere. Their older cousins tended to baby him and Finn, the youngest of the McCarthy grandchildren, and most of the time, he found it funny. Today, he wasn't in the mood for hovering or babying.

"It's all good." Riley had zero desire to talk about his mood or the fact that people were noticing he wasn't himself. Now that he knew what—or *who*—was causing it, he could begin to find a way past it. He wasn't someone who allowed himself to get mired in negativity, nor did he obsess about women. Sure, he liked women. He liked them a lot, but there'd never been one who put him into a funk or caused him to question his life choices.

Until Nikki.

Oh my God. Just shut the hell up! I met her twice!

In his mind, he was arguing with Finn. But in reality, the argument was with himself.

His cousins had altered their entire lives for the women they loved, which was great for them, but that wasn't his vibe. Not yet anyway. At only twenty-eight, he had no desire to be settled or domesticated or anything that smacked of commitment or responsibility. That's what his thirties were for.

But he couldn't deny that Finn was right. He'd become a bore lately, and that would change, effective immediately. He followed Shane inside, where the lack of freezing wind was a welcome relief.

Pulling off his gloves, he went back to where Finn leaned against the wall they'd been constructing, feeling his brother's gaze on him as he unzipped his coat and picked up the nail gun.

"You wanna go out tonight?" Riley asked as they positioned the next piece of drywall.

"Yep."

There. Back on track.

A night out with Finn was just what he needed to get himself righted. Perhaps he might meet someone who could take his mind off the disturbing thoughts he'd been having lately, although in the dead of winter, there were fewer single women on the island than during the summer. Whatever. It would be enough to go out and have some beers and laughs with his brother. Maybe some of their cousins would join them. They were always entertaining and good for many laughs.

That was all he needed to snap out of the funk.

IN A STATE OF ABSOLUTE DISBELIEF, Nikki watched her sister, Jordan, throw clothes into a duffel bag, grabbing articles off the floor and giving them a sniff before she jammed them into the bag or discarded them. When was the last time her sister had done laundry? It hardly mattered when you had more clothes than a person could wear in a lifetime, even someone who wore three or four outfits per day.

"This is a joke, right?" Nikki asked, fuming as she *felt* her blood pressure soar.

"What's a joke?" Jordan asked, oblivious as usual.

"You. Going back to *him* after what he did to you. That has to be a joke, because no self-respecting woman would ever give a guy like him yet *another* chance."

Jordan had the good grace to squirm ever so slightly. "He apologized and took down the video. He said he did it because he wanted me back."

"He posted a video of you *having sex* because he *wanted you back*? And you believe that bullshit?"

"You don't get it."

"You're right. I don't."

"I *love* him, Nik. I've *always* loved him. You know that."

That might be true, but all Nikki could think of was Jordan's utter devastation last fall when the man she *loved* had posted a video of them having sex—a video Jordan hadn't known existed until it became public. In the world of deal breakers, that would top Nikki's list no matter how much she "loved" the guy. That he'd even *recorded* such a private moment without her consent would be enough for Nikki to call it quits forever.

But Jordan had a soft spot *and* a blind spot where Zane, the rapper known only by his first name, was concerned. From the time Jordan met him five years ago, their relationship had been an unhealthy, toxic mess, and Nikki had had enough.

She marshaled her fortitude and met the gaze of the sister who looked exactly like her but was as different from her as anyone could be. "I quit."

"Don't be dramatic, Nik. You're not quitting."

"I'm not being dramatic, and I *am* quitting. I appreciate the opportunities you've given me to work as your assistant, but I'm going to pursue other interests. It's high time we started living our own lives anyway."

"You're pissed about Zane. I get it. He told me you would be."

That infuriated Nikki. She and her brother-in-law had civilly coexisted, most of the time anyway. However, after he posted the video that had—temporarily, it seemed—devastated her sister, he was dead to Nikki. If only he were dead to Jordan, too, but alas, no such luck. The definition of insanity was doing the same thing over and over and expecting different results. Her sister was completely insane to go back to him, but no one could tell her that, even the twin sister who was closer to her than anyone.

She had been anyway, until *Zane* came along and ruined so many things, including the cohesive bond the sisters had always shared. During a chaotic upbringing in which they had been shuttled between divorced parents who had fought over them for years, they'd rarely had so much as a disagreement until Jordan met Zane and went off the deep end—in every possible way.

Nikki would bet the farm that he'd never been faithful to Jordan, but even those rumors or the ever-present threat of STDs didn't seem to matter to her sister. After the video first surfaced, Nikki had felt *relieved*—right before she felt guilty for being relieved when her sister was utterly devastated. She'd hoped the video would finally be the deal breaker that would end their disastrous marriage.

During the weeks last fall that they'd spent at their grandmother's home on Gansett Island, Nikki had been hopeful that Jordan was going to end it once and for all. But then Jordan had suddenly wanted to go home to Los Angeles. Then she'd begun disappearing for entire days. Nikki checked Zane's concert schedule, found out he was in town and put two and two together to equal madness.

It was time to take herself off the insanity train. Enough was enough for her, even if Jordan wasn't there yet. She'd get there eventually. Nikki was certain of it, but she wasn't about to wait around and watch the shit show from the sidelines. She'd seen enough to last her a lifetime and to make her want to swear off men and marriage forever.

"Take a vacation," Jordan said. "You're long overdue for some time off, and I'll send you anywhere you want to go. Zane will make the jet available to you after they drop me in Houston for his show. Just say the word."

Nikki wanted to laugh at the irony of Zane making it possible for her to get as far away from him as she possibly could. That would make them both happy. He didn't like her any more than she liked him—probably because he knew she was wise to him and not buying his bullshit the way Jordan did.

"That's all right." Zane was the last person on earth she wanted to be beholden to for anything. "I'll make my own arrangements as soon as I can pack up my stuff here and get it into storage."

Jordan stopped what she was doing with the sniffing and packing. "You're serious."

"Dead serious," Nikki said, six steps beyond exasperated. This conversation was so typical as to be comical—Jordan listened to every other word Nikki said and then acted surprised when she finally heard something Nikki had already told her four times. Except it wasn't funny anymore. Not to her anyway. "It's time, J," she said gently. "We're twenty-seven and still joined at the hip."

"So what? The Kardashians are older than us and together every minute of every day. No one thinks that's weird."

If she had to hear one more word about the Kardashians, the family Jordan held up as the example all reality TV stars aimed to emulate, Nikki was going to lose her shit. "Um, *everyone* thinks they're weird. Everyone except for you, that is."

"And the twenty million people who follow their every move," Jordan said disdainfully. One of Jordan's life goals was to have as many Twitter followers as Kim. She'd been well on her way with three million followers when the sex tape exploded her numbers to ten million. In Jordan's twisted mind, Zane got credit for making her even more famous, the same way a sex tape had exploded Kim onto the national stage once upon a time.

Nikki couldn't handle her sister's twisted mind or the twisted world in which she and Zane lived and worked. However, Nikki would miss Jordan's Bel Air estate, which had been home to them both for the last three years. Nikki's apartment was totally separate from Jordan and Zane's part of the house, but she couldn't live for one more day under the same roof as that man.

No, the only roof she wanted to be under was the new one Riley McCarthy had put on their grandmother's home on Gansett Island. Although, the thought of Gansett in January did give her pause. She'd never been there in the winter, but at least she knew the roof was solid. Riley was a man of his word. Nikki had known him only fleetingly, but she knew that much, and the roof *would* be as solid as he was.

Perhaps a few weeks under that solid roof, away from the endless calamity that was her sister's life, would give Nikki the space and perspective to figure out who she was beyond Jordan Stokes's identical twin sister and faithful assistant. She needed her own life and identity. Hopefully, some time away from it all, some time in her favorite place in the world, would help her to figure out what that life might entail.

CHAPTER 2

*T*he first big difference between Gansett in the summer and Gansett in the winter was the ferry ride. *Holy crap,* Nikki thought as the ferry crested one enormous wave after another. She'd never been seasick in her life, but this trip was testing that record, especially with people discreetly throwing up all around her.

Air—she needed fresh air, and she needed it right now. She zipped up the heavy coat she had bought for the trip and pulled on a hat and gloves before stepping into the frigid air. The sky was gray and stormy, the seas churned, and the island was shrouded in thick haze as the ferry rose and fell with the tumultuous ocean.

This is what adventure feels like, Nikki thought, almost gleeful after declaring her independence from the sister who'd begun to suck the life out of her with the never-ending drama she thrived on. Standing at the rail, Nikki held on tight to remain standing. Despite their physical similarities—even their own mother mixed them up on occasion —Nikki and Jordan had always been polar opposites. While Nikki was usually content to stay home with a good book, Jordan wanted to be out and about, to see and be seen. When Nikki wanted to go for a hike, Jordan wanted to go shopping. Nikki would eat anything, while

Jordan was a vegetarian, a part-time vegan and on every fad diet that came along.

Being Jordan's assistant had exhausted Nikki. Being her sister had become almost as grueling a job. The time apart would do them both good. They were long overdue to start carving out identities separate from each other. Even after Jordan married Zane, she still spent more time with her sister than with her husband. Perhaps that was part of the reason their marriage was so toxic. If they were going to make it work, they needed her out of the way—and there was nothing she wanted more than to be far, *far* away from the Zane and Jordan freak show.

Why was she even thinking about her sister when she'd traveled three thousand miles to escape her and the madness that came with her? Although, thinking about Jordan first was ingrained in her after being her assistant for the last three years. In that time, Jordan went from a contestant on a dating show to a major reality TV star to the wife of one of music's biggest stars to sex-tape queen. Nikki's job had been to see to the myriad details that came with being Jordan.

Nikki would need an exorcism to reboot her thoughts and turn the focus away from her sister so she could figure out her own life, such as it was. She hadn't had much of a life of her own since she'd started working for Jordan. When was the last time she'd done anything that was just for her?

Yesterday, she thought, recalling how she'd stepped onto an airplane for a trip that had nothing to do with her sister. Prior to that, Nikki honestly couldn't recall the last time she had done anything that didn't in some way involve Jordan. Last fall when she'd made this trip, it had been with and for Jordan after Zane released the tape that had immediately gone viral.

Jordan had wanted to be somewhere no one could find her. Nikki had immediately thought of their grandmother's home on Gansett, where they'd spent summers with their mother and grandmother while growing up. Those had been some of the best times of their lives, and Jordan had quickly agreed to Nikki's plan to hide out on Gansett where no one would think to look for her.

Being there had been so restorative, at least it had been for Nikki, but Jordan had gotten restless after two weeks and had wanted to go home. Nikki had suspected that her sister had been talking to her husband, and thus the hasty departure. It hadn't taken much effort to discover that Zane was the reason they'd left Gansett right when things were getting interesting. If you could call a new roof interesting.

The man installing the roof had been extremely interesting. And kind. And handsome. And incredibly sexy. She'd liked talking to him, and she'd appreciated how quickly he'd fixed the leak that had damaged the ceiling in her bedroom. He was a take-charge kind of guy who got things done. As a take-charge person herself, Nikki respected that quality in others.

She'd thought of him often during the months since she'd left the island. Because Jordan had been in such a rush to leave, Nikki hadn't gotten the chance to say goodbye to Riley. That was probably why she'd thought of him so often. She'd felt bad about disappearing on him when he was putting a new roof on the house.

It wasn't like he needed her there to get the job done, but she hadn't felt right about leaving without a proper goodbye. Hopefully, she'd run into him on the island while she was there. If he was even still there. For all she knew, he could've been wrapping up a summer job and had gone back to his regular life, wherever that was. She wished she'd thought to ask him if he lived on the island year-round or only during the season.

She wished she'd thought to ask him a lot of things.

Like whether he had a girlfriend.

Nikki laughed into the brisk breeze. A sweet, nice guy who looked like he did probably had *all* the girlfriends. If she allowed herself to believe he was probably a player, she could feel better about missing the chance to get to know him better.

The ferry crested a huge wave, teetered at the top and then plunged into the trough with a stomach-dropping slide. Nikki's tenuous grip on the rail was all that kept her from falling.

A shout from her left had her looking up at a handsome, rugged-looking man rushing toward her. He wore a knit hat and a coat with the word CREW under the logo for the Gansett Island Ferry Company.

"You need to be inside, ma'am," he shouted over the wind. "It's not safe out here."

She noted a lovely Irish lilt to his voice. "People are getting sick in there. I'm better off out here."

"Not if you go overboard," he said. "I'm afraid I have to insist." He gestured toward the door, and Nikki stepped into the pervasive stench of vomit.

The man followed her in.

"See what I'm saying? I'll get sick in here. I won't out there."

"Come with me." He led her to a stairway that took them to the bridge, where the door was propped open to allow in fresh air. "Have a seat." He gestured to a seat next to the man who stood at the helm.

"It's pretty ugly out here, Seamus," the captain said. "I think we need to call it a day after this run."

"Aye, you read my mind. I'll call it in." He used his cell phone to place a call. "This is Seamus. We're suspending service for the rest of the day." He listened for a minute. "Tell them we're sorry. They'll have to come back tomorrow. It's too rough for the fuel trucks anyway." After listening some more, he said, "We'll let them know in the morning. Talk to you then." He ended the call and glanced at her. "You feeling okay?"

"Yes," Nikki said. "Thank you."

"Are you that... that girl on TV?" the other man asked. "Jordan Stokes?"

"No, I'm her twin sister."

"She's hot."

Nikki was never quite sure how to respond to comments like that about her identical twin. Jordan was hot, but Nikki wasn't, apparently. Of course, Nikki had never starred in her own sex tape, so there was that. "If you say so," she said to the grinning ferryboat captain.

"Ah, yeah, and that tape... *Whoa.*"

"Shut yer trap and drive the boat." Seamus scowled at the younger man before returning his attention to Nikki. "Sorry about that, love. Some people *talk* before they *think*."

"Apologies," the younger guy said.

"It's okay," Nikki said, relieved to see the breakwater at South Harbor coming into view. All her life, the pile of rocks that made up the entrance to the harbor had represented *home* to her. Even though they'd come only for the summers, Nikki had never felt more at home anywhere than she did at her grandmother's house on Gansett Island.

They'd had a nomadic upbringing thanks to the custody battle that had resulted in the girls spending the school year with their father and holidays and summers with their mother, whose mental health and addiction challenges had made for a chaotic childhood for her daughters.

Nikki had had enough chaos growing up to last her a lifetime. She found it interesting that while she ran from the drama that had defined their upbringing, Jordan seemed to embrace it. The peaceful vibe of the island was just what Nikki needed to regroup and figure out her next move. It worried her that Jordan seemed to be following in their mother's troubled footsteps. As much as Nikki worried about her sister, however, she couldn't live her life for her or keep her from making destructive decisions. She would focus exclusively on herself and her own life for the next little while.

Jordan had been extremely generous in the years that Nikki had worked for her, and she had enough money to live comfortably for quite some time, which was a relief. Her grandmother had told her to make herself at home at the house for as long as she wanted to be there. She would hit the grocery store to stock up on what she needed and then hibernate for the next few weeks with her e-reader. Downtime was what she needed after the last few months of high drama.

The younger captain left the bridge to use the aft controls to expertly turn the huge ferry and back it into port. Nikki never ceased to be fascinated by how easy they made that look.

She extended her hand to Seamus. "Thank you so much for letting me sit up here."

He surprised and charmed her when he kissed the back of her hand. "My pleasure. I hope you enjoy your stay on the island."

She noticed a shiny gold wedding ring on his left hand. Too bad. Otherwise, she might've asked if he wanted to get a drink. The man was too handsome—and charming—for her own good. "I'm sure I will. It's my favorite place in the world."

"Aye, mine, too. Hope to see you around town."

"Hope so. Take care." She went down two flights of metal stairs to get into the black SUV she'd rented for a month. As always, it took about ten minutes after docking before the cars toward the front of the ferry started rolling off the boat. Usually, the ferry landing was a madhouse of people and bikes and strollers and cars and forklifts and frenetic activity. Today, she drove into a ghost town.

The difference between summer Gansett and winter Gansett was… day and night. For the first time since she'd hatched the plan to come to the island, she experienced the tiniest bit of concern about being here alone during the winter. She'd promised her grandmother she'd check in daily in exchange for Gran turning on the cable and internet service. Some things a girl shouldn't have to do without. HGTV, Netflix and Instagram were at the top of her must-have list, along with the food she stopped to pick up at the island market, which was also deserted. The woman working the cash register was reading a book with her feet up on the checkout counter when Nikki walked in.

"Hey," she said. "We're closing in twenty minutes."

"I'll be quick." She moved swiftly through the store, putting the essentials in her basket—soy milk, which she was always surprised to find on the island, granola, yogurt, salad fixings, deli turkey, chicken breasts and Fritos. They counted as a necessity, as did the M&M's and the tabloid magazines she snagged at checkout.

This is a vacation, she told herself, thus the need for some reading material. "Wait one second," she said, moving to the rack that held paperback books. She picked up a couple of romances and a thriller that was being made into a movie and added them to her order. Oddly enough, she sometimes preferred paperbacks when she was on Gansett.

Netflix, books and Fritos. What else did she need to be happy? Her camera, which was never far from her side. After receiving her first thirty-five-millimeter camera from her dad at Christmas when she was thirteen, Nikki had been hooked. She never felt more inspired to take pictures than she did on Gansett, where the rugged scenery and ocean views provided an endless tableau to explore.

Suddenly, she was excited again. Tomorrow, she'd get outside, take some pictures and get back to doing the things *she* loved. While she'd been busy putting out Jordan's fires, she'd had little time for herself. Now she had nothing but time, and as she headed toward Eastward Look, her grandmother's comfortable oceanfront home, Nikki couldn't wait to be completely alone.

AFTER WORK, Riley showered and shaved and put on a flannel shirt with good jeans, classified as such because he'd never worn them to work. He even put on a tiny bit of cologne. One never knew when one might meet someone special. It was best to be prepared.

"You done primping, pretty boy?" Finn called to him. "Let's go already!"

"Showering doesn't count as primping," Riley informed his brother. "And tomorrow, we're cleaning this house."

"Shut up, Dad."

"Seriously, Finn, it's disgusting. We haven't cleaned once since Dad moved out two months ago."

"You can clean. I plan to sleep all day."

"You're helping me." Riley stepped over a pile of dirty clothes in the living room. "Most of the mess is yours."

"Life is too short to clean."

"Your life will be shorter if you don't clean that bathroom, because I *will* kill you and bury what's left of you in the backyard. You got me?"

"Whatever. Can we drink now?"

"I mean it, Finn! This place is gross, and it's freaking me out."

"Fine. Tomorrow we'll clean, but tonight we drink. Yes?"

Riley rolled his eyes at the brother who was two years younger than he was and pushed past him, taking a bottle of water from a fridge full of science experiments. Their father would flip his lid if he could see the condition of the house where the three of them had lived until their dad moved in with his fiancée, Chelsea.

The two of them were trying to have a baby, which meant his sons saw much less of him than they had during the year they'd lived together in the small three-bedroom house. It'd been spotless on their dad's watch, but since he left, things had gone rapidly downhill.

While Finn drove them into town, Riley guzzled the water that would keep him from being hungover tomorrow. "Who else is going?"

"I told Mac, and he was interested. He said he'd see if Maddie minded if he went out, and he was going to tell the others. I guess we'll see."

"Having a wife seems an awful lot like having a mother," Riley said.

"Only with regular sex."

Riley choked on his water. "Shut the fuck up," he sputtered, wiping water off his chin. "Oh my God, you're disgusting."

Finn howled with laughter.

"Don't put those images in my head."

"Speaking of Mom…"

Riley groaned. "*Stop!*"

"Seriously, have you talked to her lately?"

"Not in a few weeks. You?"

"Nada. She's been noticeably absent since she came to visit. I think she was really bummed—and surprised—that Dad is so serious about Chelsea."

"Why should she be either of those things? She's the one who left him. And Dad's a good guy. Did she think he'd be alone for the rest of his life?"

"Who knows what she was thinking?" After a pause, Finn said, "Do you think she has regrets?"

"Of course she does. That was obvious when she was here. Dad was right to shut her down and not let her rehash it all. What does it matter now?"

"You sound like you're still really pissed with her."

Was he? He hadn't given it much thought, but then again, he tried not to think too much about his mother or the way she'd chosen to end a thirty-year marriage.

"Are you?" Finn asked, glancing at him. "Pissed with her?"

"I don't know. Maybe a little. I just think the way she went about it was shitty. If you want out, get a divorce, but taking off with a younger guy and humiliating your husband of thirty years, who is a *good* guy? It's just kinda…"

"Sordid?"

"Among other things. I'm so glad we aren't still living in Westport, where the whole town knows what she did. I can't believe *she's* still there."

"Being there would be hideous with everyone knowing that."

"Definitely." Riley had stayed far away from social media since his mother had left his father. He had no desire to know what the people at home were saying about his family.

"Why are we talking about this shit anyway?" Finn asked as he hung a left into the parking lot behind the Beachcomber.

"Because you wanted to talk about having regular sex with your mother."

"Shut the fuck up," Finn said, laughing. "I never said that."

The lot, which would be full in the summer, had about five cars, one of them belonging to Chelsea and another to their father, Kevin.

"Looks like the old man's in residence," Riley said.

"As usual when Chelsea's working. Let's go see what he's up to."

Wind whipping off the water smacked his face as Riley ran after Finn, up the back stairs to the iconic white hotel that anchored Gansett's downtown, if you could call a collection of hotels, restaurants and stores a "downtown." They walked into the bar, where their dad was sitting with two other guys while Chelsea tended bar.

"Hey!" At the sight of them, Kevin McCarthy's handsome face lit up with a huge smile. His obvious adoration of them used to mortify his sons when they were younger. Now they knew to expect it—and had come to appreciate his unwavering devotion. "It's my boys. Riley, Finn, you know Shannon O'Grady, and I don't think you've met Niall Fitzgerald. These two blokes have nearly got me talked into a trip to Ireland."

"Nice to meet you." Riley shook hands with Niall as Finn followed suit. "And good to see you again, Shannon."

"Likewise," Shannon said.

"What're you guys up to tonight?" Kevin asked.

"Same as you—beer and food," Finn said. "In that order."

"Join us," Kevin said as Shannon and Niall moved over to make room for them.

"Hey, guys," Chelsea said, smiling as she came over to greet them. "Good to see you. Can I get you the usual?"

"Works for me," Finn said, bellying up to the bar on the other side of Kevin.

"Me, too," Riley said. "Thanks, Chelsea." Riley liked the woman his father had fallen for, but sometimes it was still strange to see him with someone other than their mother. Over the past year, he and Finn had mostly gotten used to the two of them together.

Chelsea put a bottle of Bud in front of Finn and an Amstel Light in front of Riley.

"Does that stuff even count as beer?" Finn asked, as he always did.

Riley ignored him—as he always did—and took a healthy drink from his bottle.

"Are you guys eating?" Chelsea asked.

"Yes, ma'am," Finn said. "I'll have a bowl of chowder and a cheeseburger with everything, please."

"I'll have the same, but make mine—"

"*Plain*," Kevin, Chelsea and Finn said together.

"One burger, no gaggers, coming right up," Chelsea said, using his favorite word to describe the gross shit everyone else seemed to put all over their food.

Riley made a face at them. *So sue me*, he thought. *I don't like my burger loaded down with crap*. "That word is trademarked."

19

"We're just messing with ya," Kevin said, nudging Riley with his shoulder. "You know that."

"I know." Riley focused on his beer, depressed to realize that it didn't matter if he was at home or out. He still felt shitty.

The feeling stayed with him as they ate and visited with their father, Shannon and Niall. Shannon's cousin, Seamus, joined them, as did Mac, Shane and Adam, all of whom seemed excited about an impromptu boys' night out in the middle of the week. His musician cousin Evan was touring in Europe this winter with his wife, Grace, and Grant was in Los Angeles, working on the movie based on the life of his wife, Stephanie.

Mac squeezed Riley's shoulders. "How's it going?"

"Good, you?"

"Excellent. I had dinner with my wife and kids and got a free pass on baths to have some beers with my boys. Life is good."

Riley found it funny that a get-out-of-jail-free card was all it took to make Mac happy. What would it take for him to say that? Riley didn't know. Maybe it was time he figured that out. The aimlessness he'd felt lately was starting to wear thin.

The bar filled up with more people he knew—his uncles Big Mac and Frank along with Big Mac's best friend, Ned Saunders. Alex and Paul Martinez came in together, followed by Joe Cantrell and Luke Harris.

"Damn," Chelsea said, smiling. "And here I thought it was going to be another quiet winter night around here."

"Nothing quiet about it when the McCarthys show up," Kevin said.

"Don't I know it?" she replied as she drew one beer after another from the taps.

"Can we put the Bruins on, Chelsea?" Finn asked, scowling at the TV where one of the entertainment shows was previewing the Golden Globes.

"I get hockey after she gets her fill of celebrity gossip," Kevin replied. "That's our deal."

Finn rolled his eyes.

Riley tipped his head, asking his brother to come closer.

"What's up?"

"Just wanted to say thanks. You know, for asking the guys to come out tonight."

"I hardly had to twist their arms."

"Still, I know why you did it, and I appreciate it."

"No problem. I figured out what's wrong with you, by the way."

"Gee, I can't wait to hear this."

"I saw this thing on TV about seasonal affective disorder. It's when people get depressed at certain times of the year. You never have liked winter very much. That could be what it is."

Riley loved his brother. He truly did. There was no one he'd rather hang out with—most of the time. So rather than laugh in his face when Finn was being dead serious, Riley only nodded and said, "Could be."

"Ask Dad about it."

"Ask Dad about what?" Kevin said, overhearing them.

Great, Riley thought. *Just what I need is a consult with Dr. McCarthy.*

"I think Riley has seasonal affective disorder."

Kevin's relaxed expression immediately sobered. "What makes you say that?"

"He's depressed and gloomy. Has been for weeks."

"Finn. Jesus. I am not depressed *or* gloomy."

"Yeah, you are. You're both."

"Finn, give us a minute, will you, son?"

"Gladly." Finn gave Riley a pointed look, silently urging him to talk to their father, and went to sit at the long table Mac and the others had made by pushing a bunch of smaller tables together.

"What's going on?" Kevin asked, signaling to Chelsea to bring them refills.

She put the beers on the bar in front of them.

"Thank you, honey," Kevin said with a warm smile for her. Then he glanced at Riley and raised that brow of his. He got a lot done with that damned brow. "So…"

"I don't know what Finn's talking about," Riley said, unwilling to discuss the funk that had begun with Nikki's sudden departure with his father, who'd want to pick it apart. It had happened. It sucked. He'd get over it. End of story. "Everything is fine."

"Haven't seen much of you since I moved in with Chelsea."

"Phone works both ways, Dad."

"True," Kevin said with a sheepish grin. "I guess I got used to you being the one to hit me up rather than the other way around. You're better than I am about keeping in touch, so it's noticeable when you stop calling."

"I've just been busy. We're hard into it at the Wayfarer and trying to meet a tight deadline. I'm exhausted after work most days, and all I want is to eat and sleep."

"You're not sick or something, are you?" Kevin asked, alarmed.

"Stop being a doctor, would you, please? I'm fine."

Kevin studied him as he took a drink of his beer. He'd told Riley once that he nursed two every night that Chelsea worked so he wouldn't get fat on beer. At fifty-two, Kevin McCarthy was a long way from fat. The guy looked forty on a bad day and was trying to have a baby with his much-younger girlfriend. Eighteen months after his marriage had ended, he'd found a whole new life with Chelsea.

"If you need me, you know where I am. Right?"

"Yes, Dad. I always know where you are. Thank you for your concern, but there's nothing to worry about."

Seamus came up to the bar to order another beer. Glancing at the TV, he said, "Hey, I brought her twin sister over today."

Riley looked up and did a double take when he saw Jordan Stokes appear on the entertainment show. Then he realized she was with Zane, the rapper ex-husband who'd released the infamous sex tape. The headline on the bottom of the screen read: *Reunited and it feels so good.*

Oh my God! She's back with that guy? After what he did to her?

Better still, *Nikki is on the island?* Riley pulled out his wallet, tossed a twenty on the bar and said to his father, "If I borrow your car, can you get a ride home with Chelsea? I'll get it back to you tomorrow."

"Where're you going?"

"Something I gotta do, and Finn drove. Yes or no on the car?" Riley was unable to wait even one more minute to get out of there.

Kevin handed over his keys. "Been years since one of you took my car."

"Thanks, Dad. I'll take good care of it." Riley bolted out of there before anyone could stop him or ask questions or get between him and…

He was in the parking lot when he stopped to ask himself what the hell he was doing rushing to see her the second he heard she was back on the island. In his father's car, which bore the citrusy scent of the cologne Kevin had worn for as long as Riley could remember, he sat staring out the windshield for a long time.

Long enough that Finn had time to come after him and tap on the window.

Reluctantly, Riley put it down. "What?"

"Where're you going?"

"I have an errand to run."

"Out at the Hopper place, by any chance?"

"Fuck off, Finn, and go back inside, will you please?"

Rather than fuck off, however, his brother leaned against the car, apparently settling in for a chat. "What're you doing, Ri?"

"It's none of your business."

"Since when is your life none of my business? We've been in each other's business *all* our lives."

Riley couldn't argue with that. But for some reason that he couldn't explain to himself, let alone his brother, Riley wanted to keep where he was going and why to himself. At least until he better understood the immediate need to go to her after hearing she was back. "Could I just please have a little bit of space? Is that too much to ask?"

"Nope, not too much to ask as long as it's not the start of a new pattern in which you act like I have no right to know what's going on with you."

"It's not," Riley said, eager to be on his way.

"Good. I'll hold you to that."

"Fine."

"Fine. Go do your little *errand*." Finn pushed himself off the car and headed back inside, his distinctive stride—part strut, part prowl—as familiar to Riley as anything in his life.

Riley started the car and backed it out of the parking space. His heart raced with excitement that he'd never felt before when it came to any woman. Why did he feel that way about one he'd seen exactly twice in his life before she disappeared without a word months ago?

Damned if he knew, but he was drawn to her anyway. He had questions, and he hoped she would have some answers. Maybe after they talked, he'd feel more settled and could put this madness—and the accompanying glum mood—behind him once and for all. That'd be a relief.

He drove toward the island's north end, where Nikki's grandmother's house was located. The last time he'd been out that way had been in the fall when the trees had been turning and the sky bright with sun. Tonight, the roads were dark and coated with a thin layer of ice that made for treacherous driving.

He slowed to a crawl. The last freaking thing he needed was to wreck his father's prized BMW in his haste to see Nikki. As he took the turn into the Hoppers' driveway, the car fishtailed, but thankfully, he was able to maintain control. Riley wondered if the elements were sending him a sign that maybe this trip to the Hopper house in the dark of night wasn't the best idea he'd ever had.

Recalling how skittish Nikki had been in the bright light of day had him worried that he might scare her by showing up this way. What if she had a gun in the house? Riley wished he had her phone number so he could call her and tell her it was him, but they hadn't gotten that far the first time around.

The porch light came on along with security lights that lined the driveway and lit up the yard.

Leaving the car running and the lights on, he got out and held up his hands, just in case she had a gun. "It's Riley McCarthy," he called out. "I heard you were back, and I wanted to see you."

A number of locks disengaged, the door opened, and there she was. Her big brown eyes were just as he remembered, the most dominant feature in a strikingly pretty face that was on full display. Her long dark hair was piled on top of her head in one of those messy buns that looked incredibly sexy on some women, including this one.

When it became clear she didn't have a gun, he put down his arms. "I didn't mean to scare you."

"What're you doing here?"

Right then, it occurred to him that the odd zing of attraction he'd felt for her had been one-sided—and he'd made a total fool of himself trekking out here in the dark to see her. "I... I'm not entirely sure."

She seemed as confused as he suddenly felt. "My grandmother told me you finished fixing the roof."

"Yes, I did."

"So..."

"I heard your sister was back together with Zane and that you were here. I wondered if..."

"What did you wonder?"

God, he was a total ass on a fool's errand. Since this couldn't possibly get any worse, he went with the truth. "I wondered if you might need a friend."

She was silent for so long, he questioned whether she had heard him. Then she said, "Do you want to come in?"

"I don't mean to bother you."

"I was watching TV and eating a frozen pizza. It's no bother."

"Let me turn off the car." He got back in the car and shut off the engine. The lights were automatic and would shut off on their own. Jogging toward her front door, he told himself to calm down and take it easy. Oh, and stop acting like a fool. That would be good, too.

CHAPTER 3

*W*ith her heart in her throat, Nikki watched Riley as he came toward the front door, which she'd unlocked so she could speak to him. And now, a man she'd met only twice was going to come into the house, where they would be completely alone. This was not good. It wasn't good at all. She didn't do things like this, didn't take these sorts of chances. Not anymore.

But he'd been so nice to her last fall. When she'd had a leaking roof and a devastated sister, he'd gone out of his way to help her. She knew the McCarthy family was well regarded on the island. Of course, none of the things she told herself in the two minutes it took for him to turn off his car and come into the house meant she was safe with him.

She'd learned that lesson the hard way—seemingly nice guys from good families weren't always what they appeared to be.

"Hi there," he said, smiling as he stepped into the vestibule, closing the door behind him.

The sound of the door latching might as well have been a shotgun blast for the effect it had on her. Alone. With a man. In a house on Gansett Island. If this went bad, no one would come to save her.

"Nikki?" He tipped his head in inquiry. "Are you okay?"

"I… I'm a little freaked out by the fact that I barely know you, and you're in my house."

"I'll go," he said without hesitation. "I didn't mean to unsettle you. I thought about you after you left, and when I heard you were back.,, I don't know what I was thinking, but I'll go."

"No," she said, her anxiety settling at his willingness to leave if that was what she wanted. The bad ones didn't go when asked to leave. They stayed. "Don't go. I'm sorry. I'm being ridiculous."

"No, you're not. You're being careful, and I shouldn't have come here at this hour. I didn't think it all the way through until I saw you were scared."

"Jordan says I'm a wimp and need to toughen up."

"That's not nice."

"She's often not nice to me," she said with a laugh that did amazing things for her pretty face. "That's her job as my sister."

"I have a brother with the same job."

She gestured for him to follow her into the kitchen, where a large pizza sat cooling on a cutting board. "Want some?"

"I'll have a slice if you can spare it."

"I'm certainly not going to eat this whole thing," she said, laughing again.

"Are you putting up a Christmas tree in January by any chance?" He gestured to the boxes surrounding a large artificial tree in the cozy living room.

"You caught me," she said with a shy, adorable smile. "Jordan was in no mood for Christmas this year, so we skipped it. I love Christmas, and I figured who would know if I put the tree up."

"Your secret is safe with me." He slid onto one of the barstools at the expansive island and took a bite of the pizza she served him, picking off the pepperoni, even though he wasn't particularly hungry after having eaten at the Beachcomber. "This is delicious."

She rolled her eyes at his compliment. "Frozen pizza is one of my few culinary specialties. What can I get you to drink? I've got iced tea, water and beer."

"A beer sounds good." He hadn't finished the second one at the bar, so one more would be okay.

She fetched two bottles of imported beer that required a bottle opener and put one of them down in front of him.

"Cheers," he said, holding up his bottle. "Welcome back to Gansett."

"Thanks." She touched her bottle to his. "It's good to be here."

They enjoyed the pizza and beer in silence for a few minutes before Riley decided to address the elephant in her life.

"Did she really go back to him?" Riley asked, hesitant to bring up what had to be a sore subject but concerned for her nonetheless.

"She really did," Nikki said with a sigh. "How did you hear?"

"I saw it on one of those entertainment shows. My dad's fiancée had it on in the bar."

"That didn't take long to get out. It must be big news in light of what caused their breakup in the first place."

"How do you go back to someone who'd do that to you?"

"Beats me, but the exposure from the video added seven million new Twitter followers and three million new Instagram fans, so in Jordan's mind, that's a win."

"I don't get it."

"Don't feel bad. I don't either." She met his gaze across the countertop between them. "I quit my job as her assistant."

"Wow. How did that go?"

"As you might imagine. She pleaded with me to reconsider, and I pleaded with her to do the same when it came to Zane. Neither of us was willing to budge, so here I am. She's in Nashville with him, or that's where she was last night. Who knows where he's playing tonight? It's no longer my job to care."

"For what it's worth, I think you did the right thing."

She gave him a measuring look. "It's worth a lot. I've been doing some second-guessing about walking away from her, but I can't take the nonstop drama anymore. She loves it. I can't bear it."

"Then you're wise to take a break."

"This isn't a break. It's a *breakup*. It's time. We're twenty-seven. It's long past time for us to lead separate lives."

"I'm twenty-eight. Almost twenty-nine, actually, and still living with my brother. The only time we haven't lived together was my first year of college. He came to the same school. We lived together after that, and we have ever since."

"That makes me feel a little better about staying with Jordan as long as I did."

"She was paying you to be there, so there is that. Sometimes I think Finn ought to pay me to live with him. He's such a slob. We were just fighting about our shithole house tonight."

Nikki laughed at the face he made. "Would you miss him if you moved out?"

"Yeah, I would, even though I work with him, so I'd still see him every day. Will you miss Jordan?"

"Not right away, but I'm sure I will eventually. Things have really changed between us since she met Zane and got the show."

"I've seen the show a few times," he confessed.

Her eyebrows lifted. "Is that right? You're not exactly the target demographic."

"There was nothing else on."

She laughed. "Good save."

"And," he said, hesitating for a second, "I was curious about what'd become of you after you left last fall."

"One reason we left was because Jordan was contractually required to return to taping the show. I wanted to stay here, but her lawyer told her to get her ass back to LA or she was going to be sued. Later, I found out she'd been talking to Zane, and he'd been pleading with her to come home so they could work things out."

"That explains why you guys disappeared overnight."

"The network sent a plane for us, so we had to go. I wanted to let you know we were leaving, but I wasn't sure how to reach you."

Hearing she'd wanted to talk to him before she left was an antidote to the funk and left him feeling unreasonably elated. "I was bummed when I realized you were gone."

"You were?"

He nodded.

"How come?"

"I liked talking to you."

"I liked talking to you, too. I thought of you after we left and hoped that you'd gotten the roof fixed without falling off. My Gran said you did a great job."

"That's nice of her to say—and PS, I'm a professional. I don't fall off."

She giggled, and the sound did something to him, something strange and unexpected. He wanted to make her laugh again, just so he could listen to the joyful noise. "I didn't mean to wound your ego."

"I accept your apology," he said in a haughty tone. "But you could make it up to me by having dinner with me tomorrow night." The words were out of his mouth before he thought through the implications of officially asking her out. To hell with implications. He liked her. She seemed to like him. After all, she'd confessed to having thought of him after she left. That meant something, didn't it?

She looked down at her plate, appearing less than thrilled to have been asked out by him. "Is anything open this time of year?"

"A few places. Domenic's, for one."

"That's my favorite restaurant on the island."

"Then we'll go to Domenic's. If you want to, that is."

"That would be nice. Thank you."

She seemed to be forcing herself to say yes, but he chose not to delve deeper into that since she'd agreed to go. "You want some help with the tree?"

"I'd love that. I was just thinking I needed a ladder to get to the higher branches."

"I'll do it for you." He took their plates to the sink, washed them and propped them on a wooden rack to dry. When he turned, he caught her watching him and saw her face flush with embarrassment. "What?" he asked, drying his hands on a dish towel. "Never seen a guy do dishes before?"

"In fact, I haven't."

"Then you've been hanging out with the wrong guys."

"That's a fact."

There it was again, that same unsettled vibe he'd sensed when he'd asked her to dinner. Someone had hurt her. Badly. The thought made him want to roar with outrage. But he suppressed that impulse and followed her into the living room, where she presented him with a Clark Griswold-worthy knot of tangled lights.

"Why do I feel like I've just been thoroughly manipulated?" he asked, crooking a brow in amusement.

That little giggle… It did things to him, weird, crazy things that made him want to settle in and get comfortable with her. Was this what it'd been like for Mac when he met Maddie or Evan when he met Grace? Had they wanted to settle in and get comfortable with a woman for the first time in their lives?

Thoughts that would've unsettled him not that long ago now had him wondering about things he never thought about as he spent forty-five minutes unraveling the lights with her sitting beside him on the sofa, helping in between fits of laughing at his frustration.

"Do we even know if these lights are any good?"

"I haven't tested them yet."

He glanced at her, feigning annoyance. "Seriously? Did we just waste an hour we'll never get back unraveling lights that don't even work?"

"Possibly?" she said with a smile.

Riley shook his head and looked away from her, even though that was the last thing he wanted to do. "Moment of truth." He went to an outlet to plug in the lights, which were all connected. "Ready?"

"Ready as I'll ever be."

He pushed the plug into the wall and watched the entire strand come to life.

Nikki clapped, her big brown eyes dancing with what could only be called joy. "That's a relief. I was pretty sure I'd be out of luck if they didn't work. Something tells me that Christmas lights might be hard to come by around here in January."

"Everything's hard to come by around here in January. We had three days around Christmas when the ferries didn't run because of the blizzard, and we ran out of *beer*. That was nearly a full-blown crisis in the McCarthy family."

"God forbid. Three days without beer!"

"You have no idea what we went through. I was afraid there might be a riot if the ferries didn't start running soon. I happened to be in town when the first boat arrived after the storm, and three huge pallets of beer were the first thing unloaded. The villagers went crazy cheering in the streets, and everyone was happy in the land that night."

"That's funny," she said, feeding him the lights as he wound them around the tree, working from the top down. "I'm picturing parades and parties."

"You're not far off. There was a tremendous sense of relief."

At six-foot-two, he had no trouble reaching the top. With her standing by his side, he realized he was a foot taller than she was.

"How many people live here year-round?"

"The *Gansett Gazette* had a story this week that reported nine-hundred and forty-nine year-round residents on the island."

"I'm surprised there're that many."

"Seems like far fewer this time of year when everyone hibernates."

"Am I a weirdo because I love winter?"

"Yes."

She laughed at his quick reply. "I know! It's so wrong, but I love the cold and the snow and Christmas and the fireplace and how everyone hunkers down to ride it out. It's my favorite time of year, especially here. In Southern California, we don't get much of a winter. But there's nowhere I'd rather be than here in the winter."

Listening to the reasons she loved winter, he decided he could easily become a fan of the season that had always been his least favorite, but only if he got to hunker down with her. "Well, I, for one, am very happy to have you as our nine-hundred and fiftieth resident."

CHAPTER 4

*R*iley arrived at work the next morning in a vastly better mood than the day before, which, of course, his brother and cousins noticed.

"Did you get laid last night?" Finn asked in front of everyone as they drank the coffee Mac brought for them every morning.

"Shut the fuck up." He said that no fewer than six times a day to the brother who alternatively amused and annoyed him.

"Well, did you?" Finn asked, undeterred.

"Not that it's any of your business, but *no*. I didn't."

"Huh… Coulda fooled me. You got that freshly fucked look to you."

Riley appealed to his cousin for help. "Mac…"

"Shut up, Finn," Mac said. "Leave him alone."

"You guys are no fun," Finn said.

Shane laughed. "I can name many, *many* people who would say otherwise about the entire lot of us. We're known for being a good time had by all."

Luke Harris snorted with laughter. "I'll attest to that."

"Everyone except Riley," Finn said. "He's a good time had by *no one* lately."

He'd had a damned good time with Nikki last night, and he was fairly confident she'd enjoyed their time together, too. He couldn't wait to see her after work.

Today, they were installing windows, which was frigid work this time of year. Riley was thankful for the intense activity that kept his brother too busy and too cold to continue busting Riley's balls. By late afternoon, they were all frozen and tired.

"Go home, everyone," Mac said at four thirty when they'd installed more than twenty windows that would provide a panoramic view of the beach from the restaurant and bar. "Get warm, and we'll pick it up in the morning."

Riley didn't have to be told twice. After stashing his tools, he headed for the main doors.

"Riley, wait up," Finn called after him. "You wanna grab dinner tonight? I'm in the mood for pizza."

"I've got plans."

"What plans?"

"The kind you make with people who are not your brother."

"Ouch. That hurts my feelings."

"You don't have feelings."

"Ha-ha," Finn said. "Seriously, though… What're you doing?"

"I'm going out."

"By yourself?"

"Nope."

"So she was glad to see you, huh?"

Riley ignored the question and kept his head down against the wind as he walked to his truck, thankful that he and Finn had driven separately today. Finn had still been asleep when Riley left at eight, eager to get his hours in so he could get to the best part of the day —*after* work.

Finn grabbed his arm and spun him around. "Come on. Don't be a dick."

"I'm not being a dick just because I don't want to talk about it."

"Even with me?"

"*Especially* with you."

"What the hell does that mean?"

"I don't want you busting my balls right now. That's what it means."

Finn held up his hands. "I'll be on my best behavior. I promise."

Riley gave him a skeptical look as he unlocked his black pickup truck.

"I will! I mean it."

"I'll see you at home." Riley got in the truck and fired it up, blasting the heat. He was frozen to the bone after the long day. Today was an exception to the norm. They were inside most of the time. According to Mac's plan, they would start on the outside of the building as soon as the weather broke. The job at McCarthy's Wayfarer would take them most of the winter and well into the spring. Their goal was to be ready to open by Memorial Day weekend, which would be a close call.

But if anyone could get it done in time, Mac could. He did an impressive job of coordinating the delivery of building supplies to the island, the timing of which could be tricky. However, the fact that Mac's brother-in-law Joe Cantrell owned the ferry company helped to simplify the process. Mac could get trucks on the boat pretty much whenever he needed to, especially this time of year, when things were quiet on the island.

On the way home, Riley stopped at the island's only liquor store and bought a six-pack of beer. He wasn't a big drinker, but he did enjoy a beer at the end of a long day at work.

When he got home, Finn was already there and had begun cleaning up. He had hip-hop playing so loudly, it was impossible to talk, which was fine with Riley.

He wanted to take pictures to document the unprecedented event of his brother cleaning, but he didn't want him to stop. So he didn't say anything. Rather, he pitched in. It took an hour, but they got the kitchen and bathroom cleaned and a load of laundry done.

Riley rewarded his brother by sharing the beer he'd bought.

They each opened a bottle and clinked them together.

Finn tipped his head back and drank most of his in one big gulp.

Riley took his a little slower. He wasn't looking to get buzzed when he had to drive soon. He'd told Nikki he'd be there around six thirty. At lunchtime, he'd made a reservation at Domenic's, not that they'd need it this time of year. But he was leaving nothing to chance tonight.

He went into his room to text Nikki. They'd exchanged numbers last night, which had been another significant development. He took comfort in knowing he'd be able to reach her, even if she had to leave for some reason. *Got out of work early. You need help finishing the tree before dinner?*

She wrote right back. Watching the little bubbles dance as she typed her reply had him holding his breath in giddy anticipation. *That'd be great! I didn't get to it today.*

Be there in thirty or so.

Sounds good! She punctuated her reply with Christmas tree emojis that made him smile.

"Is your widdle girlfriend sending you sexts?" Finn asked, attempting to look over Riley's shoulder at his phone, which Riley quickly hid from him before ducking into the clean-smelling bathroom to shower.

Standing under the warm water, it occurred to Riley that it might be time to get his own place.

FILLED WITH NERVOUS ENERGY, Nikki went around straightening up a house that didn't need straightening. She fluffed pillows in the living room and wiped down the outdated kitchen countertops that screamed for an update. What she wouldn't give to be able to get her hands on this place and put to use all the otherwise worthless info she'd gained from hours of watching HGTV.

The kitchens and bathrooms were woefully out of date and the old hardwood floors so scuffed, they barely retained the varnish. She'd thought about asking her grandmother if it would be okay to do some work on the house but didn't want to offend the older woman who'd been so good to her.

Perhaps she could work it into conversation when her grandmother called tomorrow to check on her, as she'd vowed to do every day, since Nikki was there alone.

Conversely, she hadn't heard a word from Jordan, which was indicative of an all-consuming reunion with Zane. It wasn't the first time the two of them had gone deep underground. Nikki could only hope that Jordan was using good judgment and not allowing her larger-than-life husband to push her around with the sheer force of his personality.

Nikki had to force herself not to text Jordan. The impulse was so ingrained in her as to be automatic. She resisted, telling herself that as a grown woman with her own life to lead, Jordan could handle whatever came her way. Or so Nikki hoped…

A car door closing outside alerted her to Riley's arrival. Throughout the day, she'd tried not to think too much about him, the date they had planned for tonight—the first real date she'd been on in years—or anything beyond the next few minutes. But when she'd gotten his text, her heart had skipped a happy beat from knowing she would see him again soon.

In that moment, she'd realized he represented the first significant threat to the rules for dealing with men she'd made for herself years ago—rules that had only been reinforced by the nightmare her brother-in-law had perpetrated upon her sister.

Men, she had discovered at an early age, were not to be trusted. Her parents had split after they found out that her dad had a whole other family with another woman. Almost fifteen years later, Nikki still found it hard to believe. She and Jordan had been forced to live with him *and* his new family after the court gave him primary custody over their emotionally erratic mother.

That was the first time she'd learned that men were not to be trusted, but it wasn't the last. As she went to the door to admit Riley, she vowed to enjoy his friendship without expecting anything from him. Keeping her expectations low, she'd learned, went a long way toward protecting her from things she couldn't handle.

Jordan had once accused her of being an emotional cripple. The words had hurt to hear, mostly because they were true. As she opened the door to Riley's handsome, smiling face, she wished things were different and she could be the kind of young woman to get excited about the prospect of a new guy in her life, especially a sinfully handsome, sexy, sweet man like Riley.

But Nikki wasn't a typical young woman and hadn't been for a long time. Her plan for the moment was to enjoy Riley's company until he decided she wasn't worth the effort of continuing to come around for something that wasn't going to happen.

"Hey," he said, bringing the scents of fresh air and appealing cologne in with him. "You look pretty."

"Thank you." She wanted to tell him he looked good, too, but she needed to be cautious about encouraging anything more than platonic friendship with him. Though it was nice to have a friend on the island, she had no idea how long she would be here, and it wouldn't be prudent to get overly involved with him.

Friendship she could handle. Romance? Not so much.

He wore a brown sweater with well-faded jeans that fit him to perfection. Not that she was looking as he led the way to the living room, where the tree waited for finishing touches. She wasn't looking. Well, not really…

"How was your day?" he asked, picking up where they'd left off on the tree the night before when they'd both started yawning.

"It was good. I went for a long walk out at the bluffs, took some photos, baked some vegan pumpkin bread. Nothing special."

He glanced at her. "You're vegan?"

"No, but Jordan is most of the time, so I bake like one."

"Ahh, gotcha. What does vegan pumpkin bread taste like?"

"Want a piece?"

"Uh-huh."

Amused by his enthusiasm, Nikki went to cut him a healthy slice of the bread. She'd spent years experimenting with recipes and thought the pumpkin bread had come out particularly well, but she'd have to see what he thought. She delivered it to him with a tall glass of milk.

"Thank you," he said, taking the plate and glass from her and placing them on the coffee table. He broke off a piece of the bread and popped it into his mouth as he continued to add ornaments to the upper branches of the tree. "That's really good."

"Glad you like it."

"So Jordan is vegan some of the time? What's up with that?"

"Who knows? She's a fad dieter. One day it's vegan, the next it's Paleo and then South Beach. I can't keep up. Vegan has lasted the longest, and I got so I preferred vegan baked goods. When there's less sugar and carbs, you can have *more* of whatever it is."

"That's true," he said, popping the last of his slice into his mouth. "Is there *more* pumpkin bread?"

"There is," she said, appreciating his enjoyment. "Will you still be able to eat dinner?"

"Sweetheart," he said, smiling, "one thing you should know about me is that there's never a time when I can't eat."

Flustered by the endearment as much as the devastating grin, Nikki said, "Gotcha. More pumpkin bread coming right up." She went into the kitchen and cut him another healthy slice of the bread, telling herself to stop being so easily flustered. *You're out of practice*, she thought. It'd been years since she'd spent time alone with a guy.

Not since…

No.

Her entire body went cold at the thought of the guy who'd changed her forever.

Nikki had no idea how long she stood staring out the window over the sink, lost in memories she would give anything to forget, before Riley came to find her.

"Hey," he said softly. "Are you okay?"

Rattled to have been overtaken by unpleasant thoughts that could invade her mind at even the best of times, Nikki forced a smile. "Sorry, yes. Here you go."

He took the plate from her and placed it on the counter. "You don't look all right. Is something wrong?"

"So many things," she said softly before she could take the time to decide whether she should say such a thing to a man she barely knew.

"What things?" he asked, looking at her with concern.

"It's nice of you to want to hang out with me, but you should know… I'm kind of a mess."

His brows furrowed adorably. He was so damned handsome and sexy, the kind of guy who might be capable of changing her opinion of men in general. "No, you're not."

She released a huff of laughter. "I really am. You have no idea."

"Could I tell you something that might surprise you?"

Crossing her arms, she glanced up at him, curious to hear anything he wanted to tell her. "Of course."

"After you left in October?"

She nodded.

"I was super bummed. In fact, I kinda went into a funk, if my brother is to be believed."

Nikki had no idea what to say. He'd been that sad to see her go?

"If you don't say something, I'm going to think you think I'm a weirdo."

"I don't think that," she said. "It's sweet of you to say you were bummed that we left."

"Not you as in you and Jordan. You as in *you*, Nikki. I was sad that *you* left before I had a chance to really get to know you."

"Oh," she said, venturing another glance up at him to gauge his sincerity. "Really?"

"Really. And this so-called funk lasted until I saw you again, when I seemed to miraculously shake it off."

Nikki had no idea what to do with that information.

"So please don't tell me you're a mess or anything else that'll make me sad again, because I'm really, really happy you came back to the island so I don't have to be in a funk anymore. According to my brother, I've been a total bore for months."

His earnest sweetness made her smile. How could it not? "You're very sweet, Riley McCarthy."

"Nah."

"Yes, you are."

"If you say so."

"I say so," she said emphatically, relieved that he hadn't chosen to ask her why she called herself a mess. If she had her druthers, he'd never know the reasons behind that statement.

"What do you say we get this tree of yours finished so we can go get some dinner?"

"Lead the way."

He took the plate with the second piece of pumpkin bread with him when he returned to the living room where she'd left the TV on, set as usual to her favorite network.

"Oh, I love these beach shows," she said, eager to get back to a lighthearted vibe. "I can't believe the deals these people get for houses right on the water."

"That'd never happen here."

"Right?" Real estate was at a premium on Gansett. Her grandmother's home, bought nearly fifty years ago for forty thousand dollars, was now worth millions. Or it would be if it was updated. "I love what they do with these places."

"I've never watched any of those shows," he said, winking. "It'd be like a doctor watching medical stuff."

"You don't know what you're missing. I can watch HGTV for *hours* and never get bored. I wish I knew how to do all that."

"All what?"

"Renovations. I dream about getting my hands on this place and updating it."

"I could show you how."

"Seriously?"

"Yeah," he said, laughing at her wide-eyed reaction. "I've been working construction since I was sixteen. If there's one thing I know, it's that."

"Don't tempt me. Before you know it, you'll be knee-deep in

coaching me through a new kitchen and bathrooms, hardwood floors, paint." Nikki shuddered with ecstasy at the thought. And when she opened her eyes, Riley watched her with thinly veiled desire that arced between them like a live wire.

Realizing he liked her as more than a friend made her nervous, but she didn't feel the need to run away like she would have with almost anyone else. Since the first time he'd come to her rescue when the roof had been leaking, he'd given her no reason to be wary or afraid of him. He'd been what her grandmother would refer to as a perfect gentleman in every way. And yet, even with all her instincts telling her she could relax around him, deep inside where her darkest fears lay, she retained the healthy fear that had kept her safe from men who would do her harm. She'd found out the hard way that even men she trusted could turn into monsters.

She'd known *him* for a full year before she'd realized that underneath the charming surface of a friend and boyfriend lurked a darker side he kept well hidden. Nikki shivered. Thoughts of *him* never failed to chill her to the bone, which was why she tried very hard never to think of him.

"Are you cold?" Riley asked, misinterpreting her shiver.

"I'm good."

They worked in companionable silence to hang the rest of the ornaments her grandmother had acquired over the years. When she'd sold her home outside of Boston and bought her condo in Florida to spend winters in the sunshine, her grandmother had sent most of the Christmas decorations to Gansett. Nikki had never spent a Christmas with her grandmother, as that holiday had belonged to her father, so she'd never seen most of the ornaments before now.

"I like this one," Riley said, holding up a miniature Gansett Island ferry.

"It looks just like one of the real ferries."

"Here's some McCarthy family trivia for you: My cousin's husband owns the company."

"That must be a fun business."

"It's a *lucrative* business when you consider that just about every person and thing on this island got here on one of his boats."

"True."

Riley checked his watch. "We should get going to make our reservation at Domenic's. If you still want to go."

"I do want to." She was hungry and didn't feel like a night alone. He was sweet and had been kind to her, which made her want to get to know him better.

How much better remained to be seen.

CHAPTER 5

*R*iley held her coat, which earned him more points, along with the door to his truck that he opened for her. The front of the black pickup boasted a plow blade.

Nikki had never been on a date in which the guy opened her car door. Her grandmother would wholeheartedly approve of Riley McCarthy. Hell, she already did after the excellent job he'd done on the roof.

When they were on their way to Domenic's, she said, "I meant to tell you that the roof looks really good."

"I'm glad you think so," he said. "As roofs go, that one was a bit of a beast with all the cutouts and dormers. Not to mention the sheer size of it. But we got it done."

"My grandmother was very happy with the job you guys did."

"That's good to hear. My cousin Mac says she's a really nice lady."

"She is. She had young kids to raise on her own after her husband dropped dead at work. He just keeled over at his desk. They said he was dead before anyone realized something had happened. She raised her kids on her own, including my mother."

"That's really admirable. I can't imagine having to raise kids on my own."

"She was a trouper. Fortunately, my grandfather had good insurance and owned a successful company, so she didn't have to work while they were young. But later, when they were all in school, she ended up taking over the helm of his company and ran it for thirty years."

"That's amazing. What kind of company was it?"

"Manufacturing. They make components for jet engines. My aunt is the CEO now."

"Very cool. Did your grandmother ever remarry?"

"Nope. She's never even been on a date since my grandfather died. She said she had her great love and no one could ever take his place."

Riley sighed.

And that sigh caused something inside Nikki to shift to accommodate the possibility that he might be different, better than most of the men she'd known in the past.

"I'm sad for someone I've never even met," Riley said, further cementing her instincts where he was concerned.

"There're pictures of them together at the house. You can tell just by looking at them that they were so happy."

"I'd love to see them." He turned the truck into the parking lot at Domenic's and pulled in next to a large black SUV. "You're going to get to meet my cousin Mac and his wife, Maddie," Riley said, nodding to the SUV.

"Oh cool. Gram loves him—and his father."

"Everyone does." They met at the front of Riley's truck, and he placed a hand on her lower back to usher her into the restaurant.

She told herself not to overreact to the proprietary gesture that was probably ingrained in him, but it gave her a flutter inside that she hadn't felt in so long, she almost didn't recognize the emotions coursing through her for what they were—excitement, desire, anticipation. Among the other diners, Nikki recognized Riley's cousin right away due to an obvious family resemblance. Like Riley, Mac had dark hair and piercing blue eyes.

After he checked in with the host, Riley took hold of her hand and led her to his cousin's table.

"Hey," Mac said, smiling up at Riley. "Fancy meeting you here."

"Hi there," Riley said. "This is Nikki Stokes. Nikki, my cousin Mac McCarthy and his wife, Maddie."

"Nice to meet you," Mac said, standing to shake her hand.

"You, too," Nikki said, shaking hands with both of them.

"You're Mrs. Hopper's granddaughter, right?"

"That's me, the one with the leaky roof."

"She's a doll," Mac said. "I love working for her."

"She likes you, too. She says you're a handsome devil."

"Oh dear God," Maddie said, groaning. "Do *not* tell him that. He'll be even more unbearable than he already is."

While Mac scowled playfully at his wife, Nikki and Riley cracked up laughing.

"How'd you score a get-out-of-jail-free pass tonight?" Riley asked them, adding for Nikki's benefit, "They have three kids under the age of six."

"Yikes," Nikki said.

"You know it," Maddie said, taking a healthy sip of her wine. "My mom and Ned hosted a sleepover, so we could get a night off. I told Mac we could do anything as long as I didn't have to cut anyone's food."

"You don't have to cut Mac's food?" Riley asked.

"Not anymore." She smiled up at her husband, who was an older, equally handsome version of Riley. "He's coming along nicely."

"You're a miracle worker," Riley said. "You even got him potty trained."

"I wouldn't go *that* far," Maddie said.

"I can hear you two," Mac said, making Nikki laugh.

"We'll let you get back to your date night," Riley said. "See you in the morning."

"Bright and early," Mac said.

"Yeah, yeah." With his hand on her lower back, Riley directed her toward the table the host pointed to, where menus had been left for them. Riley held her chair and waited for her to get settled before taking his own seat.

"They're funny," Nikki said.

"Yeah, they are. We all love her. She's perfect for him."

"He looks like you, or I guess I should say you look like him."

"Ew, I do not."

"Yes, you do," she said, laughing.

"I thought you liked me."

"I *do* like you."

"Then don't say I look like Mac," he said, making a face.

"That's not an insult. He's not exactly ugly."

"Yes, he is."

As she cracked up yet again, she realized she'd laughed more in the last hour than she had in years.

HE LOVED HER LAUGH, loved being the cause of it, loved the way she let go of the tension that was such a big part of her when she wasn't laughing. As he studied the menu, he wanted to keep her laughing so she wouldn't think about whatever had troubled her earlier. When he'd walked into the kitchen and found her staring out the window, lost in thoughts that were obviously upsetting, he'd wanted to wrap his arms around her and make it better.

But he'd resisted that impulse, sensing it might make things worse rather than better. The incident had confirmed his earlier suspicion that someone had hurt her badly. The thought of anyone hurting her filled him with rage that he didn't dare show her, lest he scare her off. That was the last thing he wanted to do when she seemed to be getting more comfortable with having him around.

"What looks good to you?" he asked.

"I'm leaning toward the cod."

"I was thinking about getting that, too."

The waiter came and took their orders, returning with an Amstel Light for him and a glass of pinot grigio for her.

"I haven't been here in years." She took a look around the restaurant, which was busy for an off-season weeknight. "We used to come several times each summer. It was one of our favorites."

"I'm surprised I never ran into you before. I spent a couple of summers working for my uncle at the marina. We were probably here at the same time."

"When was that?"

"About twelve years ago?"

"I was here! I waitressed at the Lobster Pot that summer."

"No way. I'm sure I must've eaten there. That's one of my uncle's favorite places, and I lived with him and my aunt. He was always trying to feed me. They used to tease me about being too skinny."

"I worked there for six summers. I wonder if I waited on you guys."

"How funny would that be? But I think I would've remembered you. Did you know my cousins?"

"I knew of the family and the marina, of course, but I don't think I ever met them. They're older than me, I think."

Nodding, he said, "They're older than me, too."

"We used to come here the second school let out." Her lips set into a grimace as she seemed to remember unhappy memories. "I couldn't get here fast enough."

"You didn't like school?"

"That wasn't it. I didn't like my father, and we had to live with him during the school year. I counted down to summer vacation on Gansett."

"That must've been difficult for you, having to live with him nine months out of the year if you didn't like him."

"It was hell. Thank God for Jordan during those years. We survived it together."

Riley was almost afraid to ask what he most wanted to know. "He wasn't… abusive, was he?"

"No, nothing like that." Sighing, she took a sip of her wine and seemed to be deciding how much she wanted to tell him. "My mom… She was an alcoholic with mental health problems that caused a lot of chaos while we were growing up. She wasn't allowed to have us on her own, which is why we came here in the summers. Our grandmother had actual custody of us in the summer."

He had questions, but he didn't ask them, hoping she would offer more.

"My dad reacted to my mom's issues by taking up with someone else while he was still married to her. By the time the whole thing came out, he had two kids with the other woman, and the court *still* gave him primary custody over my mother and her troubles."

"Whoa."

"Yeah, it was lots of fun, but it was a long time ago."

"Do you see your dad?"

She wrapped her arms around herself in that protective pose he was coming to recognize as built into her DNA. "He and his new family are no longer in our lives," she said, her shuttered expression keeping him from asking any further questions. "We haven't seen him since the day we graduated from high school. Sometimes I think Jordan ended up with Zane because of my dad."

"How do you mean?"

"She learned at an early age not to set her expectations too high."

"You must be crushed that she went back to him."

"I'm numb more than anything. That relationship has been the definition of toxic since day one. I'm glad to have him out of my life, but I sure do miss her. Even if I wanted to shake her half the time lately."

"It's got to be hard for you to see her making questionable choices."

"It is, especially since she used to really listen to me, and now it seems his voice is the only one she hears."

"I still can't believe he did what he did to her and she went back to him."

"I know. I wanted to tie her up and toss her in a closet when I realized what she was doing." She took another drink of wine. "But instead of doing that, I focused on what I could control, which is my own life, such as it is."

"How about your mom? Do you see her?"

"We're in touch with her. She's remarried and living in the south of France with an artist she met in Paris when she was there on vacation. They seem really happy."

"Good for her."

"She deserves to be happy after everything she's been through."

Riley wanted to tell her that she deserved the same. "What did you do for work before you were Jordan's assistant?"

"We were both models," she said sheepishly.

Smiling at her embarrassment, he said, "I can see that. What kind of modeling did you do?"

"I did makeup and catalog stuff. Jordan was all about the underwear. That's how she first met Zane. He was a model, too. Before his music career took off." She looked down at the table. "Because the modeling bored me, I also worked in restaurants and the hospitality business on the side. I still think about finishing college or doing something meaningful."

"You can do anything you want now."

"Yes, I can. I just have to figure out what that is."

"There's no rush, is there?"

"Not particularly."

"Then take your time and enjoy the break in the meantime."

"I've done nothing but talk about myself."

"Not true—and I'm interested in hearing about your life."

"Tell me about your life. Where did you grow up?"

"Westport, Connecticut, which is about an hour outside New York City."

"Do your parents still live there?"

"My mom does. My dad lives here now. They split a year and a half ago."

"Ouch."

"Yeah, it was sort of shocking since it came out of nowhere, at least for my brother and me it did. My dad told us later that it'd been a long time coming." He shrugged. "It was much worse when it happened to you. At least we were adults and didn't have our parents fighting over us."

"It's awful no matter when it happens," she said.

"It was pretty awful." Riley hadn't really said that to anyone but Finn. He felt comfortable telling her because she'd been through it herself. "My mom cheated on him with a younger guy. It was all so… sordid. Finn and I were just saying how glad we are to be nowhere near Westport, where our family must be the talk of the town."

"How'd you end up living on the island?"

"We came with our dad for our cousin Laura's wedding right after my parents broke up. My dad decided to stay for a bit to regroup, and when Mac begged Finn and me to stay and come to work for him, we agreed to hang for a bit, mostly to keep an eye on our dad, who was really flattened by the divorce."

"That's nice of you guys."

"We've always been really close to him, so it wasn't a hardship to hang with him for a while, but it was funny to be living with him again. We'd forgotten how anal he is about cleaning. He also likes to *communicate*. A lot." Riley rolled his eyes. "He's a shrink."

She laughed. "Ahh, that must get uncomfortable."

"Extremely." Smiling, he said, "He's a good guy, though. Finn and I both respect him more than just about anyone. And now, he's engaged to Chelsea Rose, who's a bartender at the Beachcomber, and they're trying to have a baby."

"Whoa. How do you feel about that?"

"At first, it was kinda weird, but now I'm just like whatever. It's his life, and if he wants to start all over with a new family, it's none of my business. Like Finn said, it's not like he's asking us to raise the baby for him."

She raised a brow.

"What?"

"It's okay to say that you're weirded out by the idea of having a sibling nearly thirty years younger than you."

"It is somewhat… unexpected."

"To say the least," she said, laughing. "Do you like the fiancée?"

"We like her a lot. Chelsea's great, and he's nuts about her. It's all good. I'm glad he's happy. She's quite a bit younger than him and hasn't had kids yet, thus the baby project."

"Ah, I see." She sat back from the table when the waiter appeared with their entrees. "This looks delicious."

"The food here is the best."

They ate in companionable silence that had him thinking about how easy she was to be with. Their conversation flowed effortlessly, and he found just about everything she said interesting. He couldn't recall ever being so immediately at ease around a woman, but he got the feeling she wasn't quite as comfortable with him, which rankled. It wasn't anything he could easily cite, just an overall feeling of disquiet that he'd sensed each of the four times he'd been in her presence.

Was it him or something else? Was there something he could do or say to put her at ease? He wished he knew, because he'd literally do just about anything to convince her that he could be trusted, that he was nothing like her father or other men who might've hurt her. And what did it say about him that knowing someone had hurt her made him feel so murderous? He'd certainly never felt that strongly about a woman before.

Until recently, he hadn't given much thought to the fact that he'd never been in love, but at times, he'd wondered if that particular life experience wasn't in the cards for him. Sure, he enjoyed women, had had his share of sex and had mostly coasted through life without messy emotional entanglements.

His brother had an on-again, off-again girlfriend who was thankfully off-again at the moment. Finn had definitely been in love with Missy, much to the dismay of everyone who cared about him. Riley couldn't stand Missy or the way Finn acted around her. The best part of moving to Gansett had been the demise of his brother's relationship with her.

"I was thinking about what you said about renovating your grandmother's house," Riley said, taking a chance along with a sip of his beer.

"What about it?"

"If you're serious about updating it, I could help you with that." He absolutely didn't have the time to take on another project with the Wayfarer occupying most of his waking hours, but if it meant more time with her, he'd make it happen.

"How do you mean?"

"You want to do it. I know how, and Mac is brilliant at getting what we need to the island for the business. He could help us get whatever we need for your place. I work a lot, so it would be nights and weekends, but I'd be happy to do it for you."

"That is so nice of you to offer, but I want to learn how to do it myself."

"Like the actual work, you mean?"

"Yes."

"Oh, well… I could show you anything you want to know."

"That might take a lot of time."

He shrugged. "I'm not going anywhere. Are you?"

"I don't know," she said, rolling her lip between her teeth. "I have no idea what I'm doing long-term."

Riley knew a moment of pure panic at the thought of her leaving again when he'd only just gotten her back. *Whoa…* Where had *that* come from? All he knew for certain was that he didn't want her to go, not yet anyway. "Maybe renovating the house could be your purpose for the time being, and when that's finished, you could reassess."

He was a self-serving bastard, but whatever it took to keep her around. Why that was so critical, he couldn't say. All he knew was that the gloom had lifted when she returned, and he liked how he felt when she was around. Beyond that, he didn't know anything.

She looked across the table, her big brown eyes full of vulnerability that touched him more deeply than any woman ever had. "You don't want to do that when you're already working ten hours a day."

"I wouldn't have offered if I didn't want to do it."

"You're serious." Excitement replaced the vulnerability.

"Yes," he said, smiling. "You want to know how to do renovations. I know how. I'd happily teach you—and help you."

"Why?" she asked.

The question hit him like a punch to the gut. Why indeed? "Because it would be fun."

"Really? It would be fun to do in your off time what you do all day?"

"It would be fun to teach you how." *And it will keep you here for months*, he thought but didn't say. "I also have the equipment you need," he added, waggling his brows in a teasing gesture that made her laugh and blush. Adorable.

"I'd have to talk to my grandmother. It is her house and her money, after all."

"Of course. See what she thinks. What's the first thing you'd want to do?" he asked as they perused the dessert menu.

"The kitchen," she said without hesitation.

"You'd need to set up a temporary kitchen in another room with the essentials—microwave, fridge—"

"Coffeemaker."

"Coffeemaker," he said, smiling at the excitement radiating from her. He liked that look on her a lot. "Then we get a dumpster and rip everything out."

"Chip calls that 'Demo Day.'"

"Chip?"

"Chip Gaines on *Fixer Upper*," she said, looking at him like he had six heads. "He and his wife, Jo, are super famous for their home renovations."

"Never heard of them."

"Oh my God! For real? I *idolize* them. While you teach me about renovation, I'll educate you on HGTV."

"Uhhh, okay," he said hesitantly, even if he was anything but hesitant when it came to her.

"I bet you've never heard of the Property Brothers either."

"Who?"

"Oh God," she said with mock despair. "I've got *so* much to teach you."

Yes, please, he thought. *Teach me. Teach me everything.*

CHAPTER 6

ac spied on his cousin from across the big dining room. "Riley seems to be having a nice time."

"Mind your own business," Maddie said.

"What fun is that?"

"I'll give you fun, but you have to stop staring at your cousin."

"I just hope he's being careful. The business with her sister is crazy, and I'd hate to see him caught up in that."

"He's not dating the sister. There's nothing to see over there. Focus on your own wife before she starts feeling unfriendly toward you right when this romantic dinner is about to pay off for you."

"Pay off how?" he asked, suddenly very interested in his own business again.

"You'll see when we get home."

"Check, please," he said, signaling the waiter, who came right over.

"Not yet," Maddie said, glaring at her husband. "I want dessert, please."

The waiter left them with the dessert menu, which Maddie perused in great detail while Mac tried not to pout. She loved to torture him, and it'd been weeks since they'd last had a night to spend completely alone together. Her parents had taken all three kids, even the baby, to their house for a sleepover, which was a major undertaking that included getting Thomas to kindergarten in the morning.

"Quit your pouting," she said. "I pumped myself dry for two days for *one* kid-free night. You're not going to rush me."

"Yes, dear."

She ordered a brownie sundae with two spoons as well as a glass of champagne to top off the evening.

"I like to see you relaxed and enjoying yourself," he said once he'd accepted that they wouldn't be leaving quite yet.

"I like having nothing to do but you."

Mac choked on a mouthful of beer that came out—painfully— through his nose, which made his dearly beloved laugh her ass off. "That was not nice," he said after he'd mopped up the beer that was all over him.

Fanning her face with her hand, she couldn't stop laughing.

He grunted out a laugh—how could he not? Her laughter was always infectious. Never more so than when directed at him, which was a frequent occurrence.

The sundae arrived, and Maddie dived into it like a woman who hadn't seen chocolate in months while she tried to lose the weight she'd gained carrying baby Mac.

Mac sat back to enjoy her pleasure in the dessert.

"You're supposed to be sharing this with me," she said around a mouthful of brownie.

"It's far more fun to watch you devour it."

She put down her spoon and patted her lips with a napkin. "I've had enough."

"You've barely made a dent. Get back in there, and don't give up until it's gone. My wife is not a quitter."

"Your wife isn't going to fit through the door if she doesn't lose some weight."

Mac scowled and reached for the spoon she'd abandoned. "No one talks trash about my wife, especially my wife." He held up a spoonful of brownie and ice cream. "Take a bite."

Holding his gaze, she leaned in and let him feed her a bite.

He took one for himself before dishing up another for her, continuing that pattern until the dessert was gone. Then he paid the check and held her coat for her. Before they left, they stopped by to say good night to Riley and Nikki.

"I have an appointment in the morning, so I'll be late," Mac said. "Let the others know for me?"

"Will do," Riley said. "See you when you get there."

"It was so nice to meet you, Nikki," Maddie said.

"You, too."

"You guys have a good night," Riley said.

"You do the same," Mac said, waggling his brows at his cousin.

Riley rolled his eyes. "Get lost, Mac."

"I'm going." He put his arm around his wife to escort her from the dining room.

"Why do you have to bust his balls?" Maddie asked.

"Because that's the McCarthy family credo," Mac replied as if she'd asked the stupidest question ever. "You know that."

"Maybe you could let him get through the first date with her before you start the ball-busting."

"Nope. That's not how it works. Page thirty-two of the McCarthy Family Playbook is very clear on these matters. Ball-busting shall commence upon birth and end at death."

"You're ridiculous."

"So you tell me on a daily basis." He opened the passenger door for her and waited until she was settled before leaning in to steal a kiss. "I don't like when my wife says bad things about herself, because to me, she's a freaking goddess who has given me my incredible kids. I love every beautiful inch of her, which I will show her when we get home."

Smiling, she placed her cold hand on his face. "You're very sweet."

"I'm dead serious. Eat the dessert, Madeline. Enjoy the dessert. Don't deny yourself anything you want. Ever. You got me?"

"Yes, Mac. I've got you. Now take me home before my boobs explode."

"We can't have that," he said, laughing. He kissed her again before closing the door and jogging around to the driver's side. It was colder than a well digger's ass this time of year when the days were short and the nights long, not that he would ever complain about more time at home with his wife and kids. He loved the winter, when life was slower in general than during the frantic summer, when they tried to jam a year's worth of outdoor living into three short months while he juggled two booming businesses. Thank God the marina was open only four months a year.

"What're you thinking about over there?" she asked.

"How I used to hate winter when I was a kid living here. It was so boring. Now I love it. Lots of time with you and the kids, as opposed to the summer when the marina is open and life is nonstop."

"I agree. I used to hate the winter, too, but now it has its redeeming qualities."

He reached for her hand and curled his fingers around hers. "Long, cold nights with my baby."

"Lots of snuggling."

"My favorite winter sport."

"That's your favorite year-round sport."

"Only if I get to snuggle with you."

Maddie laughed. "You should've been a politician. You always know what to say."

"Sometimes I worry that you think I'm bullshitting you when I tell you you're a goddess to me or that you're my favorite person to snuggle with."

"I know you're not," she said with a sigh.

"Why the sigh, then?"

"I didn't mean to sigh."

"Part of you doesn't believe me when I say you're the sexiest girl I've ever known, no matter what, right?"

"I just wish I could lose the baby weight. I'm heavier than I've ever been, and I hate it."

"You've also got three little kids, including an infant. It'll happen, babe."

"I just don't want it to get any worse than it already is."

Mac wished he could find the words to make her feel better. "I didn't take you out to dinner to make you feel guilty."

"I don't," she said. "Not about tonight. Just in general." She looked over at him. "Thanks for always trying to make it better."

He smiled at her and gave her hand a squeeze.

"By the way, what've you got to do in the morning?"

"My gorgeous wife. We have a rare kid-free morning. No way am I squandering that by going to work on time. I'm taking full advantage of one of the perks of owning the business."

"In case I forget to tell you later, you're the best husband I've ever had."

His low growl made her laugh. "I'd better be the only husband you ever have."

"Only one I ever wanted."

"Right back atcha, babe."

When they got home, Maddie went straight upstairs to pump. Mac locked up and texted Francine to check on the kids.

Everyone is asleep, she replied. *Hope you had a nice dinner.*

We did. Thanks again for having them.

We love having them. Tell Maddie to sleep in. We don't have anything to do in the morning after we get Thomas to school.

I will, you're the best.

He went upstairs, where Maddie was attached to the device that she called the milking machine.

"Don't look," she said, drawing the sheet over her chest the way she had back in the early days of their relationship when she'd been extremely self-conscious about her overly large breasts.

Then, like now, it truly pained him to realize that she saw herself very differently than he did. He unbuttoned his shirt, stripped down to boxers, brushed his teeth and went to get in bed with his wife. "I checked on the kids. Everyone is asleep, and your mom said to sleep in."

"Thank God for grandparents."

"No kidding. I don't know how people raise kids without them."

"We're very lucky."

"We're lucky in every possible way."

When she was finished, Mac took the bottles of breast milk downstairs to the refrigerator for her. Returning to the bedroom, he smiled at the sight of her out cold. Her honey-colored hair was spread out on the pillow, and her lips pursed in an adorable bow that made him want to kiss her. But he wouldn't disturb her when she was getting some much-needed rest. The kids ran her ragged, not that she ever complained.

Mac turned off the light and got into bed next to her, thankful as he was every night to get to share this life with her, to sleep with her and raise their kids together. Not that long ago, he'd thought he was living large in Miami, running a successful construction company and having his choice of women.

That life seemed a million miles removed from what he had now, and he wouldn't trade the present for the past, not for anything.

Maddie was the key to everything, and he hated to hear her down on herself like she'd been earlier. He needed to think of something he could do to make her feel better about herself, but damned if he knew what.

AFTER DINNER, Riley asked Nikki if she wanted to stop for a drink at the Beachcomber before he took her home.

"Sure," she said.

"Here's the thing, though. My dad is apt to be there, possibly my brother, too. I don't want you to think I'm rushing you into meeting my family."

Her stomach twisted with nerves. If they were just friends, it didn't matter if she met his family, right? "I don't mind meeting them, if you don't."

"I'd love for you to meet them."

The more time she spent with him, the more she liked him and the more he challenged the rules she'd set for herself a long time ago. No romantic entanglements. She'd been hurt enough in her life as it was. The last thing she needed was more hurt, but Riley seemed so different.

He *had at first, too. He was so nice and sweet and charming, until you said no to him and he took what he wanted anyway.*

The thoughts and the memories that came with them made her shiver.

"Are you cold?" Riley asked, tuned in to her the way no one else had ever been, or so it seemed.

"A little, but I'm fine." She was scared senseless, but she couldn't tell him that. He'd been so sweet and so kind. Not to mention, he was incredibly handsome and sexy. That'd been the first thing she'd noticed about him the day he came to the house to see about the leaking roof.

His dark hair, blue eyes, chiseled face and muscular body made her want to forget all about her stupid rules. Add his physical attributes to the warm, engaging personality, and she was nearly powerless to resist his alluring charm.

Riley McCarthy posed the first serious threat to a heart she kept well-guarded after it'd been shattered twice in the past—once by her father and again by a man who'd pretended to care about her when in fact he'd been after something she hadn't wanted to give him.

Anxiety, her constant companion for years now, had her mind racing, her stomach churning and her body feeling as if it was under attack. Fight-or-flight mode, she referred to it. Medication helped to keep it under control, but every so often, it would rear its ugly head and take her hostage the way it had for years before a doctor suggested the medication that had given her back her life.

Spending time with a handsome, sexy, charming man who was clearly interested in her brought back the anxiety she'd worked so hard to escape. Nikki had to remind herself that Riley wasn't the problem. He hadn't done anything to cause the unrest that churned within her, and it wouldn't be fair to assign any blame to him.

At the Beachcomber, he again ushered her in ahead of him with a hand on her lower back that he immediately removed when they were inside.

Nikki wanted him to leave it there, a thought that set off a new wave of tingles down her spine and more churning in her stomach.

She swallowed the tight knot that formed in her throat and took a deep breath, reminding herself that not all guys who seemed sweet at the outset were charming you into a false sense of security.

Most of them were exactly as they appeared, and, according to her grandmother, Riley's family was highly regarded on the island. They were people who could be trusted, which was why she'd let him into her house when he appeared out of the darkness last night. It was why she'd welcomed him back and agreed to have dinner with him. And it was why she was walking into the Beachcomber bar, where she would likely meet his father and possibly his brother, too.

Deep breaths.

Riley smiled at her as he snuck up on a man sitting at the bar. "Hey, old man, what's up?"

Smiling, the man said, "Who you calling old?"

"There's nothing old about him," the pretty blonde bartender said with a welcoming grin for Riley.

"Spare me the gory details," Riley said, bringing Nikki in with his arm around her shoulders, as if it was no big deal for him to put his arm around her. "Dad, Chelsea, this is Nikki Stokes. Nikki, this old guy is my dad, Kevin McCarthy, and his fiancée, Chelsea Rose. She's way out of his league, but she doesn't seem to realize that."

Kevin stood to shake Nikki's hand. "Pleasure to meet you, Nikki, and I agree completely that my lovely Chelsea is way out of my league."

"Nice to meet you, too, Dr. McCarthy." *Handsome men definitely run in the McCarthy family*, Nikki thought.

"Call me Kevin, please."

Nikki shook hands with Chelsea across the bar. "Nice to meet you."

"You, too. What're you drinking?"

"Pinot grigio?"

"Coming right up. Usual for you, Riley?"

"Yes, please. Thanks, Chelsea."

"No problem."

"Have a seat, guys," Kevin said.

Riley helped Nikki onto the stool between him and his father.

"Are you guys coming from dinner?"

"Yep," Riley said. "Domenic's was awesome as always."

"Love it there. I'd eat there every night if Chelsea didn't have to work."

"Are you saying it's better than the chowder and burgers we have here?" Chelsea asked, her brow raised.

"Nothing can beat the atmosphere here," he said, winking at her.

Chelsea laughed. "Watch out, Nikki. These McCarthy men are smooth-talking charmers."

"I'm beginning to realize that," Nikki said.

"We come by it naturally," Riley said. "It's in the DNA."

"Has she met Mac yet?" Kevin asked.

"Just now at Domenic's. He and Maddie were on a date night."

"He's the smoothest-talking one of us all," Kevin said.

"No way," Riley said. "That honor goes to his dad, Big Mac. Wait until you meet him."

"You're right," Kevin said. "My older brother is in a class all his own."

"There seem to be a lot of you around here," Nikki said.

"The whole family has gravitated to the island in the last few years," Kevin said. "My brother Mac has six children, who are all here, and my brother Frank has two, and they're both here as well."

"Every member of the family went in on the purchase of the Wayfarer at the end of last year," Riley said. "And now we're renovating it to hopefully open for the summer."

"That's really something that the entire family is involved," Nikki said. She couldn't imagine what it would be like to be part of a family that did something like that together.

"Another of my brother Mac's big ideas," Kevin said. "He's full of them."

"This was a good one," Riley said. "The Wayfarer was a gold mine back in the day before it fell into disrepair. We're excited to bring it back to life."

She could see his passion for his work in the way his eyes sparkled when he talked about it. "Do you like working with your cousins?"

"I love it," Riley said bluntly. "I've learned a ton from Mac and Shane and Mac's business partner, Luke Harris, who is a master carpenter and woodworker. In his spare time, he restores old wooden boats."

"Oh wow. That's amazing. I'd love to see his work sometime."

"Big Mac owns a couple of the boats Luke restored," Kevin said. "They're at the marina in the summer."

"Nikki has an interest in renovation and restoration," Riley said.

She felt her face heat with embarrassment. "If you can call an obsession with HGTV an interest."

"Right there with you, sister," Chelsea said. "I could watch that network twenty-four hours a day and never get tired of it. I've convinced myself I could do everything they do because I've watched so much of it."

"Me, too!" Nikki said, thrilled to have found a kindred spirit. "I told Riley that I want to renovate my grandmother's house, and he's got me thinking I could do it."

"I'll help," Chelsea said. "I'd love to. I wield a mean paintbrush."

"Thank you," Nikki said. "It's so nice of you to offer. I'll take all the help I can get. I have no idea what I'm doing, but I know just enough to be dangerous."

Riley laughed. "She's got a PhD in HGTV."

"Exactly," Nikki said.

"What does your grandmother think about your plan to renovate?" Kevin asked.

"I'm going to talk to her about it tomorrow and see if she's okay with it. I'm sure she will be. Jordan and I are her only grandchildren, so she always tells my sister and me that the house belongs to us. We don't like to think about the day when we'll officially own it, you know?"

Riley nodded with understanding. "I totally get that. You want her around for many more years to come."

"I'd rather have her than the house any day," Nikki said bluntly.

Other than Jordan, Evelyn Hopper was the most important person in her life. She'd been their touchstone during a difficult and chaotic childhood.

Chelsea quizzed Nikki about what she wanted to do to the house while the guys listened patiently, interjecting suggestions and comments.

An hour went by before Nikki came up for air, surprised to realize she already felt like she'd known Kevin and Chelsea for far longer than an hour. Like Riley, his dad was easygoing and charming, not to mention extremely handsome. He was funny and interested in what she had to say, and Nikki liked him a lot.

"Should we share our news?" Chelsea asked him when they finally had a lull in the conversation.

"I was going to ask him and his brother to lunch tomorrow, but I suppose we can tell Riley now." To his son, he added, "But don't tell Finn yet. I want to tell him myself."

"You've got my attention," Riley said. "What's up?"

"Chelsea's pregnant," Kevin said, smiling warmly at his fiancée.

The obvious love between them filled Nikki with an odd feeling of envy. What would it be like, she wondered, to have such a bond with a man?

"Wow," Riley said. "Congrats. That's awesome."

"We're glad you think so," Chelsea said, seeming relieved by Riley's support.

"Congratulations," Nikki said.

"We're going to get married at the end of the month," Kevin said, reaching for Chelsea's hand across the bar. "Uncle Mac and Aunt Linda agreed to let us borrow their hotel for a mid-winter wedding." He glanced at his son. "I'll want you and your brother to be my best men, if you're willing."

"Of course we're willing," Riley said. "I'm happy for you guys."

"Thanks, bud," Kevin said. "That means everything to both of us."

Nikki wondered what Riley was really thinking. If he was upset by his father's news, he was doing a great job of hiding it.

CHAPTER 7

*R*iley had known this was coming, and he was truly happy for his dad and Chelsea. He said and did all the right things, the things his dad expected and deserved after the lifetime of support he'd given his sons. But deep inside, in the part of him that resisted change of any kind, he still mourned for the family that'd been lost when his parents split.

No matter how much he wanted things to stay as they'd always been, that wasn't going to happen, and he could either get on board or run the risk of hurting the father who had been so very good to him. So he toasted his father and Chelsea and shared in their good news.

Nikki excused herself to go to the ladies' room.

"Nikki seems really nice," Kevin said when Chelsea went to tend to the only other customers in the bar.

"She is."

"Are you guys dating?"

Riley shrugged. "I'm not really sure. She's very… hesitant, or so it seems."

"You seem rather taken with her."

"I like her. A lot." The confession made him feel oddly exposed. He sent his dad a wry grin. "I hadn't admitted that to anyone, even myself."

Kevin chuckled. "I know that feeling. When Chelsea first showed an interest in me, I couldn't believe it for like a month."

"That's because she's *way* out of your league," Riley said, smirking.

Kevin laughed. "So far out of my league, it's not even funny. But she loves me anyway. All I can say is be patient, son. The best things in life happen when you least expect them, and if Nikki is hesitant, it's probably for good reason."

Riley nodded in agreement. He hoped that someday she'd share with him the reasons for her hesitant nature.

"Keep showing up and showing her that she can trust you," Kevin said. "That'll mean everything to her."

"Thanks, Dad."

"Any time. I'm always here if you need me."

"I know, and I'm really happy for you and Chelsea."

"Thanks." His gaze found the woman who would soon be his wife. "I'm pretty damned happy for us myself, even if I'm hoping I can do this fatherhood thing justice at my age."

"You'll be great. I have no doubt."

"That means a lot to me. Thankfully, the baby will have a youthful mother and brothers to pick up my slack."

"There won't be any slack to pick up. The baby will be as lucky as Finn and I are."

Kevin gave Riley a one-armed hug and kissed the top of his head. "Thanks," he said gruffly. "Your support and approval make all the difference."

Riley swallowed the lump that suddenly appeared in his throat. Everything had changed, but all he cared about was his father's happiness. Chelsea made him happy. That was enough for Riley.

When Nikki returned, Riley asked if she was ready to call it a night.

"I think I am. I'm suffering from a bit of jet lag with the time difference."

"No problem. I'll talk to you tomorrow, Dad."

"Yes, you will. Nikki, it was a pleasure to meet you."

"You, too, Kevin. Congratulations again."

"Thank you. I hope you'll come to the wedding with Riley. We don't stand on formality around here. Everyone is welcome."

"I'd love to come if I'm still here. Thank you." They waved to Chelsea as they left the bar and bundled up before stepping into the frigid winter air.

If I'm still here. Four words had Riley reeling as he helped her into the truck and then closed the door to jog around to the driver's side. In the short time they'd been inside the Beachcomber, the temperature had dropped significantly. The cold helped to give him something to think about besides his worries about her leaving.

"Is it even colder than it was before, or is it just me?" Nikki asked.

Riley glanced at the temperature on the dash. "Ten degrees colder than it was earlier."

"Brrr."

"Smells like snow."

"I've never understood when people say that. What does snow smell like?"

"It smells cold and damp and crisp. The more you're around it, the more you'll notice the smell." He turned up the heat and directed the truck toward the island's north end.

"So, your dad is getting married and having a baby."

"How about that?"

"I know how hard it is to see your parents moving on with other people. You don't have to pretend otherwise with me."

He glanced at her before returning his gaze to the dark road. "That's good to know." After a long silence, he added, "It helps that you get it."

"I remember what it was like to realize that the family you'd known was gone forever, replaced by something that'll never completely replace it."

"That's it," he said softly. "Exactly. I'm truly happy for my dad, but…"

"You grieve the loss of your family."

"Yeah."

"You don't say much about your mom. Do you talk to her?"

"Occasionally. Not as much as I did before everything happened."

"You're angry with her, and with good reason."

"At the end of the day," he said, "what went down between them is truly none of my business."

"But it still involves you. In that way, it's very much your business."

"I guess so."

"I remember when my parents first separated and how I wondered if we would still have birthday parties or vacations or any of the things we'd had when they still lived together."

"Did you?" he asked.

"Yes, but it was never the same again. Someone was always missing, and after we found out my dad had other kids, our feelings for him changed. My mom wasn't great about keeping the dirty details away from us. We knew far more than we should have at that age."

"As bad as my parents' split was when it happened, I can't imagine going through it as a kid and having them fighting over us."

"Whereas I think it's probably worse at your age because you thought it wasn't going to happen to your family." She shrugged. "It sucks no matter when it happens."

"It helps to talk about it with someone who gets it. My brother has been sort of weird about it. He acts like he doesn't give a shit, when I know he does."

"That's how some people choose to cope. Jordan was like that at times. It used to drive me crazy that she didn't want to dissect every detail of what was going on the way I did. I needed to understand it, but I later came to realize she needed to pretend like it wasn't happening."

"It's interesting how two siblings who are close and generally see things the same way can view something like this so differently."

"Jordan and I were always close but disagreed on more than we agreed on."

"I suppose that's true of Finn and me, too. Even though I want to clobber him half the time, I'd still rather hang with him than just about anyone else. It's always been like that between us."

"Same with Jordan and me. Half the time, I wonder what the hell she's thinking, and the other half, I need to know what she's thinking so I know how to react. It's going to be weird going through life without her to turn to for input on every little thing."

"You can still do that, can't you? She's only a text message away."

"Yeah, but she won't physically be there like she always has been. Even when she and Zane were first married, she spent more time with me than she did with him because they had totally opposite schedules."

"For what it's worth, I think you did the right thing stepping away. It'll be good for you to figure out what's important to you and for her to learn to run her own life."

"I agree, but it's hard to resist the urge to check on her or to check in with her."

"We'll keep you so busy here that you won't have time to wonder what she's up to."

"Is that right?" she asked, sounding amused.

"Oh yeah. Gansett is where it's at, even in the winter. There's always something fun going on. In fact, tomorrow night, everyone is going to my cousin Janey's house to hang out. You should come with me."

"I wouldn't want to butt in on a family thing."

"Our family's not like that. You heard my dad. Everyone is welcome. And it's a really fun group. All we do is crack up when we're together."

"That does sound fun," she said, sounding wistful. "I always wished for a big family that got along and enjoyed being around each other."

"Then you'll love the McCarthys. We're all about the fun and the hijinks. Mac is forever getting himself into trouble with Maddie and the other women. They played the best prank on the guys a while back by getting them to believe they were bringing in male strippers for Jenny Martinez's bachelorette party. The guys lost their freaking minds over it, and when they realized they'd been played… That was epic."

"Oh my God, I love that. How funny is that?"

"The guys didn't think it was funny at all. Mac proposed they get even by stealing the women's clothes while they were skinny-dipping during Evan and Grace's wedding in Anguilla. That went over like a fart in church, with the guys getting the deep freeze in the bedroom for the entire week."

Nikki shook with silent laughter.

"It's always something, especially when Mac is involved."

"Has he always been like that?" she asked.

"Pretty much. He's the oldest of all the cousins, or he was until we found out about Mallory."

"Who?"

"My uncle Mac had a daughter he didn't know about from a relationship before he met my aunt Linda. After her mother died, Mallory found a letter that told her where to find her father, and she came here to meet him."

"Holy crap. That must've been a huge shock."

"It was, especially for Mac, who got bumped out of his prime spot as the oldest cousin. But that hasn't stopped him from leading the mayhem."

"How did your uncle handle finding out he had a daughter he never knew about?"

"In typical Big Mac fashion, he took it in stride, made her part of the family and wouldn't hear of anyone treating her as anything less than a sister and cousin."

"He sounds like a really cool guy."

"He's the best."

"What about his wife? What did she think?"

"I'm not a hundred percent sure how it all went down, but my aunt Linda has been really great about making Mallory part of the family. I mean, it happened before they met, so it's not like he cheated on her or anything. He *worships* my aunt. They're so cute together. Married forty years and still acting like honeymooners."

"What must that be like?"

"I can't imagine it for myself, but they make it look easy."

"I don't think I'll ever get married."

The statement hit Riley like a fist to the gut, which immediately had him wondering why he would care if she never got married. "Why's that?" he asked, forcing a casual tone.

"I don't really believe in it. Can people really be monogamous for their entire lives? Is that even natural?"

"Who knows? I look at my uncle Mac and aunt Linda and think, yeah, it's definitely possible. They're crazy about each other after being married forever. But then I think of my parents and yours, and... I can see why you would question it." He pulled into the driveway at Eastward Look and parked. When he shut off the engine, they were plunged into complete darkness. "Then there's my cousins. Most of them have gotten engaged or married in the last couple of years, and they're all happier than I've ever seen them since they found that one person. Some of their friends, too. They make a convincing case for lifetime monogamy."

"Having a front-row seat to my sister's marriage would make anyone think twice about getting married."

Riley snorted with laughter. "That might not be the best example of a marriage to emulate. Let me walk you in."

"You don't have to."

"I know, but I want to. If that's okay..."

"Sure. Thank you." She met him at the front of the truck, and he ushered her up the stairs to the porch with a hand on her back, a gesture that'd been ingrained in him by a father who'd taught his sons to treat women with respect and admiration. *Women make the world go round, boys*, he would say, his voice always in Riley's head.

Under the glow of the porch light, she punched in the four-digit code that unlocked the door before looking up at him. "Thank you for a really fun night. I loved meeting your dad and Chelsea."

"They loved meeting you, too." He studied her gorgeous face, wishing he could look at her until he'd had his fill. That was apt to take a while. He wanted to kiss her but didn't, sensing she wasn't ready for anything like that. But he acknowledged the ever-present desire that had been with him from the first time he'd laid eyes on her in the midst of a nor'easter last fall.

Back then and in the months after she left, he hadn't let himself imagine anything more with her, because what would've been the point? But with her standing in front of him, he couldn't deny the powerful attraction and didn't want to. A strand of her hair blew across her face, and he took a chance by gently tucking it behind her ear.

She seemed to hold her breath while she waited to see what else he would do.

He let his hand drop and noted with satisfaction that she seemed slightly disappointed when he took a step back from her. "Will you talk to your grandmother tomorrow about the renovations?"

Nodding, she said, "That's the plan."

"Let me know what she says."

"I will."

"I'll talk to Mac about what's involved with getting materials."

"It's nice of you to want to help me."

"It'll be fun."

"Sure it will," she said, smiling. "Just what you want to do after full days at work."

"Helping you *will* be fun compared to working in that freezing-cold barn with my brother and cousins. For one thing, the scenery is much better here."

Her face flushed adorably, possibly from the cold, but he preferred to think it was the compliment.

"I'll text you about tomorrow night?"

"Sure, that'd be good."

Because he couldn't help himself, he leaned in and kissed her cheek. "Sleep tight."

"You, too. Thank you for dinner."

"My pleasure." He waited for her to go inside and turn the lock before he jogged back to his truck, wishing with every fiber of his being that he didn't have to leave her there alone.

.   .   .

IN THE MORNING, after sleeping better than she had in a long time, Nikki took a mug of coffee to her favorite chair in the living room next to a window that overlooked the ocean. Today, the water was gray and stormy, with frothy whitecaps and rolling waves.

As she placed the call to her grandmother in Florida, Nikki was thankful not to be on the ferry today.

"Good morning, my love," Evelyn said, her voice cheerful and animated as always.

"Morning. Have you already played eighteen holes, done yoga and painted the sunroom?"

Laughing, Evelyn said, "Not quite yet, but I'm well on my way through a rather long to-do list."

"You exhaust me."

"Keeping busy is how I stay young, darling. It's the secret to my longevity. You're up early." During the summers they used to spend together, her grandmother had marveled at teenage girls' ability to sleep half the day away.

"I don't sleep all day the way I used to, and I haven't in years, as you well know."

Evelyn laughed. "I do know that, and I worry about you on that island all alone in the off-season."

"I haven't been entirely alone," Nikki said, being intentionally coy.

"What does that mean?"

"I knew you would pounce on that," Nikki said, laughing. "Riley McCarthy stopped by the other night when he heard I was back. Last night, he took me to Domenic's for dinner."

"Oh, that's *wonderful*! I absolutely love the McCarthys. Big Mac and Linda are the most delightful people. Riley is his nephew, right?"

"Yes, he's Big Mac's brother Kevin's son. I met Kevin and his fiancée last night as well. Nice people."

"This is the best news I've had in ages!"

"Simmer down, Gram. We had dinner. That's all it is."

"But it has potential, or you wouldn't have gone out with him in the first place. I know how you think, and I'm sure you're making long lists of all the reasons why you shouldn't get involved with him."

"I'm not doing that." *Much*.

"Yes, you are. Instead of focusing on the cons, think about the pros for once. He comes from an excellent, well-respected family. He's proven to both of us that he's a hard worker who gets things done and keeps his promises. I'm sure if he's anything like Mac and Linda's sons, he's easy on the eyes."

Nikki sat back and listened to her grandmother go on, amused as always by her infectious energy.

"Is he?"

"What?"

"Easy on the eyes?"

"You could say that." Smoking hot was more like it, not that she'd ever say as much to her grandmother, who'd start planning their wedding before the day was out.

"I want you to listen to me, Nicole."

"Oh, yikes. You're bringing out the big guns here."

"Yes, I am. I've sat by and watched you live a cautious, risk-free life for years now, and I'm painfully aware of why you've felt that was necessary, but it's time to move past that and give yourself a chance to experience true love."

"*Whoa*, Gram. We went on one date, and you're talking true love."

"Do you like him, Nikki? Do you?"

Nikki swallowed the lump that suddenly made her throat tighten. "Yeah, I like him."

"Will you please, please, *please* give him a chance? I so want you and your sister to find what I had with your grandfather." She sighed, the way she often did when speaking of her late husband. "There's nothing quite like it."

"Jordan thinks she's already found that."

"Oh please," Evelyn said, scoffing. "Zane is a moron at best and a self-absorbed asshole at worst."

"Gram! You swore!"

"He drives me to it."

Nikki cracked up laughing. "He drives us all to it."

"I honestly *cannot* believe she went back to him. What has to happen to convince her that he's not worthy of her?"

"Apparently more than releasing a tape of her most intimate moments."

"I can't even... The thought of it makes me want to murder him. Let's not talk about it. My blood pressure can't handle it."

"You're taking your medication, right?"

"Yes, love, of course I am. I plan to live forever, so don't worry."

"I do worry, especially when Jordan does things that make your blood pressure go up."

"Don't fret about me. I want to talk about you and the handsome Riley McCarthy, who came running when he heard you were back."

"It wasn't quite like that..."

"Wasn't it?"

"He said he thought of me after I left and was sad that I had gone."

"This is the best news I've had in longer than I can remember."

"You're not getting ahead of yourself, right?"

"I'm old. I can do what I want. Now tell me... When will you see him again?"

"Seventy-two is not old. And he asked me to go to a get-together at his cousin Janey's house tonight."

"She's Mac and Linda's daughter. Nice girl. Worked for the vet, Doc Potter, for years. I used to take Lillian in to see her."

Her grandmother's border collie had been a fixture in their lives until she passed away five years earlier. Evelyn had refused to consider getting another pet.

"There's something else..."

"What's that?"

"I was thinking about doing some work to the house while I'm here. Maybe updating the kitchen and bathrooms? Riley offered to help, but I wouldn't want to do anything without checking with you first."

"Do it! I'd love that. I've been thinking about doing it for years. That'd be a huge help."

"Really? You wouldn't mind?"

"Of course not. The place needs a freshening up, but the thought of tackling that on an island was daunting to me. Do whatever you want. It's your house."

"Riley's cousin Mac has the inside scoop on materials and getting things on the ferry."

"Yes, he would, as his brother-in-law owns the ferry company."

"Riley mentioned that."

"Do you have pictures of this young man of yours?"

"He's not mine, and no, I don't have pictures."

"What does he look like?"

Thinking of him, Nikki felt her face—and various other parts—get warm. "He's tall with dark wavy hair that's often unruly. He wears a knitted cap a lot of the time that keeps it in check. He has blue eyes and is quite… um, well, muscular, I guess you could say."

"Mmmm," Evelyn said, sounding dreamy. "Tall, dark and handsome. Just the way I like them."

"Gram! Stop."

"What? Your old granny was young once, you know. I had a type, and your Riley fits the bill. You've seen the pictures of your grandfather as a young man."

"Yes, I have."

"He was *so* handsome and sexy."

Nikki's heart broke for her grandmother, who'd lost her beloved husband far too soon. "Do you still miss him?"

"Every day."

"Do you ever think you would've been better off if you'd never met him?"

"Not for one second. The fifteen years I had with him were the best years of my life. I wouldn't trade them for anything, even knowing how it would end. There is nothing—and I do mean *nothing* —quite like the feeling of being with the one you were born to love."

"What if I wasn't born to love anyone?"

"That's utter hogwash. Someone with a loving heart like yours was absolutely intended to love someone, and to be loved in return. Love

is the only thing in this life that truly matters, Nik. The rest is just...
well, details. The people we love are what give our lives meaning and
purpose, and the idea of you closing yourself off to that because of
what *one person* did makes me incredibly angry. Not at you, of course,
but at *him*."

"I've begun to think you're right about that."

"Of course I'm right. When have you ever known me not to be?"

Nikki laughed. "Not once ever."

"How's the anxiety been?"

"A little more active than usual, but I'm dealing with it."

"I know the subject of men and dating is fraught with anxiety for
you. But it's all about finding the *right* person, sweetheart. If your
Riley might be that person, please don't do what you do and put up
walls around your heart to keep him out. That's no way to live."

"He wants to help me take down some walls," Nikki said. "In the
house anyway."

"You should let him take down all the walls standing between you
and the possibility that this young man could mean something to you.
If he's anything like his uncle, he's a gem. Will you promise me that
you'll give him a real, honest chance to show you who he really is
before you decide anything?"

"Yes, Gram, I promise."

"This makes me happier than you could ever know. For so long,
I've wanted to see you try again."

"I haven't met anyone who made me want to."

"Until now?"

"Until now," Nikki acknowledged softly. Until Riley had come
along and made her wish for all sorts of things she'd thought she'd
never want again.

"Sweetheart," Evelyn whispered.

"Are you crying?"

"Maybe a little."

Nikki laughed as she dabbed at her own eyes. "Stop it. You're
making a mess of us both."

"This is happiness, my sweet. Pure happiness. You're going to have to give me every detail, so I can live vicariously through you."

"You should be out there dating yourself." Though men frequently sought out her company, Evelyn remained stubbornly single.

"Ack, no, thanks. I've had my great love. Now I want you—and your sister—to have yours."

"No pressure or anything."

"None at all. Let's talk renovations. I want to hear all your ideas."

CHAPTER 8

Maddie woke with a start, hours later than her kids normally had her up. She looked over at Mac, still asleep next to her, and realized she'd conked out on him the night before.

So much for a romantic night together.

She bit back a groan. What was *wrong* with her? She'd looked forward to the night alone with her husband for days and then *fell asleep?*

Maddie wasn't sure why her deepest insecurities had been having such a field day with her lately. Perhaps it was because she couldn't seem to shed the weight she'd gained having their third child or maybe it was having a five-year-old, which was the age she'd been when her father left the island on a ferry one day, not to return for almost thirty years.

Mac was nothing like Bobby Chester. He would never leave her or their children.

She knew that for certain, so why did she have those thoughts anyway?

Years of feeling not good enough had left deep wounds that even the love of the most extraordinary man couldn't completely heal. She was preprogrammed to expect things to go wrong, and reasonable or not, she never wanted to disappoint the man who'd changed her life so profoundly with his love.

He'd given her everything, and she wanted to do the same for him. She never wanted to be a source of disappointment to him, even over something silly like falling asleep early on their night alone together.

Turning on her side to face him, she rested her hand flat on the muscular abdomen that hard work had honed. Watching him sleep, she marveled at how angelic he seemed, which was a word she didn't often use to describe him when he was awake.

"I can feel you looking at me," he said gruffly, keeping his eyes closed as he reached for her.

Maddie snuggled up to him and immediately felt less wound up than she had only a few minutes ago. Even when he made her crazy with his pranks, wild ideas and over-the-top enthusiasm for life, he also calmed her the way no one else ever could.

"What're you thinking about?"

"Things that would make you mad."

His eyes popped open, blue and intense. "What things?"

"I'm sorry I fell asleep on you last night."

"Don't be sorry. You were exhausted."

"Still…"

"You aren't thinking I'm mad about that, are you?"

"I'm mad at myself. We get so little time alone, and I wasted it by sleeping."

"Madeline…" The note of warning registered in the way he said her name.

"What?"

"Stop it. Whatever you're thinking or spinning or doing in that pretty head of yours, knock it the hell off. I don't care that you fell asleep, and we have time alone every night after we put the monkeys to bed. We have a lifetime of nights together to look forward to. One night isn't going to make or break us."

"I know."

"What's this about, babe? You haven't been yourself lately."

"I don't know."

"Should you see Vic?" he asked of the island midwife who'd seen Maddie through four pregnancies, three deliveries and one excruciating loss. In a small island community like theirs, Victoria provided a wide assortment of health-related services to the moms she worked with.

"Maybe."

"Do I need to be worried?"

"No."

He cupped her cheek, compelling her to look at him. "If you hurt, I hurt."

To her mortification and surprise, her eyes flooded with tears that spilled down her cheeks.

"Maddie, sweetheart," he said, sounding helpless and baffled. "What's going on?"

"I don't know. I just feel so… afraid lately, worried that something bad is going to happen."

He gathered her into his embrace, kissing away her tears and rubbing her back. "Nothing bad is going to happen."

"You don't know that for sure."

"No, I don't, but there's nothing to worry about. Everyone is safe and happy and thriving."

"I'm sorry," she said, attempting to pull back from him, which he wouldn't allow. "I don't know what's wrong with me."

"Whatever it is, we'll figure it out together. I don't want you to be anxious or worried about anything."

"I can't seem to help it lately. Thomas is five and… it's just…"

"That's how old you were when your father left," he said, his tone flat and lacking its usual animation. "You don't honestly worry about that happening to him, do you?"

"No. Not for one second do I think you'd ever do that to him —or us."

"I wouldn't, Maddie. Where else on this earth would I rather be than right here with you and our kids?"

"Nowhere. I know that."

"But deep inside, you're still that five-year-old girl sitting in the window watching the ferries and hoping her daddy will come back, aren't you?"

His understanding, always insightful and on the mark, was one of the things she loved best about him. No one had ever *seen* her quite the way he did. "I don't want to be her."

"She's always with you, waiting for disaster to strike. You can't help that." As he spoke, his hand dipped under the hem of her T-shirt to caress her back. "But that little girl doesn't ever, *ever* have to worry about me leaving her or her children, because she and *our* children are my whole world. Nothing else matters."

Maddie hiccupped on a sob that made her feel silly and helpless at the same time. What in the world did she have to be crying about? She had the life she'd always wanted and the love of a man she couldn't have conjured in her wildest dreams.

He smoothed away her tears and kissed her softly and sweetly. "Tell me what I can do, how I can help."

"This is helping."

"I don't want you struggling with these things on your own. That's what I'm here for, to make it better and to ease your worries."

"I have no reason to worry about anything."

"No, you don't, but that doesn't mean you won't worry anyway. That's how you're wired."

"I need new wiring."

"I love your wiring just the way it is." He slid his leg between hers and began to kiss her more intently.

"I have morning breath."

"Shut up and kiss me."

"Mac! Let me brush my teeth."

"No." He moved so he was on top of her, continuing to kiss her despite her objections, which ceased to matter as he moved from her lips to her neck, the rough scratch of his morning whiskers sending tingles of sensation skittering over her skin. All he had to do was look at her in the sexy, proprietary way she loved so much for her to want him. But when he touched and kissed her with such reverence, she was utterly lost to him.

"You are everything to me, Madeline," he whispered against the achingly sensitive skin of her abdomen. "Every beat of my heart, every breath I take, everything I do and think and want, it's all for you. There's nothing I wouldn't do to make you happy and to ease your mind. Anything you want or need, I want to be the one to give it to you."

She sighed as a sob escaped from her tightly closed lips.

"Tell me what you need so I can get it for you."

"I need you." Wrapping her arms around him, she held on tight to him.

"Oh baby, you have me. I'm all yours." His tenderness and sweetness were her undoing. As he made love to her, she sobbed in his arms, her emotions a jumbled mess of happiness and despair that again had her wondering what in the world had triggered such feelings.

He waited for her, the way he always did, only letting himself go after she had come with a sharp cry of completion.

Afterward, he held her close to him.

She felt his lips curve against her neck. "I like when we can be loud."

"Mmm, loud is good."

"Maddie?"

"Yeah?"

"I want you to talk to Vic. Will you do that for me?"

She nodded. "I will."

"Today?"

"Yes, Mac. I'll talk to her today."

AFTER ANOTHER FREEZING day at the Wayfarer installing windows, Riley was ready for a cold beer, a hot pizza and more time with Nikki, who'd been on his mind during the endless hours at work. The only good thing about the cold was that it kept everyone focused on the task at hand, so they could finish up and get warm that much sooner. It kept the usual ball-busting to a minimum.

"Mac picked a good day to take off," Shane said as they cleaned up and put away their tools.

"Benefit of being the boss," Finn said.

"I must've missed that memo," Luke said. "No one told me the bosses could take off the coldest days to stay home with their wives." As Mac's partner in the construction and marina businesses, he was the other boss. However, even Luke deferred to Mac on most things.

"Mac tends to keep these things to himself," Shane said, grinning. "God forbid the rest of us follow his example."

"No shit," Luke said. "That just leads to trouble."

"Are you guys going to Janey's tonight?" Shane asked.

"I'll be there," Finn said.

"We're going," Luke said.

"What're you doing, Riley?" Finn asked.

"I'll stop by Janey's."

"Are you bringing your new *friend?*" his brother asked, batting his eyelashes and making Riley want to stab him with the screwdriver he had in his hand.

"Maybe."

"Big date last night, but no details forthcoming," Finn said.

When Finn started making kissing noises, it took everything Riley had not to sink the screwdriver into his brother's forehead.

"Leave him alone," Shane said, giving Finn a shove.

"Why should I?"

"Because someday you'll find someone who makes you want to keep the details private, and you won't want him or the rest of us up in your grill," Shane said, speaking from experience.

"That's not gonna happen," Finn said.

Luke and Shane scoffed at him.

"That's what we thought, too," Luke said, accepting a high five from Shane, who nodded in agreement.

"We all need to get some sleep while we can," Shane said. "Snow coming tomorrow into Sunday. Get those plows ready."

The sound of their groaning nearly drowned out Shane's ringing cell phone.

He lit up with pleasure as he took the call from Katie. "Hey, babe. What's up?" His smile faded, and his expression grew serious, serious enough that the others stopped what they were doing. "What'd they want?" Propping a hand on his hip, he said, "We're cleaning up. I'll be there in ten." He ended the call and stashed his phone in his back pocket.

"What's wrong?" Luke asked.

"State cops are at my place looking for me. They wouldn't tell Katie what they want."

"What the fuck?" Finn asked, saying what they all were thinking.

"We'll go with you," Riley said. "Let's go."

"You don't have to…" Shane's voice faltered.

"Yeah, we do," Riley said. "I'll drive your truck." He took his cousin by the arm and directed him to the main doors.

Luke took the time to lock up before he ran after them, jumping with Finn into the back of Shane's truck for the five-minute ride to the house he shared with his fiancée, Katie Lawry. A state police SUV along with the Gansett Island Police Department SUV that Chief Blaine Taylor drove were parked outside the house.

"What the hell is this?" Shane asked when Riley pulled up behind Blaine's vehicle.

"Let's go find out," Riley said, filled with nervous energy. There was no way Shane was in any kind of trouble, so Riley wasn't worried about that. But what could've brought the cops to his doorstep on a cold January day?

He followed his cousin inside, where Shane was greeted by a hug from Katie.

"What's going on?" Shane asked Blaine before his glance shifted to Jack Downing, one of the two state cops who were stationed on the island. "Jack?"

"We got a call from Providence Police," Jack said. "Your wife, Courtney—"

"*Ex*-wife," Shane said sharply as Katie slid an arm around his waist. "What about her?"

"She was found dead in her home earlier today."

Oh God, Riley thought.

Shane took a step back, reeling as if he'd been struck. "Did she OD?" he asked.

"We don't know that yet," Jack said, "but prescription pain meds were found in the home."

After a long silence, Shane said, "Why are you telling me? We're divorced."

"You were listed as her next of kin, Shane," Blaine said.

"What? Why? We split years ago."

"I don't know," Blaine said. "Perhaps she never thought to update the info?"

"Her parents," Shane said in a dull, flat tone. "Has someone told them?"

"Not yet," Jack said. "We were obligated to tell you first. How would you like us to proceed? We can send someone to talk to her parents, if you'd like."

Shane shook his head. "I'll do it. I'll call them."

"Shane, honey, you don't have to do that," Katie said.

"I know, but I'll do it anyway."

While he conferred with Blaine and Jack, Katie dropped the arm she had around him and leaned in to whisper to Riley, who was closest to her. "Go get Laura. Please."

Riley nodded, ducked outside and took off running the short distance to the Sand & Surf Hotel, owned by Shane's older sister and her husband, Owen. He went up the stairs to the Surf and burst into the lobby. Laura and her mother-in-law, Sarah, were standing at the reception desk and looked up with surprise at his sudden arrival.

"Hey, Riley," Laura said, smiling. She had a sleeping blond baby strapped to her chest, and her own blonde hair was piled into a messy bun. "What's up?"

"It's Shane."

Laura's smile morphed into concern.

87

"Courtney was found dead today."

"Oh dear God." Laura unstrapped baby Jonathan and handed him to Sarah.

"Katie asked me to come get you."

"Where is he?"

"His place."

"Sarah, tell Owen where I am. I'll be back as soon as I can."

"Take your time," Sarah said. "I've got the kids."

"Thank you."

Forgoing a coat, Laura headed straight to the door that Riley held for her. The two of them jogged down the street to Shane and Katie's place. Laura went in ahead of him and walked straight over to hug her brother, who clung to her for a long moment before he released her.

Seeing his cousin in good hands, Riley decided to leave so Shane could have some space in the suddenly crowded house. "Let me know what we can do."

Shane hugged him. "Thanks."

"I'll check in after a bit."

Shane nodded. He seemed dazed, although how could he not be? Courtney was in her early thirties, like Shane, and far too young to die. But her struggles with addiction had led to the demise of their marriage and now this…

After expressing condolences and support, Finn and Luke followed him out of the house, and the three of them walked through blustery wind to the Wayfarer, where they'd left their vehicles.

"This is crazy," Finn said after a long silence.

"Seriously," Luke said. "He's been through a lot with her."

"For a long time after he split from her, we wondered if he would survive it." Riley didn't like to think about how worried they'd all been about Shane during that time. "He's been so good lately."

"He'll be okay," Luke said. "He's got Katie and Laura and the rest of us. We'll get him through it."

Riley could only hope that was the case. Shane had descended into a deep, dark depression after his breakup with Courtney. That seemed like a long time ago now that he'd found a whole new life on the island with Katie.

At the Wayfarer, they parted company with Luke, who said he'd see them later at Jancy's.

Finn got into the passenger side of Riley's truck for the short ride to their place.

"Is this gonna fuck Shane all up again?" Finn asked.

"I really hope not."

"He'll blame himself. She wanted to get back with him, and he said no."

"He was with Katie then. He'd moved on."

"Still… That'll weigh heavily on him now."

"Yeah, I suppose it will," Riley said as a sinking feeling overtook him.

CHAPTER 9

*S*urrounded by the people who loved him best, Shane tried to process the devastating news the police had delivered. In his mind, Courtney had been living her new sober life, moving forward from the darkness that had plagued her in the past. Hearing she was dead, most likely from an overdose, sent him spinning back into the rabbit hole of despair that had marked his life for so long after their marriage ended. How long had she been using again? Had she been sober at all, or had she immediately gone back to her old ways after rehab, or was it after he'd refused to give her yet another chance?

And the most important question of all—why did he still care so damned much?

"What can I do for you?" Katie had been by his side from the second Jack and Blaine had delivered the devastating news.

"I don't know."

With her arm around him, she laid her head on his shoulder, offering comfort and support he didn't feel he deserved. Courtney had been his ex-wife. He didn't love her anymore, hadn't loved her in a long time. She'd lied to him the entire time they'd been together, hiding a fierce addiction that had surfaced when he discovered large sums of money missing from their joint accounts.

Until then, he'd been blissfully ignorant to the epic battle his wife was waging, completely separate from him and their marriage.

Hearing she was dead brought back a sea of memories he'd much rather forget than relive. The aftermath of their marital meltdown had been the darkest time in his life, and he had no desire to go back there.

"I need to call her parents."

"Do you want me to do it for you?" Katie asked.

"No, I'll do it." He kissed her forehead. "I'm okay." To Laura, he said, "Did you tell Dad?"

She nodded. "He and Betsy are on their way over."

"I'll be out in a minute." He got up and went into the bedroom, sat on the bed he shared with Katie and reminded himself he was a million miles removed from who he'd been with Courtney and after her. Scrolling through his contacts, he found the number for Courtney's mother that he'd never removed from his phone, even if he probably should've done it years ago.

Maybe somewhere in the back of his mind, he'd known he would need it again someday.

He put through the call, dropped his head into his hand and waited for her to pick up. Back when he'd been married to Courtney, her parents had wintered on Padre Island in Texas. He had no idea if they still did that.

"Shane? Is that you?"

"It's me."

"What's going on?"

"Mary Jane… The police were just at my house. It's Courtney."

She began to scream.

Grimacing, Shane held the phone away from his ear until she had recovered the ability to speak.

"Was it the drugs?" Mary Jane asked tearfully.

"They don't know for sure, but they found indications that she'd been using again."

"I *knew* it. I just said to Steve the other day that she had started acting strangely again, going silent for days at a time, not responding to texts. Maybe if we hadn't gone to Texas this winter—"

"Stop," Shane said softly. "Don't do that to yourself. You did everything you could think of for her. Being close by wouldn't have stopped this. Nothing could have." He believed that with every fiber of his being. "This was a fight she wasn't destined to win."

"I don't know what I should do. What should I do, Shane?"

"I have the number the state police gave me to call when we decide on funeral arrangements." When she was ready, he recited the number.

"I'll see about getting a flight home."

"The ferries aren't running today or tomorrow due to a storm coming, but I'll be over as soon as I can."

"You don't have to do that. This isn't your problem."

"I'll be there."

"You have been such a blessing to us through this, Shane."

"I wish there was more I could've done."

"You did what you could. We all did."

"I'll call you in a day or two when I can get off the island."

"Thank you."

For a long time after they said their goodbyes, Shane sat on the bed, elbows on knees, memories and despair swirling through him like a hurricane, from the first time he met Courtney his senior year of college, until the last time he'd seen her, when she'd come to Gansett pleading for one last chance to make things right between them.

He'd sent her away. He had worked so hard to put his life back on track, had fallen for Katie and was in a healthy relationship… He'd done what was best for *him*—for once. But could he have done more for Courtney? Now he would never know the answer to that question.

A soft knock on the door preceded Katie into the room. She closed the door behind her and came to sit with him on the bed. "What can I do for you?"

"Nothing. I'm okay."

"It's okay if you're not."

"I am, but it's just so fucking sad."

"Yes, it is. Your dad and uncles are here. Adam, too. If you don't feel up to seeing them, I can ask them to come back tomorrow."

"I'll see them, but first give me this." He wrapped his arms around her and held on tight to her soft sweetness, breathing in her familiar scent. Here, with her, he'd found his forever.

"I'll always be happy to give you this," she said. "Any time you need it."

"I'm going to need a lot of it in the next few days."

"I've got plenty more where this came from."

"I'm dirty from work."

"Do you honestly think I care about that?"

"I'm guessing no?"

"I don't care about the dirt. I care about *you*. I'm so sorry this has happened, Shane. My heart breaks for you and everyone who loved her."

"Thank you. In case you were wondering, I'm not going to let this suck me back into the rabbit hole."

"I wasn't wondering, but that's good to know."

"Let's go spend a few minutes with Dad and the others. He'll be worried about me."

"Let me know when you want me to kick them out."

"I will." He got up and took hold of her hand, holding on tight when they walked out of the bedroom to join the others, who now included his dad, Uncle Mac, Uncle Kevin, cousin Adam, brother-in-law, Owen, and Ned Saunders, an honorary uncle to all the McCarthy cousins.

His dad, Frank, came over to him and wrapped his arms around him. "I'm so sorry, son."

"Thank you, Dad." Shane felt weird accepting condolences for a woman he'd been divorced from for quite some time. But he understood that people wanted to pay their respects, and he needed to let them. Knowing how his father had worried over him during the dark period, Shane was determined to reassure him. "I'm okay, Dad. Don't worry."

Frank gave a gruff laugh, as if to say, *That'll be the day*. Since their mother died when Shane was seven and Laura nine, Frank had been mother, father and friend to them. "What can I do for you?"

"Nothing right now. I'll go over in a day or two when I hear from her mom about the arrangements."

"Her poor mom. Did everything she could and then some."

Shane nodded, his throat closing around a hot ball of regret and despair. He accepted hugs from Ned, his uncles, cousin and brother-in-law.

Big Mac reduced him to tears when he hugged him and said, "You were a good husband to her, Shane. You did all you could."

"Thank you," he said gruffly, glancing at Katie.

"I think Shane could use a little time to himself to process what's happened."

"Of course," Frank said. "We'll go, but we'll check on you tomorrow?"

"That'd be good, Dad. Thanks. And thanks, all of you, for coming over. I appreciate it."

Laura hugged him tightly. "Call me if you need anything. Anything at all."

"I will, thanks."

They filed out the door that Katie closed behind them. The sound of the lock engaging filled him with relief.

"I can go stay at the hotel if you need to be alone," she said.

"Hell no. You're staying right here with me where you belong."

"I have no idea what to say or what to do for you."

He put his arms around her. "Just love me. That's all I need."

"That's the easiest thing I've ever done."

MAC AND MADDIE had scored Victoria's last appointment of the day. The pretty midwife came breezing into the exam room with her long dark hair in a high ponytail and her dark eyes shining with happiness.

Maddie had teased her about smiling nonstop since she and Shannon O'Grady had committed to each other and were planning a life together.

"Oh, I get *both* of you," Vic said, typing on the laptop that sat on a rolling desk that she toted around the clinic like a dog on a leash. "This is a nice surprise. Everything all right?"

"I've been feeling a little… off… lately, and Mac wanted me to come see you, so here I am."

Vic's brows knitted with concern. "Off how?"

Mac took hold of Maddie's hand. "May I?"

Maddie shrugged. "Go for it."

"She's been really down on herself over the weight she gained with Mac and kind of weepy and worried about things that aren't going to happen."

"I just can't seem to bounce back the way I normally do," Maddie added.

"Does she have postpartum depression?" Mac asked.

"I think we would've seen signs of that before now." Victoria sat on a stool and crossed her legs. "Any chance you could be pregnant again?"

"*What?*" Maddie asked, her voice so high, it could make dogs bark. "No. *No way.* Mac is *four months old!*"

"Um, well, technically," Mac said, stammering, "it's not… well, it's entirely *possible.*"

"No, it is not!"

When Victoria began to laugh, Maddie wanted to punch her—and Mac. Mostly him. If she was pregnant, she was going to kill someone, and he was the most likely candidate.

"Sorry," Vic said, making an effort to recover her composure. "It's just you two are funny. After four pregnancies, you ought to know where these babies are coming from by now."

Maddie began to cry.

"Aw, babe, don't," Mac said, putting his arms around her. "We don't know anything for sure, and if you are pregnant, we'll have another baby. It'll be okay."

"It will *not* be okay! I have three children under age six as it is, and I'm the size of a rhino with massive boobs! I can't have another baby. At this rate, I'll never lose the baby weight I've already got!"

"So what?" Mac made an effort to control the fury he always felt when she put herself down. "You're perfection."

"For what it's worth, I'd kill to have a fraction of your curves," Vic said.

"You can have my so-called curves," Maddie said. "I don't fit in any of my clothes!"

"I'll buy you new clothes."

"Mac! You don't get it."

"Make me understand."

"You still look exactly the same as you did the day we met, and me… I'm…"

"More beautiful than you have ever been to me." He turned to her, seeming to forget they weren't alone as he cupped her cheek. "*You're* the one who doesn't get it, Madeline. I understand that the extra pounds make you feel down on yourself, but I don't see them. When I look at you, I see *you*, my beautiful wife, the mother of my children, my best friend, the love of my life. That's *all* I see."

"Sigh," Victoria said, fanning her face.

"I'm an awful person," Maddie said as tears streamed down her face. "My sweet sister-in-law would give anything to be pregnant, and all I can think about is my fat belly." She choked on sobs.

Mac drew her into his embrace. "Do you see what's going on here, Vic?"

"I see, and I think a quick pregnancy test might be in order."

Maddie moaned. "This can't be happening."

As FRANK LEFT Shane's house with his brothers and Ned, Big Mac said, "Let's get a drink."

Frank, Kevin and Ned followed him into the Beachcomber, where the daytime bartender, Lucy, was on duty.

"Hi, guys." She put cocktail napkins on the bar in front of them. "Usual?"

"Yes, please, sweetheart," Big Mac said with a warm smile for the young woman. "Thank you."

"What's it say about us that we have a 'usual' with every bartender on the island?" Kevin asked.

"That we're good about supporting the local economy?" Big Mac said to grunts of laughter from the others.

"Ain't it the truth?" Ned said.

"I'm so sorry this has happened, Frankie," Kevin said, hand on Frank's shoulder.

"Me, too. Shane has been doing so well. I hope this isn't going to be an awful setback for him."

"Is it wrong of us to be worried about Shane when poor Courtney is dead?" Mac asked.

"It's only natural for us to be worried about him," Kevin said. "He's ours. We can worry about him while we feel sad for her and her family."

"'Tis an awful tragedy, no matter how ya look at it," Ned said.

"I feel awful for her parents," Frank said. "They're good people who did so much to try to help her. And they were there for Shane through it all. It's just so terrible. Fucking drugs…"

Mac blew out a deep breath. "Thank God none of our kids ever got wrapped up in that shit."

"There but for the grace of God," Kevin said, sighing. "We are blessed."

"Indeed," Mac said. "I wonder if there's a program or something we can donate to that would help other people like Courtney to get the help they need. We could donate in her name."

"That's a great idea," Frank said. "I'll talk to Mary Jane about that when I see her this week."

"Count me in on that," Ned said. "Happy ta give to the cause."

"Thanks, buddy," Frank said, squeezing Ned's shoulder.

"So you're going over for the services?" Kevin asked Frank.

"I'm going. For better or worse, she was my daughter-in-law. My son loved her very much, despite her challenges. And there's no way I'd let him go through this without all the support I can muster. I'm sure Laura will go, too."

"We'll all go," Mac said.

"You don't have to do that," Frank said, moved by his brothers' support.

"Yeah, we do," Kevin said.

Ned nodded in agreement.

Frank released a deep sigh. "We can't let Shane go off the deep end again."

"He's so much stronger now than he was then," Mac said. "We all see it. It's not just Katie, although she's been a big part of it. He's really grown into himself since he's been here. Mac tells me all the time that he couldn't run the construction business without Shane."

"It's good for him to spend his days with his cousins and closest friends," Frank said.

"He has support around him he didn't have the last time, not that you and Laura didn't do all you could," Kevin said. "But now he's got the entire tribe, and there's no way any of us are going to let him falter. We've got him, Frankie."

"Love you guys," Frank said gruffly. "I'm so damned glad to have you nearby at times like this."

"We love you, too," Mac said. "And we love Shane. We'll get him through this."

Knowing his brothers and friend had his back—and his son's—made Frank feel a thousand times better than he would have without them around to tell him everything was going to be okay.

CHAPTER 10

*R*iley showered and changed into clean jeans and the striped sweater his mother had sent him for Christmas. He put on a little cologne and was on his way to a clean getaway when Finn emerged from the shower, towel around his waist and dripping all over the place.

"Off to see your girlfriend?"

"She's not my girlfriend."

"Yet."

"Okay, see you later." Riley was in no mood to spar with his brother tonight, not when he'd been waiting all day to see Nikki again.

"You going to Janey's?"

"That's the plan."

"Are you bringing her?"

"Probably. Don't be a dick if I do, you hear?"

"I'll try not to be."

"Try hard." Riley zipped up his coat. "And mop up the puddle you made on the floor, will you?"

"Yes, Mommy."

Rolling his eyes, Riley went out the door before Finn could say something else to irritate him. On the drive to Eastward Look, Riley ruminated over the way his brother had been getting under his skin lately before his thoughts naturally turned to Shane. He'd lived through a nightmare with Courtney, and now this…

Riley hadn't known Courtney very well. He'd met her at their wedding and seen her a few times after that at family events. He remembered how happy Shane seemed with her, how his cousin had had his arm around his wife any time she was nearby. And he recalled how low Shane had been after it all went sideways. The entire family had been gravely concerned about him. Riley knew that Kevin had spent many a day trying to get through to his nephew, without success. Only when Laura begged Shane to come help with the renovations to the Surf had his cousin seemed to rally.

Witnessing Shane's unbearable agony had been a good reminder of the many reasons it paid to remain stubbornly single. At the time, he couldn't have imagined giving another person the power to flatten him the way Courtney had done to Shane.

But as he pulled into the long driveway that led to Nikki, he began to understand that something had shifted in him since he met her last fall, a door had opened to the possibility of taking that kind of chance. Then she'd disappeared before he'd gotten to know her. And why her and not the hundreds of other women he'd known in his life?

That was a mystery he couldn't easily solve. All he knew was that something about her made her different from everyone else, and he wanted to know her better—perhaps better than he'd ever known anyone else.

The thoughts, coming one right after the other, frightened him. This was all new territory for someone who'd gone out of his way to avoid anything that smacked of commitment or permanence.

He was still sitting in the dark staring at her front door when his phone rang, startling him. The caller ID showed his former boss's name.

"Hey, Clint," Riley said. "How's it going?"

"Not so great, to be honest. I'm just coming off another shitstorm of a week in which everything that could go wrong did."

"Wow, sorry. What happened?"

"Incompetence, negligence and downright stupidity, to name a few things. Listen, Riley... I know you and your brother are happy out there on your island, but I could sure as hell use you guys back here. I just fired another foreman, and I've got another one hanging by a thread. I need people I can freaking count on, and I'm willing to double whatever you're making now to get you back on the job."

"I, um... I don't know what to say."

"Say yes. Come back and bring your brother. I *need* you guys."

Clint Davis had been very good to Riley and Finn, employing them from the time they were in college until they took vacation to come to Gansett for Laura's wedding and ended up staying when Mac offered them jobs. They'd also wanted to stay close to their dad in the immediate aftermath of their parents' breakup. A few months turned into a year, and now they were well into a second year on the island.

"Let me talk to Finn and my cousin, who we're working for now. We're into some pretty big things out here with a new family business in the works."

"I'll take whatever I can get. Let me know, okay?"

"I will. Sorry things are fucked up there."

"Me, too. I'll look forward to hearing from you guys."

"Take care, Clint."

Long after he ended the call, Riley sat in the cold, pondering the complexities of timing. Then Nikki opened the inside door and turned on the porch light, and the sight of her cleared every thought that wasn't about her from his mind. He got out of the truck and jogged to the stairs, taking them two at a time in his haste to be with her again.

"Hey," he said, smiling when she opened the storm door for him.

"Hi there. I saw your lights coming down the driveway. Were you on the phone?"

He followed her into the kitchen. "Yeah, sorry. My old boss called."

"No worries. I knew it was you. The big yellow plow on the front of your truck is a giveaway every time."

"I'm going to need it tomorrow night, according to the weather reports."

She opened a beer for him and put it on the counter. "What'd your old boss want?"

He noted that she'd gotten some Amstel Light for him. "Me. And my brother. Back to work in Connecticut, for double what we're making now."

"Oh." She turned to the stove. "Are you going?"

Did she seem disappointed or was that wishful thinking on his part? "I don't know. I like what I'm doing here, and I think Finn does, too." He hadn't intended to tell her about his ex-boss's call, but he found himself spilling the details anyway. "Something smells good."

"I hope you don't mind that I cooked."

"Trust me. I don't mind. What'd you make?"

"Nothing fancy. Just pasta."

"Works for me. Thanks for doing that." With her face flushed from the heat of the stove—or at least he thought it was that—he wanted to put his arms around her. He wanted to hold her and kiss her and show her how happy he was to see her. But something stopped him from acting on those urges. He'd already accepted that the first move, if there was one, would have to come from her.

He hoped that someday she'd tell him what had hurt her in the past, so he could do his best to make sure nothing ever hurt her again. Caring that much about a woman was definitely a first for him, but something about her made him want to shelter her, to protect and comfort her.

"Riley?"

He realized he'd been staring at her. "What? Sorry."

"Is something wrong?"

"Wrong? No, definitely nothing wrong." He took a step toward her, drawn to her like he'd never been to anyone else.

She seemed breathless as she looked up at him while standing guard over a pot of sauce.

He reached out to swipe a smudge of sauce from her cheek, smiling as he did it.

"Jordan says I'm the messiest cook ever."

"I think you're the sexiest cook ever." There. He'd done it. Thrown down a gauntlet. Changed the ballgame. He held his breath, waiting to see if she'd meet him halfway. Hell, he'd take a quarter of the way after months of thinking about her and days of dancing around the fact that he wanted her. Badly.

She glanced up at him, looking madly vulnerable. "You really think so?"

He took another step toward her. "I really, really do." Running a finger over her face, he focused on the pink hue that had left her with a rosy glow.

"I... um..." She swallowed hard. "I kinda suck at this."

"No, you don't."

"Yes, I really do."

Riley shook his head and moved his hand ever so slightly to cup her cheek and tilt her face upward. It cost him tremendously to wait for some sign, any indication that she wanted him to kiss her. He thought he'd go mad in the seconds it took for her lips to part and her gaze to shift to his lips.

He took that as a green light to proceed, but he moved carefully, not wanting to spook her or ruin his chances with her by asking for too much too soon. The last freaking thing in this world he wanted was to scare her, so he gave her the softest, sweetest, gentlest kiss he'd ever given anyone, completely unprepared for the wildfire that sweet kiss set off inside him.

With both hands now framing her face, he leaned his forehead against hers, hoping she would come back for more.

Her hand curled around his neck, and her fingers in his hair made him tremble from the effort it took to hold back, to wait for her.

Then she licked her lips, and the movement of her tongue over her bottom lip moved into first place as the single most erotic thing he'd ever seen. Without making a conscious decision to proceed, he came down as she moved up, their lips meeting in a frenzy of need that had him pulling her closer to him, greedy for more after waiting so long to taste her.

The metal spoon she'd used to stir the sauce fell to the floor with a clatter that he ignored as her tongue met his in a sensual, desperate dance.

Holy shit. Hottest. Kiss. *Ever.*

With his hands on her ass, he lifted her, deposited her on the counter and leaned in for more, kissing her until his lips were numb and his dick was so hard, it ached. *Too much, too soon.* The refrain echoed through his mind, reminding him he needed to take it easy with her, to respect the hesitancy he'd sensed in her from the beginning. Though it was the last freaking thing he wanted to do, he eased out of the kiss, turning his focus to the elegant length of her neck.

"You are so sexy, so beautiful, so sweet," he whispered, making her shiver. He loved that little shudder that rippled through her.

"Riley…"

"Hmm?"

"The pasta… It's boiling."

"The pasta isn't the only thing that's boiling."

She laughed and eased him back from her with her hand on his chest before jumping down from her seat on the counter to tend to the stove.

Riley didn't know what to do with himself or the rampant desire that gripped him like an extra heartbeat, and there was no way he could hide what the encounter had done to him. So he leaned back against the counter, crossed his feet at the ankles and focused on breathing as he watched her intently.

By the time she turned to face him, he had himself more or less under control—until she rolled her plump bottom lip between her teeth and fixed her gaze once again on his mouth. It was all he could do not to groan out loud.

"I… I haven't done anything like that in a long time," she said, each word seeming to cost her something vital.

"Why not? You're quite good at it."

Her eyes widened with surprise.

"You didn't know you're good at it?"

"I..." She shook her head and wrapped her arms around herself in that protective thing she did.

He wondered if she knew she was doing it. Standing up straighter, he held out a hand to her. "Come here."

"I'm here."

"Closer. Only if you want to, that is."

He watched her screw up the courage to step back into his embrace. With his arms around her and her body flush against his, where there'd be no doubt in her mind how their kisses had affected him, he rested his hands on her shoulders. "Tell me why you think you're not good at this," he said, punctuating his words with kisses to her forehead and lips.

"I haven't done a lot of it. Something happened... when I was in college."

"Do you want to tell me about it?"

She shook her head and then closed her eyes when they filled with tears.

"Nikki, sweetheart." Devastated by her tears, he hugged her close to him and buried his face in the fragrant silk of her hair. "Please don't cry. You don't have to tell me."

"I do have to. It wouldn't be fair not to."

"Not now. Not if you aren't ready."

"I want to be ready... for you, for this. I want..."

"What do you want, sweetheart?" Now that he was allowed to touch her, he couldn't seem to stop himself from sliding his fingers through her hair or rubbing soothing circles on her back. "Tell me what you want so I can get it for you."

"I want you."

He smiled down at her, filled with giddy elation that was all new to him. "That's the best news I've had all day."

"It's just that I don't know how... I dated a guy in college who... He got tired of waiting for me to put out and took what he wanted."

"Oh my God," he said, his elation of a minute ago turning to rage at the thought of someone hurting her that way. "I'm so sorry that happened to you, Nikki."

"It was a long time ago, but sometimes it feels like it only just happened. I've mostly kept my distance from men and dating ever since."

"I can't say I blame you. Tell me he was charged at least."

"He was. It was a total nightmare. I ended up leaving school."

"I'm so sorry you had to go through such an awful thing."

She smiled up at him, and the ground seemed to shift beneath his feet as the most profound feeling of falling overtook him. He'd never experienced anything like it.

"Whatever happens between us is completely up to you. I'll never ask you for anything you don't want to give."

"You have no idea how much that means to me."

He traced his fingertip over her soft cheek, his stomach and heart aching for her and what she'd been through. "I wish I could have five minutes alone with the guy who hurt you."

She looked away, seeming to collect herself before returning her gaze to him. "I wanted you to know why I'm so... weird."

"You're not weird."

"Yes, I really am."

"No, you're really not." Keeping his eyes open, he kissed her again, returning to the initial soft sweetness in light of what she'd told him.

"I don't want to be weird with you."

Riley laughed as he hugged her, bewitched, enchanted and getting deeper by the second into something that had the power to change his life.

HOT DAMN, the man could kiss. *Sweet fancy Moses,* as Gram would say. Nikki wanted to dance with glee around the kitchen. She'd kissed the sexy, thoughtful, handsome, *sweet* Riley McCarthy, and she'd survived it. She hadn't done anything overly embarrassing besides shed a few tears that had come mostly from the sheer relief of having gotten that first kiss out of the way, confirming the hum of attraction she felt for him wasn't at all one-sided.

He'd said and done all the right things when she told him about what'd happened in college and how it had affected her ever since.

As they ate the spaghetti and salad she'd made, she was thankful she'd decided not to make garlic bread. Now that she'd kissed him once, the only thing she could think about was when she might get to do it again. Thank goodness garlic breath wouldn't be a concern.

Everything was different between them now, the air charged with an aura of expectation and anticipation that made her unable to focus on anything but the lips that had kissed her with such tenderness.

"Quit it," he said gruffly after taking a sip from his beer.

Startled, Nikki said, "Quit what?"

"Staring at my lips."

Mortified, she had no idea what to say to that until those sinfully sexy lips curved into a smile that had her toes curling inside her fleece-lined slippers. He was teasing her, and she'd fallen for it.

"Stare all you want, because that means I get to do it, too."

"You want to stare at me?"

"Hell yes, I want to stare at you. I've been trying not to since the second I first saw you."

"And that's taken some effort, has it?"

"You have *no* idea."

She hid her smile behind her hand.

He took hold of her other hand and brought it to his lips. "The best thing to happen to me since last fall was you coming back. You should've seen me when I heard you were here. I was out with my brother and our cousins, and I basically ditched them and took off with my dad's car, which I haven't done in years."

"You must've really wanted to see me."

Giving a gentle tug on her hand, he had her rising from her seat to move to his lap. He wrapped his arms around her and nuzzled her neck. "I really, *really* wanted to see you."

"I wanted to see you, too," she said, feeling breathless from the kisses he placed on her neck. "The whole way from LA, I hoped you'd still be here. I had no idea if you would be."

"I think you're the reason I stayed. I hoped you might come back."

"I guess I ought to thank Jordan for going back to Zane. Otherwise, I wouldn't have any reason to be here."

"I'm not sure we should go that far, but I'm glad you had a reason to come back."

"So am I."

"Today was a really rough day but being here with you made it better."

She smoothed her fingers through his hair. "What happened?"

"My cousin Shane found out his ex-wife died, possibly of a drug overdose."

"Oh God, that's terrible. Is he okay?"

"He's shocked, of course, and really upset."

"The poor guy. Have they been divorced for long?"

"A couple of years now. He found out after they were married that she was addicted to prescription pain meds, and things kind of went downhill from there. For a long time, he was in a really bad place. He's been a lot better lately…" Riley took a deep breath and released it slowly. "Sorry, I don't mean to unload on you."

"Don't be sorry. You're worried about him, which is very sweet."

"We're all worried about him. It's such a shock for him and such a sad loss for her family. And while I'm sad for him, I feel selfish, too, because all I can think about since I kissed you is when I'm going to get to do it again."

Smiling, she touched her lips to his. "Do you still want to go to your other cousin's house tonight?"

"Not as much as I did earlier." His hands moved over her in a gentle caress that had her thinking about *more* for the first time in years. No one had ever made her feel the way Riley did with a few heated kisses.

"What would you rather do instead?" she asked, loving the way his blue eyes went dark with desire.

"More of this." He kissed her again. "But I want you to meet my family, too."

"We could go for a little while."

"Mmm," he said against her lips. "Okay."

"Riley…"

"Hmm?"

"You have to stop kissing me if we're going to your cousin's."

"Don't wanna stop kissing you."

Nikki couldn't recall the last time she'd enjoyed anything more than the feel of Riley's strong arms around her and his sweet lips devouring hers. "Just for now. You can kiss me more later."

"Promise?"

She nodded, charmed by him. "I promise."

CHAPTER 11

*F*inn McCarthy was out of sorts, an unusual state of being for a Friday night. He lived for Fridays and a whole weekend to do whatever he wanted, but with a snowstorm looming and his brother spending all his free time with his *girlfriend*, Finn's usual weekend elation was missing.

"What crawled up your ass and died?" his cousin Janey asked as she moved around the kitchen preparing trays of food for the family due to descend any second.

"Huh? Nothing."

"You're all dark and stormy and pissed. How come?"

"I'm not pissed, dark *or* stormy."

"You're all of the above, so don't try to deny it." She bumped him with her shoulder on the way to the sink. "I know you too well."

Janey was a couple years older than he and Riley, and the three of them had run around together as kids, getting into all sorts of trouble. Those had been good times. He took a deep drink from his beer bottle, knowing she was someone who wouldn't be easily turned off the scent of disquiet within him.

"What's going on, Finn?"

"Nothing." He nudged at the floor with a toe of the Timberland boots he favored this time of year. "Much."

"Do I have to drag it out of you?"

He laughed, because if anyone could do that, Janey could. "Missy's been calling and texting—a lot. She wants me to come home."

"Ugh," Janey said, her reaction not unexpected. "I thought you'd moved on from her."

"I have. I *did*."

"So why are you still talking to her?"

"We were together five years."

"And it's been over for two. Why're you looking to go backward?"

"I'm not, but she says we're both older and wiser now, and it'd be different this time."

"Different how?" Janey asked as she dumped ranch dressing into a bowl surrounded by veggies.

"We wouldn't be quite so…"

"Horrible together?" Janey asked, raising a brow in amusement.

"Yeah," Finn said, huffing out a laugh.

Janey wiped her hands on a dish towel. "Can I tell you a little story from my own biography?"

"Sure." Finn opened a second beer and leaned against the counter.

"David and I were together for thirteen years, so long we lost all sense of perspective. It wasn't until we were with other people that we were able to see what'd been missing in our relationship. The first night I spent with Joe as more than friends was a major revelation."

Cringing, Finn held up a hand. "Stop right there. No disgusting details that'll scar your baby cousin for life."

"Shut up," she said, laughing. "And *grow* up, will you?"

"That'll never happen."

"Yes, it *will* happen, and when it does, I'll be the first one there waiting to say, see, I told you so. Missy is the *past*, Finn. If you were meant to be with her forever, you wouldn't have spent the last two years apart. Trust me when I tell you, when the right one comes along, you will *know* it— and you won't want to spend one *day* away from her, let alone two years."

Her husband, Joe, walked into the kitchen with a pajama-clad child in each arm, their hair still damp from the bath he'd given them.

Janey lit up at the sight of her little family and took her daughter, Vivienne, from Joe, who snuggled their son, PJ. "Are my babies all ready for night-night?"

"No," PJ said.

Joe laughed. "That's his only word so far. Some kids start with Dada or Mama. Ours starts with no."

"That's awesome," Finn said, laughing.

"Not if you're his parents, it isn't," Joe said, tickling his son, who responded with a deep belly laugh.

"No bedtime riling," Janey said, kissing her son and handing her daughter back to Joe.

"Say good night to cousin Finn," Joe said.

"No," PJ replied.

"Am I allowed to laugh?" Finn asked.

"Not if you want to live," Janey said, scowling. "He has to get another word one of these days, doesn't he?"

"No," Finn said, earning a punch to the biceps from his cousin.

As Joe went upstairs with the kids, Finn's cousin Mallory arrived with her fiancé, Quinn James. She hugged her sister, Janey, and then hugged Finn, too. He marveled at how Mallory had fit right into the family after learning that Big Mac was her father. Now it was like they'd always known her.

"What'd we miss?" Mallory asked, pouring herself a glass of seltzer as Quinn helped himself to a soda.

"I'm giving our baby cousin Finn a lecture on the downside of recycling," Janey said.

"There's a downside to recycling?" Quinn asked, popping a carrot into his mouth.

"There is when we're referring to relationships that've run their course but keep coming around for new drama," Janey said with a pointed look for Finn, who scowled at her.

"Ah," Mallory said. "Gotta agree with my sister here, Finn. Some things are better left in the past where they belong."

"So I've been told," Finn said, returning Janey's pointed look.

"I firmly recommend waiting for the right one to come along," Mallory said with a warm smile for Quinn. "There's nothing quite like getting it exactly right."

Quinn took her hand and brought it his lips. "What she said." The look he gave her was positively indecent.

Finn was quite certain that in all their years together, he'd never looked at Missy in quite that way. "No need to rub my face in all your happiness, people," Finn said in a teasing tone, ready to change the subject.

"You'll get your turn, Finny." Janey ruffled his hair and kissed his cheek. "And I, for one, can't wait to see that happen."

"Don't hold your breath," Finn said, not in any particular rush to settle down.

The house began to fill with family members, each of whom inquired as to whether anyone had spoken to Shane. Everyone was concerned about him in light of the day's events. *What a bitch*, Finn thought, *to lose someone the way he'd lost Courtney, more than once now.* The awful senselessness of it all had contributed to Finn's general feeling of gloominess. Courtney had been a beautiful, sweet woman, and what'd happened to her—and to Shane—was heartbreaking. It made Finn want to steer well clear of anything resembling true love.

Speaking of true love, when his dad arrived with Chelsea, he asked for a second alone with Finn. The three of them stepped into the dining room, which was the only room in the downstairs part of the house that wasn't overrun by McCarthys and their friends.

"What's up?" Finn asked Kevin.

Kevin glanced at Chelsea, smiling. "We wanted to let you know that we're expecting—and we're getting married. At the end of the month."

"Oh," Finn said, feeling all the air leave his body in one big whoosh. "That's great. Congrats."

"I was hoping you and your brother would stand up for me."

"Sure." Steeped in a sense of the surreal, he leaned in to kiss Chelsea's cheek and to hug his father. "Happy for you guys."

"Thanks, bud," Kevin said, smiling at his intended. "We're pretty damned happy for us, too."

It had been a very long time since Finn had seen his father look so happy. *When the right one comes along,* Janey had said, *you'll know it.* His father with Chelsea—that was what finding the right one looked like, he decided, even as he continued to grapple with the way his parents' marriage had ended.

Life was too short to spend it unhappy. Finn honestly believed that, but his parents' divorce had rocked him nonetheless, and the shockwaves continued to reverberate almost two years later. With hindsight, he could see how miserable they had been for a long time before they split, but since he hadn't lived at home since leaving for college, the breakup had still surprised Finn and his brother.

Riley arrived with Nikki a few minutes later and came over to where Finn stood with their dad and Chelsea. "Hi there," Riley said, his arm around Nikki. "You know my dad and Chelsea. This is my brother, Finn. Finn, this is Nikki Stokes."

Gorgeous, Finn thought, *even more so than her famous sister, if that's possible.* "Nice to finally meet you," Finn said, shaking her hand.

"You, too."

Raising a brow, he gave her an assessing look. "I'm going to call you Nicholas."

She returned his assessing look with one of her own, immediately earning his respect. "And I will call you Finnbar."

Riley cracked up laughing at the same time Finn, Kevin and Chelsea did.

"Touché," Finn said, raising his beer bottle. "To Nicholas."

"I'll drink to that," Riley said meaningfully as Nikki's face turned bright red.

She elbowed him playfully in the gut, making him gasp and taking her up another notch in Finn's estimation.

"Did you hear we've got a wedding to go to later this month?" Riley asked.

"I just got that memo."

"We'll need a bachelor party," Riley said, eyeing Kevin shrewdly.

"Oh no, we won't," Kevin said.

"Oh yes, we will," Finn said. "No one gets out of that ritual. Not in this family."

"I don't think we should," Kevin said, his expression serious. "With Shane and everything."

"We absolutely should, and Shane would agree," Riley said. "We'll show our respect for him and for Courtney, and then we will continue to live. That's all we can do, or so says my father, the shrink."

"I hate when they use my words against me," Kevin said to Chelsea, who laughed behind her hand.

"You can't laugh at them," Kevin said. "You're either with me or you're with them. You can't have it both ways."

"I'm with you, babe," Chelsea said, curling her hand around Kevin's arm.

"Suck-up," Finn said, teasing.

"He's my baby daddy. I need him."

If you'd asked Finn a couple of years ago if his dad would want more kids, he would've said no way, but then along came Chelsea, and everything changed. Like Janey said, being with the right one made all the difference.

Missy was not the right one for him. He knew that. Hell, she knew it, too, but they continued to stay in touch out of habit more than anything else. It was probably time to cut that cord and move on, even if the cutting of the cord would be painful.

Seeing Riley obviously enthralled with Nikki made Finn wonder about what might be around the next bend for him. As far as he knew, Riley had never been serious about any woman, but he was putting out vibes that had Finn wondering if Nikki might be the one for Riley.

Things were changing all around him, whether Finn wanted the changes or not. It was high time he made some changes of his own, beginning with ending things once and for all with his ex-girlfriend.

SHELL-SHOCKED. That was the word of the day for Mac McCarthy Junior. Maddie was pregnant. *Again.* And, after their appointment at the clinic, he'd heard the news about Shane's ex-wife, and shock had been compounded by more shock. Both sets of grandparents had offered to stay with their kids so they could go to Janey's, but after the appointment at the clinic, they'd decided to stay home.

After calling Shane to express his condolences and check on his cousin, Mac went through the motions of helping Thomas and Hailey get ready for bed, giving them baths and wrestling them into pajamas. They were in the mood to fool around, and he wasn't, which made for a stressful hour.

"Daddy cranky," Hailey said, taking him by the face and puckering her sweet lips into a frown that made him laugh.

"No, I'm not."

"Yes, you are," Thomas said.

"Maybe a little," Mac conceded.

"How come?" His son studied him in the intent way that often made Mac want to squirm. The child watched his every move, mimicking what he did and said—and *how* he did and said *everything*. He'd never been more *seen* by any human being in his life than by the son who'd come into his life when the boy was nine months old.

"No reason, buddy. Nothing to worry about. Whose turn is it to pick a story?"

"Mine," Hailey said as Thomas groaned.

"No princesses," Thomas said.

"Yes, princesses," Hailey said.

They compromised on one princess and one Star Wars story that left everyone happy. Mac tucked them into their beds and kissed them good night, leaving them with stern warnings about *staying* in bed. That had been their biggest challenge lately.

He went into the bedroom he shared with Maddie, who was breastfeeding Mac as tears rolled unchecked down her face. Her tears broke his heart. "Is he asleep?" he asked, leaning in for a closer look at the baby who everyone said looked just like him.

"I think so."

Mac moved carefully to pick him up without waking him. Gazing down at the perfect, sweet face of his son, Mac couldn't help but be thankful for their many blessings. No, they hadn't been planning to have more kids, but they also hadn't been as careful as they could've been since baby Mac was born.

As he settled the baby in his crib, he blamed himself. He should've been more careful Maddie had her hands full with three little ones, and the thought of a fourth was taking her right over the edge. And how could he blame her? He worked all day—and in the summer, he worked *two* jobs. She was the one home with the kids, so most of the work of child-rearing fell to her.

He'd hire a nanny or someone to help her, especially in the summer when he was also working at the marina. And he'd cut back his hours wherever he could, give more responsibility to Luke, Shane, Riley and Finn. The latter two had proven they were no longer the babies of the family and were capable of much more than he'd asked of them so far.

Returning to their bedroom, Mac found Maddie right where he'd left her, staring at the far wall with the tears continuing unabated.

"We can't tell Adam or Abby about this," she said.

His brother and sister-in-law had been grappling with fertility challenges. "We'll have to tell them eventually."

"I don't want them to ever know."

"Maddie," he said, sighing as he sat next to her.

"It's not fair. She wants a baby more than anything, and I can't seem to *stop* having them. And if you laugh, I'll stab you in your sleep."

"I'm not laughing. I swear."

"You're getting a vasectomy," she said. "This is it."

"Okay."

"I thought you said no one was cutting your junk ever."

"I've changed my mind."

"That's good, because I was prepared to do it myself with the kitchen scissors if I had to."

Mac winced. "No need to get violent. I'll do it."

"Mac…"

"What, honey?"

"What the hell are we going to do with *four little kids?*"

"We're going to love them and raise them and lose our minds for the next ten to fifteen years, but we'll get through it. Together."

"They're all going to be teenagers."

"I know that."

"*At the same time!*"

"Just think, we'll get it over with all at once." He paused, considering whether he should tell her about Courtney when she was already so raw, and decided talking about it might help to give them both some perspective. "I want to tell you about a girl I used to know, who was married to Shane. Only he didn't know she was an addict until it was way too late. She was a sweet girl, pretty and funny, and he loved her so much."

"Courtney, right?" She hadn't met Courtney because Shane's marriage had been over before she and Mac got together.

Mac nodded. "Today we heard she died, possibly of an overdose."

"Oh God, Mac…" She began to cry again. "Is Shane okay?"

"I talked to him a little while ago, and I checked with Laura, too. Katie is with him, and he's coping as well as can be expected."

"And here I am sobbing over another baby when you'd think I'd learned my lesson after we lost Connor. I said I would never overreact to being pregnant again after that. You see why I'm not liking myself very much lately?"

Mac leaned in to kiss her. "It's a good thing I like you enough for both of us. I wanted to tell you about Courtney to remind us both that we need to count our blessings, all the time, even when we're overwhelmed. As long as we have each other, there's nothing we can't handle, even four kids."

"You make me believe that."

"You can believe it. We'll get some help, so you don't have to do it all yourself during the day when I'm at work."

"I hate to say I might need that."

"I'll get you whatever you need, and we'll continue to count our blessings, because we are so very, very lucky."

"I know that. I honestly do. I don't want you to think I'm not grateful."

"I know you are, babe. Anyone would be overwhelmed by this news."

"Let's not tell anyone for a while, okay? By the time they find out, it won't be like we literally got pregnant one second after Mac was born."

"You got it," Mac said, laughing as he gathered her into his embrace. "Whatever you want."

"I'm never having sex with you and your super sperm again."

"Yes, you are."

"Never again."

"You know how much I love a good challenge." Cupping her cheek, he said, "Kiss me."

"No, that's probably enough to get me pregnant again."

"The good news is that can't happen for the next eight months or so. We can have all the fun we want in the meantime."

"After that, no more."

"Kiss me."

"Mac…"

"Hmm?" He was busy kissing her neck and working his way to her lips.

"Do you promise you'll love me even if I never again look the way I did when we met?"

He raised his head and looked down to find her caramel eyes gazing up at him with wild vulnerability. "I promise I will love you no matter what. I like you better with some curves. You were too thin when we met, too worried about everything and not properly taking care of yourself because you were too busy caring for Thomas. I love every inch of you. I love every curve, every valley, every hollow and every bit of smooth, silky skin. There will never come a time when I don't love you or want to make love to you more than I want anything else in my entire life."

Maddie sighed and wrapped her arms around him as he settled on top of her. "I'm sorry to be this way. It's the old insecurities coming back to haunt me."

"You can be insecure any time you need to be, and I'll be happy to put your mind at ease."

"Even after all this time, sometimes I still can't believe…"

His lips skimmed over hers in the lightest possible caress. "What can't you believe?"

"That you picked me."

"You crashed into me. You didn't give me much choice."

She smiled at his familiar reply, as he'd hoped she would. "*You* crashed into *me*."

"Semantics," he said, pushing her nightgown up and pressing his cock against the heat between her legs. They had the who-crashed-into-whom "argument" frequently, and it never got old to think about the day they met. "And if you'll recall, I loved you when you were bruised and bloody and scabby."

"Yes, you did." She ran her fingers through his hair, making him tremble with need.

"I've loved you and wanted you and needed you every day since. I always will, Madeline. No matter what." He pushed into her, desperate to show her how much he loved her in every way he possibly could. Though he understood where the insecurities came from, it pained him to know she still suffered from them. If he could, he would use the power of his love for her to wipe away everything that had ever hurt her and replace those memories with the joy she had brought to his life.

She clung to him and met his every deep thrust with a welcoming lift of her hips.

"I can still remember every detail of our first week together," he whispered, his lips brushing against her ear and making her shiver. "Right down to the bar that poked me in the back on that awful pull-out sofa bed. I remember feeding orange sweet potatoes to Thomas and our first kiss when you were dreaming and the first time we made love and how I had to get Janey to buy us more condoms."

Maddie laughed and then gasped when he drove into her again.

"That was the best week of my entire life, and every week since then has been even better. And it's all because of you."

"I love you, Mac. So much. I never want you to think—"

He kissed her with deep, coaxing strokes of his tongue. "I know exactly why this happens every now and then. I get it, babe. Any time you need to be reminded of how I feel about you, you just let me know. I'm always happy to tell you."

With her hands on his face, she compelled him to meet her gaze. "I remember everything about that week, too. From the first second you forced your way into my life to the way you took care of me and Thomas and covered my shifts at the hotel and made me feel safe for the first time in my life."

Her words took his desire for her from slow burn to open flame. He reached down to where they were joined to caress her until she exploded, her inner muscles clamping down on his cock, taking him with her until they were gasping and clinging to each other in the aftermath.

"So much for keeping my distance from you and your super sperm," she said dryly.

"Don't do that. Don't ever do that."

"As if I could."

"Today was a huge shock to both of us, but it's going to be okay. Tell me you know that."

"I do know it. Thank you for always doing what you do to talk me off the cliff."

"I need you right here with me, not out on a cliff worrying yourself sick."

"Love you, Mac."

"Love you more, Madeline. Close your eyes and get some sleep. I'm right here, and I'm never letting go."

CHAPTER 12

*R*iley introduced Nikki to most of his family. Everyone was there except for Mac, Maddie, Grant, Stephanie, Shane and Katie and Evan and Grace, the latter two traveling on tour in Europe with Buddy Longstreet as Evan's musical career continued to exceed his wildest expectations.

"Your cousin is *touring* with Buddy Longstreet?" Nikki asked, incredulous.

"Yep," Riley said. "He's been pursuing the dream for years, and when his song 'My Amazing Grace' topped the charts, Buddy asked him to tour."

"Wait, that song… Evan McCarthy! I had *no idea* he was your cousin! I *love* that song."

"When he's home, we treat him like he's no big deal so he won't get too big for his britches," Adam said.

"Truth," Janey said. "He's already unmanageable. Thank God for his wife, Grace. She keeps him in line."

"And Grant is an Academy Award-winning screenwriter," Riley said. "Did you see 'Song of Solomon' by any chance?"

Nikki stared at Riley. "No way."

"Yes way. He's working on a new film now that tells the story of his wife Stephanie's efforts to get her stepfather out of prison," Riley said.

"He was unjustly incarcerated," Adam said. "She fought it for fourteen years."

"Grant's friend Dan Torrington got involved," Janey said.

"*The* Dan Torrington?" Nikki asked. "Even I've heard of him."

"The one and only. Stephanie's stepfather, Charlie, is out. He lives here on the island and is engaged to Owen and Katie's mom, Sarah. They're so happy together."

"When will the movie be out?" Nikki asked. "I want to see it."

"Another year or so," Adam said. "It's in production now."

"What about you?" Abby asked. "Tell us your story."

"My story is boring compared to everyone else's," Nikki said.

"There's a lot to be said for boring," Abby said.

Janey hooted with laughter. "Is she calling you boring, bro?" she asked Adam.

"Not at all," Abby said with a pointed look for her sister-in-law. "Nothing about him is boring. In fact—"

Janey held up a hand to stop her. "Say no more."

Nikki laughed at their antics. "I got what you meant. Believe me, I appreciate boredom after suffering through the insanity of the last few months with my sister."

"Is she really back with him?" Abby asked with a kind but pained smile.

"Sad to say she is," Nikki said. "And no, I don't get it either. On the list of deal breakers, you'd think publishing a sex tape of your wife without her knowledge or consent would be right at the top, but apparently not for her."

Riley took hold of her hand and gave it a squeeze.

"That must've been difficult for you," Janey said.

"It was awful—and it was *my* deal breaker. I quit my job as her assistant and got the hell out of there. As much as I love her, I just couldn't do it anymore."

"She'll wise up," Janey said, perching on the arm of the love seat Nikki shared with Riley. "Eventually."

"I don't know," Nikki said, the old anxiety resurfacing when she allowed her thoughts to stray in her sister's direction. "He has this weird hold on her that I don't understand."

"Things like that tend to burn out sooner rather than later," Adam said.

"Usually," Nikki said. "But this has been a couple of years of madness. I thought it was over when he released the tape. I realized she'd never stopped communicating with him, so I wasn't entirely surprised when she went back to him, but it was devastating nonetheless."

"I'm really sorry," Janey said. "It's hard to watch people you love make bad decisions."

"It really is. My grandmother has always said that the only thing we control is ourselves and our own actions, so I got myself the heck out of there. I've spent enough time managing her life. It's time to focus on my own for a change."

"Good for you," Abby said. "What do you think you want to do?"

"I have no idea! I'm hoping to figure that out while I'm here."

"She's going to oversee some renovations to her grandmother's home, for one thing," Riley said.

"Oh, that's cool!" Abby said. "You should talk to Syd. She's got a decorating business on the island. They would've been here, but their baby Lily conked out early." Abby snapped her fingers. "And Lizzie James. They just did an amazing renovation of the kitchen and living spaces at the Chesterfield. They operate it as a wedding venue, but the renovations are beautiful. She gave us a tour the other day."

"I'd love to see it," Nikki said.

"Give me your number, and I'll set something up," Abby replied.

"Stick with us," Janey said, squeezing Nikki's shoulder. "We'll help you figure it out."

Sitting among Riley's cousins and their significant others, Nikki believed these strong, dynamic people could take over the world if they set their minds to it.

The party broke up a short time later. On the way out, Riley told Finn about the call from their old boss in Connecticut.

"What'd he want?" Finn asked.

"Us. Back to work."

Finn winced. "Not the best timing with the Wayfarer and everything."

"That's what I told him. I have a feeling if we don't go back now, we aren't going to be welcome back later."

His words struck a note of panic in Nikki. Not that she had any standing in his life after a few nights together and a couple of heated kisses, but the last thing she wanted to hear was that he was leaving any time soon.

"How'd you leave it with him?" Finn asked.

"That I'd talk to you and get back to him."

Finn ran his fingers through his hair, something Riley did, too, when he was thinking. "I suppose we can at least take the weekend."

"I guess so."

"Let's talk about it tomorrow."

"Sounds good."

After thanking Janey and Joe for having them, Riley and Nikki followed Finn into the frigid night.

As Riley drove them back to Eastward Look, Nikki's anxiety began to kick in. She'd loved kissing him earlier, had thought about it throughout the evening they'd spent with his fun and funny family, but now she wondered what would happen when they were alone again.

He reached over and took her hand, linking his fingers with hers. "Are you okay?"

"Uh-huh," she said, although his question made her wonder if she was putting out anxiety vibes that he was picking up. "I liked your family."

"They liked you, too. That was somewhat of a skeleton crew. You should see what it's like when everyone is here in the summer. It's utter madness."

"Sounds like fun."

"It is."

"You seem to really like being around your family."

"I do. I always have. And now we're into this business together at the Wayfarer, which is cool. Everyone contributed whatever they could, so we all have a stake."

"That's really awesome. You're lucky to have such an amazing family."

"And I know it. Believe me. My dad and his brothers have always been exceptionally close, which meant all the cousins were, too. It was a nice way to grow up."

"Sounds like it."

"Finn and I are the youngest. They called us 'The Babies' until we were in high school, or at least that's how it seemed, and we begged them to stop."

"That's funny."

"Wasn't funny at the time, but it is now."

"What're you going to do about the ex-boss in Connecticut?"

"I don't know," he said, sounding torn. "He's such a good guy. He gave me my first real job right out of college, and when Finn graduated two years later, he hired him, too. He taught me so much and was always so fair. Finn and I have a ton of respect for him."

"That doesn't mean you have to upend your current life for him, does it?"

"No, but he sounded pretty desperate." Riley took the right-hand turn into the driveway that led to Eastward Look and brought the truck to a stop.

"You want to come in?"

"Only if you want me to."

"I want you to."

"Okay, then." He released her hand and shut off the truck, plunging them into darkness.

Nikki got out of the truck and hustled through the freezing air to get into the warm house. "I want hot chocolate with a shot of Baileys. Any interest?"

"I'll have the hot chocolate, but hold the Baileys. I've got to drive."

"Coming right up."

· · ·

As he followed Nikki into the kitchen, Riley sensed her nervousness, which was confirmed as he watched her go through the steps of making their drinks. Her hands had the slightest tremor, and she could barely look at him.

Two steps forward, one step backward… That was how it seemed to him anyway, which, in light of what she'd shared earlier, was more than understandable. He didn't want to do anything to make her uncomfortable or, God forbid, frightened. Riley wanted more of her sweet, sexy kisses, but only if she wanted more, too.

One thing he knew for certain, he'd never met any woman who interested him the way Nikki did, with her intriguing mix of loyalty, vulnerability, anxiousness, sexiness, charm and humor. She was easy to talk to and to be with and flat-out fucking beautiful, and the more time he spent with her, the more he wanted her.

"Hey, Nik." He'd said the nickname before he consciously decided to call her that, but he liked the way it felt as he said it.

She looked up from the pot she was stirring on an old gas stove. "Yeah?"

"Has there been anyone else?" He hoped she knew what he meant.

Shaking her head, she said, "I've tried. A couple of times. But I couldn't go through with it."

His heart ached for her.

"Don't pity me. I don't need that."

"I don't pity you, but I'm very sorry it happened to you."

"So am I." She glanced at him, and he saw the vulnerability she tried so hard to keep hidden. "I wish it wasn't an issue for me, but it always is."

"It's part of what made you who you are, and I happen to like who you are. A lot."

"I told you I'm kind of a mess, Riley," she said softly. "I quit my job, I'm somewhat homeless, I have no idea where I'm headed or which end is up. I'm scared of sex, I have awful anxiety, and…"

He wrapped his arms around her from behind, pushing her hair out of the way so he could kiss her neck. "Quit trying to scare me off. It's not going to work."

At first, she went tense, but then she relaxed against him, and he felt elated by the trust she had granted him by allowing him to hold her in such a familiar way.

"You might be leaving…"

"As long as you are here, I'm not going anywhere."

"Your former boss—"

"Can kiss my ass. He's got nothing on you." Reaching around her to kill the flame under the pot, he turned her to face him. Tipping her chin up, he kissed her as gently as he possibly could. "This, with you… I want this."

She rested her hands on his chest and looked up at him. "I want it, too. But you're going to have to be patient with me. I'm no good at it."

"I believe we've demonstrated that's not true."

"Yes, it really is."

He shook his head and kept his eyes open when he kissed her again, laying his lips on hers in an effort to refresh her memory about what they'd done earlier and how much they'd both enjoyed it.

She slid her hands up and wrapped her arms around his neck, her mouth opening to accept his tongue.

Riley wanted to howl from the thrill of her tongue rubbing up against his. He'd never felt anything like the almost-electrical charge that went through him as she returned the kiss with an eagerness that made a liar out of her. She was very, *very* good at this.

She withdrew slowly from the kiss. "The, um… hot chocolate."

All he could see were her swollen, kiss-dampened lips and the high flush that turned her cheeks a light shade of pink. He'd never seen anything more beautiful. He was still gazing hungrily at her when she handed him the mug of steaming chocolate with a dollop of whipped cream on top.

She spiked hers with a shot of Baileys. "Let's go admire our tree."

Riley followed her into the living room. "Does the fireplace work?"

"Uh-huh."

"Do you want me to make a fire?"

"I'd love it. You have to open the flue thingie."

Smiling, he put his mug on the coffee table. "I know." He knelt on the hearth, opened the flue and built a fire using the wood in the box next to the fireplace. The wood was nice and dry, so it caught quickly.

"I'm always afraid to do that when I'm here by myself," she said when he rejoined her on the sofa. "One time, I filled the house with smoke, and the fire department had to come."

"You forgot the flue thingie."

"Don't mock me. It was traumatizing. I thought the house was burning down."

Riley curled his lips inward so he wouldn't be tempted to laugh.

"I can tell you're mocking me."

"I'd never do that," he said, curling a strand of her long dark hair around his finger.

"It's okay. You can. It's kind of funny. Now… At the time, not so much."

"How old were you?"

"Sixteen? I think… My grandmother was out to dinner. Jordan and I were home alone. Of course, on Gansett, when something like that happens, the whole island knows in a matter of minutes. It sort of scared me off fireplaces for the rest of my life."

"I bet you were a very cute sixteen-year-old."

"I had freckles."

"Adorable." He drew her closer to him, close enough to kiss the unmarked skin on her face. "Where were they? Right here?" He kissed her cheek and the tip of her nose. "Or was it here?"

"Pretty much everywhere," she said, sounding breathless.

"I'm going to need to see pictures."

Nikki's smile lit up her entire face.

Riley had the odd thought that he could look at that face forever and never get tired of the view. Taking her mug from her, he put it next to his on the coffee table. "I want to kiss you some more, but you have to tell me it's what you want. Anything that happens between us will only happen if you want it to."

"I want to kiss you, too." This time, she was the one who leaned in, who touched her lips to his and took the lead.

She tasted like chocolate and Baileys. She tasted like desire, the purest, simplest desire he'd ever experienced. One kiss at a time, this sweet, vulnerable woman was changing him and redefining what he wanted.

Riley was far more accustomed to confident, overtly sexual women who saw what they wanted and took it. He'd always found that kind of confidence sexy, but now he wanted something different. He wanted Nikki with her mix of moxie and vulnerability. More than anything, he wanted her to trust him, so he forced himself to go slow, to savor rather than devour.

She had her arms looped around his neck, so when she reclined on the sofa, he had no choice but to go with her. Not that he objected... But the new position made it impossible for him to hide his reaction to her.

"Nikki," he whispered, his lips gliding over hers. "Hey."

Her eyes fluttered open.

"Hi there."

"Hi, yourself."

Her damp, swollen lips curved into a smile that touched him deeply, in places no one had ever reached before. In that moment, he began to accept that she had already changed his life. Possibly forever. Was he ready for that? Probably not, but it seemed to be happening whether he was ready or not.

"You're staring."

"You're so damned gorgeous. I can't help but stare."

She ran her fingertips over his face. "I could say the same about you." When she shifted beneath him, he groaned from the effort to hold back.

"Nikki... I don't... Is this..." Sighing, he dropped his head to her chest.

Laughing softly, she ran her fingers through his hair.

"You're making a fumbling fool of me."

"What's on your mind?" she asked.

"Well..." He pressed against her, letting her know exactly what was on his mind. "I heard what you said earlier, and I just want to be sure this isn't too much, too soon."

"I really like kissing you."

"I really like kissing *you*."

"It seems we're on the same page here…"

"I like being on the same page with you, but you're going to have to be the one to *turn* the page."

Smiling, she dipped her fingers under his sweater and ran her fingertips lightly over his back in what quickly became the most erotic caress of his life. Why was it, he wondered, that this woman's touch was so different from every other?

She drew him into another kiss, this one more intense than any of the others, and Riley's resolve to go slow was sorely tested. He wanted to touch her and kiss her everywhere. He wanted to bury himself inside her.

Her words from earlier echoed in his head, reminding him to proceed with caution, which was the last thing he wanted to do with her warm and willing as she kissed him without any hint of restraint. If this was a test of his resolve, he was about to fail miserably.

"Nikki," he said, taking a deep breath between kisses and shifting to his side so he was facing her. He brushed her hair back and cupped her cheek, running his thumb over the flush of color that gave her a rosy glow. "Tell me what you want."

"I want to keep kissing you." Under his sweater, her hand moved from back to front, sliding from his belly to his chest and leaving a trail of fire behind.

"You're making me kinda crazy here."

"Am I?"

"Yeah," he said on a nervous laugh. "Just a bit."

"I appreciate that you're being careful with me, but…"

"What?"

"I want more."

Riley's heart felt like it was performing cartwheels that left him breathless and impossibly aroused. For the longest time, he hadn't understood why his cousins wanted to tie themselves to one woman for the rest of their lives when they could've had *all* the women. Lying on the sofa, wrapped up in Nikki, he was beginning to get it. "How much more?" With other women, he'd let things happen organically. With her, he needed certainty.

"Touch me, Riley."

He gave her sweater a gentle tug. "Could we take this off?"

She hesitated, but only for a second before nodding and helping him to remove her sweater, and then took his off, too.

Taking in the sight of her full breasts contained only by a lacy, sexy bra, Riley drew her into his embrace, trembling from the power of his desire for her. "Nik... You're so soft and sexy. I'm trying really hard to hold back here..."

"I'm okay."

"Are you sure?"

Nodding, she drew him into another kiss, using her tongue to outline the shape of his mouth as her hand caressed his chest.

Riley held perfectly still, allowing her to do whatever she wanted while he tried to keep his head—and other parts of him—from exploding.

CHAPTER 13

*S*ince the assault in college, Nikki had never been entirely "comfortable" with a man the way she was with Riley. Everything about him was different, and not just because he was so sweet and sexy and easy to talk to. It was more than that. After having met his father, brother, cousins and many of his other family members, she felt a sense of safety with him that had been missing in the past.

Other guys she'd dated hadn't seemed to care about truly getting to know her or introducing her to their families. It'd been about one thing and one thing only.

Riley wasn't like that. While he seemed to find her appealing, the same way other guys had in the past, he saw more than how she looked or how she might perform in bed. He saw *her*, Nikki. Not Jordan's identical twin or another easy conquest. In that way, there was absolutely nothing typical about Riley McCarthy, and that realization had her wanting things that had been impossible for her since that long-ago night changed everything for her in ways she still hadn't fully shared with Riley.

Talking about what'd happened *after* that night was too painful, even all these years later. As they often did, the memories came flooding back to remind her that she would never be "normal" again, the pain searing her as it always did, forcing her to pull back from Riley when that was the last thing she wanted to do.

"What's wrong?" he asked.

"I..." Oh God, please, no. Her chest tightened with the telltale signs of the dreaded panic attacks that had crippled her in the days and weeks after the assault and the nightmare that'd followed. She pushed herself up to a seated position and focused on getting air to her lungs before the panic could take over.

"Tell me what you need," he said, putting an arm around her.

Nikki went through the mental checklist she relied upon at times like this—everything is okay, you are safe, nothing is wrong, breathe. Just breathe. Sometimes the checklist worked, other times it didn't. As tiny dots danced before her eyes, she feared this was going to be one of the latter cases.

"Nikki," Riley said, giving her a gentle shake. "Talk to me. What's wrong?"

She continued to focus on the burning need for oxygen and the ache in her chest.

Riley rubbed her back. "What do you need, sweetheart? Whatever it is, I'll get it for you."

His words as much as his tender care helped to loosen the stranglehold the panic had on her. Air came rushing back to her starving lungs, sending tears of relief and mortification cascading down her cheeks.

Riley held her through it, whispering soothing words and giving her gentle caresses that were all about comfort.

If she hadn't already been falling hard for him, his compassion would've done it. When she could speak again, her first words were an apology.

"Please don't." He brought her head to rest against his chest as his fingers slid through her hair. "It's my fault. I got carried away—"

"No." She couldn't bear to hear him blame himself. "It's me. There are other things, about what happened in college, that I didn't tell you, things I never talk about with anyone." A sinking feeling of utter despair came over her. "I'll understand if this is way too much for you."

"I'm not going anywhere."

"You're a good guy, Riley. You deserve to be with someone who isn't a complete mess."

"Don't say that. You're not a mess."

"We're only scratching the surface here. It's really okay to walk away. I swear I won't hold it against you."

"I sent a text to my boss Luke's wife, Sydney, earlier. She's the interior designer that Abby mentioned. I thought she might be able to give us some ideas about how we can redo the kitchen and bathrooms. Once we have a design, we can order the materials and get started on demo. Did your grandmother give you a budget?"

"She—I… You don't have to do this."

"Do what?"

"Help me with the house. I'd totally understand if you…"

"Left and never came back?"

Aching, she nodded.

"Because that's what's happened in the past? Things got tense, and the guy took off, never to be seen or heard from again?"

She stared at him, stunned by his insight.

"You're not getting rid of me that easily. As much as I like kissing you and holding you and being with you like this, I like talking to you and laughing with you and thinking about what we might do to bring this magnificent old house back to life. I like all of that as much as I like this." He touched his lips to hers in a sweet, undemanding caress.

She'd known he was different. He'd just proven it to her.

"And when you're ready to talk about whatever has you so troubled, I'll be there to listen. I'm not going anywhere."

"Your old boss wants you back in Connecticut."

"I told you—as long as you want me here, I'm not going. I'll let him know on Monday." He hesitated before adding, "Unless I'm reading this all wrong, and you really don't want me and that's what caused whatever just happened here."

"You're not reading anything wrong, but I don't want you to feel obligated to me."

"I don't." He kissed her again and reached for her sweater to help her back into it before donning his own. "I'm going to go, but I'll call you tomorrow to let you know what Syd has available, okay?"

"Okay."

"Make sure you close the glass doors to the fireplace before you go to bed." The fire had died down, but glowing embers remained.

"I will." Nikki stood on legs that felt wooden and followed him to the door as a sense of desperation descended upon her. She couldn't let him leave like this. "Riley."

He turned to her, zipping his coat and donning a gray knit hat.

"Despite how it might've seemed for the last few minutes, I had a really good time tonight. I loved meeting your brother and cousins and the others."

"I had a great time, too." He put an arm around her waist and brought her in close to him. "And I *will* call you tomorrow."

She raised her hands to his face and kissed him. "Thank you for being awesome."

"I didn't do anything."

"You did. More than you'll ever know."

He hugged her tightly and then kissed her forehead. "Get some sleep. Text me when you wake up. Okay?"

"Okay." Nikki stood in the door and watched him dash through the cold to his truck, keeping the lights on until he was on his way. Then she turned off the lights, locked the door and went into the living room to close the glass doors to the fireplace. She sat on the sofa, which was still warm from their bodies.

It'd been years since her last panic attack, long enough to lull her into a false sense of security, thinking that unsavory stage of her life was in the past. Now she knew otherwise.

She normally tried not to let memories of Griffin invade her thoughts, but as if seven years hadn't gone by, he was right there, front and center, torturing her with regrets and guilt. Years of therapy had helped her cope, but tonight's events had her wondering if she'd made any progress at all.

Riley would come back, because that was who he was. But once he realized what he was up against, he'd quietly disappear from her life. That was what'd happened with the other two guys she'd dated since Griffin. They'd quickly figured out that she was going to be too much work and moved on, which had been fine with her. In fact, it'd been a relief both times.

But with Riley…

She took a deep breath and blew it out.

If he quietly disappeared, she'd miss him. Possibly forever.

DRIVING HOME ON DARK, bending roads, Riley asked himself what the hell had happened back there. Everything had been fine one second and not fine the next. What'd caused her to panic? He'd followed her lead, so he was almost positive he hadn't done anything that scared her.

The not knowing was going to drive him mad.

He arrived home, where Finn was watching an old episode of *The Office* and drinking a beer.

"Did you strike out?" Finn asked.

Riley wanted to tell him to shut the fuck up, that he was in no mood for his crap, but he didn't say either of those things. Instead, he went straight to the bathroom and then into his room.

"What's wrong?"

Riley looked up to find Finn standing in the doorway, still holding the beer bottle. "Nothing."

"Okay, if you want to play it that way, but you forget that I know you, and I could tell the second you came in the door that something was up. Are you already fighting with her? Isn't this supposed to be the rose-colored-glasses portion of the program?"

"I'm not fighting with her."

"If you say so."

"It's not that." Riley hadn't intended to confide in Finn, but he needed to tell someone, and for all his asshattery, Finn had his back. "She's been through some things, traumatic things…"

"Oh damn," Finn said, leaning against the doorframe. He wore only basketball shorts, and his dark hair stood on end in typical weekend fashion. "I'm sorry to hear that. She seems like a really nice girl."

"She is. She's… I really like her. A lot."

Finn fanned his face dramatically. "Is my widdle boy in love? *Finally?*"

"I never said that."

"You didn't have to. It's all over your face when you look at her."

"Not sure that means much coming from you, who loves to tell me I've got ugly all over my face."

Finn laughed. "I do like to say that, but tonight, I noticed something different. Something I haven't seen before."

"It's different with her."

"It has been since the leaky roof."

"Yeah." Why try to deny it when it was the truth?

"So what happened tonight?"

Riley thought about what he should say. He wanted Finn's advice, but not at the expense of Nikki's privacy. "Things got a little… intense."

"How so?"

"We were, you know, fooling around a little, and she kind of panicked."

"Panicked how?"

"She couldn't breathe."

"Damn," Finn said, exhaling his way through the single word.

"I swear to God, Finn, everything that happened between us, she was into as much as I was. It was all good until it wasn't."

"Did she tell you what happened?"

"Not really, but she gave me an out. She said she'd totally understand if it was too much for me."

"*It* being what?"

"There was an incident with a guy back in college." He played it down to protect her privacy. "I don't know the details, but she said there's really been no one since then."

"Whoa. So you're basically navigating an emotional minefield."

"I guess."

"And you don't even have all the info on what happened. You could go online—"

"No. I'm not doing that, and neither are you, you hear me?"

"I hear you, but how are you supposed to handle this if you don't even know what you're dealing with?"

"I'm going to handle it by focusing on other things. She wants to renovate her grandmother's kitchen. I'm going to help her do that."

"What about the fact that you're hot for her?"

"It may come as a shock to you that I *can* control myself."

"That's not what I mean, Riley, and you know it. You *like* this girl. She likes you, for some unknown reason. Does this mean you're hands-off until she figures things out that happened years ago?"

When Finn put it like that, the challenge before him seemed rather daunting. "For now."

"Is that realistic?"

"Is what realistic?"

"Hear me out. You like her. She likes you. Something happened to her a long time ago that makes her panicky when it comes to guys. What's the endgame for you in that scenario?"

"I don't know yet. All I know is that I want to find out. I like being around her. If she's not capable of bells and whistles right now, then that's fine. I'll wait."

"For how long?"

"For as long as it takes." Riley surprised himself as much as his brother with the emphatic statement.

Finn stared at him for a long moment before he cleared his throat. "I wish you the best. It's clear that you care about her, but if it doesn't seem like it's going to happen, get out before you get hurt. Will you do that, please?"

Riley didn't want to tell him it was already far too late for such warnings. If it didn't work out with Nikki, he was going to hurt like hell. "Yeah, I will." He said what his brother needed to hear. "Don't say anything about this to anyone, okay?"

"I never would. No one loves to bust your balls more than I do, but I know that this is different."

"It really is."

"Be careful, Ri," Finn said.

"I will."

"Get some sleep. The news said tomorrow night's gonna be a snowmageddon."

"Hey, Finn? Thanks. You know, for listening."

"Any time." Finn left the room, closing the door behind him.

For a long time, Riley lay awake reliving the special joy of kissing Nikki and wondering if he'd ever get to do it again.

DESPITE THE EMOTIONAL overload of the night before, Nikki slept surprisingly well and woke to a text from Riley.

Syd can see us at noon if that works for you? She said to bring pictures of the kitchen for now, and if you decide to use her, she can come take measurements later.

That works for me!

I'll pick you up at quarter till.

Thanks. See you then.

Nikki wanted to add something about what'd happened the night before, but he didn't seem to be dwelling on it, so she wouldn't either. He'd already proven himself worthy of her time and attention by following up on his promises. That put him hundreds of points ahead of any other guy she'd ever dated.

For the first time in days, Nikki sent a text to her sister. This was the longest they had ever gone without talking. Even when Jordan had been on her honeymoon, they'd texted just about every day.

Thinking about you and hoping all is well.

Nikki sent the text and put down her phone to spend the next few hours cleaning out kitchen cabinets full of mismatched plates, glasses and other items collected over fifty summers.

An hour into the project, Evelyn called for her daily check-in.

"Gram, you're a pack rat."

"I am not," Evelyn said indignantly.

"Yes, you are, and I can prove it. I'm switching to FaceTime." She switched the call over and smiled when her grandmother's pretty face popped up on the screen. "You have a collection of rooster pitchers."

White curls framed a youthful face, and blue eyes danced with glee at the sight of her granddaughter. "I love roosters."

"Do we need thirty of them?"

"You're not going to make me part with my roosters, are you?"

"I'm afraid so. Their time has come and gone."

"You're breaking my heart."

"Really?"

"No, I'm just teasing," Evelyn said. "Most of the stuff in that house I wouldn't even miss, so you can decide what to keep and what to get rid of. I only care about the photos and the things you girls made for me over the years. Don't get rid of those treasures."

"Like this?" Nikki held up the dead starfish she'd painted yellow and decorated with stick-on eyes at an island summer camp years ago.

"That's Starry! You were so proud of him. Don't you dare get rid of him."

"You're an overly sentimental pack rat."

"Sticks and stones, darling. Tell me you're doing more than cleaning out the cabinets. Where's your friend Riley?"

"He was here last night. We went to the party at his cousin's house. It was fun."

"Isn't Janey great?"

"She's very nice, and her husband is, too."

"Joe is a sweetie, and when you live on an island, it's always good to be in tight with the man who runs the ferries."

"Very true."

"Did he kiss you?"

"Who? Joe? No! He's married."

"Nicole Elizabeth, do not get sassy with your old granny. You know I'm talking about Riley."

Giggling at the face her grandmother made, Nikki said, "He might've kissed me, and I might've let him."

"Did you now?" Evelyn's smile lit up her face. "This is such good news."

"It was until I had a panic attack."

"Oh no. Oh, honey."

"It wasn't the worst one I've ever had, but it messed up our evening. He was great about it. Very sweet." Nikki couldn't bear to think about it. "But, you know. It was embarrassing."

"You can't help it. You don't need to be embarrassed."

"When you're making out with a hot guy who you really like and then suddenly you can't breathe—and not in a good way—it's definitely embarrassing."

"I'm sorry that happened, honey. I'd rather hoped the panic attacks were a thing of the past."

"You and me both. It was a major bummer, to say the least. But Riley… He was really amazing. I tried to give him an out, but he said he'd talk to me in the morning, and I've already heard from him. He's taking me to see his friend Sydney, who's an interior designer. She can help me come up with a plan for the kitchen renovation."

"Your Riley sounds like a lovely young man."

"He is. I just hope he's not so weirded out by me and all my issues that I've ruined any chance of something coming of it."

"You should tell him the rest, honey. It would help him to understand."

"I hate to think about it, let alone talk about it."

"I know, but it would be unfortunate if your chance to make something of your friendship with Riley got sidetracked because he doesn't have all the info he needs to truly understand you."

"You're right," Nikki said, sighing. "I know you are, it's just…"

"Hard."

"Yeah."

"People like to say that time heals all wounds, but some wounds run so deeply that all the time in the world can't cure them."

Nikki blinked rapidly, trying to contain the tears that appeared out of nowhere. You'd think she'd be used to that by now. Before Griffin and the assault, she'd never been ruled by her emotions. Afterward, she'd been an emotional disaster area.

"Talk to him, Nikki. Tell him the whole story. Give yourself—and him—an honest chance at true happiness. If it's the real thing with him, I promise you'll never regret taking that chance."

"Thank you, Gram."

"Don't thank me, honey. All I want is for you and your sister to find what I had with your grandfather. Then I could die happy."

"Stop! Don't even say it."

"I'll die happy many years from now. Better?"

"No. You can't ever die. I won't allow it."

Evelyn laughed. "Enough of that morbid business. Tell me more about my new kitchen."

CHAPTER 14

*R*iley pulled into the driveway at Eastward Look right on time. He'd been to the gym and to the grocery store to shop for what he needed to make dinner for Nikki later. Depending on Finn's plans for the evening, he'd either invite her to their place or bring it to hers.

He still had questions about what exactly had happened last night, but for now, he was choosing not to dwell on that. Rather, he planned to focus on the renovations she wanted to do and how he could help her. That was far less complicated than thinking about why their great night had gone so wrong.

He'd texted to let her know he was on his way, so she came out when she saw his truck in the driveway.

She wore a white turtleneck sweater under a down vest with jeans and duck boots. Other than the hint of dark circles under her eyes, she looked fresh and pretty and much better than she had the night before when the devastation had dampened her natural sparkle.

"Thanks for doing this," she said, saving him the trouble of thinking of a way to say hello that didn't include the questions he was dying to ask. *Are you okay? How did you sleep? Will you please tell me what happened last night?*

"No problem. Syd is great. You'll love her. She's married to Luke, who's Mac's partner in the construction business—and the marina. They're like brothers from another mother."

"I'm looking forward to meeting her and Luke."

"They also have a baby girl named Lily. Luke is crazy about that baby. He shows us pictures every day at work."

"That's cute."

"He waited a long time to get married and have a family. Mac told me that he and Syd were together for four years when they were younger, but then she went to college, met someone else and married that guy. They had two kids together, and when the kids were seven and five, their car was hit by a drunk driver. The kids and her husband were killed. She lost her whole family that night."

"Oh my God. That's so awful."

Riley noticed tears in her eyes and was touched by her compassion for a woman she'd never met. "She and Luke saw each other again a year or so later. They've been together again ever since, and now they have Lily."

"I give her credit for picking up the pieces that way and taking another chance with Luke. That couldn't have been easy for her."

"From what Mac said, it wasn't, but Luke never gave up on her. He never stopped loving her, even when she was married to someone else."

"That's very sweet." After a long period of quiet, during which Riley still wanted to ask her if she was okay, she said, "There was more to what happened to me in college than what I told you last night."

"Oh," he said, feeling woefully unprepared for this. His dad would know exactly what to say and how to deal with whatever she had to tell him. "Okay…"

"After we see Syd, maybe I could buy you lunch and we could talk?"

"Sure." He rubbed the tight knot of stress that formed in his chest as he tried to imagine what she would say and how it might change everything.

. . .

SYDNEY WELCOMED them into her home with a gracious smile as she held her baby girl on her hip. Her long reddish-blonde hair was captured in a high ponytail, and the house, while stylishly put together, was clearly devoted to the baby and her toys.

"Pardon the mess," she said. "Lily has been on a tear this morning."

"No problem," Nikki said. "I appreciate you seeing me on short notice."

"When Riley told me you're Mrs. Hopper's granddaughter and want to do some renovations to Eastward Look, I jumped at the chance to meet with you." She put Lily down on an activity mat on the floor. "I've always loved the lines of that house and have been dying to see the inside."

"Come over whenever you'd like. I'd be happy to show it to you."

"I'll take you up on that."

"I absolutely love this room," Nikki said, taking in the scenic ocean views through big plate-glass windows.

"Thank you. It was one of my first designs. Can you believe that used to be a wall?" she asked, gesturing to one of two big windows.

"No, I can't. Good move to bring in the view."

"I thought so, too. Riley says you're interested in redoing the kitchen and bathrooms at your grandmother's house?" She picked up an iPad from the coffee table and began to make some notes as she kept a watchful eye on Lily.

"Yes, they're original to the house, which means 1950s."

"Are you thinking complete gut of the kitchen or partial or what?"

"My grandmother said to go for it, so probably complete."

"That's exciting! We can reconfigure it any way we want with a full gut."

"I have a few ideas about how we might do it. I took some photos of what's there now, so you can see what I mean."

They spent the next hour going through photos and discussing options, while Riley offered construction advice.

"I'd like to show you the kitchen we just did at the Chesterfield,"

Syd said. "It's similar in size and scope to yours, and Lizzie wanted a coastal theme, too."

"I'd love to see it. If you've had house curiosity about my grandmother's home, I've had it for the Chesterfield."

When Lily began to fuss, Syd scooped her up off the floor and snuggled her, immediately calming the baby. "Jared and Lizzie James have done such a beautiful job of restoring and renovating the public rooms. I'm sure Lizzie would be happy to show you. She's very proud of it, and rightfully so."

They made plans for Syd to come to Eastward Look on Monday morning, and from there, they'd drop by the Chesterfield.

"I'll give Lizzie a heads-up," Syd said. "I hope you don't mind if I have my little peanut with me. She's my full-time business associate."

"Of course not," Nikki said. "She's adorable."

"We quite agree."

The baby had her mother's strawberry-blonde hair. Where Syd's eyes were blue, her daughter's eyes were more gray than blue. They were wrapping up the meeting when a handsome dark-haired guy came in through the sliding door off the kitchen.

Lily squealed at the sight of him.

"Daddy is very popular around here."

"I'm coming," Luke said from the kitchen, where he stopped to wash his hands before joining them.

"Luke, this is Nikki Stokes, Mrs. Hopper's granddaughter. Nikki, my husband, Luke Harris."

"Good to meet you." Luke shook Nikki's hand and took Lily from Syd. "I love your grandmother."

"We have that in common. She's awesome."

"Yes, she is."

After they filled Luke in on the purpose of their meeting, he said to Riley, "You don't get enough of this stuff eight hours a day?"

Riley shrugged. "What's a few more hours to help a friend?"

"A long-ass day," Luke said, teasing.

"I can handle it," Riley said. "We're only young once. Have you been working on a boat?"

"Yep. A 1957 Century Coronado."

"Riley told me about your boats." Nikki asked, "Could I see?"

"Sure." To Riley, he said, "Hit the barn on the way out. It's unlocked. I'm going to spend some time with my girls before naptime."

"How do you have time for restoring boats after working eight hours a day?" Riley joked.

"Ha," Luke said, grinning. "Touché." Bouncing the baby on his lap, he smiled when she giggled. "I'm not doing as much of it as I used to. Now I have much better things to do with my time off."

"I need to come see the latest with the Wayfarer," Syd said. "I haven't been there in weeks. I bet you guys have gotten a lot done."

"We're getting there," Luke said. "Still got miles to go."

"We'll get it done for the season," Riley said. "Has Mac said any more about hiring someone to run the place for us?"

"He's put out some feelers, but nothing yet. It's a big deal for someone to move out here for what's basically a seasonal job."

"And an intense one at that."

"What kind of person are you looking for?" Nikki asked, feeling a spark of interest—and excitement—at the thought of being involved in a project like the Wayfarer.

"Someone with banquet, food and beverage experience, some management," Luke said. "I haven't seen the full job description. Mac has it."

Nikki licked her lips and took the plunge. "I think I'd like to see it."

"Really?" Riley asked, his brows lifting.

Nodding, Nikki said, "I worked for a banquet facility for seven years while I was in high school and college, I worked summers at the Lobster Pot, and I managed my sister's very high-profile career for the last three years. I think I might be qualified."

"Wow," Luke said. "That'd be amazing."

"I'll text Mac and ask him to send it to me," Riley said.

Nikki fanned her face and then laughed. "Did I really just say I might be interested?"

"I think you did," Sydney said, laughing with her.

"Be prepared," Luke said. "Mac will probably pounce if you show an ounce of interest. We need someone in that job like last week to start the ball rolling on hiring for the summer, buying equipment and generally getting things organized."

"The manager's office was the first thing we finished," Riley added as he typed on his phone. "Sent the text."

"Gulp," Nikki said.

"This is awesome!" Sydney clapped her hands. "This is a great place to live and work. I've met some of the best friends I've ever had here."

"Same," Luke said. "Island life is the bomb if you can handle the winters."

"I love the winters," Sydney said, blushing as she glanced at her husband.

"The summers are crazy with the marina *and* the construction business," Luke said. "I only have one job in the winter."

"Lily and I love having Daddy home more, don't we, sweet girl?"

The baby gave her a gummy smile that did weird things to Nikki's insides. What would it be like, she wondered, to have a life like Syd and Luke's, to know they'd walked through fire to find each other a second time, to end up with the kind of happiness they clearly shared?

When Lily began to yawn, Nikki and Riley said their goodbyes and then walked out to the barn that Luke used as a workshop. He held the door for her, and she walked into the smell of varnish and paint thinner and turpentine. On a trailer in the center of the vast space was the nearly completed restoration of a gleaming wooden boat.

"Oh my goodness," Nikki said, flabbergasted.

"I know, right? He does incredible work. He usually keeps before pictures on the bench," Riley said, going to look. "Here they are."

Nikki went to join him. "*That* is the same boat?" she asked of the wreck in the pictures.

"No way."

They flipped through a photo album of before-and-after pictures.

"That's the one he recently did for my uncle," Riley said. "My aunt Linda gave it to him for their fortieth anniversary."

"It's beautiful. He's got a real gift."

"Yes, he does. He's in hot demand."

"Why doesn't he do it full-time?"

"I asked him that once, and he said that before Mac started the construction business, he used to spend all winter working alone on boats, and that turned him into a bit of a weirdo loner. He prefers working with us to being alone all the time, so the boat business is more of a hobby these days."

"Is this whole island full of talented people, or does it just seem that way to someone who feels like she has no real talents?"

"You have talents."

"Like what?"

"You must've been super organized to run Jordan's career for her."

"I was."

"That's a true talent and not something you should dismiss as no big deal."

"I think I'm a pretty good cook, too."

"That pumpkin bread was really good, as was the pasta sauce."

Smiling, she said, "I'm glad you liked it. I also take really cool photos."

"I'd love to see them sometime." He put a hand on her shoulder. "You're a *really* good kisser, too."

"Does that count as an actual talent?"

"Oh yeah. For sure."

She looked up at him. "I'm glad you came back today. I wouldn't have blamed you if you hadn't."

"Not coming back never occurred to me."

She reached up to bring him down for a kiss. "Means a lot."

Riley put his arms around her and hugged her.

That's where Luke found them when he returned to the barn. "Sorry to interrupt," he said. "I would've knocked, but it's my barn."

Riley laughed and released her.

Nikki felt her face get hot with embarrassment. "Your work is amazing."

"Thanks. It's fun."

"We're going to head out," Riley said. "I'm sure I'll talk to you later on."

"Snow's coming around six, or so they say. We'll see. Get a nap this afternoon. Could be a long night."

"Will do."

"Nice to meet you, Luke."

"You, too, Nikki."

Riley put his arm around her as they walked to his truck, and Nikki felt a profound sense of relief to realize that nothing had changed between them after her panic attack. He was sticking with her, and for that, she was thankful. She liked him more than she'd ever liked any guy, and over lunch, she would tell him the truth.

If only the thought of revisiting the darkest days of her life didn't make her feel so sick.

RILEY TOOK her to The Oar, which was open for lunch and dinner on the weekends during the winter. He and Finn tended to stick closer to town when they went out, so Riley hadn't been there in a while.

"I love this place," Nikki said, gazing at the thousands of painted oars that graced every available surface inside the restaurant. Tucked into a cozy corner, they had the place more or less to themselves when it would be packed to the gills on a summer day.

"My name is on a couple of them," he said of the oars. "We used to do one every summer when I worked at my uncle's marina."

"Jordan and I used to talk about doing one for Eastward Look, but we never got around to it."

"Have you heard anything from her?"

Nikki shook her head. "I texted her last night just to say hi, but she hasn't replied."

"I suppose no news is good news, right?"

"I'd like to think so, but who knows with them."

When the waitress came to take their order, they both requested lobster rolls with fries along with draught beer. Riley requested his lobster roll without mayo.

"Is it a lobster roll without mayo?"

"Mayo is the biggest gagger of all the gaggers."

"What the hell is a gagger?"

"The gross stuff that people have to put on food to make it edible."

"Do you mean *condiments*?"

"Everything except ketchup, which doesn't count as a gagger."

"Good to know," she said, clearly amused by his food rules.

"Having lobster will be like summer in January," Riley said.

"I love summer in January. Thank you again for taking me to meet Sydney and Luke. They're really great people."

"They are. He's a good guy to work with and for. I really like him."

"I can see why. I can't stop thinking about what you told me about her and what happened to her family. I really admire the way she's put her life back together."

"According to what I've heard from Mac and others, it didn't happen overnight. Took a long time."

"I can only imagine." Nikki took a sip from her beer. "I admire her because, as you might've already figured out, I'm still trying to put my own pieces back together."

He laid his hand over hers on the table. "Anything you want to tell me, I want to hear. I want to know you, Nikki. Really know you."

Curling her fingers around his, she said, "You're very sweet, and that helps." She licked lips that'd gone dry the way they always did when her anxiety kicked in. "I went to college in Chicago and met Griffin at freshman orientation. We were in the same group and hit it off the first day. I had no idea who he was until after school started and someone told me he was a big star on the basketball team. He never told me that. I took that as a good sign that he wasn't caught up in his own hype, you know?"

"I can see that, for sure."

"Anyway, we hung out here and there, and I remember my roommate asking me if I was his girlfriend or his buddy. I honestly didn't know, and I wasn't in any great rush to make it into something. I was busy adapting to school and being away from my sister for the first time in my life."

"Where did she go to school?"

"She didn't. She decided to pursue the modeling career, so she stayed in California." She took a deep breath, forcing herself to continue to tell a story that filled her with dread and despair and every other emotion. "Junior year, we started actually dating and Griffin asked me to go to a party with him at his fraternity. My friends in the dorm were jealous because everyone wanted to go to that party, and it was invite only. I felt special, which is ironic in hindsight. Right away, I realized I was in way over my head at that party. People were drinking anything and everything, and I'd never been much of a drinker. I had a vodka tonic to go along with the group, but I didn't really like how it tasted, so I didn't drink much of it. The party got really wild, and I decided to leave. I had no idea where Griffin was, so I got the hell out of there and walked back to my dorm. I remember how cold it was and how stupid I felt for having gone there in the first place."

Their food was served, and while Nikki wasn't sure she could eat, she took a few tentative bites. "My roommate had gone home for the weekend, so I was asleep when someone pounded on my door at four in the morning. It never occurred to me that it would be him. I figured it was someone from the dorm who'd gotten locked out of their room or something. I still think about what would've been different if I hadn't opened that door."

Riley signaled for the waitress. "Would you mind boxing this up to go for us?"

"Of course. Is everything all right?"

"Yes, thanks. We'll take our check, too."

"Coming right up."

"We don't have to go," Nikki said softly.

"I don't want you to have to do this in public. I'm sorry I didn't think of that before."

"Don't apologize. I didn't think of it either."

He signed for the check, pocketed his credit card and helped her into her coat.

"I was supposed to treat you."

"Next time."

He helped her into the passenger side of his truck, and before he could close the door, she stopped him with a hand to his face. "Thank you for knowing what I needed before I did."

"You don't have to thank me. I needed to get out of there, too." He handed her the to-go bag, gave her a quick kiss, closed the door and went around to the driver's side. As he drove them back to Eastward Look, he held her hand, tighter than usual, as tension came off him in waves that had her worrying that maybe she shouldn't tell him the rest.

When they were back at the house, he put their lunch in the fridge and guided her into the living room with a hand on her lower back.

The protective, proprietary way he touched her gave her the courage to tell him the rest of the story when they were seated together on the sofa.

CHAPTER 15

"*Y*ou can probably figure out for yourself that he forced his way into my room and, in a drunken frenzy, basically attacked me. My funny, charming boyfriend turned into someone I didn't recognize, and I was so shocked and scared. I had no idea how to fend him off." She wiped away tears that infuriated her. "The next couple of hours were a blur. I don't remember much about it until my roommate came back later that morning to find me huddled on her bed and him passed out in mine.

"At first, she thought congratulations were in order, until she realized my face was bruised and swollen and put the pieces together. Her dad is a big lawyer in Chicago. She called him and asked what to do. He advised against contacting campus police. He said they'd be likely to bury it because Griffin was a basketball star. Her father called the Chicago police. They showed up with paramedics for me and arrested him. I didn't understand the implications then, but I certainly know now what happens when law enforcement is brought in and how the ball starts to roll before you're even aware of what's happening."

Riley wrapped his arms around her and held her close to him, rubbing her back and offering comfort and support that meant the world to her.

"My friend's father was a tiger on my behalf. He went to bat with the cops. With him on the job and the evidence of a violent assault backing up his claims, they charged Griffin with first-degree sexual assault, felony battery, breaking and entering. The press coverage was relentless. I couldn't go back to school. People were angry with *me* because he was in so much trouble."

"That's unreal."

"I would've thought so, too, if I hadn't experienced it. It was a nightmare. His parents hired an attorney who tried to make me sound like a total slut who'd been out to land the big man on campus. My friends spoke out to say that wasn't true, but they were no match for a big-name attorney who had the press hanging on every filthy lie he told about me. My grandmother came and got me and brought me here. I recovered physically, but emotionally, I was a disaster. I just kept thinking that the only mistake I'd made was opening the door to him."

"You didn't do anything wrong, Nikki," he said fiercely. "None of this was your fault."

"I knew that intellectually, but I still questioned everything I'd said and done since I met him. Had I given him some sort of indication that he could do that to me and get away with it? Had I led him on? We'd been friends for two years before we started dating, and I'd never seen any sign of this in him. How could I have missed it?"

He covered her lips with his finger. "You didn't do anything wrong."

Nikki closed her eyes and leaned her forehead against his, breathing in the rich, appealing scent of cologne and soap that would forever remind her of Riley. "My Gram and I hunkered down here, and after a couple of months in my favorite place, I began to feel more like myself again. I started to think about going back to school— somewhere else—and starting over. The trial was more than a year away, and I knew I'd have to testify, but I tried not to think about that too much. My grandmother had gotten me a therapist, and we met twice a week by Skype, and I'd been making real progress when…"

"What, honey?" Riley sounded as tense as she felt.

"Griffin… He… He took his own life."

"Oh my God. Oh no."

"If I thought what'd happened before that was a nightmare…"

"I can't even imagine."

"People blamed me."

"*How* could they blame you?"

"I don't know, but they did. Just when I was starting to get back on my feet, this happened, and I was right back to day one. I grieved for him, even after what he did."

"You grieved for the version of him that'd been your friend."

"Yes, exactly." His understanding made this so much more tolerable than it might've been otherwise. "It didn't make any sense to me in light of everything that'd happened, but my therapist helped me to see that grief is messy and often doesn't make sense. I grieved for the young man who'd made a terrible mistake and ruined his life in the process."

"You grieved because you're a kind and loving person who understands that no one is all bad or all good. My dad always says that."

"Your dad is very wise."

"I'm so sorry you had to go through such an awful thing, Nik."

"Last night… When we were kissing…"

"You don't have to say any more. I get it."

"It had nothing to do with you." She drew back so she could see his face. "It's really important to me that you know that."

"I understand."

She swallowed hard and glanced up at him. "For the first time since everything happened, you make me want to take a real chance on things I thought I'd never want again."

"For the first time *ever*, you make me want to take a real chance on something I've never wanted before." He kissed her gently and then leaned his forehead against hers, the moment charged with possibility and promise.

Nikki waited expectantly, hoping he might kiss her again.

"I don't know about you, but I'm starving. How about we eat those lobster rolls and then spend the afternoon packing up your kitchen?"

"Sure," she said, swallowing her disappointment. "That sounds good."

THEY WORKED for hours in the kitchen, filling plastic bins she brought up from the basement with items she'd decided to keep and making piles of things she would donate to the thrift shop in town. As they worked, they hashed out a variety of different layouts and scenarios for a reconfigured kitchen, which Riley drew up on a pad of lined notebook paper.

"It's not to scale or anything," he said, showing her his drawing. "But does that about capture it?" The drawing detailed her wish to remove the walls that separated the living and dining rooms from the kitchen, opening up the downstairs area into one big room.

"I love that! You never told me you were an artist."

"I'm hardly an artist. Lots of drafting courses in college made me a fairly competent sketcher."

"I think it's really impressive."

God, he wanted to kiss her and hold her and make love to her and… *Whoa, rein it in, man.* Hearing what she'd been through with Griffin had touched him deeply and made him aware of how careful he needed to be with her going forward. He'd never been in a situation remotely like this and honestly had no idea how to navigate his way through it.

His mind had been spinning ever since she told him the full story earlier, thinking about what had happened and how it must've affected her. *One step at a time*, he told himself. The saying *slow and steady wins the race* also came to mind. He focused on enjoying her company while keeping his hands to himself.

Riley took a call from Mac at four. "Hey, what's up?"

"Just making sure you're available to help out tonight. We're meeting at the marina at eight to get organized. The state sent over sand trucks that're out now."

"I'll be there."

"Take a nap. Gonna be a long night from what the forecasters are saying."

"Will do. See you at eight."

Nikki went to the window to look out on the encroaching darkness. "It's snowing!"

"That's why Mac called. We're plowing tonight. He wants me to take a nap."

"If you need to go, I can finish this on my own. No problem. I really appreciate all your help."

"I was going to make you dinner. I even went to the store."

"You can make it for me tomorrow. Right now, you need to rest up."

"If you wouldn't mind if I borrowed your sofa for a couple of hours, I could nap here."

"My sofa is your sofa." She went to the window for a closer look at the thick gray clouds. "Snow is one of my favorite things. I didn't see much of it growing up in Southern California."

"If you had to spend long, dark nights plowing it, you wouldn't love it so much."

With her hands on his back, she steered him toward the sofa. "Lie down."

"Only if you lie with me."

"Can we watch a movie?"

"If you want to." He stretched out on the sofa and held out his arm to her, snuggling her in close to him and hoping his body wouldn't betray him and give away just how much he wanted her.

She pulled a blanket over them and settled in to watch a chick flick while he tried to slow his racing heart and mind enough to rest up for the long night ahead. But with the soft silk of her hair brushing against his face, the heat of her abdomen singeing the palm of his hand, her scent filling his senses and her nearness making him hard as a rock, sleep proved elusive.

It was torture being this close to her and not being able to touch her the way he really wanted to. For the first time in his life, someone else's needs took precedence over his own. His leg slid between hers, which did nothing to assuage the ache in his groin.

"You're not sleeping," she said, sounding amused.

"I am most definitely *not* sleeping."

She giggled, and the sound of her laughter went straight to his overcommitted heart. "I'll move to the other sofa."

Riley tightened his hold on her. "Don't go."

"You need to sleep."

"I'll sleep when I'm dead."

"Don't say that before you go out into a snowstorm."

"I'm used to it. I've lost a lot of sleep to plowing this winter."

They fell into a comfortable silence as she watched the movie, and he tried to think about anything other than the soft, warm, fragrant female who made him yearn for things he'd never wanted before.

THE ALARM on Riley's phone woke them both at seven thirty. Nikki was surprised she'd slept when having him wrapped around her had put every cell in her body on full alert. Outside, the wind howled and snow pinged off the windows.

Groaning, he tightened his hold on her. "Don't wanna."

"You gotta."

"Don't wanna."

She elbowed his belly playfully and then turned onto her back. "Time to get up."

"Come with me."

"Is that okay?"

"Sure. If you want to. Wouldn't blame you if you didn't."

"I'd love to."

He playfully tapped her chin with his finger. "You're crazy."

"It'll be an adventure." She got up and folded the blanket that'd covered them.

"You don't get out much if you think plowing snow is an adventure."

Nikki laughed. "You're very grumpy when it snows. I'm seeing a whole new side to you."

"I need food and coffee. I'll call in a pizza to Mario's. What do you like on it?"

"I'll eat anything."

"Anchovies and hot peppers. Coming up."

"No anchovies!"

"By anything, you mean anything but anchovies?"

"Exactly."

Shaking his head, he smiled at her and called in the order while she brewed a pot of coffee and filled a thermos that she'd put in the pile to get rid of. They bundled up and headed out into the driving snow, laughing as they ran to the truck where the snow had begun to accumulate on the hood.

Riley scooped up a handful of snow and chucked it at her right as she turned to say something to him, resulting in the snow hitting her square in the face. As she sputtered with outrage, he lost it laughing and got in to start the truck before she could retaliate.

She got into the passenger side, wiping snow from her face as she glared at him. "That was mean."

"I threw it at your back. You're the one who turned around."

"I see how it is. I'll exact my revenge when you least expect it."

"Easy, killer." Riley turned the truck around and dropped the plow to clear the driveway as they moved through the snowy night.

"How can you see where you're going?"

"Instinct. I know these roads very well."

"There's no chance of you driving me off a cliff at any point in this adventure, is there?"

"No chance at all," he said. "You're perfectly safe with me."

Nikki knew that truer words had never been spoken, but now she feared that by sharing her story with him, she'd ensured that they might never get past the dreaded "friend zone." Maybe she should come right out and tell him she wanted him to be her boyfriend or significant other, which seemed like a more grown-up term. Whatever the word, as long as he came away understanding that she wanted to be much more than "just friends" with him.

He wanted her. The substantial evidence of his desire had been pressed against her back earlier. But would he ever do anything about wanting her after what she'd told him?

The roads were a mess, so it took twenty minutes to make the short trip into town. At Mario's, Riley left the truck running when he ran in to pick up the pizza. Then he headed for the marina, where he was supposed to meet the others.

"Bust out that pizza," he said. "I'm starving."

"You can't drive in the snow and eat pizza at the same time."

"Wanna bet? That's why I got two smalls instead of a large. Easier to eat small slices while driving in the snow."

"Clearly, you've done this before," she said as she put a piece of sausage pizza on a napkin for him.

"A few times."

At the marina, Riley parked next to several other trucks with plows that had been left running. The garage doors to the marina restaurant had been thrown open, and the big space was lit up.

Nikki followed him inside, where the first person they encountered was his brother.

"Nicholas."

"Finnbar."

"Nothing better to do on a Saturday night than play in the snow?"

"Apparently not."

A big, strapping guy came over to them with brown bags full of freshly baked chocolate chip cookies for each of them. "I'm Uncle Mac," he said, shaking her hand. "Everyone calls me Big Mac."

"I'm Nikki. Nice to meet you."

"You, too. You're one of Evelyn's granddaughters, right?"

"That's right."

"She's good people."

"I agree. She thinks the world of you and your family."

"That's nice to hear." To Riley, he said, "Auntie Lin made the cookies. She said to tell you guys to be careful out there."

"Tell her thanks from us," Riley said.

"Will do." Big Mac moved on to talk to others, but Nikki found herself watching him and the way he interacted with family members and friends.

"He's one of my favorite people in the whole world," Riley said. "No one is more fun than he is."

"He seems great."

"When he bought this place more than forty years ago, it was a falling-down wreck that he transformed into a booming business. I have mad respect for what he's done here. People come back every summer just to see him."

"I love your family."

"I do, too."

Mac whistled to get everyone's attention, updated them on the dire forecast and then handed out assignments and portable radios that they used only when it snowed. "Stay alert and take a break if you need it," Mac concluded. "Let's get to it."

"It's no fair that Riley gets to bring a girl," Finn said. "I wanna girl to bring."

While the others cracked up laughing, Riley smacked his brother upside the head. "Girls want nothing to do with you. You've got cooties."

"Ha, bro," Finn said, punctuating his words with a low, dirty laugh. "You know that isn't true."

"Dad, tell The Babies to shut up and get to work, will you?" Mac said.

"Boys, shut up and get to work," Big Mac said, smiling as he delivered the order.

More pushing and shoving ensued with Finn nearly succeeding in knocking Riley off his feet, before Riley rallied and pushed Finn head-first into a drift.

"You fucker," Finn said, coming up sputtering.

Before he could charge after him, Riley grabbed Nikki's hand and said, "Run!"

He had her safely in his truck and was getting in the driver's side when he was hit square in the head with a massive snowball.

Nikki couldn't stop laughing at the murderous expression on his wet face.

"That son of a bitch," Riley said as he got into the truck, giving his brother the bird as they drove out of the parking lot.

"You guys are funny."

"*I* am funny. *He* is a pain in the ass."

"I hate to break it to you, but he's funny, too."

"No, he isn't. You can't like me and think he's funny. It's the law."

"Good to know," she said, biting back the urge to laugh, knowing he wouldn't appreciate it. *This is fun*, she thought. More fun than she'd had in years. And they weren't even doing anything all that special. Turned out that driving around in the snow with Riley McCarthy was every bit the adventure she'd hoped for. They listened to music, sang along to cheesy country songs, ate pizza and chocolate chip cookies, drank coffee and kept each other awake as the snow continued to pile up.

CHAPTER 16

"Why do I feel like we're fighting a losing battle here?" she asked around two in the morning.

"Because we are." They were out by the bluffs, and he drove into one of the parking lots that he was supposed to be clearing. He parked and killed the headlights, but kept the truck running for the heat. They could hear the roar of waves crashing against the rocky shore below.

"I'm glad I'm not on the ferry tonight." She shivered at the thought of how rough the ride would be.

"Are you cold?"

"Nope. I'm fine."

"Bust out more of those cookies."

As they ate the delicious cookies and watched the snow swirl around them, Nikki experienced a feeling of contentment so new and unexpected that it took her breath away for a second. She'd done the right thing taking this break on Gansett, even as she acknowledged it would've been boring without Riley to entertain her.

Sealed off from the storm swirling around them, Nikki had the confidence to broach the subject that'd been on her mind for hours. "Could I ask you something?"

"Anything you want."

"After what I told you earlier… Does that make you want to keep your distance from me?"

He stared at her, his expression fierce. "No," he said forcefully. "Absolutely not. If you had any idea…" Shaking his head, he cut himself off.

"What?" she asked, her throat going dry as her heart began to pound.

Grasping the wheel, he tightened his grip as tension made his jaw pulse.

She placed her hand on his shoulder, and even through the padding of his coat, she could feel how rigid his muscles were. "Tell me."

His eyes seemed to get even bluer. "If you had any idea how much I want you, you'd probably jump out of this truck and run home to get away from me."

It took every bit of courage she could muster to meet his intense gaze and then to shake her head. "No. I wouldn't."

They stared at each other for an endless beat in which time seemed to stand still and significant decisions were made. The sound of his seat belt releasing echoed through the cab as he moved toward her at the same time she moved toward him, getting tangled in her own seat belt.

He grunted out a laugh as he freed her and dragged her into his arms, pizza boxes and bags of cookies going flying as they came together for the single most combustible kiss Nikki had ever experienced. Lips and tongues and teeth and hands, driven by pure, pulsing desire that had her pulling him closer. Frustrated by the thick layers of coats and sweaters that stood between them, Nikki tipped her head to improve the angle of the kiss.

Then he was lifting her and bringing her down to straddle his lap. *Much better*, she thought as she wrapped her arms around his neck and opened her mouth to his tongue.

He unzipped her coat and pushed it aside, his hands dipping under her sweater and straight up to her breasts. His thumbs coasted over nipples gone tight from his touch as much as the pervasive chill in the air. Riley never missed a beat in the kiss when he reached behind her to unfasten her bra. When he cupped her bare breasts, she gasped, breaking the kiss so she could breathe.

"Too much?" he asked.

"Not enough."

Riley groaned and pressed his mouth to her neck, which set off a new wave of shivers that racked her entire body. "God, Nik... You're so hot, and you make me crazy. From the first time I ever saw you, I wanted you."

She squirmed on top of him, needing to get closer to the rigid length of him. "I wanted you, too. I thought about you every day after we left."

He captured her lips in another panty-melting kiss that was compounded by the light pinch of his fingers on her nipples.

Nikki had the presence of mind to wonder if they were going to do it right here in his truck when the cab was lit up with headlights set to high beam. A horn blared right outside the window.

"Fucking Finn," he muttered. A series of beeps had Riley swearing viciously. "I'm going to fucking kill him."

The walkie-talkie crackled to life. "Riley is making out when he's supposed to be plowing."

"He's dead."

"Ignore him," Nikki said, sliding her lips over his. "He's just jealous."

"Riley," Mac said over the radio. "Quit making out and plow the snow."

"I want to make out," Luke said. "I'm going home."

"No one is going home until the snow is gone," Mac said.

"Screw you," Luke replied. "You're not the boss of me. I'm going home."

"I wanna go home, too," Finn said.

"Yes, please go," Riley whispered.

"Riley won't quit making out," Finn said.

Nikki laughed even as Riley continued to kiss her as if they'd never been interrupted. "How long do we have to stay out here?"

"Supposed to be all night."

"That's too bad." She moved suggestively on top of him, letting him know what she wanted while trying not to think about anything other than him and what was happening right here and right now. She refused to allow the past into one of the most perfect nights of her life.

"Fuck it. I'm done plowing." He deposited her into her seat. "Buckle up." Shifting the truck into reverse, he turned toward the parking lot entrance and headed for the road, flying past Finn's truck, which sat idling a few feet away.

"Was it something I said?" Finn asked over the radio.

"Going home," Riley said into the radio.

"He's got better things to plow than snow," Finn said.

"Shut up, Finn," Mac said, sounding increasingly annoyed, "and *plow the damn snow!*"

A deep rumbling laugh echoed through the radio. "Son, you're losing control of the troops," Big Mac said.

"Who gave you a radio?" Mac asked.

"I took one."

"I gots one, too," another voice said.

"Who is that?" Nikki asked, trying not to laugh her ass off.

"Big Mac's best friend, Ned Saunders."

"Everyone shut up and plow," Mac said, "or I'm going home, too."

"Maybe we should all go home," Finn said, "and come back out in the morning. This is a losing battle."

The snow continued to come down harder than ever.

"Fine," Mac said. "Go home. Everyone back out at eight, and I mean it. No screwing around."

Finn's laughter came through the radio. "Us? Screw around? Oh, wait. You're talking to Riley. He's the one screwing around when he's supposed to be working."

"I'm going to kill him, and I'm going to make it hurt," Riley muttered.

Nikki laughed so hard that tears filled her eyes.

"Riley?" Finn said. "Hello, Riley? Come in, Riley? What are you doing, Riley? Where are you going, Riley? I'm following you."

As he drove, Riley kept a hand on her thigh, squeezing her leg to let her know they were going to pick up where they'd left off the second they got to her house.

She couldn't wait.

THIS IS REALLY GOING *to happen*, Riley thought, frustrated by the fact that he had to drive slowly so he wouldn't kill them both before they could get home.

Even Finn and his shenanigans couldn't rattle him. Not with Nikki sitting next to him, warm and willing and sexy as all fuck. He was so hard, he ached from wanting her, and they were still miles from the house while the snow seemed to intensify, as if it knew how badly he needed to get her home.

Forty-five minutes after leaving the bluffs, they pulled into the driveway at Eastward Look, and there was no sign of Finn following them. They'd lost him a while back, thankfully.

Riley turned off the radio and shut down the truck. "Wait for me," he said, getting out to run around and help her lest she fall and get hurt at this critical juncture.

Inside, they shed coats, boots, hats and gloves into a pile on the floor of the foyer.

Riley hooked his arm around her waist and picked her up.

Her arms and legs curled around him, holding on tight as he walked them upstairs, kissing her as he took the stairs two at a time. "Where're we going?" he asked between kisses.

"End of the hall."

In the bedroom, he lowered her onto the bed and came down on top of her. "You can still say no," he said gruffly, his lips hovering above hers.

"I'm not saying no."

"You can say no at any time, and everything stops."

A huge lump lodged in her throat, forcing her to swallow hard. "That means everything to me," she said, drawing him into another kiss.

After that, there were no more words.

Riley helped her out of her sweater, and then she returned the favor.

The bra he'd unhooked earlier hung loosely on her shoulders.

His gaze heated with desire as he pushed the cups aside and slid the straps down her arms, his fingers gliding over sensitized skin. Then he tugged on the button to her jeans and began to move with more urgency as he removed them, leaving her covered in only a thin layer of silk.

"I've never seen anything more beautiful than you are," he whispered, bending over her to press a kiss to the valley between her full breasts. "And I've never wanted anything more than I want you."

As he drew her nipple into the heat of his mouth, Nikki buried her fingers in his hair, needing to hold on to something. She wanted to touch him but couldn't seem to make her hands move while he tormented first one nipple and then the other.

"Riley," she gasped.

"What, honey?"

"You're making me crazy."

"That's kind of the idea." His lips skimmed down her body, over her belly and…

Oh God. She'd never done that… Was that his… *Oh my God.* The three words echoed through her mind like a chant and a cry for mercy. He pushed her underwear aside. His tongue stroked her most sensitive flesh, while his fingers slid into her, the combination taking her to the brink of orgasm so fast, she could barely keep up. He backed off, clearly intent on torturing her, before doing it again and again until she was half out of her mind and begging for relief.

When it happened, the orgasm blew through her in a flash of heat, leaving every part of her humming with relief and a kind of giddiness she'd rarely experienced. The soaring high left her feeling like anything was possible, that she could overcome the past and move forward with joy and the kind of pleasure she'd lived for so long without.

She could do this.

But only with him. Only with Riley.

Then he was gone, standing to pull off his clothes, help her out of her panties and retrieve a condom from his wallet. Rolling it onto a long, thick erection, he never took his eyes off her. He came down on top of her, kissing her furiously before withdrawing slowly. "Is this still good?"

"Mmm, *so* good. Don't stop."

"I won't stop, sweetheart."

She loved when he called her that, especially when he looked at her with such affection as he said it. The sensation of falling, of stepping off a cliff into the unknown, overtook her as he pushed into her, stretching her to the absolute limit.

Jordan always said the lean guys came packing, and that thought, out of nowhere, almost made her laugh at the worst possible moment.

"Talk to me. Tell me you're okay."

"I'm okay." She smoothed her hands over his back and down over his ass, giving a gentle tug to encourage him. "I'm very okay." For so long, she'd known that eventually she'd have to do this again, hopefully with someone she cared about and who cared about her. One stroke at a time, Riley was repairing her broken heart, putting the pieces back together and bringing out emotions she'd never experienced before.

"You feel so good," he whispered, his lips skimming over her neck. "So, *so* good." Raising himself up on his muscular arms, he gazed down at her, watching over her as he made love to her.

His concern and tenderness were just what she needed to let go of her painful past to focus on a future that suddenly looked a whole lot brighter than it had in a very long time.

THIS, Riley thought, *is life-changing*, that elusive *thing* people talked about but couldn't ever seem to quantify. *This* had to be experienced to be fully understood. Gazing down at her, he saw dark hair spread out on a white pillow, the olive tone of her smooth, silky skin, swollen lips, dark pink nipples and big brown eyes gazing up at him with trust and affection. His heart filled to overflowing with emotions, all of them tied up in her.

"Nik…"

"*Yes,*" she said, sounding as breathless as he felt.

God, he hoped this meant as much to her as it did to him.

Her eyes closed, her lips parted, her fingers dug into the flesh of his back, and her internal muscles tightened.

Riley picked up the pace, moving faster until she cried out from the powerful release that took him along with her on the ride of his life. Afterward, he collapsed on top of her, and even his worries that he might be crushing her couldn't seem to permeate the bliss.

Her arms around him kept him from moving as he focused on breathing and stopping his head from spinning. "Still okay?" he asked when he could speak again.

"Mmm-hmm. Very okay."

"Very okay is very good."

"Yes, it is." Her hand moved in soothing strokes on his back, the gesture comforting and arousing at the same time.

He breathed in the fresh, clean scent of her, committing the fragrance to memory because he never wanted to forget a single detail of this first time with her. When he could summon the strength to move, he wrapped his arms around her and brought her with him when he turned onto his back.

Nikki reached for the down comforter and pulled it up, enveloping them in a cozy, warm cocoon that he wanted to wallow in for days. They'd come up only for air and food. Outside, the wind continued to howl, rattling the storm windows as the icy snow pinged against the glass. In a few hours, he'd be required to go back out and help clean up after the storm. But for right now…

He smoothed a hand over her back, reveling in the softness of her skin.

"Thank you," she whispered after a long period of silence.

"For what?"

"For making that so perfect for me. I've sort of dreaded it for all this time."

"You made it rather perfect for me, too."

"Really?"

"Um, you couldn't tell by my… *enthusiasm?*"

Her low chuckle rumbled through his chest. "You were rather enthusiastic."

"You inspired my enthusiasm. Remember when you said you suck at this stuff?"

She gave a small nod.

"You really, *really* don't."

"That's good to know." Kissing his chest, she said, "Could I ask you something?"

"Anything you want."

"Have you had… a lot of girlfriends?"

"Not really. There've been… How to say this?"

"Hookups?"

"Yeah, that, but not what I'd refer to as an actual girlfriend."

"How come?"

"I never met anyone I wanted to spend that much time with, until last fall when this gorgeous girl needed my help with a leaking roof. Then she left without saying goodbye, and I was so afraid I'd never see her again."

"I'm really glad I came back."

He kissed her shoulder and playfully nibbled on her neck. "So am I. You have no idea how glad I am. I thought about going after you, but that would've required asking Mac to ask your grandmother where you were, which would've involved my entire family."

She raised her head off his chest, her eyes wide with surprise. "You really thought about trying to find me?"

"I more than thought about it. I did a search for you online, but that led nowhere. Other than a few mentions of you in relation to Jordan, you don't exist online."

"That's intentional. We've had to be really careful about people being able to find us, especially since the tape went public. I was panic-stricken at first that all the publicity would bring back everything that happened with Griffin, but Jordan and Zane are big enough stars that the story stayed focused on them. I kept waiting to be dragged into it, but thankfully it never happened."

"Thank God for that."

"I know. Gram and I were so afraid of having to relive that nightmare yet again. There's been some really weird stalker stuff that led Jordan to hire security for when she travels." Her brows furrowed. "When she isn't dodging them, that is."

"Why would she dodge her security if people are stalking her?"

"Good question. I had to tell her detail where to find her when she took off to join Zane on tour. They were pissed, to say the least."

"Who hired them?"

"My grandmother did, against Jordan's wishes, but I was all for it."

"Is it okay to say that I'm really glad you're nowhere near the madness that is your sister's life?"

"Yes, it's okay to say that. I'm glad to be away from it, too. But you should know… That's not the only reason I came here."

"No?"

"I was also hoping to see you again. All the way across the country and on the rocky ferry ride, I just kept wondering if you'd still be here. I didn't know anything about you other than you were Mac's cousin, and my grandmother adores him. If you hadn't come to find me, I was prepared to try to track down Mac and ask him how to get in touch with you."

Ridiculously moved to hear that she had been willing to go to such lengths to find him, Riley tightened his hold on her and kissed the top of her head. "I'm really glad I came over as soon as I heard you were back."

"So am I. But now I'm kind of afraid…"

"Of what?" he asked, alarmed to hear her say she was afraid. He never wanted her to be afraid of anything ever again, even if that wasn't possible.

"Your old boss made you a hell of an offer."

"He's got nothing on you." He moved both hands down to squeeze her ass, laughing when she gasped in response. "I swear I'm not going anywhere, Nikki. Not as long as you want me here with you."

"I'm apt to want you here with me for quite some time," she said, squirming on top of him.

His cock went hard inside her. "Hold that thought for a second," he said, easing her off him so he could deal with the condom—and get another one.

CHAPTER 17

*H*aunting dreams tormented Shane McCarthy as the storm raged outside. He tossed and turned, running from a past that wouldn't let him escape. He woke with a start when he cried out in his sleep.

Katie put her arms around him and drew him into her loving embrace.

A sob erupted from his chest, which made him angry and afraid at the same time. Crying over your ex-wife was never a good idea when you were in bed with your beloved fiancée. But Katie understood what Courtney had once meant to him and wouldn't hold his out-of-control emotions against him. Or at least he hoped she wouldn't.

Tears flooded his eyes and spilled down his cheeks. All he could seem to think about was the Courtney he'd first known, the sweet, sexy, smart, funny woman he'd fallen head over heels for way back before he knew that she was hiding a secret addiction to pain meds. He'd had two years of bliss before it all caved in around him, leaving him buried under an avalanche of agony and despair and debt.

He mourned the woman he'd met in college, who'd been so bright with potential with a zest for life that had fully enraptured him. The loss of his mother when he was seven had wounded him deeply.

Courtney's love had healed the long-festering wounds he'd carried with him for so long. Meeting her had been like having the sun come out after years of cloudy days.

"What can I do?" Katie asked, her tone as gentle as her touch.

"I'm sorry." He wiped his face and tried to get himself under control. "I'm not being fair to you."

"Shane, honey, please... Don't worry about me. You're heartbroken and understandably so."

"I didn't love her anymore. Not the way I love you."

"I know that. You don't have to say it. I know." She cradled his head against her chest and ran her fingers through his hair, providing the love and comfort he could get only from her.

"I'm thinking about the Courtney I first knew, before it all went bad."

"Tell me about her."

"It's okay, babe. We don't have to talk about it. It's enough to be able to hold on to you this way. I'd be losing my mind if I didn't have you."

"You'll always have me, and if I didn't want to hear about her, I wouldn't ask. If you want to talk about it, I want to listen."

Shane took a moment to gather himself. "I have all these things in my head that I haven't thought about in a very long time."

"It's only natural that those memories would come back now."

"I haven't thought about the beginning in years. The good times were totally eclipsed by what came later."

"Tell me about the good times. I really want to hear, and I promise I won't hold it against you."

Her sweetness and the hint of humor in the midst of the darkness made it possible for him to air out his grief. "The first time I ever saw her was at a basketball game. I was with my friends, she was with hers. We had friends in common and ended up going out after the game. I sat next to her, and we started talking. That one night was all it took. We were pretty much together from that point on. I'd... I'd never been in love before. It was... I can't describe it."

She kissed his forehead. "You don't have to. I know the feeling."

"I sort of lost that version of her in what came later, but those first few months were just incredible. Back then, I couldn't have imagined any scenario that didn't have us together for the rest of our lives."

"I know you must blame yourself for a lot of what happened with her, but it wasn't your fault. You know that, don't you?"

"Yeah."

"Shane? Tell me you know it's not your fault."

"I do know, but I wish I could've done more. I'm haunted by the last time I saw her when she came here asking for another chance and I said no."

"Because you were already involved with me and had worked really hard to pick up the pieces of your life after she left you."

"Still… I can't help but wonder if she spiraled again after that. Did I do the wrong thing sending her away?"

"Shane, honey. Stop. Please don't do this. You nearly bankrupted yourself trying to get help for her, and then she left you without so much as a conversation. After you spent years getting back on your feet, she showed up to say she'd had no choice and never would've left you if it'd been up to her. You did what anyone would've done in that situation. You said no more. It wasn't up to you to continue to prop her up, especially after she divorced you the way she did."

"You're right."

"You've worked so hard to put the darkness of those years in the past. I don't think Courtney would want her death to undo all the progress you've made. That would only compound the tragedy."

"Thank you for being so understanding. I'm not sure I would handle it as gracefully as you have if the roles were reversed."

"You would, because you love me every bit as much as I love you."

"I love you so much. You're saving my life tonight. I hope you know that."

"I owed you one from the time you saved my life."

"Best day ever," he said of Owen and Laura's wedding day when he'd saved Katie from a rip current. He kissed her and leaned his forehead against hers.

"It was for me, too, except the part where I nearly drowned and took you down with me."

"All's well that ends well."

With her hands on his face, she studied him. "Are you going to be okay?"

"Eventually. I promise I'm not going to nearly drown and take you down with me."

"I won't let you. I'm right here, and I want to help in any way I can."

"That makes everything better." He tried to relax his racing mind so he could get some sleep. "Hey, Katie?"

"Hmm?"

"Why don't we ever talk about getting married?"

Only because he was still cuddled up to her did he feel her body go rigid as her breathing slowed. "We talk about it."

"No, we really don't." When she had no reply to that, he said, "Do I need to be worried about anything?"

"No! Of course not. We can get married. If you want to."

"That doesn't sound very convincing."

"It's just that everything is great the way it is. Do we need a piece of paper to make it better?"

"We don't need it, but I sort of thought that we'd make it official at some point."

"We will."

"But not now?"

"Don't we have enough on our plate right now without adding to it?"

Shane had no idea how to respond to that, so he went with the simplest answer he could come up with. "I suppose we do."

She released a deep breath that sounded an awful lot like relief to him. What the hell was that about? And how was it possible that he now had even more to worry about than he'd had earlier?

For the first time since he'd worked for his cousin, Riley ignored his alarm when it went off at seven thirty. He had far better things to do than plow snow, and while he momentarily felt bad for letting down the others, they'd get by without him. Then he remembered that Shane was off the grid, and guilt set in. They were already down one member of their team, and if he didn't show up, everyone else was going to have to be out there that much longer.

Sometimes having a conscience freaking sucked. He was about to get up when his phone chimed with a text from Mac.

Make it noon. The snow is still coming down too hard to bother.

Oh, thank God. A stay of execution.

"Do you have to go?" Nikki asked, her voice husky with sleep.

"Nope." He curled up to her back, helped himself to a handful of breast and pressed his hard cock against her back. The sound of her voice had made him hard this time. That was all it took. "Mac said it's still snowing too hard to bother."

"Speaking of too hard…"

"Shall I bother?"

Laughing as she groaned, she said, "You're going to break me."

"Never." He kissed the back of her shoulder and left a trail of kisses down her backbone. Then he turned his attention to her ass, kissing and nibbling until she strained against him. "Like this," he said, arranging her on her hands and knees. He quickly rolled on a new condom, the last one he had, and entered her from behind, stopping when she went tense. "Does it hurt?"

"Only a little. It's okay, though."

"Are you sure? We don't have to." They'd already done it three times, and the fact that he wanted her again made this the craziest and best night of his life.

"It's okay. Just go slow."

"I can do slow." At least he thought he could. The desire she inspired in him made it difficult to do anything as simple as think when he had her naked in a bed with him. Her eager enthusiasm for everything they did only made him want her more. He was beginning to understand why his cousins had changed their lives for the women they loved. If this was what it was like for them…

Nikki cried out and came hard, clamping down on him and making him see stars as he lost any semblance of control. They landed in a sweaty, heaving pile on the bed, arms and legs intertwined.

Pressing his lips to her shoulder, he closed his eyes and tried to calm the racing beat of his heart.

The next thing he knew, his cell phone was ringing in the tone he'd set for Finn. Riley groaned and reached over Nikki to grab the phone from the bedside table.

"What?"

"Where are you?"

"None of your business."

"Everyone is here to plow, and Mac is looking for you."

"Fuck," Riley muttered under his breath. His eyes were gritty from the lack of sleep, and his muscles protested even the slightest movement. "I think I might be sick."

"Sex flu does not count as an actual illness."

"Seriously."

"You want me to tell Mac?"

"Would you? And can you leave out any mention of the words 'sex flu'?"

Finn snickered. "I'll see what I can do. It may be *hard* to restrain myself."

"Try."

"Yeah, yeah. You owe me one."

"Whatever."

"So I take it things went well after I saw you at Makeout Point last night?"

"Bye, Finn."

"Come on—"

Riley ended the call and felt Nikki shaking with laughter under him. "It's not funny. He is not funny."

"Yes, it is, and yes, he is." She turned over to face him.

He pushed the hair back from her face, which was flushed. Her lips were swollen, and as she ran the tip of her tongue over them, he felt a new surge of lust. That couldn't be healthy, but he'd never felt better.

"It's okay if you need to go to work."

"I can sit this one out. Finn will cover for me."

"Will he ever let you hear the end of it?"

"Nope," he said, leaning in to kiss those swollen lips. "But you're absolutely worth the aggravation."

"YEAH, so, Riley's not feeling good," Finn said to Mac. It took all his restraint not to mention the words "sex flu."

"Great," Mac said, scowling and obviously skeptical of Riley's sudden "illness." "Now we're down *two* people. I'll call in my dad and Ned. They'll be thrilled to have an excuse to play in the snow."

While Mac went to make his calls, Finn helped himself to the coffee his cousin had made behind the counter at the marina restaurant. This place held so many memories for Finn. Some of the best times of his life had been spent here with his larger-than-life uncle and the older cousins he'd idolized as a kid.

Those had been good times, but now was better. Hanging out with his cousins as an adult, working with Mac and having the others close by made for a satisfying life. He liked knowing Janey was around if he needed a female perspective. The two of them had always been close, but this was the first time they'd ever lived near each other year-round.

Clint had made him and Riley a good offer. No doubt about that. He'd be crazy not to jump on it, especially since Clint was desperate and probably willing to make some other concessions. A company truck would be nice, among other things.

But when Finn thought about leaving before the Wayfarer was finished or not working next to Mac, Shane, Luke and Riley every day, Clint's offer didn't look quite as good. Riley wasn't going anywhere as long as Nikki was around. Finn had never seen his brother so gone over a girl. Riley was more of a short-term kind of guy, but this thing with Nikki had long-term written all over it.

His phone chimed with a text from Missy.

I'm snowed in and lonely. Wish you were here. When are you coming home?

Finn sighed as he read the message. She was nothing if not persistent. *Not sure yet. Might be here for a while.*

She replied with a pout face emoji. *Can I come visit?*

It's not the best time. We're working long hours on a big new job. I wouldn't get to see you very much. And it's freezing here.

I miss you and I love you. I don't know what to do.

We agreed to see other people...

Do you have someone else? Is that what's going on??

No! I'm not seeing anyone. All I do is work and sleep. Speaking of work, I've got to go plow snow. Can we talk later?

Yeah, I guess.

As Finn stashed the phone in his back pocket, his uncle Mac walked in with Ned Saunders, both of them appearing delighted to have been called in to help. They must've been together up the hill at Big Mac's when Mac called them. Finn wished he shared even a fraction of their enthusiasm. He hated plowing snow.

Big Mac came bearing gifts—a huge tray of doughnuts Auntie Linda had made for the men.

Finn began to actively drool at the sight of them. Those doughnuts had been a cornerstone of his childhood, and the smell of them could take him back to perfect summer days, working the docks with his uncle, crabbing, Wiffle ball and doughnuts—as many as he could consume in a day without making himself sick. To this day, the smell of sunscreen and fried dough took him right back to those blissful days.

He grabbed two off the tray and went to fill his to-go mug with coffee. You couldn't have doughnuts without coffee.

"All right, everyone," Mac said. "Listen up." He handed out assignments to his father, Ned, Finn and Luke.

When Frank and Kevin arrived, they were greeted with rousing applause and teasing abuse.

"Desperate times must truly call for desperate measures if we need a shrink and a judge to plow snow," Finn said, earning a cuff to the head from his father and then one from his uncle.

"Where's your brother?" Kevin asked over a mouthful of doughnut.

"He's 'sick,'" Finn said, making air quotes with fingers covered in sugar.

"Is he now? What're his symptoms?"

Lowering his voice, Finn said, "I believe it's lack of sleep from an overabundance of sex, but don't quote me on that."

"Well, good for him," Kevin said, grinning.

"If you say so."

"You're not happy for him?"

"Of course I am. I just hope he isn't getting into something that's going to leave him crushed if she takes off again."

"True, but she seems equally into him."

"I guess we'll see, won't we?"

"Let's go, boys," Mac said. "We need to get this island up and running."

"When do the ferries start up again?" Luke asked.

"Joe said they're hoping for later this afternoon when the wind dies down," Mac said.

The reminder that the ferries were shut down and there was no way off the island made Finn feel itchy and confined in a way he hardly ever had since he'd moved to Gansett. It was a weird feeling to know he couldn't leave, even if he wanted to, which he didn't. But still… weird. Island life wasn't for everyone, but he'd taken to it rather swimmingly. No pun intended.

During the long lonely night with the wind howling and the snow piling up, he'd thought about Clint's offer to come back to work for him in Connecticut for twice what he was making now, and Missy's pleading requests that he come home to her.

As he got into his truck and secured his coffee mug in the cup holder, Finn had to admit he was tempted. However, something was stopping him from jumping at Clint's offer. Perhaps it was Missy and knowing she wanted him to come home that had him hesitating. Their relationship had been a roller coaster of ups and downs. More downs than ups, if he was being honest. While he had genuine feelings for her and definitely missed her, he wasn't sure he wanted to revisit that situation.

He wasn't sure what he wanted, and the mental debate of *should I stay or should I go* was getting exhausting. Did he honestly want to put down roots on the island and stay forever? Would he wake up ten years from now and realize he'd missed out on a number of opportunities by settling for a "safe" job working for his cousin in a place where he was surrounded by family members?

Or would he be better off going back to the mainland for a few years and maybe return to the island after he got married? Gansett would be a good place to raise kids someday—someday far off in the distant future.

For now, he decided, he would stay put. He'd like to see the renovations to the Wayfarer through to the finish since that was a family effort he wanted to be part of. When that was finished, he'd see where things stood with Clint and the job offer in Connecticut. Missy wouldn't be happy, but after a year and a half, what was a few more months on the island? The third reason to stay was to keep an eye on Riley, who was off the rails over a woman for the first time ever.

Finn worried about Nikki's troubled sister crooking her finger and Nikki running to bail her out of yet another scrape. If or when that happened, Finn would be there to deal with Riley.

In the meantime, Finn dropped his plow and went to work. The snow wasn't going away on its own.

CHAPTER 18

That weekend was right out of a dream come true for Riley. When they weren't in bed, they worked on the kitchen, boxing up the things collected over a lifetime of summers on the island. Cups bearing the logos of Mario's Pizzeria, Beachcomber Hotel dish towels, a package of napkins from the Oar bar that Nikki said someone must've stolen. Underneath the counter, they unearthed a huge platter bearing the branding of the original Wayfarer.

"Whoa," Riley said, holding it up. "Can we have this for the new place?"

"It's all yours."

"I want to do something cool with this, like make it the centerpiece of the new bar or something."

"That's a great idea." Nikki tipped her head. "I think there might be a framed picture of the original building in the attic. I remember it from when I was a little kid and Jordan and I would play haunted house hide-and-seek up there."

"Haunted house hide-and-seek sounds horrifying."

Laughing, she said, "It was fun."

At two o'clock Monday morning, the old house creaked as the wind continued to whip. From what they'd heard earlier from Finn, the ferries were still shut down due to exceptionally high seas. They were trapped, and there was nowhere in the world he'd rather be trapped than in Evelyn Hopper's kitchen. He wore only a pair of boxer briefs while Nikki bent over and gave him a flash of delectable ass when the shirt of his she wore rode up her back.

"Nice view," he said, moving into position behind her and pinching her ass.

She let out a squeak of laughter and stood, holding another item from the Wayfarer, this one a pitcher with the logo etched onto the glass.

"Did you people blatantly steal from every establishment on the island, or does it just seem that way?" Riley asked, amused.

"I have no idea if my Gram is a closet kleptomaniac, but knowing her, she found this stuff at yard sales and added it to her collection. She loves a good yard sale."

"Isn't she somewhat well-off?"

"Uh-huh, and still loves a bargain more than anyone I've ever known. She shops for clothes at thrift stores and drives a used car. She's super frugal and raised us to be, too. I followed her example while Jordan discovered a taste for the high life."

"I think I'm going to like this Gram of yours."

"I know she's going to love you. She appreciated you fixing the roof last fall." She handed him the pitcher. "Take this to the new Wayfarer and use it with our blessing."

"I'll do that." He kissed her. "Thank you."

"I'm starving. Are you hungry?"

"I could eat."

She opened the fridge and freezer to examine their options while he examined her toned, tanned legs under the T-shirt that just barely covered her spectacular ass. She turned to consult with him and caught him looking.

Riley offered a sheepish smile. "Sorry. Just enjoying the view."

When she returned his smile, the hint of shyness coming from her invoked fierce feelings of protectiveness. It occurred to him, standing in her grandmother's kitchen in his underwear, that he would go to war to keep her from ever being hurt again. He had never experienced anything remotely similar to the feelings she aroused in him.

He was in love with her.

Perhaps he had been since that first day last fall when she'd met him at the door, arms wrapped protectively around herself, as if that could somehow keep danger away.

"Riley?" She tipped her head and gave him a perplexed look. "What's wrong?"

Clearing his throat, he said, "Nothing." He couldn't very well blurt that he loved her out of nowhere. There was a time and a place for such pronouncements, and the middle of the night in her grandmother's kitchen hardly seemed like the right place. All at once, he felt the way he often did on the ferries, when the deck seemed to move beneath his feet, tipping him off balance and sending him scurrying to find something to hold on to.

The counter behind him lent the sturdy support he suddenly needed.

"How do you feel about frozen pizza?" she asked.

"Is it plain cheese?"

"Would I offer you a pizza with gaggers on it?"

"I would certainly hope not."

"I know better by now."

While the pizza cooked, he helped her box up two more cabinets full of mismatched cups and bowls and kitchen junk. She'd decided to go through it all after the renovation rather than before so it wouldn't take forever to prepare. In the meantime, she'd been texting with Sydney about ideas and plans. Being snowbound had given Sydney time to dive into the design of the new kitchen, and Nikki's excitement over the initial plans had been contagious.

Riley couldn't wait to start the job and to help make her vision a reality.

They ate the pizza sitting on stools at the large kitchen island, a bottle of red wine sitting on the counter between them.

"What do you think about remodeling the island rather than

getting a new one?" she asked, a spot of sauce decorating her bottom lip.

Grinning at her enthusiasm for the pizza as well as the project, Riley dabbed at the sauce with a napkin. "How do you mean?"

"What if we resurfaced the bottom with bead board and topped it with the same thing we use on the countertops?"

Currently, the island boasted a laminate surface that differed from the tile on the countertops.

Riley bent to take a closer look at the island, which had drawers on the front side. "I think we could do that. Would you paint the drawers to match the white cabinets?"

"That's what I'm thinking—or what if we painted the island an accent color? Maybe a cool blue?"

As Riley pretended to give that deep thought, he rubbed at the stubble on his chin. "You're very daring."

Nikki rolled her eyes. "That hardly counts as daring. You need to watch more HGTV."

"No, I really don't," he said, laughing. "I live HGTV every day at work."

She frowned as she glanced down at her plate. "It's okay if you don't want to deal with me and my kitchen after a long day at work. It's really too much to ask of anyone who works as hard as you do."

Pushing his plate aside, he said, "Come here."

"I'm right here."

He crooked his finger. "Closer."

Seeming perplexed, she stood and took the two steps that closed the distance between them.

Riley drew her in between his legs and wrapped his arms around her, burying his face in her hair and breathing in the refreshing scent that was permanently etched upon his soul after this weekend. "I want nothing more than to deal with you and your kitchen, and PS, it's not too much to ask. I'm looking forward to it."

"It's okay to tell me if you change your mind."

"Not going to change my mind," he said, drawing her into a kiss that made his head spin. Would it always be like that with her? Would every kiss be somehow *more* than he'd ever imagined possible? As he kissed her, he ran his hands over her back and down to cup her ass under the hem of his shirt before lifting her onto his lap.

"Riley!" She broke the kiss, gasping. "We're going to break the stool."

"No, we're not." He tried to resume the kiss, but she turned her face.

"Yes, we are. They're as old as the house."

Without actively making a plan, Riley stood and lowered her to the floor, making sure she made a gentle landing as he came down on top of her. "Better?"

Looking up at him with big eyes full of emotion, she nodded.

"We have to maintain some semblance of control here," he whispered, kissing her neck and rolling her earlobe between his teeth. "We're out of condoms."

"I'm safe if you are."

Her words hit him like a punch to the gut, sucking all the air out of him in one big whoosh. "Are you saying…"

"We don't need condoms?" Her saucy reply and the expression to match were his undoing.

"Holy Christ. Hang on to your hat. Things are about to get crazy."

She was still laughing when he kissed her with the kind of ravenous hunger he hadn't known he had in him until her, until she made him want her in a way that had him thinking of white picket fences and forever. Whatever it took to keep her and the feelings that came with her in his life permanently.

A short time ago, thoughts like those would've terrified him and had him running for his life from the threat of being tied down, of being beholden to someone other than himself. But the idea of being tied down by *her* or beholden to *her* didn't scare him at all. Rather, it filled him with a kind of ebullient joy that made him feel like he could climb mountains and scale tall buildings. It made him confident that he could do anything he set his mind to, as long as she was in his life, his bed and his heart.

The only thing standing between them was the thin cotton of his boxer briefs, but she quickly dispatched them and wrapped her hot hand around his cock, stroking him until he was forced to bite his own lip—hard—to keep from exploding in her hand. Words like *desire* and *passion* had never meant much to him until she showed him the true meaning of both words. Desire whipped through him, making every part of him aware of her and the craving need she inspired in him.

And when she guided him into her body with nothing between them, he staggered from the punch of emotion and the sheer pleasure that had his arms giving out, bringing him down on top of her without a thought as to whether she could withstand his weight.

She more than withstood it, wrapping her arms and legs around him and making him feel welcome, more at home with her than he'd ever been anywhere.

"Nik," he whispered. "This is…" God, she'd turned him into a stammering fool.

"Mmm, for me, too." She soothed him with her fingers in his hair, her hand on his back and the lift of her hips as he moved in her.

He'd never had sex that felt like a nearly religious experience. Raising himself on his elbows, he used his hands to sweep stray strands of hair from her face as he gazed down at her and saw everything he was feeling reflected back at him in the gorgeous brown eyes that looked up at him with such wonder.

"I love you." The words were out of his mouth before he took the time to question whether the time was right. Fuck that. The time had never been more right.

"Riley." She blinked back tears. "I love you, too."

Saying the words, hearing them back from her… *Best moment of his life*. Hands down. He leaned his forehead against hers, fighting his way through the emotional firestorm. "I'm really, really glad your grandmother's house sprung a leak."

She laughed even as she groaned from the deep thrusts of his cock.

Making love to her, without a condom, knowing she loved him… It would take a lot to top this.

.   .   .

191

BEING IN LOVE, Riley soon discovered, was an all-consuming proposition. If he wasn't working long days at the Wayfarer, he was with Nikki, helping her prep the kitchen for the renovations or spending hours making love to her, going without sleep so he could have more of her.

Mac had a dumpster delivered to Eastward Look, and they would start with demo tomorrow.

After a full week of burning the candle at both ends, he was thrilled to have another weekend to spend exclusively with her. Unlike last weekend, which had happened spontaneously, this time, he packed a bag. He was getting ready to leave his house and head to hers when Finn came in, bringing a blast of cold air with him.

"Oh, hey, look who it is," Finn said, his tone dripping in sarcasm. "My former roommate and ex-brother."

"Ha-ha, you can't get rid of me that easily."

"Where're you going, or do I need to ask?"

"You know where I'm going."

"I hope you're at least getting some if you're spending every night there."

"Don't," Riley said, unreasonably pissed at the crass comment. In the past, it would've rolled off his back, but not when Nikki was involved.

"Don't what?" Finn went into the kitchen and popped open a beer. The house was an absolute disaster, but Riley couldn't be bothered to take the time to deal with it. "Do what we do? If the rules are changing, you need to clue me in, bro."

"This is different."

Finn leaned against the counter, arms crossed, beer in hand, and gave him a good looking over. "Different how?" He took a swig of beer, downing half of it.

"Different in the sense that I don't want to talk about it. I've got to go. Have a good weekend."

"That's it? You're outta here? See you Monday at work?"

Riley zipped his coat and turned to his brother. "What do you want me to say, Finn? Whatever it is, just put it out there."

"It's just that we used to hang out and stuff after work, on the weekends, and now I never lay eyes on you except for when we're working. I'm just checking as to whether you're planning to be gone all weekend."

"I am. Is that a problem?"

"No problem, but since Dad's getting married and you're shacking up with Nikki, maybe I should head home rather than hanging out by myself here."

"What about the Wayfarer? Mac is counting on us to get it done in time. And besides, I thought you'd decided to stay."

"Plans change, and I'm sure Mac can find someone to replace me."

"I thought you were excited to be working on a project with the rest of the family."

"I was." Finn shrugged. "Things change. The offer from Clint is intriguing. I'd like to buy my own place at some point. Could happen a lot faster if I went back to work for him. And besides, how often have we talked about how we went to college to be engineers and are working as carpenters?"

That topic had come up a lot since they moved "temporarily" to Gansett and ended up staying when Mac offered them jobs. At first, it had been about sticking close to their dad after the shocking end to their parents' marriage. But that excuse had gone away a long time ago, when their dad started seeing Chelsea.

"What're we doing here, Ri?" Finn asked. "We came for a wedding and never left. Is this it? Did we choose this life, or did it choose us? I've been thinking a lot about that lately. And Missy wants me to come home."

"Oh, for fuck's sake, Finn. Do not make decisions based on what *she* wants."

"Why not? She's been part of my life for a long time, and people do grow up and change."

"If you go back to her, you're settling."

Finn raised a brow. "And you're such an expert on women and relationships now?"

193

"I only know what it was like when you were with her, and I'd hate to see you go backward after all this time."

"The universe seems to be sending me all the signs I need that it's time to go home. Maybe things with Missy will work out. Maybe they won't, but I'll never know if I don't go home."

"I don't want you to go."

Finn laughed. "You won't even notice I'm gone."

"That's not true. I like working with you and having you here."

"You've got better things to do than hang out with your brother these days. It's all good. We don't have to be joined at the hip for the rest of our lives. In fact, it's probably long past time that we went our separate ways."

Riley wanted to argue, but he couldn't. Finn was probably right. They'd been lucky to stay in each other's daily lives for this long. "Just think it all the way through before you do anything, will you?"

"Sure. I've got an entire weekend with nothing to do but think."

An idea occurred to Riley. "Any interest in helping me gut a kitchen tomorrow?"

Finn groaned. "Seriously? Don't we already do that shit forty-plus hours a week?"

"This will be fun, and it's demo. You love to smash things."

"Yeah, I do. I'll come by. What time is safe to not see anything that'll scar me for life?"

"Any time after noon. We like to sleep in."

"Aww," Finn said, dabbing dramatically at his eyes. "My widdle boy is all married and shit."

Riley rolled his eyes. "Whatever. See you tomorrow?"

"Yeah, yeah. I'll be there. Tell Nicholas she's going to have to feed me if she wants my free labor."

"I'm sure she'll be fine with that. Hey, we need to make a plan to do something for Dad before the wedding."

"I'll send a text to the others to save the night before and figure out where we should have it."

"Sounds good. Have a good night."

"You, too, although we both know you will."

Riley flashed him the bird on the way out the door. What did it say about him that he couldn't imagine life without Finn smack in the middle of it? Other than his first two years of college, they'd never lived more than an hour from each other and had lived together for years. Their lives were extremely intertwined, not that he'd ever given much thought to that. It had just worked out that way.

At the thought of Finn leaving Gansett, Riley began to better understand the odd feeling of separation that Nikki had described when she talked about leaving Jordan to pursue her own goals. As he drove toward Eastward Look, he couldn't wait to see Nikki, to kiss her, to talk to her about Finn, to make love to her. Every night this week, she'd met him at the door, he'd lifted her into his arms and carried her straight to bed. Sometimes they didn't resurface until the morning, when he would wake up starving and realize he'd missed dinner and never even noticed.

It was utter madness.

The only thing marring what had been an otherwise spectacular week was Nikki's growing concern over the fact that neither she nor her grandmother had heard a word from Jordan, despite frequent attempts to reach her.

When the truck fishtailed on Sunflower Road, he realized he'd been speeding and slowed down lest an accident keep him from her any longer than he'd already been away. Workdays had never seemed longer than they did lately with her waiting for him.

While he worked, she made great progress in cleaning out the kitchen and had finalized the design plans with Sydney after they visited the Chesterfield to meet Lizzie James and tour the recently completed renovations. Nikki had come away bubbling with praise for what Lizzie and her husband, Jared, had done to the estate and full of ideas for things she'd like to do at Eastward Look.

Sydney was taking care of ordering the new cabinets and appliances, while Riley was working through Mac's channels to procure the building supplies. It was all moving forward. Now, if he could only keep his hands off her long enough to get it done.

He turned into the driveway, saw the light she'd left on for him, and his heart lurched. Rubbing the aching spot on his chest, he still couldn't believe the way he felt about her. If this was the feeling that had his cousins acting moonstruck over their spouses, he finally got why they all seemed to have lost their minds in recent years.

It was a feeling he would do almost anything to hold on to.

He got out of the truck and jogged to the stairs, the last obstacle in a very long day of obstacles that had kept him from her. The excitement that came from knowing they had three nights and two full days together reminded him of being a kid on Christmas morning, only this was way, way better.

She'd told him days ago to quit knocking on the door.

He punched in the code and stepped into the foyer. "Nik?"

"Coming!" she called from upstairs.

After leaving his coat and boots in the foyer, he stopped short at the sight of her coming down the stairs, her face flushed with excitement, her eyes bright and her smile warming him all the way through.

He held out his arms, and she took the leap from the third stair straight into his embrace, wrapping herself around him in a tight hug that put all her best parts into contact with his best parts. Riley walked them straight upstairs.

"Wait," she said, laughing as she kissed his face. "I have things to show you."

"I've waited all damned day. You can show me later." He'd never behaved this way with any other woman. In the past, civilized sex had usually happened at the end of a date that included dinner, drinks, maybe a movie or dancing. It had never been about the raw *need* that Nikki aroused in him. Back then, sex had been a satisfying physical release. With her, it was all that and more than he could ever put into words. "You've cast some sort of spell on me. I'm never like this."

"Like what?"

"Afraid I'm going to *die* if I'm not inside you within the next five seconds."

"We can't have that," she said, faking alarm.

"No, we really can't."

CHAPTER 19

*H*e put her down next to the bed and tugged at the sweatshirt she wore over yoga pants. "Get naked as fast as you can. The situation is critical. Code red."

Nikki giggled as she raised her arms to help him remove the shirt. "Funny you should mention red."

Riley's eyes bugged when he caught sight of her lacy red bra. "*Whoa*," he said, nuzzling into the deep valley between her full breasts, which might be his favorite spot on her body, but it was hard to choose just one favorite. "You are so fucking hot."

"Didn't expect that under my so-called work clothes?"

"Not at all. You've totally distracted me from my goal." He pushed his hands into the back of the formfitting yoga pants and shoved them down over her hips to reveal a matching red lace thong. Dropping to his knees, he put his arms around her and kissed her toned belly.

She buried her fingers in his hair to hold him there, and for the longest time, he simply breathed her in, the physical urgency tempered by something far sweeter.

Love for her beat through him like a live current, touching every part of him. He looked up at her gazing down at him and ran his hands over the backs of her legs, up to grasp her supple bottom.

"Lie back," he said gruffly, arranging her the way he wanted her with her feet and ass at the edge of the mattress. Bending over her, he pressed his mouth to her core through the thin layer of silk that covered her.

She jolted in response, and goose bumps covered her skin while she waited to see what he would do.

Everything about her appealed to him, including the rich feminine scent of her arousal. He breathed her in before moving the thong aside to worship her with his tongue and fingers. After a week of nights with her, he knew exactly what it took to make her come so hard, she screamed from the power of it.

He kissed his way up the center of her, releasing the front clasp of her bra and using his lips to push the cups aside.

"Riley…" Her hand closed around his cock and guided him into her.

He'd planned to draw it out some more but couldn't stop himself from taking what she offered. Sliding into her was like experiencing all the benefits of heaven without having to die first. If he could stay right there forever, he'd never need anything else ever again. "What've you done to me?" he whispered, his lips touching hers. "I want you all the time."

"I want you just as much."

Gathering her into his embrace, he held her tight against him as they moved together. As if someone had suddenly given him the answers to every question he'd ever had, he understood that she was the one, the *only* one for him. She would occupy the center of his life for as long as he lived, and nothing would ever be right unless he had her with him.

He wondered how that had happened so quickly, but in reality, it hadn't been quick. Months had passed after they first met, and all that time, Riley had thought about her. It had been happening then, too, only he hadn't known it at the time.

The heat they generated together threatened to consume him. His sweat mingled with hers as they reached the apex at the same instant, leaving him breathless and demolished, as if he'd run a marathon. A week of sleepless nights caught up to him in the hazy, sweet aftermath, with her head on his chest, her hair brushing against his face, her scent filling his senses with the essence of her. He couldn't recall a time when he'd been more relaxed.

Her hand moved in lazy circles on his abdomen.

Utter perfection.

SHE WAS BECOMING ADDICTED to him. He walked into her house fresh from an after-work shower, and the only thoughts in her head were *Mine. Now. More.* After years of avoiding the complications of men and sex, she couldn't get enough. But it wasn't just the physical aspects with Riley, although those aspects were life-changing.

It was everything else. That she could talk to him—really talk to him—and he listened intently to her, valued her opinions, made her laugh. And he'd fully embraced her plan to renovate the house, even though helping with what had to be the last thing he wanted to do after working long hours on an even larger renovation project.

He was good and decent and sexy as all hell, and she was crazy about him. Crazier by the minute. She barely recognized the person she'd become with him, but she liked this new spontaneous version of herself who stayed up all night having sex and laughing and talking and then dragged through her days like she'd been partially sedated.

The change in his breathing indicated he'd fallen asleep, which he needed even more than she did. She worried about him getting hurt at work because he was so tired from losing sleep with her.

I can sleep when I'm dead, he'd joked the other night, but she didn't want to think of him as anything other than beautifully alive and all hers.

Nikki didn't think she would sleep, but she awoke when Riley stirred, realizing two hours had gone by.

Riley's stomach growled loudly.

Laughing, she said, "That's one hell of an alarm clock."

"You want to go somewhere?"

Nikki groaned. "Not even kinda. How about I make us some pasta while I can still cook?"

"That's fine with me." He ran his index finger down her backbone, making her jolt when he didn't stop at her waist. "I was thinking that you should come stay at my place while yours is torn up. Then you wouldn't have to live in a war zone."

"What about Finn? Would he mind?"

Riley's brows furrowed. "He's thinking about going back to Connecticut."

"Does that bum you out?"

"Kinda. I wasn't expecting him to say that, but I think he's sort of lonely since my dad moved in with Chelsea and I started hanging out with you."

"He's lost his best friend," she said sympathetically. "I know how that feels, and it sucks."

"No word from Jordan?"

She shook her head.

"Is there someone you could call to check on her?"

"There're a few people who work for Zane, but I'm trying to disengage. Reaching out to them brings me back in. I keep telling myself if something was wrong, it would make the news."

"Have you checked online?"

She looked somewhat sheepish when she nodded. "Nothing."

"No news is good news, right?"

"Usually, but I can't help but feel anxious the longer she goes without reaching out to me or our grandmother. Although, she knows we don't approve of her going back to him, so maybe that's why she's gone silent."

Trailing his index finger down her arm, he said, "I'm sorry you're worried."

She offered a weak smile and linked her fingers with his. "Seems to be the new normal where Jordan is concerned. Anyway, it's her loss. She would be so excited to hear that I've been seeing you."

"Is that what you're doing?" he asked, grinning. "*Seeing* me?"

"Seeing *all* of you."

Laughing, he drew her in even closer to him, until she was half lying on top of him, their legs intertwined. "You think she'd approve?"

"Definitely. She knew I really liked you when we first met."

They stayed wrapped up in each other for a long time, until his stomach growled loudly again and made them laugh.

"How about we see about some dinner?" she asked.

"My stomach says yes, please."

Nikki sat up and reached for the flannel shirt he'd had on earlier, fastening only two of the buttons.

Riley found a pair of sweats in the bag he'd brought and put them on.

They went downstairs, made dinner, polished off a bottle of wine and ended up back in bed an hour later.

"I thought we were going to get some work done tonight," he said after they'd made love again.

"Eh," she said, yawning. "We'll work tomorrow."

"I recruited Finn to help with demo, so we need to be decent by noon."

"Define decent."

He squeezed her ass. "None of your good parts showing."

"All my parts are good," she said indignantly.

"Mmm, they certainly are."

She loved how he constantly touched and caressed her, as if he couldn't be near her without touching her. One stroke at a time, he was repairing the wound on her soul that Griffin had left there. And while she didn't expect she'd ever "get over" that, every minute she spent with Riley proved she was capable of having a real, loving relationship with a man. For a very long time, she'd doubted whether that could ever happen. Now she knew that not only could it happen, it could change her life in all the best ways. "Thank you," she said softly.

"For what?"

"This. All of it. You have no idea what it means to me to be here with you this way."

"I can't believe you're thanking me. I feel like I should be down on my knees in front of *you*. This has been the best week of my entire life."

With her hand on his face, she drew him into a kiss. "I feel so lucky to have met you."

"Me, too, babe. So fucking lucky, it's not even funny." Gazing into her eyes, he kissed her again. "I love you. I've never said that to anyone but you, and I'm really glad I saved it for you."

She blinked back tears. "I love you, too, and I've never said that before either. I was waiting for you."

He hugged her fiercely, and during the most perfect moment of her life, the old insecurities came roaring back to remind her not to get too comfortable. How could something so amazing possibly last?

RILEY AND NIKKI slept until ten, lolled about until close to noon and then dragged themselves out of bed to shower and get dressed before Finn arrived.

"Today," she said, flexing her biceps, "is what Chip calls 'Demo Day.'"

"Tell me again who Chip is," he said, focused on getting another cup of coffee into his system so he could begin to function.

Nikki stared at him, agape. "*Who is Chip?* What rock do you live under, Riley McCarthy? Chip Carter Gaines is the master renovation guy on *Fixer Upper*, one of the best TV shows *ever*."

"Until I met you, I'd never heard of him or the show."

Looking absolutely adorable with a big sledgehammer resting on her shoulder, she shook her head, seeming as gutted as her kitchen soon would be. "I knew you were too good to be true."

"You'll have to educate me."

"Oh, I will, and before long, you'll know all about Demo Day and shiplap and everything you ever wanted to know about Waco, Texas."

"Can't wait. In the meantime, are you going to use that sledge-hammer or just stand there looking fierce and pretty all day?"

She struck a playful pose. "Do I look fierce and pretty?"

He replied with a low growl that had her taking a step back.

"We said no touching during demo." She sent him a coy look over her shoulder as she turned to face the wall that was coming down. "We have rules."

Crossing the small distance between them, he wrapped his arm around her waist and hauled her back against him and nibbled the ticklish spot on her neck. "Rules were made to be broken."

She screamed with laughter and tried to break free of him.

"Don't let me interrupt," Finn said as he came in bearing a tray of coffees and a bag of what looked like Aunt Linda's doughnuts.

Riley released Nikki and lunged for the doughnuts.

"I see where I rate," Nikki said. "Second to a bag of doughnuts."

"These aren't just any doughnuts," Riley said, dead serious.

Finn held them out of his brother's reach. "I'll trade you doughnuts for assurances that I'm not going to see or hear anything that can't be unseen or unheard in this house of ill repute."

"Deal," Riley said. "Gimme."

Finn handed over the bag. "Don't be a pig. Offer one to Nicholas."

"Thank you, Finnbar," she said, helping herself to a doughnut.

"Welcome."

"Where'd you get these?" Riley asked over a mouthful.

"Auntie Linda made them for Uncle Mac, Ned, Dad and Uncle Frank, and I happened to stop by to see what they were up to. I told her what we were doing, so she made some for us."

"She's the best," Riley said, reaching for a second.

Taking in the sledgehammer on Nikki's shoulder, Finn said, "You ought to put that down before you hurt yourself."

She scowled at him, turned toward the wall Riley had spray-painted an X onto and let it rip into the drywall, taking a huge chunk of it out in the first hit.

"Not bad," Finn said. "You've got real potential."

"Shut it, or I'll pretend this wall is your head," she replied.

Riley snorted with laughter. "That's my girl. You tell him."

"I thought you people wanted my help," Finn said, pretending to be offended.

"We do," Riley said. "Help me get the old cabinets out."

The two of them took crowbars to the cabinets, pried them off the wall and walked them to the dumpster. They were too old to save, which they did whenever they could. Donating outdated but still working items was something Clint had advocated when they had worked for him, and Mac practiced as well. Recycle and reuse was a central theme of the renovation game.

By four o'clock, the kitchen had been taken down to studs. The old appliances were picked up and hauled away by Joshua Banks, the pastor at one of the island churches, who was going to find a good home for them.

Nikki opened three beers and sat next to Riley on the sofa while Finn flopped into one of the easy chairs. "Thank you both for giving up a weekend day to help me."

"It was our pleasure," Riley said.

"It'll be *your* pleasure, I'm sure," Finn said, adding a teasing grin. "Happy to help, but I'm going to need food, and I'm going to need it soon."

"Me, too," Riley said.

"I'd offer to cook for you boys," Nikki said, "but I seem to be out a kitchen."

"Let's go to Mario's," Finn said.

"Yum," Nikki said. "My treat."

"You bet your ass it's your treat," Finn said. "The pizza is on you for the indefinite future."

"Good to know," Nikki said, laughing.

A loud knock sounded at the unlocked door, followed by Kevin McCarthy calling out, "Anyone home?"

"Come in, Dad," Riley said, giving the others a quizzical look. What was he doing here?

"Finn told me you guys were working over here, so we thought you might be hungry." Kevin and Chelsea came in bearing pizza boxes and bags along with a twelve-pack of beer.

"Is he telepathic?" Finn asked.

"I think he might be," Riley said. "But I've never loved him more than I do right now."

"What's that about?" Kevin asked.

"We were just talking about going to Mario's, and they were going to make me pay," Nikki said, standing to take Kevin's and Chelsea's coats. "So we're all happy to see you."

"Judging by the dumpster, you got a lot done today," Kevin said as he sat on a love seat with Chelsea and served up pizza onto paper plates that Mario's had provided.

"We've got the kitchen ready to rock and roll," Riley said.

"And we found out that Nicholas wields one hell of a sledgehammer," Finn said, gesturing behind him. "Used to be a wall there until she showed it who's boss."

"I put a serious hurt on it," she said, proud of how hard she'd worked, even if every muscle in her body ached as a result.

Riley smiled at her, and she could tell he wanted to kiss her.

He lit the fire, and they passed an entertaining couple of hours in which Nikki heard stories from Riley and Finn's childhood, including their extremely profitable lemonade stand as well as their lawn-mowing, snow-shoveling and car-detailing businesses.

"How old were they when they started all these businesses?" Nikki asked in amazement.

"Like twelve and fourteen, I think," Kevin said.

"We were younger," Finn said around another mouthful of pizza. "Ten and twelve. We like money, and the doc kept us on a short leash."

"Didn't want them to grow up to be useless," Kevin said.

"It worked with me," Riley said, tending to the fire. "Not so much with Finn. He's completely useless."

"I believe I proved otherwise today, didn't I, Nicholas?"

"Yes, Finnbar. You were very useful today."

Finn smiled victoriously at his brother. "Your girl digs me."

"No, she doesn't," Riley said, scowling at his brother as he rejoined Nikki on the sofa.

Chelsea laughed at their antics. "I'm a little concerned for our baby, Kev, and the things these two will teach him or her."

"We won't let them near the baby until he or she is at least eighteen."

"Good plan," Chelsea said.

"The first time they need babysitters, it'll be like *Riley, Finn, help us,*" Finn said in a high-pitched voice.

"God forbid we're ever that desperate," Kevin said.

Chelsea covered her mouth to hold back laughter.

"You guys won't be surprised to hear that your uncle Mac has us fully organized to go to Courtney's funeral on Thursday," Kevin said. "Right down to ferry reservations for enough cars to get us all there."

"I'm sure Joe had more to do with that than Uncle Mac did," Riley said.

"Joe was apparently a big help with the ferry part of the program. Chels and I are staying on the mainland for a few days so she can pick up her wedding dress and I can get a new suit. We've got a few other details to tend to."

"Oh crap," Finn said. "We need suits, too."

"Give us sizes and measurements, and we'll hook you up with something new," Kevin said.

In one of the boxes from the kitchen, Nikki found an unopened bag of marshmallows that they toasted in the fireplace and used to make s'mores for dessert.

Chelsea began to yawn around nine. "I'm a good time had by all lately."

"First trimester is exhausting," Kevin said. "Let's get you home to bed."

"I'm out, too," Finn said. "Thanks for a fun night, Nicholas."

"All the thanks go to Kevin and Chelsea for bringing the pizza and beer."

"It was a pleasure," Kevin said. "I can't wait to see the renovations finished."

"It's going to be beautiful," Riley said, slipping an arm around Nikki.

"I hope so," she said, nervous but excited to see her choices come together in the new kitchen. "There's no way I could do it without your help."

"And mine," Finn called on his way out the door.

"You're the one making it all happen," Nikki replied.

"Hey!" Riley's outrage made her laugh. While the others dashed through the cold to their cars, he said, "Do you want to go to my place?"

"Since we've been well fed, let's stay here where we can be alone."

"I won't argue with that."

CHAPTER 20

They stood at the door until both vehicles had left the driveway. Then Nikki shut off the outside lights and locked up. "That was really fun."

He followed her back to the sofa. "Yes, it was. Nice of my dad to cater."

She pulled a cable-knit blanket over them. "Very nice. He's very sweet and obviously crazy about Chelsea."

"He has been from the start. At first, it was kind of odd for us to see him with someone else, but now she's one of us."

"Do you hear from your mom?"

"Yeah, we're in touch. We text and stuff."

"What's her name?"

"Deb."

"Your entire demeanor changes when you talk about her. Do you realize that?"

"It does?"

She nodded.

Reclined against a pile of pillows with her snuggled up to him, Riley ran his fingers through his hair, attempting to bring some order to it. "I'll never understand why people don't just get divorced if they want someone else. Why cheat?"

"I don't know. I don't get it either." She looked up at him. "No matter what happens between us, I promise I will never do that to you."

"And I will never do it to you." He drew her into a kiss that quickly went from soft and sweet to needy. "I feel like it's been *days* since I woke up with you."

"Days and days," she whispered. "Let's go to bed."

ON THURSDAY, Riley and the rest of the McCarthy family took the first boat off the island to attend Courtney's funeral, which was held in a cathedral in Providence. They filled four rows in the crowded church, surrounding Shane with their unwavering support.

Shane had remained stoic throughout the emotionally charged service, and Katie never left his side or released her tight hold on his hand during a very long day.

The usually jovial group was subdued on the ferry ride home.

"It was so good of you all to come," Shane said. "I really appreciate it, and I know Courtney's mom did, too."

"Nowhere else we would've been today," Big Mac said.

"We're all so proud of you, Shane," Linda said.

Shane's eyes filled as he shook his head. "Don't be proud of me. I didn't do anything."

"You tried to save her," Linda said gently. "You did as much as anyone could."

"She's right, son," Frank said. "The only one who could truly save Courtney was Courtney. You did everything you could and then some."

"This is just the saddest freaking thing," Janey said in a low tone that only Riley and Finn sitting next to her could hear. "I can't bear it for him."

"He's going to be okay," Finn said. "We'll all be there for him, and we'll get him through it."

"I thought you were planning to go back to Connecticut," Riley said.

"I talked to Mac, and he begged me to stay until the Wayfarer is finished. Besides, I don't feel right leaving when Shane's dealing with all this, and what's up with him anyway?" Finn gestured to Mac, who was on the phone as he paced from one end of the cabin to the other.

"No idea," Riley said. "He's been agitated all day."

"He doesn't like leaving Maddie and the kids on the island, especially this time of year," Janey said. "He was afraid he wouldn't be able to get back to them."

"You left Joe," Finn said.

"And we told Maddie to call him if she needed anything, but Mac frets nonetheless."

"Something else is up with him," Riley said. "He's been acting kinda weird all week."

"He's always weird, if you ask me," Janey said, grinning.

"You have to say that," Finn said. "You're his baby sister."

Janey rolled her eyes. "And he never lets me forget it. I have two kids, and he still can't deal with the fact that I have sex, regularly, with his best friend."

"Ewww," Finn said, cringing. "Don't be disgusting."

"Nothing disgusting about it, my friend," she said suggestively.

A shout went up from the other side of the cabin, where Adam sat with Abby. She was holding her cell phone and staring at it with huge eyes as Adam leaned in to see what it said. Then he looked at her, seeming equally dazed.

"What's going on?" Janey asked her brother and sister-in-law.

"We just got a text," Abby said, her eyes filling with tears and her hands shaking. "They... They have a baby for us."

The group erupted into cheers and surrounded Adam and Abby to share in their excitement. Luckily, they had the cabin more or less to themselves.

"It's a boy," Adam said, leaning in to see the phone, every bit as emotional as his wife as he read the text. "The family he'd been promised to is unable to take him, so it's happening fast. We can pick him up the day after tomorrow."

Janey took the phone from Abby, whose hands were shaking so hard, she could barely hold it. "The message says you need to reply if you are willing to accept the child."

"Say *yes!*" Adam said. "Tell them we'll be there!" As Janey typed in their response, he pulled his wife into his arms and let out a happy whoop. "We're having a baby!"

"And life goes on," Big Mac said, squeezing Shane's arm. "Life goes on."

BY THE TIME the ferry docked in South Harbor, Mac was on the verge of a full-on anxiety attack. Leaving Maddie and the kids alone on the island in the dead of winter had freaked him out, because there was always a chance he wouldn't be able to get back if the ferries stopped running. There'd been no question about going to the funeral to support Shane, who was not only his cousin but his close friend and coworker.

He and Maddie had debated about her going with him, but Hailey had a fever the day before, so Maddie hadn't felt right about leaving their daughter with a sitter for a long day, and with baby Mac still breastfeeding, they would've had to bring him with them. In the end, they'd decided she should stay home while he went to the funeral by himself. But he hadn't had an easy moment since the morning ferry pulled out of port, leaving the most important people in his life behind on a remote island in the dead of winter.

"Mac." Only his father's hand on his shoulder kept him from leaping the three feet from the still-moving ferry onto the island. "What the hell is wrong with you today? You're like a cat on a hot tin roof."

"Nothing's wrong."

"Mac."

The way his father said his name had him turning to face Big Mac. At six foot two, Mac was no shrimp, but his father still had two inches on him. He also had an ability to stare him down that no one else, except Maddie, had.

"What's going on, son? And don't say it's nothing. I know you too well to believe that."

"I don't like leaving Maddie and the kids on the island, especially this time of year." He glanced at the dark clouds that had loomed all day. The crossing had been bumpy, but not as rough as it could've been.

"What else?"

"That's it." Mac glanced longingly at his truck parked a hundred yards away. "Can I go now?"

"You can go when you tell me what else is going on."

The cars began rolling off the ferry. Uncle Frank tooted as he and Betsy drove by with Laura and Owen in the backseat. They'd left their kids with one of the women who worked for them at the hotel, which was quiet this time of year.

Knowing defeat when it stared him in the face, Mac sagged as he glanced up at his dad. "Maddie's pregnant."

His father seemed momentarily stunned before he recovered. "Oh. *Well*. Congratulations."

"Thanks. I think."

"That's why you were so tense about going today."

"One reason. She's been really tired, and I'm sure she's had a long day. The thought of them being here and me not being able to get back to them for whatever reason... Stressed me out."

"I get it."

"The pregnancy is very new. We're not telling anyone because..." He still had trouble saying Connor, the name of their son who had died in utero.

"I won't say a word. I promise." His father hugged him, speaking gruffly in his ear. "You're a wonderful husband and father, and I couldn't be prouder of you."

Damn the man! He had Mac on the verge of bawling his head off. "I had the best possible example," Mac replied.

"Everything okay?" Adam asked as he, Riley and Finn approached them.

"Yeah," Big Mac said, releasing Mac. "Everything is just fine."

"It is now." Mac stepped onto the island and breathed a deep sigh of relief. Waving to the others, he jogged to his truck and was on his way home within seconds. The ten-minute ride to Sweet Meadow Farm Road seemed to take twice that. Even though he'd texted with Maddie all day, the vision of their home lit up like a power plant was the best thing he'd seen since he'd left nearly twelve hours earlier. Every freaking light in the house was on, probably thanks to Thomas, who they were constantly telling to turn off the lights when he left a room.

Mac bounded up the stairs, taking them two at a time, opened the sliding door from the deck and stepped into bedlam. Toys were scattered about the living room, little Mac was bawling his head off as Maddie walked him while also supervising Thomas and Hailey, who were apparently supposed to be cleaning up but were fighting over a truck. The kitchen table was covered with the remains of what looked like a spaghetti dinner.

Filled with relief, he blew out a deep breath. Business as usual.

Hailey was the first to spot him, and she let out a cry of happiness as she ran for him on pudgy legs. Her blonde curls bounced, and her face reflected her pure joy at seeing her daddy after a long day.

Mac scooped her up and made her squeal when he kissed her neck. She smelled like peanut butter, spaghetti sauce and little girl. Most important, the fever was gone. "How's my baby girl?"

"Daddy, Thomas got in trouble for stealing my toys."

"I didn't steal nothing," Thomas said, sticking his tongue out at his sister.

Mac squatted down and brought Thomas into his embrace, kissing the top of his head. "How about I make you guys a deal? I'll help you clean up this mess and take your baths and read you *three* bedtime stories if you promise no more bickering. Do we have a deal?"

"Okay, Daddy," Hailey said.

Three stories were a powerful bargaining tool.

"All right," Thomas said begrudgingly.

"You guys get started, and I'll help as soon as I say hi to Mommy."

"No kissing," Thomas said, making a disgusted face.

"Yes kissing," Mac said, cuffing his son's chin. "Lots of kissing."

"Gross," Thomas said.

Mac couldn't wait to remind him of that when he reached the age when kissing was no longer gross. Standing upright, he went to his wife, taking the baby from her. "Hi, honey, I'm home."

"Thank God," she said, weariness clinging to every inch of her.

Mac leaned in for a kiss and was surprised when she pulled back.

"I stink like sour breast milk and a variety of other substances that can't be easily identified."

"I don't care what you smell like. I want a kiss from my gorgeous wife."

"It might be time to get you some glasses. At your advanced age, vision is the first to go."

Smiling, he hooked his free arm around her waist and gave her an uncompromising look. "Kiss me before I die from wanting you to."

Shaking her head at his shameless appeal, she gave him a gentle peck. "There."

"You can do better. I'll expect a do-over at bedtime."

"Thanks for the warning."

"Is this guy fed?" he asked of the baby, who had settled the minute Mac showed up, something that happened often enough that Maddie cried "no fair" at least once a day. It certainly didn't break his heart that his son seemed to favor him over everyone else, not that he would ever admit that to the baby's devoted mother.

"He's drunk on breast milk and ready for bed."

"Go on up and take a bubble bath. I got this."

"You haven't even taken your coat off yet, and you must be hungry. There's a plate for you warming in the oven."

"Go. I got it. Relax. You're off duty."

"In case I forget to tell you later, I really love you."

"I'll remind you to tell me again."

She left him with a giddy grin and went to kiss Thomas and Hailey good night. "Be good for Daddy and help him with baby Mac."

"We will, Mommy," Thomas said. He took his big-brother duties very seriously when it came to Mac. Not so much with Hailey, whose job it was to be a constant thorn in his side, or so it seemed to Thomas.

With Mac supervising, they picked up the toys and returned them to the toy box and containers.

"Good job, buddy," Mac said to Thomas, who'd done most of the work.

They went upstairs to put the baby down before Mac supervised Thomas and Hailey in the tub. As usual, he got as wet as they did, just like he had the long-ago first night with Thomas when he'd been brand-new to babies and baths. Now he was a seasoned professional.

By the time he read the three stories he'd promised and got them tucked into their beds, Mac was ready to drop from the long, emotional day. He went downstairs and had a few bites of the dinner Maddie had left for him and locked up before going back upstairs to shut off the rest of the lights. Unbuttoning the dress shirt he'd worn to the funeral, Mac stepped into the master bedroom, where Maddie was in bed reading a home decorating magazine. He took off the wet shirt and T-shirt under it, tossing them on the foot of the bed.

"My hero," she said, welcoming him with a warm smile. "Is everyone in bed?"

"For the moment." Bedtime was often a rolling event with a variety of ups and downs until everyone was asleep. "Fingers crossed they stay there."

"How was it?" she asked.

"As awful as you might imagine."

"And Shane?"

"He seems okay. It's going to take a while, I suppose." He sat next to her on the bed and linked his fingers with hers, feeling like he could finally breathe again after a long, stressful day off the island. "I was out of my mind leaving you guys here while I went to the mainland."

"We were fine."

"I know, but the thought of not being able to get back to you for whatever reason made me nuts."

She released his hand and held out her arms to him. "Come here."

He crawled into her outstretched arms and breathed in the sweet scent of summer flowers that reminded him of their beginning. "I was thinking about the first time I ever gave Thomas a bath."

"You got as wet as he did."

"I still do. My shirt is soaked."

"Your hair is wet, too," she said, laughing.

"Some things never change."

"I've never been as happy to see you as I was tonight."

"You're really tired?"

"It's insane! I wake up tired, and I feel like I'm slogging through quicksand all day long."

"Hopefully that'll pass after the first three months."

"I hope so, too, or the inmates are going to overtake the asylum around here."

"Nah, we won't let that happen." He forced his mind and body to relax. Everything was fine. They were okay, so he was okay. "Big family news on the ferry ride home."

"What's that?"

"Adam and Abby got a text from the adoption agency. They've got a baby boy for them. They're picking him up the day after tomorrow."

"Oh, Mac. *Oh my God*. That's the best news I've ever heard!"

"I know. They're so excited—and shocked."

"We'll have to help them get ready. They'll need everything. Between all of us, we can get them what they need to start with."

"I'm sure they'll appreciate that. Let me up so I can brush my teeth. I'm ready to end this long-ass day."

He went into the bathroom to finish getting ready for bed, sliding into his side five minutes later and immediately reaching for her.

She turned off the light and snuggled up to him. "Were there a lot of people at the service?"

"It was packed."

"I never knew her, and I feel so sad about her death."

"I know. I do, too. Makes me so damned thankful for what I have with you."

"Me, too."

"I told my dad about the baby—or I should say, he got me to tell him."

"And how did he do that?" she asked, sounding amused.

"In his usual Big Mac way. He could tell I was wound up today being off the island while you guys were here. He promised not to say anything about it."

"I don't mind that you told him. Everyone will find out soon enough. They probably think we're like a couple of bunnies."

Mac snorted with laughter. "Let them say whatever they want. I'm more than happy to be like bunnies with you."

"It's not funny."

"Yes, it is." He tipped her chin up to receive his kiss. "It's hilarious."

"Easy for you to laugh. You're not the hare in this metaphor."

"You're not a hare. You're a queen. My queen. The mother of my five children, the center of my universe, the love of my life."

"Don't be sweet and charming when I'm trying to be depressed."

Laughing, he kissed the pout off her lips.

"Thank you for saying we have five children."

"Connor counts. He'll always count."

She nodded. "Yes, he will."

"Close your eyes and get some sleep while you can."

"Only if you will, too."

"I'm not going to have any trouble sleeping tonight," he said. "Being stressed out all day is exhausting."

"I love you, Mac, and I love the way you love us."

"I love you, too. You and our babies are everything to me."

CHAPTER 21

*L*ong after Katie had gone to bed, Shane sat in the dark, a glass of bourbon in hand, his heart and mind full of Courtney after the funeral. Her family had given her a beautiful send-off that paid tribute to her life and her struggles in the most respectful way possible. His amazing family had rallied around him the way they always had, making an awful week less so with their unwavering support and encouragement.

And Katie… She'd been incredible, rarely leaving his side in the days that'd followed the dreadful news. He couldn't have gotten through the shock and despair without her there to light the way.

If only he could stop thinking about the odd vibe he'd gotten from her the other night when he'd asked her why they never talked about getting married. They'd been engaged for more than a year, and until their conversation three nights ago, neither of them had ever mentioned setting a date to make it official. He'd been waiting on her to bring it up without even realizing it. Now he suspected she never would've brought it up if he hadn't.

Had he gotten complacent? Should he have mentioned it before now? The not knowing had been working on his already shredded nerves during the last few days. Of course, he understood that after growing up with a violent, abusive father, legally binding herself to any man was a bigger deal to her than it would've been for anyone else.

But he'd shown her, every day of their lives together, that she would never have anything to fear from him. He wanted only to keep her safe, happy and loved for the rest of her life. Had he done a good enough job of telling her that? Of making sure she knew that there was nothing he wouldn't do for her?

He'd downed the last of the bourbon and was thinking about going to bed when Katie came out of the bedroom, looking sleep-rumpled and adorable in a silk nightgown he'd bought her for Christmas at Tiffany's shop. As it always did, his heart gave a happy little jolt at the sight of her. She loved to tell people that he'd saved her life, but the opposite was true. She'd saved his life in every way that mattered.

She came to him and slid onto his lap, making herself at home in his arms.

He'd loved Courtney. God help him, he had loved her. But he'd never loved anyone or anything the way he loved Katie Lawry.

"Can't sleep?" she asked.

"Haven't tried yet."

She kissed his face and smoothed the hair back from his brow. "You ought to try. You have to be exhausted after the last few days."

"I am."

"Let's go to bed."

When she would've gotten up, he stopped her by tightening his arms around her. "Hey, Katie?"

"Hmmm?"

"The other night when I asked you about whether we're going to get married one of these days, I got the feeling that the question upset you. And I was just wondering if there's anything I need to be worried about."

"*No*," she said emphatically. "You have nothing at all to be worried about where I'm concerned."

"You don't either. I hope you know that."

"I do, Shane. Of course I do."

"Then let's set a date for our wedding."

For a long moment, she was so still that he wondered if she was breathing.

"Katie?"

"You know I love you more than anything, right?"

His heart sank as he said, "I think so."

"I do. I love you and our life together. It's more than I ever dreamed of for myself."

"Are you afraid to marry me, Katie? Do you think things will change between us after we exchange vows?"

"No," she said, but less emphatically than before.

"That's what happened to your mom, right? Your dad was wonderful until after the wedding?"

"Yes, but—"

"That's not going to happen to you or us. I swear to you, Katie. You're perfectly safe with me. If you marry me, my only goal will be to make sure you never, ever regret it. I'll do whatever it takes to make you happy. You will *never* be unsafe with me." With his hand on her cheek, he turned her to face him and kissed her gently. "We got a tough reminder this week about how we never know what's around the next corner. Time is so precious, and it's time for us to take the next step together. Marry me, Katie. Please, marry me."

She closed her eyes, took a deep breath and let it go before opening her eyes. "Okay."

"You're sure?"

Nodding, she said, "I'm sure." She kissed him. "Thank you for understanding how difficult it is for me…"

"No need to thank me. I get it."

"I love you, Shane."

"I love you, too, and I can't wait to marry you. What're you doing Memorial Day weekend?"

"No plans that I know of."

"How do you feel about a sunset wedding on the same beach where we found each other?"

"I think that'd be lovely."

He kissed her and then hugged her tightly. "It's a date."

ADAM WENT LOOKING for Abby and found her in the attic, wearing only a thin cotton nightgown as she sorted through boxes. "Babe, what're you doing up here? It's *freezing*." His breath came out as puffy clouds in the frigid air.

"I'm looking for the baby clothes I bought ages ago, before we found out it might never happen."

"Sweetheart, we can do that tomorrow. We have all day, and it's too cold to be up here without a coat."

"I want to do it now. It'll only take a few minutes. They're in one of these boxes. I just have to figure out which one."

Resigned to no one sleeping until she found what she was looking for, he went downstairs to get coats for both of them and joined in the search. In the sixth box he opened, he found tiny little shirts, blankets, sleepers and socks so small, they would fit on his finger. All at once, the enormity of what was happening hit him in a tidal wave of thoughts and emotions.

He was going to be a *father*.

Abby was going to be a *mother*.

They were going to be *parents*.

They had a *son*.

Dear God. *We have a son!*

"Abby," he said softly. "Here it is." He held up a onesie that said "I Love Mommy" on it.

"Yes! That's it." Her brown eyes glowed with the kind of excitement that reminded him of how she'd been before the sky caved in on them with the devastating polycystic ovary syndrome diagnosis stealing her joy, her zest, her optimism. She'd been overjoyed since they received the text from the agency, followed soon after by a photo of the baby who would be their son. Having his Abby back was the greatest gift he'd ever received, even better than the news about the baby.

"Can we please take this downstairs?" he asked, shivering.

"I'll follow you."

Adam lifted the heavy box and carried it down the stairs, setting it on the foot of their bed.

Abby closed the door to the attic and came into the bedroom, shivering from the cold. "Brrr." She took off the coat he'd made her put on and tossed it on a chair.

He put his arms around her and drew her into a tight hug. "This is really happening."

"I still can't believe it," she said, clinging to him. "The agency said it could take *years*."

"We have a *son*, Abs." He withdrew from her only enough to place his hands on her face before he kissed her.

"A son. We have a son. Maybe if we keep saying it, we'll believe it by the time we get to meet him."

"When did you get all this stuff?"

"I've been collecting it for years, since I first opened Abby's Attic. Any time something came in that I'd want for myself, I added it to my collection."

He'd had no idea she'd been making preparations for a baby for years. "What're we going to name him?" They hadn't had these sorts of discussions before now out of fear of further jinxing themselves.

Besides, what was the point of talking baby names when every doctor they consulted had said pregnancy was unlikely for her due to the PCOS. They had continued to seek out treatments, and she'd undergone a number of grueling procedures, but so far, their efforts hadn't yielded the desired results. Each month, her period arrived with frustrating regularity, when one of the hallmarks of PCOS was erratic periods. The irony hadn't been lost on them.

"What do you like for names?" she asked, sitting on the bed to go through the items in the box. "All of this will need to be washed in special laundry detergent."

"Why does it have to be special?"

"Because the regular stuff is too harsh for babies' sensitive skin."

"How do you know that?"

"I don't know," she said, laughing. "I just do."

"Are there books I should read? I don't know anything. What if I break him or do something wrong or—"

"Adam," she said, laughing as she pulled on his arm, urging him to sit next to her. "Calm down. We'll figure it out the same way everyone else does."

"Everyone else has *nine months* to prepare for this. We have *two days*." He placed his hand on his chest. "I think I might be hyperventilating. Am I hyperventilating?"

She dissolved into helpless laughter, the kind that engaged every inch of her body in convulsions as she fell back onto the bed.

It had been, he realized, a very long time since he'd heard her laugh like that. Even if she was laughing *at* him, it was the best sound he'd ever heard. She finally got herself under control, for the most part, but remained stretched out on the bed, the I Love Mommy onesie clutched in her hand.

"What do you think of Callahan?" she asked, referring to her maiden name.

"Callahan McCarthy has a nice ring to it." But then another thought occurred to him. "People will call him *Cal*, which is your ex-fiancé's name, so that's a no-go."

"How come? Cal doesn't mean anything to us."

Scowling, he said, "You really want to name your son after your ex?"

"I wouldn't be naming him after my ex. I'd be joining my family name to yours. I like it."

"I don't know if I could handle that name in our lives every day..."

"Awww, are you still jealous over a guy I was done with before we ever got together?"

"Yes."

She lost it laughing again.

God, he loved her.

"What if we made Callahan his middle name, so Cal wouldn't be his nickname?" she suggested.

"I could live with that, but we're left with the need for a first name."

"Let me think about it."

Adam put the baby clothes she'd taken out back in the box, and they got in bed, turning on their sides to face each other. "Are you going to be able to sleep between now and Saturday?"

"Probably not. Are you?"

"I doubt it. The only time I've ever been more amped was the day I came back to Gansett after selling my company in New York. I was beyond excited because I was going to finally be able to see you again."

"A baby is more exciting than I'll ever be."

He brought her hand to his lips and kissed it. "Nothing will ever be more exciting than you are, but this comes pretty damned close."

Smiling, she said, "Should we give him an A name like we both have?"

Adam curled his lip with distaste. "Do we really want to be *that* family?"

"What's wrong with all of us having names that begin with A?"

"So many things. My brothers would be merciless."

She rolled her eyes. "What about Adam McCarthy Junior?"

"That's an A name, in case you think I'm not paying attention here. And I'd rather give him his own name."

"Well, we definitely can't have another Mac."

"Hell no. There're already far too many Mac McCarthys in this world."

"What about Liam? I've always loved that name."

Adam thought about that for a second. "I like it. Liam Callahan McCarthy? His initials would be LCM."

She took a deep breath and let it out, tears flooding her eyes and spilling down her cheeks. "Liam Callahan McCarthy," she whispered. "Our son's name is Liam Callahan McCarthy."

Adam moved closer to her, brought her into his arms and kissed away her tears. "No more tears. We've had enough of them to last a lifetime."

"These are happy tears."

"Well, those are certainly allowed."

"I just want to say…"

"What do you want to say, sweetheart?"

"I'll never have the words to tell you what it's meant to me that you've treated my problem as if it were *our* problem."

"It was—and is—*our* problem. You are not alone, Abby Callahan McCarthy. You will never be alone again. You will always have me—and Liam."

"That's all I need."

RILEY WENT straight from the ferry to Nikki's. Twelve hours off the island away from her felt like an eternity, and he couldn't wait to see her. He'd skipped going home to change out of the dress pants and button-down he'd worn to the funeral, because he was so eager to get to her.

He came to a skidding stop in the driveway and was out of the truck a second later, warmed by the light she'd left on for him. Inside, he called for her, but she didn't reply. He went upstairs and heard the shower running. Not wanting to scare her, he was about to knock on the bathroom door when her cell phone rang.

Checking the screen, he saw the name Davy and experienced the harsh sting of jealousy for the first time in his life. He felt ridiculous, knowing he didn't need to be jealous of anyone. The phone stopped ringing and then immediately started up again with another call from Davy.

Riley took the phone with him, knocked loudly on the bathroom door and walked into the steam-filled room. "Just me. Not an ax murderer."

She lit up with pleasure, while every cell in his body responded to the delicious sight of her naked body surrounded by steam. "Thank goodness it's *only* you."

Forcing himself to focus on something other than her sexy body, he said, "Somebody named Davy wants to talk to you. He called twice in the last ten seconds."

Her face lost all expression.

"Who is he?"

"Zane's manager." She turned off the shower and took the towel he held for her, wrapping it around her.

Riley handed her the phone and noticed that her hands trembled ever so slightly as she returned Davy's call.

"Hey, what's up?" she said when he answered.

Riley thought about stepping out of the room to give her privacy, but something about the rigid way she held herself made him stay.

Nikki sat on the closed lid of the toilet when her legs seemed to go out from under her. "How bad?" she asked, followed by, "When?" She dropped her head into her hand as she listened to what he was saying. "I don't have any way to get there. I'm on a freaking island, Davy." Looking up at Riley, she said, "What time is it?"

"Seven thirty."

"Yes," she said to Davy. "I can be ready by then. I'll meet the plane at the airport." After another pause, she said, "You're not the one who needs to apologize—for a lot of things. I'll see you soon." She ended the call and sat perfectly still for a full minute before she looked up at Riley. "Jordan and Zane had an altercation in a hotel in Charlotte, North Carolina, where his band was performing. She's in the hospital with a concussion and a broken arm. He's in jail."

"Oh my God, Nik. I'm so sorry."

"She's hysterical and asking for me, so Davy's sending Zane's plane for me. They'll be here by ten."

"I'll go with you."

"You're sweet to say so, but that's okay. I know you have work, and your dad is getting married. I don't know when I'll be back."

"Tomorrow's Friday, so no big deal, and the wedding isn't for two weeks yet. I'll go with you, and I'll worry about getting myself back here in time for work on Monday."

"She won't want you to see her if she's a mess."

He met her gaze straight on. "I'm not going for her."

Closing her eyes, she shook her head. "I never should've left her. If I had stayed…"

"This still would've happened, Nikki. You said it yourself—they're toxic together. Maybe this'll be the time that she says enough."

She looked up at him, her despair obvious. "I thought the sex tape would do it, so I've learned not to get my hopes up."

Riley held out a hand to her. "Come on. Let's get you dressed and packed, and then we'll run by my place to grab some clothes. Everything will be okay. I promise."

She gave him a weak smile. "Don't make promises you can't keep."

"I never do. We'll get you to your sister, and that'll make everything better for both of you."

CHAPTER 22

*J*ust after ten, Nikki boarded the private plane with Riley following right behind her. Though she felt bad about him missing a day of work on her behalf, she was thankful for his company and his support.

"Are you sure Mac won't be mad if you miss work tomorrow?"

"I'm sure. I texted him, but he's probably already asleep. It'll be fine. Finn will let him know what's going on, so don't worry." Riley took a good look around at the luxurious interior of the private plane. "So, this is how the other half lives, huh?"

"Don't be impressed. The person who owns this ostentatious plane is a flaming asshole."

"I already knew that, but the plane is kind of cool. I've never flown private before."

The pilot and flight attendant came into the cabin to say hello to Nikki.

"Nice to see you, Jesse," Nikki said to the pilot.

"Wish the circumstances were better," he said grimly. "We'll get you to your sister as fast as we can."

"Thank you."

"This is Mel, our flight attendant. Let her know if you need anything."

"Thank you both."

"We'll be airborne shortly."

Nikki and Riley strapped themselves into side-by-side white leather seats.

"Zane likes his gold, huh?" The plane was finished with gold on every available surface.

"He bought the plane after his first gold record," Nikki said, clearly unimpressed.

As they taxied for takeoff, Riley reached for her hand. "Are you okay?"

"I'm strangely numb after all the crazy crap that's happened since she met him. She's going to tell me that this it, she's done with him forever this time." She shrugged. "I've heard it all before."

"Maybe this'll be different."

"Maybe, but I'm not optimistic. He has some sort of weird hold over her that I've never understood. She has to be strong enough to break that bond, and so far, she hasn't been."

"What about your grandmother? Should you call her and tell her what's going on?"

"I'll call her in the morning."

"She won't see it online or on TV before then, will she?"

"No, she goes to bed early and gets up early. I'll catch her before she watches the news. I wonder if it's already all over the internet."

"You want me to look?"

She shook her head. "I'll find out soon enough."

The plane flew down the runway and lifted smoothly into the air, leaving Gansett Island behind as they climbed through thick clouds that made for a bumpy few minutes. When they cleared the clouds, they found a sky sprinkled with stars.

"I hope this flight is a metaphor for what happens next with Jordan," Riley said. "A patch of bumpiness followed by clear skies."

"That would be nice."

At his suggestion, they snuggled into the same chair and watched a movie to make the time go by faster. Nikki couldn't have said what movie it was or what it was about, but the mindless activity and his steady presence helped to pass the ninety minutes it took to fly from Rhode Island to North Carolina.

Nikki moved into her own seat for the descent and landing. Davy was waiting on the tarmac when they came off the plane. In his mid-thirties, Davy was tall and blond with a wiry build and always seemed to be vibrating with nervous energy. Nikki had thought he was on something the first few times she met him, until she realized the nervous energy came from trying to manage the unmanageable Zane. "Davy, this is Riley. Riley, Davy."

The two men shook hands.

"How is she?" Nikki asked.

"In a lot of pain, but she didn't want to take anything for it until you get there."

"Let's go," she said, climbing into the backseat with Riley. "Hurry." The thought of her sister in pain because of the man she loved made Nikki feel murderous. If she had ten minutes alone with Zane, she'd be tempted to stab him in the throat. It was probably just as well that he was in jail. "Does he know you sent the plane for me?" Nikki asked.

"Nope."

"Will he be pissed?"

"Fuck him if he is."

Realizing that Zane's own people were fed up with him, too, made Nikki feel slightly better.

Riley squeezed her hand.

Nikki was really glad he was there, and even more so when they arrived to find a massive crowd of reporters and photographers outside the hospital.

"Crap," Davy said. "We tried to keep a lid on it, but it's hard to keep a lid on anything these days."

"Can we find another way in?" Riley asked, seeming unnerved by the sheer volume of people waiting for news about Jordan.

"I'll try the back." Davy pulled around to the emergency entrance, which was deserted. "She's in room four forty-one. Go on up. I'll park and meet you. Leave your stuff. I'll take you to a hotel when you're ready."

Nikki appreciated that Riley let go of her hand only long enough to get out of the car. The second they were both out, he took hold of it again, letting her know he was right there with her. She'd never had that kind of support to lean on before. She was always the strong one, the one everyone else turned to in times of trouble. It was a refreshing and welcome change to have someone there just for *her*.

In the elevator, he put his arm around her, giving her exactly what she needed.

"I'm glad you came," she said.

"Me, too."

He walked her to Jordan's door. "Go ahead. I'll be right out here. Take your time."

She went up on tiptoes to kiss his cheek and then went into her sister's darkened room, where the only sound was that of sniffling. It broke Nikki's heart to know her sister's heart had been broken yet again by the man she loved. "Hey," she said, making an effort not to recoil at the sight of her sister's bruised face. One cheek was almost totally black and blue, and her lower lip had been laid wide open. Her arm was encased in a bulky cast and resting on a pillow. "I'm here."

Jordan began to sob, wincing from the pain the movement caused her.

"Easy," Nikki said, taking her hand. "Don't move. I'm right here, and you're going to be okay."

"No," Jordan said as tears slid down her face. "I'm not going to be okay."

"Yes, you are."

"I didn't even last two weeks on my own without you," she whispered.

"No one is keeping score, least of all me." Taking a tissue from a box on the bedside table, Nikki gently wiped the tears from Jordan's face.

"This is it, Nik. I swear to God. I'm done this time."

"I'm glad to hear you say that," Nikki replied, although she'd believe it when it happened.

A nurse came in and asked if Jordan was ready for pain meds. "Yes, please."

The nurse gave her a shot of something into her IV. "Now get some rest," she said on the way out of the room.

"I know you have good reason not to believe me," Jordan said, resuming their conversation. "But I mean it. I never want to see him again after this."

"The only thing that matters is getting you better so we can get out of here. Wait until you see what I've done to Gram's house on Gansett."

Jordan's eyes began to get heavy. "Did you see your roofer friend again?"

"Uh-huh. He's here with me."

Jordan's eyes flew open. "Really?"

Nikki nodded.

"Tell me. I want to hear the whole story."

While Jordan closed her eyes and listened, Nikki told her about Riley.

RILEY WAS LEANING against the wall outside Jordan's room when Davy joined him a few minutes after Nikki went in. "What happened tonight?" Riley asked him.

"I'm not sure exactly. There were some technical issues during the show last night, and he was a bear all day. We were supposed to leave for tonight's show, when we heard a disturbance inside their room. Next thing I knew, Jordan was in the hallway screaming for help with blood running down her face and her arm hanging at a weird angle. I could tell right away it was broken."

"Son of a bitch," Riley muttered. How any man could do that to a woman was beyond him, but to call Zane a man was giving him far too much credit. "I hope he's at least spending the night in jail."

"I have no idea," Davy said. "I'm not taking his calls. He doesn't know it yet, but I'm done working for him. I've put up with a ton of shit from him, and so has Jordan. I've had enough. I'll be surprised if she hasn't after this, too."

"We can only hope so."

"Yeah," Davy said. "Nikki did the right thing getting off the crazy train when she did."

"You can't tell her that. She feels responsible, like she could've done something if she'd been there."

"Nah, it's not her fault. Zane's got real issues that he's going to have to do something about before his life and career go up in smoke. We've got thirty thousand fans losing their collective minds because tonight's show was canceled at the last minute. Gonna cost a fucking fortune to give them all refunds. And then when they hear where he is and why…" Davy shook his head. "PR nightmare, and he'll deserve all the bad press he gets. Jordan is a sweet girl who can do better."

"You won't get any argument from me—or her sister."

"Figured she had to be at the end of her rope. Zane has that effect on people." Davy glanced at him. "Didn't know Nik had a boyfriend."

His familiarity and use of her nickname grated on Riley. "It's a relatively new development."

"Hmm, well, good for her. She's a nice girl, and so is her sister."

"Yes, she is. I'm looking forward to getting to know Jordan."

"I'm going to get a coffee. You want one?"

"Sure, sounds good. Just cream for me."

"You got it."

A few minutes after he walked away, Nikki came out of Jordan's room and stepped straight into Riley's arms.

"How is she?"

"Terrible. Her face is bruised and swollen, her lip is split, and her arm is in a big cast."

"I'm so sorry, babe. I feel so bad for both of you."

"She says this is it, and maybe I'm being overly optimistic, but it sounds different this time."

"I really hope so, for your sake as much as hers."

The nurse that had given Jordan the pain meds approached them.

"She'll be asleep for four or five hours if you want to get some rest while you can. You can leave your number at the nurse's station, and someone will call you when she's awake."

"Thank you," Nikki said.

After the nurse walked away, Nikki glanced at Riley. "What do you want to do?"

"I'm with you. Whatever you want. If you want to hang here, we can."

"We may as well get some sleep while we can. Where's Davy?"

"He went to get coffee. He'll be right back."

"I'll text him." She pulled out her phone and dashed off a text.

Davy came back a minute later—without coffee. "Figured if we're going to get some shut-eye, we don't need coffee."

"Good call," Riley said.

"I'm just going to check on her one more time," Nikki said. "I'll be right out." She went into the room where Jordan was sleeping peacefully. Leaning over the bed, she kissed her sister's forehead. "I'll be back in a little while." She gently smoothed some stray hairs, aching once again at the bruises that darkened Jordan's pretty face. "Love you."

Feeling bruised on the inside, Nikki forced herself to walk away so they could all get some rest. When she stepped out of the room, Riley put his arm around her and kept it there until he helped her into the car.

"Found a place that's close," Davy said, handing them hotel keycards.

Riley took them from him.

"Thank you for everything you've done for us, Davy," Nikki said.

"Least I could do. And besides, better I help you than find Zane and wring his fucking neck."

"True," Nikki said, "although a little neck-wringing might do him some good."

"For what it's worth, all his boys are fed up. We love Jordan, and after what he did to her... He's got a rude awakening coming his way."

"That's good to know, but I'm sorry that I don't really care what happens to him."

"Fair enough."

They traveled a couple of blocks and pulled into a hotel parking lot.

"I can leave you the car keys," Davy said when they prepared to part ways.

"We can walk back," Nikki said, giving the other man a quick hug. "Thanks again for everything."

"Call me when you're ready to get out of here. I'll make the plane available to take you anywhere you and Jordan want to go."

"Appreciate it. We'll be in touch."

Riley carried both their bags and ushered her inside.

Nikki was too emotionally drained to do anything but follow his lead. Inside the nondescript hotel room, Nikki sat at the foot of the king-sized bed, more exhausted than she'd been in years.

"So, I took a look online while you were in with Jordan," Riley said, sitting next to her. "I really think you ought to call your grandmother as soon as possible."

"It's bad?"

"It's everywhere."

"She'll panic if I call her now."

"What if she can't sleep and turns on the TV?"

"You're right. I'll call her."

He handed over her phone.

She had no memory of giving it to him. God only knew where it would be if he wasn't there to make sure she didn't lose her phone or her mind. Finding her grandmother's number at the top of her list of favorites, she made the call and held her breath, waiting for Evelyn to answer.

"Nicole?"

"Everything's fine."

"Clearly that's not true, or you wouldn't be calling me in the middle of the night."

"Jordan's in the hospital. There was a… situation with Zane. It's all over the news, and I didn't want you to hear it that way."

"What kind of situation?"

"The kind that puts her in the hospital and lands him in jail."

"That son of a bitch."

"My thoughts exactly. I'm with her in Charlotte. Davy sent the plane for me and has been super nice and helpful."

"Which is the least he can do as the chief enabler of that bastard."

"He's quitting. Zane doesn't know it yet, but Davy is done. He and the rest of Zane's posse are really upset about Jordan getting hurt. They all love her."

"Of course they do. What're her injuries?"

"Concussion, broken arm, bruises on her face."

"Oh my God. I want to come there and *murder* him."

"I know the feeling, but I'd rather act like he's dead to us."

"That's a better plan. How long will she be in the hospital?"

"I'm not sure yet, but Davy said we can have the plane to get out of here as soon as she feels up to it."

"And how are you holding up?"

"I'm good. Riley came with me. He's been a big help."

"Is that right?" Evelyn said, sounding thrilled. "I'm so glad to hear you're not alone."

Nikki glanced at Riley, who gave her a small smile. "I'm definitely not alone." After promising to update her grandmother as soon as she had more information, she said good night.

"Come on, sweetheart." He stood and gave her a tug to bring her with him. "Let's get you into bed. You're about to topple over."

For a woman who prided herself on competence and independence, Nikki was more than willing to let him help undress her, put one of his oversized T-shirts on her and walk her into the bathroom to brush her teeth before tucking her into bed. He kissed her cheek. "Close your eyes. I'll be right here."

When he slid into bed next to her a few minutes later, Nikki curled up to him, grateful for his love, his strength, his support and, most of all, his friendship. "Thanks for coming."

"Nowhere else I'd rather be than wherever you are."

ikki's ringing cell phone woke Riley out of a dream that included her and a group of dark-haired kids running with them on a beach. There'd been a dog, too. As she took the call, he ran his fingers through his hair and tried to process the meaning of the dream.

Nothing like getting ahead of yourself, he thought, even as the dream took root in his heart, refusing to be dismissed or ignored. What would've been inconceivable not that long ago was suddenly within reach. He couldn't imagine himself on that beach or in that family with anyone else but Nikki.

"Jordan's awake." She got up to take a shower while he ordered coffee and room service breakfast. If Zane was paying for their stay, Riley figured they ought to take full advantage.

When she was finished, he took a quick shower but didn't bother shaving. He moved quickly, knowing she'd want to get to her sister as soon as possible.

Within thirty minutes, they were walking into the hospital rested, fed and caffeinated, prepared to support Jordan in any way necessary. They'd brought their bags with them in case Jordan got released.

Leaving Riley in the waiting room with a thriller he'd picked up in the gift shop, Nikki went to see Jordan. A few minutes later, Riley's phone rang with a call from his father. "Hey, Dad. What's up?"

"I got your text, and I saw the news. I'm just wondering how Nikki and Jordan are?"

Riley should've expected to hear from his dad, who would naturally be concerned. "Jordan is in the hospital with a concussion, broken arm and facial bruises. Nikki is in with her now. We're waiting to hear how long she'll be here and what the next step is."

"You did a good thing going with her, son."

"There was never a question in my mind about letting her go alone."

"Will they come back here when Jordan is released?"

"I don't know anything yet."

"Well, keep me posted. I just wanted to check on you guys."

"Glad you did. Thanks, Dad. I'll text you and Finn when I know what's up."

"Sounds good. Love you, buddy."

"Love you, too."

Riley returned to his book and was two chapters in when Nikki reappeared, seeming hesitant. "How's she doing?" he asked.

"Better. They're going to release her today."

"That's great news. Are you bringing her home to Gansett?"

Her devastated expression stopped his heart. "She wants to go to LA."

A sinking sensation, the likes of which he'd never experienced so profoundly, overtook him as her words registered. She wasn't coming back to Gansett. Not now anyway. Her sister would need someone with her while she recovered, and naturally, Nikki would want to be that person.

"I'll be back as soon as she's on her feet again. I promise." Her expressive eyes begged him to understand what she had to do.

Riley forced a smile even as something inside him broke at the thought of being separated from her for who knew how long. "I'll hold you to that."

Three hours later, Riley took off on a flight to Providence while

Zane's plane took Nikki and Jordan to LA. He'd barely managed to get a quick kiss goodbye from Nikki before she ran off to see to the details of getting Jordan home. She'd promised to text him as soon as they landed.

As the plane gained altitude, Riley had the worst feeling that he'd made a terrible mistake by not staying with her. But he had a job and a life to get back to, not that his life on Gansett would be all that appealing without Nikki. The time they'd spent together made up the best days of his life. What would he do if she never came back? He'd go after her. That's what he'd do. No matter what, he couldn't let her get away a second time, not before they had a chance to see what might be possible.

ON THE MOST EXCITING day of her life, Abby McCarthy woke with a stuffed head, scratchy throat and the starting of a cough. Refusing to let anything as pedestrian as a common cold ruin this day, she took cold meds and was sitting next to Adam in his car as they waited to drive onto the nine-o'clock ferry. The day was blustery and stormy, and normally, Abby wouldn't go near the ferry on a day that promised a rough ride. Today, she barely noticed the whitecaps or the waves crashing against the South Harbor jetty.

An infant car seat they'd borrowed from Laura, who had three of them, was mounted in the backseat. They had spent two hours online yesterday ordering everything they needed for the baby and would make do with borrowed items until their delivery arrived. With Adam's siblings and cousins having babies one right after the other, they had most of what they needed. And, if necessary, they could improvise.

After the word got out about the baby, congratulatory texts full of ideas and suggestions had come flooding in. For example, Maddie's sister, Tiffany, had told them to use a dresser drawer until they had a bassinette.

Adam had referred to that as "good old Yankee ingenuity."

"What're you thinking about over there?" he asked.

"Yankee ingenuity."

"The dresser drawer idea is brilliant."

"Even if it's not how I pictured bringing home a baby, it is a pretty good idea."

"It doesn't have to be perfect, Abs. The only thing that matters is we already love him. He's not going to remember that we brought him home to a dresser drawer."

"True."

He reached for her hand and held on tight until he had to let go to back the car onto the ferry. She was always glad that he was the one to do that, as she was sure she'd drive the car right into the harbor if she had to do it.

They were seated in one of the passenger cabins when Adam took a call from his father, putting it on speaker so Abby could hear, too. "Hey, Gramps, how's it going?"

"*Daddy!* Where are you guys?"

"On the ferry and getting ready to leave."

"Mom and I could not be more thrilled for both of you."

"Thanks, Dad. We're pretty thrilled, too."

"We can't wait to see pictures and to hear his name."

"We'll send both as soon as we can."

"We'll be waiting. Love you guys. We're so, so happy for you."

"Thanks, Dad. We love you, too. We'll text pictures." Adam ended the call and stashed the phone in his pocket. "I think he might be as excited as we are."

"I'm not surprised. That's how he is."

"I got a text from Ned, too, letting me know that he couldn't be happier for us."

"Our son will be surrounded by more love—and grandparents—than he knows what to do with."

"And cousins. Lots and lots of cousins."

"They'll keep him from being a lonely only child."

"He'll never be lonely in this family."

"Aye, there're the happy parents," Seamus O'Grady said in his lilting Irish brogue. "We're all so delighted for you both."

"Thanks, Seamus." Adam shook Seamus's hand. "We're a little excited, to put it mildly."

"I can only imagine. I just want to say…" He paused, seeming to choose his words carefully. "Despite how it transpired, becoming a parent was one of the greatest things to ever happen to me. I have a feeling it will be for you two as well."

Adam and Abby both stood to hug Seamus. He and his wife, Carolina, had taken in two young boys after their mother passed away.

"Thank you," Abby said, dabbing at tears. "We so appreciate all the support we've been getting."

"It might be a little tossy out there today, but we'll get you to your wee one safely. Don't worry."

"We're in good hands with you at the helm," Adam said.

"See you on the other side."

After a long blow of the horn, the ferry departed from its South Harbor berth a few minutes later. Once outside the breakwater, the ferry bobbed and weaved, cresting the waves and then sliding into the trough in a stomach-turning drop.

"You okay?" Adam asked.

"Yep. I've got my eyes on the prize." Glancing at him, she said, "Remember the last time we shared a rough ferry ride?"

His grin lit up his sinfully handsome face. "When you were drunk and swearing off men? How could I forget it? That day changed my life forever."

"I was *tipsy*, not drunk."

"Whatever you say."

"That day changed my life forever, too. Sometimes I wonder what would've happened if I'd taken an earlier boat or you'd taken a later one."

"Thank goodness we ended up on the same boat."

Resting her head on his shoulder, she held on tight to his hand as the seas seemed to get rougher the farther away from the island they got. "I found you when I was at the end of my rope when it came to men and romance and all the nonsense that went along with it."

"I was right there at the end of the rope with you. Perfect timing."

"This feels like perfect timing with Liam, too. Nothing is working on the medical front, so now we have a chance to be parents another way."

"It is perfect timing. He needs us. We need him. We've got this."

"You think so?" she asked, raising her head off his shoulder.

"I know so. We're going to be awesome parents."

"I sure hope you're right."

"When have you ever known me not to be?" he asked with that cocky McCarthy grin he shared with his father, uncles, brothers and cousins.

The hour-long ferry ride and the forty-five-minute drive to Providence seemed to take two days. When they finally arrived, Adam carried the car seat inside, where they were met with hugs from Maura, the social worker who'd been to visit their home on Gansett Island and had walked them through the reams of paperwork involved in the application.

"Congratulations, Mom and Dad," Maura said, smiling.

"Thank you so much," Abby said. "When can we meet him?"

"I just need a few final signatures, and then I'll take you to see him."

They signed the forms and waited while Maura notarized them and made copies for the file she handed them. She'd explained that it would take six months for the adoption to be finalized, and they would be notified of a court date in the next few weeks.

"Are we allowed to know about his biological parents?"

"They're a teenage couple unequipped to care for him, but they want you to know they love him very much. This was a difficult decision for them, but they believe it's the right thing."

"They aren't going to change their minds, are they?" Adam asked, giving voice to their greatest fear.

"I have no way to know that for sure, but I don't believe that's a concern in this case. You're aware of the six-week period during which the biological parents can change their minds. If you'd prefer for us to care for him until then, we can do that. We've had other adoptive parents do that so there'd be no chance of them getting attached before the six weeks are up."

Filled with despair at the thought of that scenario playing out, Abby glanced at Adam and noticed tension in the set of his jaw. He didn't like the thought of that any more than she did.

"What do you want to do?" he asked her.

The thought of going home without their baby was unimaginable after the excitement of the past few days. "I'm willing to risk it if you are."

He nodded. "Whatever you want is what I want."

Even knowing they could be setting themselves up for disaster, Abby wanted to meet her son.

Adam took her hand and held on tight as they followed Maura to a conference room, where another member of the agency staff was waiting with the baby.

Abby took one look at the tiny bundle, wrapped in a striped receiving blanket and wearing an oatmeal-colored knit cap on his tiny head, and fell in love with his scrunched little face. Later, she wouldn't have been able to describe the woman who put the baby into her arms. From the second she set eyes on his little red face, she couldn't see anything but him—and his father, who put his arms around her as tears ran down his face.

"Hi there," Adam whispered, running a fingertip gently over the baby's cheek.

His tone perfectly matched the way she felt—*awestruck*.

"He's so beautiful." Abby raised the cap to reveal a thatch of dark hair. "He even has dark hair like we do." She had no idea how long they were in that conference room, staring and touching and drinking in the sight of the baby they had longed for. When she thought back to that day, it would be a blur. The only thing she would clearly remember was his face. Liam's face, and his big gray eyes looking up at her with questions and curiosity and wisdom.

Adam took a selfie of the three of them and sent a quick text to his family and Abby's, introducing them to Liam Callahan McCarthy. His phone began chiming with responses, but he tucked it into his pocket. They had better things to do than respond to texts.

"Do we really get to take him?" Abby asked Maura without taking her gaze off the baby. A feeling of disbelief continued to envelop her. Was this really happening? Would she wake up to find it had all been a lovely dream?

"You get to take him and keep him," Maura said, amused by the questions. "Congratulations to the new family."

"Thank you so much for everything you did for us, Maura," Adam said.

"It's been a pleasure to help make your family complete. We'll be checking in with you, and we're required to do two more home inspections before the adoption is final. I'll call you next week to schedule them. According to the chart, he's been fed and changed, so he should be in good shape for the journey home to the island."

"Well, here goes nothing," Adam said with a nervous laugh.

Abby's usually calm, cool and competent husband was anything but as he took the baby from her and placed him in the carrier.

Working together, they made several attempts before they had him properly strapped in. The baby didn't seem to mind that they had no idea what they were doing.

Abby sat in the backseat with the baby while Adam drove them back to the ferry. She kept waiting for the baby to get fussy, but he seemed content to watch the world go by. He was a trouper all the way to the island. Whereas the high seas made her feel queasy, the motion lulled Liam to sleep. He snoozed on his mother's shoulder for most of the ride home.

"This wasn't how I pictured it happening," she said to Adam, "but I can't imagine anything more exciting than this day has been."

"I couldn't agree more. Best day of our lives."

"Tied for first with that other day on the ferry."

He leaned over the baby to kiss her. "I'll give you that."

CHAPTER 24

For two weeks after Riley got back from North Carolina, he did nothing but work—all day at the Wayfarer and every evening at Eastward Look. On the second day after Adam and Abby brought home their new son, Riley stopped by after work to visit his new baby cousin, who was settling into his new home. His parents were tired but elated, and their joy had only made Riley's discontent more profound. He kept the kitchen project moving forward in Nikki's absence, hoping it would make her happy to return to an almost-renovated kitchen. He was leaving some of everything for her to do, since she'd wanted to learn how to do it. Some nights, Finn helped him, but most of the time, he worked by himself.

Having something to do every waking minute kept him from going crazy wondering when he might see her again.

They texted frequently and talked every day, but she never said anything about returning to the island, and he didn't want to make things more difficult for her by asking questions.

So while she took care of Jordan in Los Angeles, Riley went slowly insane on Gansett Island. He worked until he couldn't stay awake another minute and then stumbled to the sofa most nights and crashed until the morning, when he would start the cycle over again.

He'd tried to sleep in Nikki's bed one night, but the scent of her shampoo on the pillowcase and the memories of the nights they'd spent there together had been too much for him to handle.

What if she never came back? What if the time they'd already had was all they'd ever get? How would he survive having had her and then losing her? He wouldn't. It was that simple. If she didn't come home soon, he'd go to her.

Of course, those who knew him best were tuned in to the fact that he was a hot mess. They gave him as much space as they could, but Mac called him aside at the end of the second week.

"Your friend Nikki who you recommended for the manager's job. What's her story?"

"I… I'm not sure."

"I'm ready to hire someone, and you recommended her, so I wanted to give her a shot. Is she coming back?"

"I don't know that either."

Mac gave him a knowing look. "Is this why you've been such a gluebag at work lately?"

Riley shrugged. What did his cousin want him to say? He wasn't about to admit to being a heartbroken fool.

"It's clear to everyone that your head's not in the game. I can't have that, Riley. That's when people get hurt. Take the weekend and get it together. Come back Monday ready to focus."

"I will," Riley muttered. "Sorry."

"You don't have to be sorry." Mac squeezed his shoulder. "I've been where you are when I was first with Maddie, and it totally blows."

"Yeah, it does. I feel like I'm losing my mind."

"Go after her, then. Do what you've got to do, Riley. No offense, but you're not much good to me in your current condition."

"I know. I really am sorry. I'll get it together. After the wedding this weekend, I'll figure out what I'm going to do."

"Let me know what you decide, and ask her to get in touch with me if she's still interested in the job."

"I will. Thanks, Mac."

"We'll have some fun tonight. Blow off some steam. It'll be good for everyone. The winters are way too long around here."

"Definitely. I'll see you later."

"We'll be there."

The guys were taking over Mario's to celebrate Kevin's wedding, which was the next day.

"What was that about?" Finn asked when Riley rejoined him.

"Nothing."

"Hopefully he was telling you to get your head out of your ass."

"He didn't use those exact words."

Finn laughed. "But the message was the same. Check out this text I just got from Clint." He held up his phone. "He sent it to you, too."

You two are killing me. Would love to have you back, but since I haven't heard from you, I've got to move on. Pulling the trigger on some new hires. Let me know if you ever get back this way.

"To translate—we're now officially stuck here for the time being," Finn said, his voice echoing in the cavernous building.

Being "stuck" on the island didn't look as good to Riley as it would have a few short weeks ago. "We need to finish what we started here anyway. Then we can move on."

Finn released a deep sigh. "Missy's going to lose her shit when I tell her I'm here until May, possibly June."

"Missy needs to move on the same way Clint did."

"Try telling her that."

"Maybe you should tell her exactly that."

"Eh," Finn said. "You know how I hate to burn a bridge."

Rolling his eyes, Riley said, "That's a bridge you should've blown up a long time ago." They parted company a short time later to go home and clean up for the party. Since he'd been more or less living at Eastward Look while he worked on the renovations, he went there instead of the house he shared with Finn. He felt closer to Nikki when he was at the house she loved so much.

On the way, he stopped to buy a six-pack of beer and a bag of ice for the cooler he'd brought to the house. At the front door, he punched in the four-digit code Nikki had told him was her birthday—

and Jordan's. In the foyer, he took off his dirty work boots and hung up his coat, yearning to see her coming down the stairs, dark hair piled on top of her head, wearing the yoga pants and T-shirt she called her "work clothes" and brimming with excitement to see him. But the house was silent and empty, devoid of life without her there to make it a home.

He ached for her. Taking one of the beers to the sofa, he put his feet up on the coffee table and leaned his head back, exhausted in more ways than one. His phone vibrated with a new text from his uncle Frank, confirming the time of the party.

Riley replied to Frank and then opened a new text to Nikki, whom he hadn't heard from since yesterday. For a long time, he thought about what he could say that didn't include *I miss you, I love you, I need you, When are you coming back* and *Please tell me what's going to become of us*. Since he couldn't say any of that, he decided to go with something totally random.

What's your position on dogs?

His heart gave a happy jolt when he saw that she was responding.

In general, or as pets?

As pets.

She sent thumbs-up, heart and dog emojis.

With or without cats?

Without.

Good answer. Cats freak me out. They know too much.

True. How was work?

Fine. Glad it's Friday.

Is everyone excited about the wedding?

Yeah. Everyone except me, he wanted to say but didn't. The last thing he wanted to do was make her feel bad about how she'd left things with him.

What's your position on the color yellow?

In general, or in particular?

As in a paint color for the kitchen...

That'll look good.

Glad you agree.

His phone chimed with another text, this one stopping his heart.

What's your position on kids?

He told himself to stay cool and not read too much into an innocuous text, but that was a huge challenge when he wanted to read *everything* into that innocuous text. In an attempt to keep from overreacting, he went with witty over serious. *In general, or as pets?*

As pets. Definitely. She added a laughing emoji.

No objections but would prefer they not outnumber the adults in the house.

Good call.

The ache, which had been a dull roar in the area of his breastbone, intensified with every text they exchanged, making him wonder if missing someone could bring on a heart attack.

His phone lit up with a new text. *Have I told you twins run in my family? My dad is a twin and so are my mom's cousins. Although identical twins don't run in families. That's a biological anomaly.*

Are you warning me?

LOL, just providing full disclosure.

Because he couldn't go another second without hearing her voice or seeing her sweet face, he switched over to FaceTime. The room was dark enough that she wouldn't know he was at her place. He wanted to surprise her with the work he'd done to the kitchen in her absence. He hoped she'd come back at some point and he'd get the chance to show her.

She popped up on his screen looking pretty and fresh and sexier than any woman had a right to be. Everything about her did it for him and had from the first time he'd ever seen her.

"Hey," she said, smiling.

"Hey yourself. You look gorgeous."

"No, I don't. I'm all sweaty from yoga."

He held back a groan as images of her bending into interesting positions assailed him, making him instantly hard for her. It was all he could do not to beg her to come home to him.

"You look tired. Are you okay?"

"I've been better. You're way too far away."

"I know," she said, sighing. "Believe me, I feel the same way about you. Three thousand miles is way too far."

"How's it going?" he asked, because he couldn't *not* ask. He had to know.

"She's doing better every day. The broken arm is the biggest issue. Makes it hard for her to do the simplest things."

"Glad she's doing better."

"She talked to a lawyer today about filing for divorce, which is the first time she's actually used that word. Maybe now he really will be her *ex*-husband. Finally."

"That's a step in the right direction."

"I'm cautiously optimistic."

"How're you holding up?"

"I'm okay, but I miss you. I wish I was there slamming my sledge-hammer into walls, among other things." That last part was said in a sexy, suggestive tone that added to his torment.

"You have no idea how much I miss you and wish you were here." Filled with despair, he dropped his head into his hand. *Come back*, he wanted to say. *Please come back to me.* It took everything he had to hold in words that were burning to be said. "So Mac told me today he's ready to hire a manager for the Wayfarer. He wants to know if you're still interested."

"That would be a dream job. Could I let you know what's going on in a couple of days?"

"Sure." There was so much he wanted to say, but he couldn't. Not now. "I suppose I ought to grab a shower and get ready for my dad's party."

"Oh, that's tonight. I'm sure it'll be great. He'll appreciate the effort you and Finnbar put into it."

Nothing is great without you. Everything sucks. Every fucking thing. Even hearing you call my brother Finnbar hurts. "Yeah."

"Riley..."

He needed to go before he said something stupid or desperate. "I'll talk to you tomorrow? Not sure when. Things will be chaotic with the wedding."

"Text me when you can. I'm thinking of you. All the time."

It helped to know she was thinking of him, but still he ached. "Same, babe. I'll see you."

"Bye."

NIKKI PUT down her phone and leaned against the wide kitchen island. He looked awful, and that was entirely her fault. She'd left him with no idea of when they might see each other again. He'd been nothing but supportive and had never once made it about him, which she appreciated more than he'd ever know.

She'd never felt more torn between what she *needed* to do and what she *wanted* to do. And God, she wanted him with the kind of yearning she'd never imagined possible until she'd been forced to walk away from him to care for her injured sister.

Jordan came into the kitchen, stopping short at the sight of Nikki hunched over the island. "What's wrong?" she asked, her skin golden from an afternoon at the pool. The bruises on her face had faded to a pale yellow, and her lip was slowly healing.

"Nothing. You need something?"

"A refill." Using her broken arm to hold the insulated water bottle against her body, she used her other hand to unscrew the top. A week ago, she couldn't have managed that on her own. Using the filtered-water dispenser on the door of the fridge, she refilled the bottle. "You should go back to Gansett," she said, as if that wasn't the biggest thing she could say to her sister. "I can get by on my own."

"No need for you to get by on your own," Nikki said, forcing a smile.

Jordan leaned against the counter. "I know you're here because you're afraid I'll go back to him, but that's not going to happen."

"That's *not* why I'm here."

"It *is* why you're here, and I'm telling you, it's not necessary. I've deleted him, blocked him, and my new lawyer is requesting a restraining order, so he can't come anywhere near me."

Nikki stared at her sister in mute shock. She'd never seen or heard

Jordan so resolute about removing Zane from her life, even after the tape was released. Then, she'd just been flattened. Now, she was finally furious. Nikki wanted to sing hallelujah.

"I am *never* going back to him. I swear on my life. It's over."

For the first time, Nikki truly believed her.

"As much as I appreciate everything you've done, I can tell you're dying to be somewhere else. You should go, Nik. I promise I'll be okay without you."

"The press…"

"I hired a publicist today to deal with the inquiries. I told her to put out the word that I'm not talking about Zane now or ever. They'll go away when they realize they aren't going to get anything from me."

"Who are you, and what've you done with my sister?"

Jordan smiled. "Your clueless sister finally got a big, fat wakeup call in a hotel room in Charlotte. I'm only sorry it took me so long to figure out what you and everyone who loves me already knew."

"We only want what's best for you."

"Believe it or not, I want that, too. It'll take me a while to figure out what's best for me, but I'm determined to move past this and to be rid of him. I also made an appointment with Yvonne." Jordan referred to the therapist they'd seen during their parents' contentious divorce.

"I'm really, really proud of you," Nikki said softly.

"I don't deserve that. Not yet anyway, but I hope at some point, I'll deserve it."

"You do deserve it." Nikki went to her and hugged her, careful not to jar her injured arm. "I just want you to be safe and happy and loved."

"I want that, too." Jordan gave her a playful shove that ended the hug. "Go back to your boyfriend, Nik. You know you want to."

She wanted that more than anything, and now that Jordan was telling her to go, she felt excited again for the first time in weeks. "His dad is getting remarried tomorrow."

"If you get a flight out tonight, you can get there in time for the wedding. In fact, let me handle the arrangements for you for a change."

"I can get my own plane ticket."

"I want to do this for you. Please let me. You're always there for me when I need you, even if that means putting your own life on hold. From what you've told me about Riley, you have a real chance of happiness with him. The last thing I want is to stand in the way of that."

The thought of seeing Riley again—*soon*—filled her with the sort of joy she'd rarely experienced until she'd met him.

"Are you sure you'll be okay by yourself?"

"I'm positive."

"In that case, I'd be happy to let you send me back to Gansett."

CHAPTER 25

*R*iley forced himself to rally for his dad, who was on top of the world with happiness that gave Riley hope. It seemed like every guy in town had come out to celebrate Kevin, including Big Mac, Frank and Ned, along with Mac, Adam, Shane and Grant, who'd flown home with his wife, Stephanie, from LA for the wedding. In addition, Luke Harris was there, along with Blaine Taylor, Seamus O'Grady, Owen Lawry, Joe Cantrell, David Lawrence, Quinn and Jared James, Alex and Paul Martinez, Niall Fitzgerald, Shannon O'Grady and Chelsea's brother, Andrew Rose.

Mario's served up an Italian buffet that Riley and Finn had arranged in advance, along with an endless flow of beer and whiskey.

After everyone had eaten and a dozen pitchers of beer had been consumed, Riley stood with Finn and whistled to get everyone's attention.

As he sat among the men he loved best in the world, Kevin's broad smile lit up his handsome face. Not that long ago, Riley had wondered if his father would ever smile again. Then he'd met Chelsea.

"As the best men, it's our job to make sure Dad gets hammered tonight, so someone give him a refill," Riley said.

Kevin put his hand over his glass. "If I go home hammered, Chelsea will leave me. That might make for a crappy wedding."

His comments were met with raucous laughter from the unruly group.

"Dad, Finn and I are happy for you and Chelsea and looking forward to being big brothers to our new baby brother or sister. However, we would like to say for the record that we think it's extremely unfair that you're getting a second wife and family when some of us still haven't had a first one."

Wild whoops and hollers followed the comment, especially from Kevin.

"That said, we love you, and we wish you and Chelsea all the best. To Kevin!"

"Good job," Finn said. "And excellent point."

Riley toasted his brother. Maybe his father wasn't allowed to get wasted, but there was nothing stopping him. Whatever it took to dull the relentless ache that refused to let up.

HUNGOVER AND GROUCHY after overindulging the night before, Riley showered, shaved and prepared to put on the dark suit his dad had bought for him on the mainland. Kevin had refused the reimbursement Riley had offered, saying it was his fault Riley had needed the suit in the first place.

His cell phone rang while he was wiping the last of the shaving cream from his face. Hoping it was Nikki, he saw MOM on the screen. *Uh-oh.* "Hey," he said, "what's up?"

"I haven't talked to you in a couple of weeks, so I figured I'd check in."

On Dad's wedding day, he wanted to ask but didn't. "We've been working a lot on the new Wayfarer. Trying to get it done for the season. It's going to be close."

"Riley…"

"What do you want to know, Mom?" he asked, resigned to talking about it even when he really didn't want to."

"I'm just…" She sounded weepy and sad. "I heard your dad is getting married."

"Yes, in about two hours." *This is what you wanted!* Riley loved his mother. She'd been an awesome, involved, hands-on mom to him and Finn, but he wasn't prepared to be her counselor on the day his father was getting remarried. "In fact, I need to run. I'm supposed to be at Dad's in twenty minutes."

"I won't keep you, then. Please tell your father… Tell him I send my best wishes."

"I will."

"Love you, Ri."

"Love you, too, Mom." Riley ended the call and groaned. God, that'd been awkward. What did she want him to say? She'd been the one to end the marriage. What had she expected his dad to do? Sit around and feel sorry for himself for the rest of his life? The guy his mother had been involved with hadn't worked out. No doubt she had regrets, but she'd made her own decisions, and now she had to face the consequences.

He didn't want to think about that today, not when his dad deserved his full focus and support. On the way to pick up his dad, he decided he'd share his mother's good wishes after the wedding and not before. There was no need to bring Kevin's ex-wife into this day and resurrect old hurts when Kevin was about to commit to a new life with Chelsea.

Riley sure wished Nikki could be there to help him celebrate. Even a joyful event like his dad's wedding was something to be endured rather than enjoyed without her there to share in it with him. That was what it had come to. He was fully aware that he couldn't continue in this state of agonizing limbo. Later on, he'd talk to Mac about taking a few days off to go see Nikki and hopefully talk her into coming home. He had no desire to move across the country, but he would if it meant he got to be with her. Something had to give before he succeeded in nail-gunning his own hand—or someone else's—to a wall in his utter distraction.

When Riley pulled into the driveway at the small house Kevin shared with Chelsea, his dad came running out, sporting a big, dopey grin and a blue plaid bow tie. "It's today!"

"Get in and shut the door. You're freezing me out."

"I can see you're in your usual festive mood of late."

"I'm hungover."

"And whose fault is that?"

"Yours. If you weren't getting married, I wouldn't have been at a bachelor party last night."

Kevin laughed. "Your logic is as screwed up as the rest of you." He glanced over at Riley. "What can I do for you, son?"

"Nothing. Don't worry about me. This is your big day."

"I will always worry about you, and I've tried to give you space the last couple of weeks, but it isn't easy for me to see you obviously suffering."

"I'm okay. I swear. Today is your day and Chelsea's. Don't make it about me."

"Do you love her, Ri?"

The question hit him like a sharp arrow to the heart. "Yeah."

"Then go after her."

"I'm going to. Tomorrow." Even waiting one more day to see her was apt to kill him.

Kevin nodded in approval. "Good. That's the right thing to do. If you didn't, you'd always wonder what might've been. I don't want you to have regrets."

"I already do. But it's nothing that can't be fixed." At least he hoped that was still the case. He drove Kevin to Big Mac and Linda's to hang out before they went down the hill to the hotel for the wedding. Uncle Frank was already there with his fiancée, Betsy Jacobson, who hugged Kevin.

"We're so happy for you guys," Betsy said.

"Thank you," Kevin said, accepting hugs from Big Mac, Linda and Frank.

"Champagne for everyone," Linda said. "Let's get this party started!"

"Where's Finn?" Riley asked.

"Here I am," his brother said as he came in, shedding his coat and accepting the glass of champagne their aunt handed him.

Linda raised her glass to Kevin. "Here's to true love and happily ever after."

"I will happily drink to that," Kevin said.

Riley smiled as he touched his glass to his dad's, determined to celebrate his father's joy even as his own heart ached.

The bride was stunning in a sexy white dress and her long, curly blonde hair contained in a sleek updo. Carrying a bouquet of white roses and lilies, Chelsea came toward them on the arm of her brother, glowing with happiness and love for Kevin, who had been brought to tears by the sight of his lovely bride. They exchanged heartfelt vows in front of a roaring fire in the great room of McCarthy's Gansett Island Inn.

Standing between his dad and brother, Riley was oddly emotional watching the bride and groom exchange vows and pledge their lives and their love to each other.

Uncle Frank, a retired superior court judge, presided over the nuptials and had the assembled family members and friends laughing one minute and crying the next.

"Kevin, Chelsea," Frank said, "anyone who has spent even five minutes in your presence can attest to the love and commitment you have for each other. It is my great honor as Kevin's older and wiser brother to pronounce you husband and wife. Kev, you may kiss your bride."

As Kevin raised his hands to Chelsea's face to kiss her, the main door opened, bringing with it a whoosh of cold air.

Riley looked to see who it was and nearly stopped breathing when he saw Nikki. For a second, he thought he might've conjured her through sheer desire to see her, but no, it was really her, and his entire family stood between them as Kevin and Chelsea accepted congratulations and heartfelt best wishes from their guests.

"Uh, bro," Finn said. "Nicholas is back."

"Do you honestly think I need you to tell me that?"

Finn busted up laughing. "Want me to help you get to her?"

"Hell yes, and use all the dirty tricks we learned playing hockey."

"I'm on it. Follow me." Finn blazed a path through the crowd, tossing the occasional elbow as needed.

Riley followed him, his heart beating so hard and so fast, he feared he would pass out before he got to her.

Seeming to realize something was up, the crowd parted to let them through.

Finn got to her first. "Nicholas, I'm so happy to see you. You have no idea what I've been through with this one since you left."

"Nice to see you, Finnbar." She removed her coat and handed it to Finn.

In one quick second, Riley took in the sight of her, recording each detail—clingy black dress, sexy-as-fuck heels, spiral curls, lipstick. Christ have mercy, she was hot, and he loved her madly. Riley pushed his brother aside and wrapped his arms around her, relief pulsing through him like an extra heartbeat. As he breathed in her familiar scent, the tightness in his chest loosened, and the ache finally receded. "What're you doing here?"

"I hoped it would be okay if I crashed."

"You were invited, but that's not what I meant. What're you doing *here*? On Gansett? Where's Jordan?"

She looked up at him with those bottomless brown eyes that had haunted his dreams over the torturous weeks without her. "Jordan is in LA figuring out the next steps in her life, and I'm here on Gansett."

"Why?" he asked, though he suspected he already knew. He wanted to hear her say it.

"Because you're here."

"I've never been so happy to see anyone in my entire life," Riley said.

"Neither have I."

He took her by the hand and led her into his aunt Linda's office, closing the door behind him so he could kiss her the way he was dying to without his entire family watching. After the longest, sexiest, deepest kiss of his life, he said, "You can't ever leave me again. I was totally fine before I had you, but I'm not fine at all without you. I almost went crazy."

She clung to him, kissing his face and neck. "I was just as crazy without you, and I don't want to be anywhere but where you are."

"Love you so much, Nik," he whispered, his voice thick with emotion.

"I love you just as much, Riley."

They were the best words he'd ever heard.

No one could party like the McCarthys, even in the dead of winter. The champagne flowed as a delicious dinner of prime rib and lobster was served. As the waitstaff cleared the tables, Riley stood up and tapped his knife against a crystal glass to get everyone's attention.

"My co-best man and I would like to thank everyone for being here tonight to help us welcome Chelsea into the McCarthy family. Chelsea, you've been around us long enough to be fully aware of what you're getting into."

Chelsea nodded and laughed. "I'm not scared."

"She hasn't seen our full potential yet," Mac said, rubbing his hands together. "Now that they're married, it's back to business as usual."

Big Mac gave his oldest son a smack upside the head that brought down the house.

"As I was saying," Riley continued, "Finn and I want to be the first to welcome you to the family and apologize in advance for whatever might happen next."

"Got it," Chelsea said, giving him a thumbs-up.

Kevin smiled and kissed her.

With Nikki sitting next to him and gripping his hand under the table throughout dinner, Riley had finally been able to relax and enjoy the wedding, even if he burned to get her alone. Soon enough, he'd told himself. Soon enough.

"I just want to say that it's obvious to me and Finn and everyone else in this room that we're witnessing true love here, and true love is so hard to find and even harder to hold on to." Glancing down at Nikki for a second, he said, "When you find it, you should hold on to it with everything you have, the way Dad and Chelsea have. I love you both and wish you a long and happy life together. Finn, your turn, and I apologize in advance for whatever he says."

Riley sat, put his arm around Nikki and kissed her.

"Dad and Chelsea," Finn said, "I'm not the sickening romantic that my brother has become since Nicholas came along, but let me just add that you guys are a great couple, and we love you both. Congratulations and best wishes for many years of happiness. To Kevin and Chelsea."

"I'm going to shoot him," Riley muttered.

"Don't do that," Nikki said. "I've got better things to do than bail you out of jail."

"Like what?" he asked.

Whispering in his ear, she said, "You."

"Don't do that to me when we can't be alone for hours."

She flashed a coy grin that made him want to say to hell with the fucking wedding. But he couldn't do that when the groom was his dad and he was one of the best men.

Owen invited the bride and groom to the dance floor and, with Niall's help, played a cool, sultry acoustic version of "Beginnings" by Chicago, one of Kevin's favorite songs.

"God, this song," Finn said. "How many millions of times did we hear this as kids?"

"Ten million," Riley said. "Easily."

"I've never heard it," Nikki said.

"Seriously?" Finn said. "Then you can't marry into the family. Sorry."

"Finn!" Riley said.

Finn busted up laughing. "Relax, bro. For some reason, she totally digs you. Not even I can scare her off."

"That's right," Nikki said. "So go away and leave us alone."

"You're the best girlfriend I've ever had," Riley said.

"She's the *only* girlfriend you've ever had."

Finn's life was saved by Adam and Abby, who were walking baby Liam and stopped by to say hello.

"Nikki, this is my new cousin Liam, and you remember his parents, Adam and Abby."

"Congratulations," Nikki said, giving the baby a longing glance. "He's beautiful."

"We're quite smitten," Abby said.

"Looks like you guys are figuring out the parent gig," Riley said.

"Slowly but surely," Abby said. "Good thing Liam doesn't know we're clueless."

"You know what the best part of adopting is?" Adam asked, gazing at his son with obvious adoration.

"What's that?" Riley asked.

"No waiting six weeks after the birth to get *back in the saddle*," Adam said with a dirty grin for his wife.

While Finn, Riley and Nikki laughed, Abby slugged his arm. "*Adam!* Shut up!" To Nikki, she said, "I apologize for him."

"No need," Nikki said. "That was funny."

"Nothing funny about it," Adam said, waggling his brows.

Abby glowered at her husband. "On that note, it's time to get Liam home to bed," Abby said.

"She said *bed*," Adam said.

Ignoring him, Abby said, "Please give your dad and Chelsea our best."

The bride and groom were completely caught up in each other.

"Will do," Riley said.

"They're so cute," Nikki said. "And that baby is adorable."

"They were told they couldn't have children and decided to adopt. They got really lucky when another couple couldn't take the baby."

"I'm so glad it worked out for them."

"Me, too. They're a great couple." Lowering his voice, he said, "Here's a little family gossip for you. Long before Abby was with Adam, she dated his brother Grant."

"Which one is Grant?"

Riley pointed him out. "He and his wife, Steph, spend the winters in LA. They came home for the wedding."

"How did he feel about his brother dating his ex?"

"He was so happy with Steph by then that he didn't mind. It's all ancient history now."

"How is Shane doing?"

Riley looked over to where Shane was seated at a table with Katie, Laura, Frank, Betsy, Joe and Janey. "He seems okay. I'm sure Courtney's death is still weighing heavily on his mind, but we've been rallying around him and making sure he stays focused on the present."

"You have a really great family, Riley. I hope you know how lucky you are."

"I do." Fortified by champagne and the thrill of having her back by his side, he took it a daring step further. "Maybe someday you'll be a McCarthy, too."

Smiling, she said, "Wouldn't that be something?"

He'd gone from the lowest of lows to the highest of highs, and all it had taken was having her walk in the door. "Have you been to the house yet?"

She shook her head. "Jordan got me a private flight straight to the island. There was a delay leaving LA, which is what made me late. I came right here from the airport."

"I'm glad you haven't been there yet. I've got something I want to show you." He leaned in and kissed her, lingering despite the roomful of people around them. His love had come home. Nothing else mattered.

EPILOGUE

*W*ith almost everyone staying at the hotel that night, it wasn't easy to sneak out, but once his father and Chelsea left at eleven, Riley decided to make his move. He'd quit drinking hours ago so he could drive them home. He and Nikki donned coats, said their goodbyes and headed out into icy, windy darkness.

Riley bundled her into his truck and ran around to the driver's side. "I still can't believe you're back in my truck where you belong. I'm not going to wake up and realize I dreamed this, am I?"

"I'm really here, and I'm staying this time. I talked to Mac about the job, and he said it's mine if I want it."

"And do you?"

"I really do. I'd love to be part of getting the Wayfarer back up and running again."

He cranked the heat and reached for her, crushing his mouth to hers. Kissing her felt as natural to him as breathing. He couldn't get enough. "We're going to spend the rest of the weekend in bed. Just so you know."

"Thanks for the warning, but that works for me."

Riley forced himself to let her go, to focus on driving when all he wanted was more of her. Once they were on their way to Eastward Look, he reached for her hand, loving the way her fingers wrapped around his. "I was going to come get you tomorrow."

"Were you?"

"Yep. Ask my dad. I told him that earlier."

She squeezed his hand. "I believe you, and I would've been really glad to see you."

By the time they pulled into the driveway at Eastward Look, the sexual tension in the car was so thick, it threatened to consume him. He wondered if she had any idea how completely she owned him or how desperately he wanted her.

He released her hand so they could get out of the truck and then put his arm around her so she wouldn't trip in those crazy-ass heels. When she teetered precariously, he scooped her up and carried her the rest of the way.

Her laughter echoed through the vast yard and filled him with joy. There was simply no other word to describe it.

"Get the doors," he said.

She punched in the code, and when they were inside, he put her down only long enough to remove their coats before picking her up again.

"Riley! I can walk."

"But this is so much better. Hold on to me." He could tell he surprised her when he walked toward the kitchen rather than heading straight upstairs. "Get the light."

She flipped the switch and gasped at the sight of the new white cabinets, half-finished subway tile backsplash and silvery-white quartz countertop, with one piece still waiting to be installed by her. "Riley... Oh my God! You did all this?"

"With a little help from Finn. Are you happy with it?"

"I'm *thrilled*! I can't believe you did this."

"I hoped you wouldn't mind if I kept going. I didn't know how long you'd be gone."

"Of course I don't mind. But I still want you to show me how to do it all."

"I left most of the tile and finish work for you to do. I'll teach you anything you want to know, but not tonight."

"Why?" she asked, the picture of innocence. "Is there something else you'd rather do tonight?"

Nodding, he kissed her as he carried her upstairs, breaking the kiss only to put her down next to the bed.

She slid her hands into his suit coat and wrapped her arms around his waist. "In case I forgot to mention it, the suit is hot as hell."

"It's nowhere near as hot as those heels are."

"You like them?"

"Whimper." He kissed her again, giving her deep thrusts of his tongue that she answered enthusiastically. They began pulling at clothing, laughing when her dress got stuck halfway off before clearing her head.

While she frantically freed buttons on his shirt, Riley feasted his eyes on the sight of sexy, lacy black underwear.

"Focus, Riley. The goal is naked here."

"I'm focused." He nuzzled the tops of her breasts, which spilled out of the cups of her bra. "I'm very, *very* focused."

Giggling, she tugged on his belt and nearly unmanned him in her efforts to get him out of his pants.

"Go easy down there, tiger, or this'll be over before it starts."

"Then help me!"

"Gladly." He whipped off his pants and boxer briefs and followed her into bed, coming down on top of her lush softness and breathing in the intoxicating scent of her. "I'll remember three very distinct things about my father's wedding," he said as he kissed her neck.

"What three things?"

"One, that he and Chelsea are truly happy."

"Agreed."

"Two, that you came back to me."

"I couldn't stay away another minute. Missing you was killing me."

"Same. You've got me completely addicted to you."

With her hands on his face, she said, "What's the third thing you'll remember?"

"That the day my dad got married was the same day I knew for certain that I'm going to spend the rest of my life with you."

"Riley," she whispered.

"It might be too much, too soon, but all you had to do was walk into the room to make everything that was wrong right again."

"It's not too soon. I want the same thing you do. I want you and a life with you."

"Here on Gansett Island?"

She nodded. "This is our home. Gansett Island and Eastward Look are home."

"Gansett, Eastward Look and *you* are home. Home is nothing without you, sweetheart."

Nikki wrapped her arms around his neck and gasped as he entered her in one smooth thrust. "Yes, Riley. God, *yes*. I missed you so much."

"Missed you, too. But now you're back, and I'm never letting you go again."

"That's more than fine with me."

Keep reading for A Gansett Island Christmas, a novella that takes place during a snowstorm that might keep the McCarthy family from being able to spend the holidays together.

A GANSETT ISLAND CHRISTMAS

*J*aney Cantrell stood in the window and watched the snow come down in a total whiteout. She wanted to scream at the weather gods—not today! Not on Christmas! She looked forward to this day all year, and the snow was scuttling her plans. This would be the first Christmas of her life that she didn't spend with her parents and siblings. The thought of missing out on the McCarthy family madness made her want to cry.

Right away she felt silly for being sad. What did she have to be sad about? She had her wonderful husband, Joe, as well as their children, P.J. and Vivienne, who would celebrate her first Christmas. She had what she needed.

Except...

Evan and Grace were home, and Stephanie and Grant were back from a few weeks on the west coast...

Janey hadn't gotten the chance to see any of them yet. Plus, her brother Mac's baby son Malcolm the third—another Mac McCarthy, God help them all—would celebrate his first Christmas today, too. Janey wanted photos of him with Viv to commemorate the day.

She shook her fist at Mother Nature. As New Englanders, they hoped every year for a white Christmas, but no one asked for a *blizzard* on Christmas!

"What's the matter, babe?" Joe asked as he joined her at the window, taking a good look at the snow that had shut down the ferries for the day. "It sure is pretty."

"No, it isn't!"

"Um, yes, it is, and I thought you loved snow."

"I do love snow, but not when it ruins my Christmas."

"Aww, is my baby sad that she can't be with her mommy and daddy and her new sister and big mean brothers today?"

"Yes! I've never had a Christmas without them, and I don't want to start now."

"So what you're saying is that your wonderful husband and the two beautiful children he's blessed you with aren't enough for you?"

"Yes, that's exactly what I'm saying."

Joe laughed. "You could at least *try* to spare my feelings."

"Oh stop. You're as bummed as I am that we won't get to see the family today."

"You're right. I am, but we'll still have a nice day together." He put his arms around her. "The kids are down for naps. We can snuggle in front of the fire. It'll be great."

"No, it won't," she said, trying not to sound as whiney as she felt.

"Now, you're officially hurting my feelings. I'm very good at snuggling, as you well know."

"Yes, you are, but today I want my family. It's Christmas, Joseph. It's wrong that we're so close to them but can't see them."

"As much as I'd love for you to have everything you want for Christmas, there's no way I'm taking babies out in this. It's not safe to drive, Janey."

"I know!"

"Are you going to pout all day?"

"Not all day, but for a little while longer."

"I'll allow that." He tugged on her hand to lead her from the window. "But while you pout, I want my Christmas snuggle with my wife."

Janey followed him to the sofa and sat while he added wood to the fire. Outside the wind howled and the snow pinged against the windows. "It's only *two* miles."

"What if we get stuck? Then what?" He stood and came to sit next to her on the sofa. "You'll survive one Christmas without your family."

Evan and Grace, Adam and Abby and Grant and Steph would probably brave the roads because they didn't have babies to worry about. It would be so much fun! She wondered if Mac and Luke were as bummed as she was to be stuck at home with babies while everyone else got to go home for Christmas.

"Did you hear from your mom?" she asked Joe. "Did they make it to Ireland?"

"Safe and sound."

"Did the boys love the flight? They were so excited for their first plane ride."

"They did love it. Mom said they didn't want to sleep on the plane because they didn't want to miss anything."

"Caro and Seamus must be exhausted."

"She said they're hoping they can convince the boys to sleep for a while when they get to Seamus's mom's house."

"I hope so." Janey texted her brother Mac. *This weather sucks!*
I know, he replied.
Whose big idea was it to have babies?
Not mine, that's for sure.

Janey replied with laughing emojis. Her brother's aversion to babies being born on the island was well-known—and he had good reason with one chaotic delivery after another. She'd had Viv on the ferry, for crying out loud. Nothing ever went according to plan when it came to babies on Gansett Island.

What are you guys up to? Mac asked.
Joe wants to snuggle. Janey awaited his predictable reply.
Ewww. Gross.
Nothing gross about it...
Everything about that is gross.
What r u doing?

Walking the floor with Mac. He's cranky.

That's going around today.

Thomas is so excited to play in the snow. We told him he has to wait until it stops blizzarding.

That's not a word.

Did you get what I meant? If so, it's a word.

I'm going to snuggle now.

Barf.

"What's he barfing about?" Joe asked when he joined her on the sofa.

"Me snuggling with you."

"Nothing barfy about it."

"That's what I told him."

"Thank you for defending me, babe." He wrapped his arms around her. "Let's make out while we can."

"Don't you want your Christmas present?"

"Making out with you is all the present I need. Now kiss me."

"But I got you something cool."

Joe sighed. "Will it still be cool after you kiss me?"

Janey giggled at the pathetic face he made. "Yes, I suppose it will be."

"Then…"

"Oh, all right. If I must." Smiling, she laid her hand on his handsome face, which was even more so thanks to the stubble on his jaw, and kissed him.

"Mmm, more of that, please."

While her babies slept and the wind howled outside, Janey decided since she couldn't fight Mother Nature, she may as well enjoy the stolen interlude with her sexy husband. There were worst things that could happen on Christmas than having nothing better to do than make out with Joe Cantrell.

RED HAIR SPLAYED out on a white pillow was one of Luke Harris's favorite sights, especially on Christmas morning with the wind howling outside and baby Lily back to sleep after an early-morning feeding.

"Luke," Sydney said, gasping. "Do something."

"I am doing something. I'm doing *you*."

She laughed, which made her internal muscles clamp down on his cock.

He saw stars. There was nothing in this world he loved more than making love to his gorgeous, sexy wife.

"So we're just going to stay like this all day?"

"You got somewhere else to be?" God, he loved her. He loved their life and their little girl and the home they'd made together. When he thought of all the Christmases he'd spent alone, wishing for the things he had now... That seemed like another lifetime.

"No, but..." She squirmed, seeking relief he wasn't in the mood to give her. Not yet anyway.

"Relax, sweetheart."

"How am I supposed to relax when you're doing *that*?"

"What am I doing?"

"Nothing!"

He flexed his hips. "Feels like something to me."

Sydney's fingers dug into his back as her legs encircled his hips. "She's going to wake up, and won't you be sad then that you didn't take care of business while you could."

"Is that what this is? Business?"

"*Luke!*"

He laughed. How could he not? She was so damned cute and sexy and all his. The only girl he'd ever wanted. "Maybe we'll make a little brother or sister for Lily. Wouldn't that be a Christmas miracle?" They'd been having sex without protection for months, but so far, they hadn't succeeded in conceiving again. But they'd had a hell of a time trying.

"Can't talk right now. My husband is torturing me."

He nuzzled her neck, making sure his chest hair brushed against her breasts, which were extra sensitive from feeding Lily. "You love when your husband tortures you." Christmas was a tough day for her, a reminder of the husband and children she'd lost. His goal today was to keep her too busy to let the past intrude to make her sad. Plus, they were celebrating their anniversary, too.

She gasped. "Luke... *please...*"

He raised himself up on his arms and began to move. "Is this what my baby wants?"

"Yes," she said, eyes closed, lips parted. "Yes, yes, *yes.*"

Feeling her body tighten with impending release, he let himself go, losing himself in her and the magic they created together. He'd never experienced anything remotely like the way she made him feel, especially when she wrapped her arms around him and held him through the aftermath.

"That was mean," she said after a long silence.

He grunted out a laugh. "How do you figure? Didn't it end well?"

She poked his side. "How can you still be surprising me after all this time?"

"Baby, I have only *begun* to surprise you."

"That's what I'm afraid of. Now you've done it. I'm completely exhausted, and all I want to do is sleep."

"So sleep." He kissed her, lingering over the sweet taste of her lips. "I've got Lily."

"Mmm, I might take you up on that."

"We've got nowhere to go and nothing to do but relax."

"Are you sad to be missing Christmas with the McCarthy's?"

"Nah, it's okay. I had Christmas with them for years. Now I want to spend Christmas with my two best girls." He slid her hair through his fingers. "Are you missing your folks?"

"A little, but they're having fun in Wisconsin, and they'll be back tomorrow."

"If they can get here."

"True."

"So it's just you and me and Lily." He kissed her. "Best. Christmas. *Ever.*"

THE DAY BEGAN for Mac McCarthy at five a.m. when baby Mac decided he'd had enough sleep. Unfortunately, his parents did not agree, and were trying to keep their two older children asleep for another hour or two so their day wouldn't be a complete disaster.

Mac picked up the baby from the bassinette next to the bed he shared with Maddie and walked him to the window to check the weather.

As predicted, the blizzard had arrived overnight, and the wind was blowing so hard the snow came down sideways.

Trapped.

No grandparents to take turns with the baby.

No cousins to entertain Thomas and Hailey.

No one to cook them a delicious dinner.

No opportunity for him and his brothers to gang up on Janey.

Worst. Christmas. *Ever.*

As if he could read his father's thoughts, baby Mac patted his daddy's face with a chubby hand.

Mac nibbled on the baby's fist and got the deep belly laugh he loved so much. He went to enormous lengths to make his son laugh as frequently as possible just so he could hear that joyful sound.

"Are you trying to remind me to count my blessings, buddy?"

"Is he answering you?" Maddie asked.

"We have our own language, don't we, pal?" Mac asked the baby, who looked at him like he was crazy. "We don't understand why people are so excited about a white Christmas that ruins everyone's plans."

"You'll survive one Christmas without your mommy."

"I don't know if I will," Mac said, sitting on the bed.

"You're a grown up now, Mac. You have your own family. If we have to spend the holiday just the five of us, then so be it."

"Why do you have to be so mean to me?"

Maddie laughed, rolled her eyes at him and reached for baby Mac, bringing him to her breast to feed him.

Mac loved to watch her feed their babies. She was an amazing mother and wife, and he felt lucky every day to be taking this journey with her.

"Why don't you go back to sleep for a while?" she asked.

"I'm awake now. That ship has sailed."

"It's gonna be a long-ass day around here."

"Yep, and no grandparents to help. It's us versus them."

"And there're more of them than there are of us."

"Whose big idea was it to let them outnumber us?"

Maddie laughed and shook her head. "Not the best idea we ever had."

"I don't know about that." Mac smoothed his fingertip over the baby's foot. "This guy may turn out to be the best idea we ever had. How can we go wrong with another Mac McCarthy?"

"Is that a rhetorical question?"

"Come on, admit it. The world needs more Mac McCarthys."

"You're delusional."

Mac laughed. "You love me."

"For some reason, I really do."

"Will you take good care of me today, so I don't miss my mom too much?"

"Don't I take good care of you every day?"

"I'll need extra care today, especially at nap time."

"I see where this is going. You do realize that's how we ended up outnumbered around here, don't you?"

Mac nuzzled her neck and then kissed her. "It was so, *so* worth it."

Big Mac McCarthy stood at the big sliding doors that looked out over the deck and the Salt Pond below. Through the driving snow, he could just barely make out the marina that was boarded up for the off-season, and the hotel that was closed for the holiday. They had some bookings coming in later in the week, but for now, all was quiet in their waterfront fiefdom.

He drank from his mug of coffee and tried to shake off the morose mood that had descended upon him since waking to the raging blizzard that would keep the kids from coming home for the day. That was particularly vexing since all of them were close by, but the snow would leave them stranded.

Usually Big Mac loved snow. Today, not so much.

The thought of Christmas without his kids and grandkids made him sad and put a serious damper on his holiday spirit.

"Ugh," Linda said when she joined him downstairs and took a look at the weather. "What the heck am I going to do with all the food I bought for today?"

The lights flickered.

They held their breath while they waited to see if the power would go out.

It didn't, not yet anyway.

"Please tell me we have gas for the generator," she said.

"All set."

"I suppose we can postpone Christmas dinner to tomorrow or the next day."

Storms tended to settle in over Gansett Island, lasting for days sometimes. "Won't be the same without the kids underfoot." He still missed having little ones at home on Christmas morning. They'd grown up shockingly fast, and Christmas wasn't the same without them waking up at the crack of dawn to see what Santa had brought.

Those had been the best years, but these years, with their kids settled into happy relationships and five grandchildren—and counting—to spoil were pretty great, too. On days like today, his mind wandered back in time to when he and his brothers, Frank and Kevin, still lived at home with their parents.

His folks had been gone a long time now, but holidays always brought back fond memories of precious time with family.

The phone rang and Linda went to grab it. He heard her talking to his best buddy, Ned, about the weather.

"We'll miss you guys today," she said. "You, too. Here he is." She handed the phone to Big Mac.

"Hey," he said. "Merry Christmas."

"Ya don't sound too merry."

"Not gonna get to see my kids today. Bums me out."

"I hear ya. Not a holiday without the little ones."

"What're you guys doing?" Big Mac asked.

"Same as you. Poutin' about not gettin' ta see our babies."

"Damn snow."

"Thought ya loved it?"

"I do til it messes with my plans."

Ned laughed and then went silent for a few seconds. "What if…"

"What?"

"Nothin. Just an idea I had."

"What idea is that?"

"Let me think on it a little more, and I'll let ya know if I can make it happen," Ned said.

"What're you talking about, old man?"

"Gotta run. I'll call ya back later."

The line went dead, and Big Mac stared at the phone. "What the heck?"

"What's Ned up to?" Linda asked as she made a pot of coffee.

"Hell if I know. He's up to something, though."

Linda's cell phone made a sound he hadn't heard before. She picked it up to check it. "It's an alert from Blaine," she said of the Gansett Island police chief. "Asking people to stay off the roads today."

Big Mac sighed. If the police were asking people to stay home, that meant the roads were bad.

Then the lights flickered again, and this time the power went out.

"Christmas is doomed."

"Don't be silly," Linda said. "We have each other, a fridge full of good food and a generator. We'll be fine."

They would be fine, but the holiday wouldn't be the same without the kids.

"Wʜᴀᴛ ᴅᴏ you think you're doing?" Francine asked, following Ned to the mudroom where he donned his heaviest parka and pushed his feet into boots.

"I gots an idea."

"What kind of idea?"

He kissed her cheek. "The kind that's gonna save Christmas."

"You're not going out in this."

"I ain't goin' far, so don't worry."

"Ned, seriously, it's a blizzard. You have no business being out there."

"This ain't nothing. I been out in much worse over the years."

"That was before you had a wife at home who will worry about you."

That gave him pause. Until the last couple of years, he'd never had anyone at home to worry about him. Now he had his dream girl, and knowing she would worry made him question the sanity of this mission. But then he thought about how depressed Big Mac had sounded. It had reminded Ned of how his best friend had been after he suffered a head injury a few years back.

Ned couldn't bear to hear him so down, and if there was something he could do to fix it for everyone, then that's what he'd do.

"Ned…"

"I'll be back before you miss me," he said. "Promise."

"What'll I do if you don't come back?"

"Call Blaine. But that won't be necessary. I'll be back."

She sighed. "You're a crazy old fool."

"Ya knew that when ya married me." He kissed her again. "Pack up yer stuff to go to Linda's."

"We're not going to Linda's. We're staying home like our son-in-law the police chief told us to."

"We're going to Linda's. Get yerself ready and pack us a bag just in case we get stuck there. I'll be back to getcha soon." This idea got better with every passing minute.

"Ned—"

"Get ready," he called over his shoulder as he went out into the howling wind and snow to fire up the woody station wagon he used as a cab. After pulling out of his driveway, he discovered the roads were bad. Worse than bad, in fact. But he knew this island better than anyone and took it nice and slow. He made his way past the Southeast Light, which was barely visible through the snow.

Ned wondered if Slim and Erin had made it back to the island ahead of the storm or if they'd hunkered down in Florida to wait it out. Big Mac would know. He kept tabs on their pilot friend Slim.

He crept along at five miles an hour, the station wagon fishtailing here and there. Francine might've been right about this being a fool's errand, but if he could pull it off…

He went by the entrance to Martinez Lawn and Garden. Alex and Paul were no doubt hunkered down with their families, their houses walkable to each other even in the blizzard.

Half an hour after he left home, what should've been a five-minute ride landed Ned at the home of Gansett Island Town Councilman Royal Atkinson. Ned parked the car but left it running as he dashed through the snow to ring the doorbell.

The rotund councilman pulled open the door. "Ned? What the heck are you doing out in this?"

"I need a favor."

ADAM MCCARTHY WOKE up cold and realized the power had gone out while he and Abby were sleeping. "Crap."

"What?" Abby asked, her voice sleepy and sexy.

He curled up to her. "We're going to have to share body heat. We lost power."

"I love sharing body heat with you."

"We'll have no choice but to stay in bed all day so we don't freeze."

She laughed at his shameless ploy. "There are worse ways to spend Christmas than snuggled up to you in bed."

"Far worse ways."

"It won't be the same without naked boy, naked girl," Abby said, referring to last Christmas when Adam's nephew Thomas and his cousin Ashleigh had coined a new term when they ran through the family gathering completely naked.

"We can play naked boy, naked girl all by ourselves. It's my favorite game." He worked his hand under her T-shirt.

She screamed. "*Adam!* Your hand is freezing!"

"Warm me up."

She shivered. "It's too cold."

"I'll go downstairs, build a fire and then come back for you."

"Hurry. I'll freeze without you."

"I'll be quick." He got out of bed and grimaced at the smack of cold air that greeted him. "Damn, this house gets cold quick."

"Gonna be a long day without heat. I told you we should've gotten a generator when they had them at the hardware store."

"Yes, dear, you did." Adam jammed his feet into fleece-lined slippers and pulled on a thick sweater over a long-sleeved T-shirt. At this rate, he'd need a parka inside the house before much longer.

"You can also say that from now on I'll act immediately on all my wife's good ideas."

"Nice try. Going downstairs now." He darted down the stairs and went directly to the fireplace, thankful that he'd heeded Abby's suggestion to bring in firewood last night, just in case they needed it. He built the fire and had it going strong within a few minutes.

Then he went back upstairs to get Abby.

"All set, sweetheart. Let's go." He held up a down blanket that he wrapped around her when she got out of bed.

Downstairs, Adam pulled cushions off the sofa and set them up with a bed by the fire.

"My hero," Abby said, when they were snuggled up in front of the fireplace.

"Your hero should've bought the generator when he could."

She patted the hand he had on her belly. "My hero can't be perfect *all* the time."

Adam laughed. "I promise to do better in the future."

Linking their fingers, Abby held on tight to his hand. "Do you think someday we'll have little people waking us up way too early on Christmas?"

"I do. I really, really do. I see that for us."

"You're so sure."

"I am sure. It's going to happen. It's just a matter of when."

"Sometimes I think I should move on and let it go."

"Don't do that yet. I'll let you know when it's time for that—but it's not going to happen."

"I wish I had your confidence."

"You don't need it. I'll be confident for both of us."

"It's too bad we won't get to see the kids today," she said, sighing.

"We'll see them tomorrow. Go back to sleep for a little while. We've got nothing to do and nowhere to be. There's no one I'd rather be marooned with on Christmas than you."

"Me, too."

Adam was on his way back to sleep when the phone rang. Groaning, he untangled himself from Abby and grabbed the phone off the coffee table where he'd left it the night before. What the heck did Ned want so early? "Hey, Ned, what's up?"

"Merry Christmas," Ned said, speaking loudly over a whirl of noise in the background. "Pack yerselves up. I'm comin' to getcha."

"Huh?"

"Just get ready. I'll be there soon to take ya to yer mama's. Pack a bag. Just in case I can't getcha home tonight."

"Uhh, okay..."

The line went dead.

"What did he want?"

"He's coming to get us to take us to my mom's."

"Coming to get us *in a blizzard*? Seriously?"

"That's what he said." Wondering what Ned was up to, Adam said, "Looks like we'll get to see the kids after all."

WHILE ON THE phone with Big Mac earlier, Ned had recalled the estate sale Mrs. Chesterfield's heirs had held right before they put her home on the market. Ned had scooped up her old Cadillac. Royal had bought the oversized sleigh that Ned now navigated over snow-covered roads. The one thing he hadn't anticipated was the wind that made it difficult to see where he was going.

Royal had made two of his sturdiest workhorses available to Ned, saying they could handle anything, including a blizzard. He'd also sent Ned with oats to feed them and filled the sleigh with red plaid blankets to keep Ned's precious cargo warm. He was giddy with excitement as he turned the sleigh with the jingling bells toward his home to pick up his first passenger. There was nothing he wanted more than to make the ones he loved happy on Christmas.

Approaching his house, he saw Francine looking out the window, her eyes wide with what he hoped was delight. He brought the sleigh to a stop and jumped down into snow that came up to his knees.

Inside the door, he knocked the snow off his boots. "Doll! Getcher coat on! We're goin' for a ride."

"You have lost what's left of your mind," she said.

"Aww come on! It'll be fun. Doncha want to see yer babies on Christmas?"

"Of course I do, but—"

"No buts. Get yer coat on, grab yer bag of presents and let's go. I gotta lotta stops ta make." He helped her into her coat and kissed her before wrapping a scarf around her neck and face. Gathering up her bags of gifts, the picnic basket full of food and the bag he'd told her to pack—just in case they couldn't get home later—he hustled her out of the house.

He helped her into the sleigh, tucked a blanket around her and stashed her things in the back compartment, covering them with another blanket.

"This is the craziest thing you've ever done!" She had to yell so he'd hear her over the wind.

Ned directed the sleigh back to the road and headed for Adam's house. "Tisn't it fun though?"

"Oh yeah. Lots of fun."

"Ya mean that?"

"You're still crazy, but it is fun. Leave it to you to figure out a way to save Christmas."

A few minutes later, he guided the horses for a right-hand turn into Adam's driveway.

"Are you kidding me?" Adam called from the doorway.

"Let's go!" Ned said. "We're on a schedule!"

Adam and Abby came running through the snow, bags in hand and got in behind Ned and Francine.

"This is *awesome*!" Adam said.

"Glad ya think so. Ready?"

"Ready!"

"Bundle up and hold on."

Fifteen minutes later, they pulled up to the McCarthy's White House, and Ned helped Francine down from the sleigh. He carried her bags and opened the gate to the white picket fence that was crusted with snow. Adam and Abby followed them up the walk.

Big Mac threw open the door and the euphoric expression on his face made Ned's day complete. *"You gotta be kidding me!"*

"I ain't kidding ya." Ned handed over Francine's bags to Linda. "I gotta go to town. Call Tiffany, Mallory, Grant and Evan. Tell 'em all to get ready."

"I want to go with you," Big Mac said. "Give me one minute." He ran to grab his boots, parka, hat and gloves and kissed Linda.

"Crazy old fools," Linda said, but she couldn't hide her delight.

"Get dinner in the oven, doll," Ned said. "The kids are comin' home!"

"We're on it," Linda said, glancing at Francine, who nodded.

"Don't get your fool selves killed out there," Francine said. "That'd put a damper on the day."

Ned laughed and kissed her. "Doncha worry 'bout us. We may be fools, but we're hardy fools. Ya ready?" he asked Big Mac.

"Ready. Let's do it."

The two men ran out into the storm and climbed aboard the sleigh for the ride to town to collect the kids.

"This is *awesome*," Big Mac declared when they were underway.

"Tisnt it? These horses are fearless." He guided the horses through a huge drift. "What'd ya hear from Slim?"

"They stayed in Florida for the holiday with Erin's folks, but they'll be up for a visit in the next few days. He said they were waiting out the storm."

They plowed through the snow, undeterred by the drifts, the wind or the cold, arriving in town about half an hour after they set out. First stop was the pharmacy where Evan and Grace lived in the loft upstairs. "Go get 'em," Ned said to Big Mac.

Big Mac was halfway up the stairs when Evan and Grace came out, bundled up and carrying bags of presents.

Evan had his guitar slung over his back. "You guys are crazy," he said, laughing at the sight of the sleigh.

"Ned's the crazy one," Big Mac said, relieving Grace of the duffel bag she carried. "I'm just along for the ride."

"Bundle up, kiddos!" Ned said. "Let's go get yer sister."

They stopped to pick up Mallory and Quinn as well as Grant and

Stephanie before heading to Tiffany's place.

She sent Ashleigh out first, and Ned snuggled her in next to him.

"You can help me drive," he told her. The little girl who looked just like her mama had him wrapped so tightly around her little finger it wasn't even funny.

Big Mac helped Tiffany with her bags and carried baby Adeline, bundled into a snow suit.

"Am I really taking my babies out in a blizzard?" Tiffany asked when she climbed in next to Grant, who helped to tuck blankets around her and the baby.

"We can't let a little bit 'o snow ruin our Christmas," Ned said, turning the sleigh to head back to the White House.

"Did you tell Blaine where to find you?" Big Mac asked Tiffany.

"He's working, so I texted him. Needless to say, he wasn't pleased to hear we were going somewhere."

"He'll catch up to ya later. No sense you girls bein' home alone if ya don't hafta be."

"I'll let you tell him that," Tiffany said.

"Mommy," Ashleigh said. "I'm driving!"

"Oh dear God," Tiffany said while everyone else lost it laughing.

NED DELIVERED the group from town to the White House with instructions for them to call Mac, Janey and Luke to put them on notice that they were coming for them.

They went first to Mac's house.

"If I forget to tell you later," Big Mac said as they headed down Sweet Meadow Farm Road, "thank you for this."

"We couldn't have Christmas without our babies," Ned said. "Wouldn't have been the same."

Ned brought the sleigh to a stop in Mac's driveway. "Go get 'em!"

Big Mac bounded up the stairs to Mac's deck. His son met him at the sliding door. "What're you two up to now?"

"We're saving Christmas. You guys ready?"

"We aren't really taking a baby out in a blizzard, are we?" Maddie asked, eyeing the storm with trepidation.

"It's only a mile," Big Mac reminded her. "We'll have you bundled up so tight you won't even know you're out in a blizzard."

"Right," Maddie said skeptically. "If you say so."

"Have you ever known my dad not to be right?" Mac asked.

"Not once, ever," Maddie said with a warm smile for her father-in-law."

"Mommy!" Thomas said. "There's horseys out there! Can we go? *Can we?*"

"Let's go," Maddie said, seeming to realize when she was outnumbered.

Mac held Hailey, Maddie carried baby Mac and Thomas took care of himself while Big Mac juggled bags of gifts, a suitcase and a diaper bag.

"Off to the Cantrells," Ned said, directing the team with the assistance of Ashleigh and now Thomas, too. He tried not to notice that the storm seemed to be intensifying. They were so close. He couldn't quit now. Fifteen arduous minutes later, they pulled into Janey's driveway. "Hurry," Ned said to Big Mac. "It's getting worse."

"I'm hurrying."

Janey let out a scream of delight when she saw the sleigh. "Joe! Look! Oh my God! This is *fabulous!*" She carried baby Vivienne while Joe brought P.J. They wore backpacks and had bags of gifts hanging from their arms.

"Cantrells get the prize for most ready to roll," Ned said when they were loaded up.

"Janey was so excited to hear you were coming, I practically had to sit on her to keep her inside until you got here," Joe said. "She even got Mr. Davis next door to agree to come over and check on the menagerie a couple of times. Oh, and Luke called to say thanks for the offer, but they're staying home."

"Good thing cuz I don't think we coulda gotten there." Ned directed the sleigh toward the White House. "Off we go!"

"This might be the craziest thing we've ever done," Maddie said.

"If this is the craziest thing you've ever done," Big Mac said, "you kids need to get out more."

"No shit," Ned muttered.

"Don't encourage her Dad," Mac said. "She's wild enough for me as she is."

It took twenty minutes, but they finally pulled up to the open gate at Big Mac's house. With two babies on board, Ned had become more anxious with every passing minute, but they'd done it. They'd gotten them all.

He and Big Mac helped everyone inside and went back with Mac and Joe to grab the bags.

"Can we stow the team in the barn?" Ned asked Big Mac.

"Yep. Let's do it."

They went back out into the storm to detach the horses from their harnesses and put them up in the barn-shaped garage that also doubled as a workshop. They filled buckets with oats and water, rubbed down the horses and covered them with dry blankets.

"Will they be okay out here?" Big Mac asked.

"Royal says they're low maintenance and will be fine as long as they're outta the elements and have food and water." Ned petted their long snouts. "Ya boys did good work. Ya saved Christmas."

"With a little help from our good friend Ned," Big Mac added.

"They did the hard part." Ned spotted the camping supplies piled in the corner of the garage. "We oughta grab the air mattresses and sleeping bags. I have a feeling we're gonna need 'em tonight."

"Good thinking."

Carrying sleeping bags and deflated air mattresses, the two men made their way through waist-high drifts to the back door. Inside, they stashed their cargo, kicked off their boots and shed layers of heavy wet outerwear.

Big Mac opened the door to the kitchen, and the roar of voices, laughter, screaming babies and Christmas music greeted them. "Now *that*," he said, grinning at his best friend, "is more like it."

"Merry Christmas, good buddy." Ned raised his hand for a high five.

Big Mac returned the high five and then hugged him. "Best Christmas present anyone ever got me."

"CAN you tell me what the *hell* we're doing in this madhouse?" Quinn asked Mallory, amused by the antics of Thomas, Ashleigh and Hailey, whose excitement bordered on mania.

"We're enjoying my second Christmas with my new family."

"Is that what we're doing?" His eyes went wide when Ashleigh jumped on Thomas's back and took him down into a heap.

They landed with a thump and promptly cracked up laughing.

Quinn released a deep breath. "I keep thinking I should've brought my medical bag."

Mallory laughed at him. "Didn't you grow up in a big family?"

"I did, but my big family is nowhere near as crazy as yours."

"Isn't it *wonderful*?" Mallory had been devastated to realize Christmas would be canceled due to the weather and elated to get the call about Ned coming with the sleigh.

"Wonderful. Hmmm, okay. If you say so."

"We don't have to stay if you don't want to."

"I'm just teasing you, sweetheart. I know how badly you wanted to be right here in the middle of this madness."

"I really did. I know we were having a nice quiet day, but I had so many of those before I knew my family."

"It's fine. I promise."

"So you'll be okay if I go help Linda in the kitchen?"

"I'll be fine. The guys are watching football in the den. I'll go in there where it's safe."

Mallory kissed him. "This is the best Christmas of my life."

"Because you have your family. I get it."

"Not just because of them, but because I have you, too."

"Every day is like Christmas since I met you."

"That's very sweet of you to say, but thankfully not every day is as loud as Christmas with the McCarthys."

"Very true. Not sure I could handle that."

"At least they have a doctor and a nurse in residence, just in case."

"Let's hope they don't need our professional expertise today."

He'd no sooner said the words, when Ashleigh and Thomas rolled across the floor, taking out Hailey, who bumped her forehead on the coffee table.

"Spoke too soon." Mallory scooped up her niece and held her tight as she howled. "Get some ice," she told Maddie who came running when she heard her daughter crying.

"Mac!" Maddie called. "Talk to your son about roughhousing."

Mac, who had baby Mac in his arms, said, "I love how he's *my* son when he's misbehaving and *her* son when he's charming."

"Move it," Maddie said to her husband, taking Hailey from Mallory. "My poor baby. Did your brother knock you down?"

Hailey, who had a knot forming on her forehead and a quivering chin, nodded.

"A little ice will make that boo-boo go away," Mallory told her, kissing her cheek.

"Auntie Mallory knows these things," Maddie told Hailey. "She's a nurse."

Maddie went to sit with Hailey and the ice pack while Mallory joined Linda, Stephanie, Abby, Grace and Francine in the kitchen.

"What can I do to help?"

"How are you with a potato peeler?" Steph asked.

"That's my holiday specialty," Mallory replied. She took the potato peeler from Steph and eyed the ten-pound bag. "Where's Janey?"

"Upstairs nursing Viv," Grace said.

"I can't believe we're all here and carrying on as if there's not a huge storm going on outside," Abby said. "Our house was freezing!"

"Ours, too," Mallory said. "We were bundled under ten blankets, and I was still cold."

"Good old Ned," Linda said. "Leave it to him to find a way to save Christmas."

"Crazy old fool," Francine muttered, eyes brimming with affection for her husband.

"Your crazy old fool saved the day," Linda said.

"Yes, he did," Francine said, shaking her head. "He never ceases to surprise me."

"He's the best of us all," Linda declared.

"He sure is," Steph said. "Did anyone hear from Laura and the others?"

"Frank, Betsy, Shane, Katie, Sarah, Charlie, Kevin, Chelsea and the boys all stayed at the Surf last night with Laura and Owen and the kids," Linda said. "Big Mac talked to them earlier, and they're hunkered down with a generator."

"I'm glad they can all be together," Grace said. "Did you talk to Charlie?" she asked Stephanie.

"We had Christmas Eve with him and Sarah," Steph said of her stepfather. "After so many years apart on Christmas, we'll take what we can get."

Tiffany came into the kitchen holding Adeline. "I got a text from Blaine in all capital letters with multiple exclamation points that said, 'ARE YOU FREAKING KIDDING ME?!?!!!!,' when I told him where we are and how we got here. I said it was all Ned's fault."

The others laughed at that.

"Poor Blaine out serving the community, thinking his family is safe at home," Linda said. "And you're actually cavorting in the snow with babies."

"He was worried about us being home alone in the storm," Tiffany said, "so at least we're not home alone anymore."

"There is that," Maddie said, smiling at her sister's reasoning.

Tiffany was an expert at manipulating her alpha husband who was slavishly devoted to her.

"How late does he have to work?" Francine asked.

"Not too much longer. He's mostly making sure people heeded his advice to stay home."

"Everyone did except his wife and her family," Grace said, giggling.

"I'm going to hear about this," Tiffany said.

"Ya think?" Francine asked, laughing.

"Ohhh, maybe he'll spank me for disobeying him," Tiffany said, shivering.

"Good lord," Francine said as the others howled with laughter. "I have no idea where she came from."

THEY OPENED PRESENTS, drank eggnog, sang Christmas songs and took turns going out into the cold for more firewood. Babies were passed from one set of arms to another, and the volume remained just below deafening.

Big Mac couldn't remember a better Christmas.

Dinner for twenty-five—counting Blaine, if he made it—took some doing, but under Linda and Francine's oversight, they had a ten-pound beef tenderloin with all the fixings on the table by two o'clock.

Big Mac sat at the head of the table and took in the faces that surrounded him—Linda, who made it all happen. Mac, Maddie, Thomas, Hailey and baby Mac. Mallory and Quinn. Grant and Stephanie. Adam and Abby. Evan and Grace. Janey, Joe, P.J. and baby Vivienne. Ned, Francine, Tiffany, Ashleigh and Adeline.

When he thought back to his wedding day, now forty-one years ago, Big Mac never could've imagined what would come of his life with Linda.

She reached for his hand under the table and they shared a smile. "Unbelievable, isn't it?"

"Best Christmas ever. Look at them—everyone has the one they love most by their side."

"Except Tiffany, but hopefully he'll be here soon."

"He'll be here the minute he can get free," Big Mac said. "Wild horses couldn't keep him away from his wife and girls."

"Wild horses brought his wife and girls through the snow to grandmother's house," Linda said in a sing-song voice.

"That they did. Ned to the rescue."

"Best friend we ever had."

"He sure is."

Ned sat at the other end of the table, holding hands with Francine like the newlyweds they still were.

"We need a toast," Linda said.

"I'm on it." Big Mac stood, cleared his throat.

"Oh no," Mac said, groaning. "Here we go."

"Hush," Big Mac said to his oldest son. "I'd like to propose a toast to family—the best gift any of us can get on Christmas."

The others raised their glasses in support of that.

"And to Ned, our cab driver extraordinaire, who made it possible for us to be together today."

"To Ned!" everyone said.

Ned's face turned bright red. "Aww shucks," he said, waving off the praise. "Twas no big deal."

"Twas the biggest of big deals," Big Mac said. "To all of us. Thank you again for coming up with a way to save Christmas."

"My pleasure," Ned said, smiling widely.

The front door slammed shut and boots landed on the floor with a loud thump. In came Gansett Island Police Chief Blaine Taylor, hands on hips, hair standing on end. "What in the name of god is wrong with you people?"

"So many things," Quinn said, earning an elbow to the ribs from his beloved.

"What part of 'stay off the roads' wasn't clear to you?"

Tiffany got up to greet her husband with a kiss. "You're just in time for dinner, honey."

"Don't try to kiss your way out of this, Mrs. Taylor. You took our babies out *in a blizzard!*"

"They were perfectly safe. Ned knows these roads better than anyone, even you."

Blaine glowered at her.

"Maddie, can you please watch Addie for a minute while I have a word with my husband?" Tiffany asked.

"I've got her," Maddie said.

Tiffany took Blaine by the hand and dragged him along behind her, pushing him into the half bath in the hallway.

"What do you think you're doing?" Blaine asked.

"This," Tiffany said, pinning him against the sink to kiss him, "is a much better use of your mouth than scolding everyone."

His fingers dug into her hips. "Everyone heeded my instructions except my own family. What does that say for my authority?"

"If you drop it for now, I'll let you spank me when we get home." She rubbed against him shamelessly. "If you want to, that is."

The low, tense growl that came from deep inside him nearly made her laugh.

"Do we have a deal?"

"How soon can we leave to go home?"

"My husband, the police chief, said no one should be on the roads tonight, so we might have to stay here."

"If you're offering a spanking, we're going home."

"We'll see about that. If it's not safe, I'm not taking my babies out in the storm."

His eyes bugged. *"But you were fine with taking them out earlier in a freaking sleigh?"*

"In a sleigh during the daylight with Ned, the most qualified driver on Gansett? Yes, I was fine with that."

The scowl that overtook his handsome face made her laugh. "You don't scare me."

"Good," he said, wrapping his arms around her. "Even when you're working me shamelessly, I'd never want you to be afraid of me."

"I'm so happy you're here. Wasn't the same without you."

"I couldn't believe it when I got your text that you were here. Leave it to Ned."

"We've been saying that all day. Ashleigh loved the sleigh ride."

"I'll bet she did. What did my little Addie think of it?"

"She slept right through it."

"I need to see my girls, but I can't go out there in this condition." He looked down at his hard cock, which stood out in prominent detail under his jeans.

"I could take care of that for you," she said, tugging his button and unzipping him. Before he could form a reply, she had her hand wrapped around the steely length of his erection and was stroking him.

"Fucking *hell*, Tiff," he said, gasping.

She stopped the movement of her hand. "Are you saying no?"

"Fuck no, I'm not saying no."

She smiled. So predictable. And she loved him madly.

His hands framed her face, and he kissed her senseless as she stroked him. He broke the kiss to suck in a deep breath before he came in her hand. While he continued to breathe hard, she reached around him to wash her hands. Then she tucked him back into his pants and patted his chest.

"You should be nice and relaxed now."

"I have no idea what I ever did to deserve a wife like you," he said, kissing her softly.

"You loved me—and my daughter—like no one else ever has. That's what you did."

"Loving you two and Addie is as easy for me as breathing."

"That makes us very, very lucky." She kissed him again. "Merry Christmas, love."

"Merry Christmas, my disobedient sweetheart."

AFTER THE GUYS handled kitchen cleanup, Mac got out the Twister game and taught the kids how to play with Adam and Evan's assistance. As often happened on holidays at the McCarthy's house, the game descended into a wrestling match that pitted Adam against Evan with Thomas and Ashleigh "helping" by jumping on top of them.

"If they knock my tree down, I'll kill them," Linda said, as she always did.

"Boys, if you knock your mother's tree over, she'll kill you," Big Mac said.

"How old are they again?" Quinn asked.

"Old enough to know better," Janey said. "But that's never stopped them."

"Get him, Thomas!" Mac said to his son, who had Evan in a headlock.

"No fair," Evan gasped. "I'm being double-teamed."

"Throw an elbow," Grace said.

"Hey," Abby said, laughing. "Don't hurt my husband. I need him." Just as she said that, Ashleigh's foot connected with Adam's groin, and he went down in a boneless pile, moaning.

The others howled with laughter, especially after Abby offered to kiss it better.

"Taken down by a widdle, widdle girl," Evan said, rubbing his eyes dramatically. "Poor baby."

"We beat him, Uncle Evan," Thomas said.

"With Ashleigh's help." Evan high-fived Ashleigh.

"That's the only way you can win," Adam croaked. "With the help of toddlers."

"We aren't toddlers," Thomas said. "*Hailey* is a toddler."

"My apologies," Adam said.

"When can we play naked boy, naked girl?" Mac asked.

His wife let out a scream. "*Mac!*"

"We're not allowed to play that anymore," Thomas said solemnly. "But Mommy still gets to play it with Daddy cuz they're married."

"My mommy plays naked boy, naked girl with Blaine *all the time*," Ashleigh said.

After a heartbeat of complete silence, Grace snorted with laughter that took down everyone in the room.

As DARKNESS FELL over the salt pond, Ned wandered to the big windows to check the weather. The snow continued to fall unabated, with easily two feet accumulated on Big Mac's deck.

Linda joined him, curling her hands around his arm and resting her head on his shoulder. "I can't thank you enough for organizing us today. You gave us all a priceless gift."

"Ahh, doll, think about all the years I had no one but you and yer family and how welcome ya made me here. Twas the least I could do fer ya."

"We love you."

"Love ya, too, gal, but I hope ya still love me when I tell ya yer gonna be puttin' up twenty-five of us tonight."

"We've got plenty of room, and if it means having everyone home for Christmas, then so be it." She turned to face the gathering. "Listen up, everyone! You're all staying put tonight, so here's what we're going to do. Mac, Janey, Tiffany and Mallory—you get the four bedrooms upstairs."

"Why do they get bedrooms?" Evan asked, pouting.

"Because three of them have babies and the other has a fiancé who is still new to this family. Since we'd like to keep him around until the wedding, they get a bedroom." Linda ensured her tone left no room for negotiation.

"Thank you, Jesus," Quinn said, grinning.

Mallory stuck her tongue out at Evan.

Linda loved to see her fitting right in with the siblings she'd discovered later in life.

"Thomas, Ashleigh and Hailey can have the kid's room," she said, referring to the bedroom she'd turned into a room for her grandchildren. "Ned and Francine, you get the pull-out sofa in the den. The rest of you get air mattresses and sleeping bags down here."

"We're being discriminated against for not having kids," Grant said.

"Yeah," Adam said. "No fair."

"That means no naked boy, naked girl for us," Grant said.

"Shut up, Grant," Stephanie said, putting her hand over his mouth.

"Honestly," Linda said. "When are you all going to grow up?"

"Not today," Evan said, accepting a high five from Grant.

They got busy settling little ones, blowing up air mattresses and making beds.

"We can use dresser drawers for the babies," Linda said.

"That's freaking brilliant," Tiffany said.

"No kidding," Maddie said. "She must be an expert on babies or something."

"Believe it or not, this is not my first circus," Linda said.

"That's a good word to describe this day," Quinn said, making everyone laugh.

It took an hour, but they got Thomas, Ashleigh, Hailey and P.J. bathed and into pajamas. They were tucked into Linda and Big Mac's bed for a story read to them by Big Mac before their moms came to collect them and put the sleepy kids to bed.

Babies were deposited into towel-lined dresser drawers in the rooms assigned to their parents who snuck downstairs for a nightcap before calling it a night.

"Spiked eggnog for everyone," Janey declared.

"You're breastfeeding," Joe said.

"Oh my God," Evan said, making retching noises. "Do not talk about her breasts in front of us."

"Seriously," Grant said. "So gross."

"Nothing gross about it, boys," Joe said, grinning. "Your sister has one hell of a rack."

"*Joseph!*" Big Mac's bellow rang across the living room from his perch in front of the fireplace where he added more wood.

"Oh shit. Didn't see you there. Sir."

Mac and his brothers lost it laughing.

Smiling, Janey stood so Joe could sit and then climbed into his lap. He wrapped his arms around her.

"Thank you for defending my ta-tas," she said, laying a hot kiss on him while her brothers groaned and threw pillows at them.

"Your ta-tas are well worth defending, babe."

"*Mom!*" Grant said on a long whine. "Make her *stop*."

"Jane Elizabeth, stop disgusting your brothers."

"Why would I stop now when I'm *so* good at it?"

"Let's go to bed," Joe said, waggling his brows suggestively.

"You're at *mom's* house," Mac said disdainfully. "This is a no-sex zone tonight."

"Is it?" Maddie asked, raising a brow.

"Oh, um, well…"

That set off more laughter.

"My sides hurt from laughing," Mallory said, hands on her ribs.

"Mine, too," Stephanie said. "I had no idea holidays could be like this until I met this family. Thank you, guys."

"We couldn't be happier to have you as one of us," Big Mac said.

"Totally agree with the old man," Grant said, kissing his wife.

"Who you calling old, boy?" his father asked.

"Evan," Linda said, "will you play for us?"

"Sure."

"Quietly," Maddie said.

"You got it." Evan tuned his guitar while the others snuggled up to their loved ones.

Grant slung one arm around Stephanie and the other around Grace, so she wouldn't feel left out.

"Don't get too comfortable with my brother, Mrs. McCarthy," Evan said, glowering playfully at Grant.

"Shut up and play," Grace told her husband as she leaned her head on Grant's shoulder.

"No respect," Evan said, strumming the guitar and listening intently until he was satisfied with the sound. He sang a lovely, moody take on "Joy to the World" that brought tears to his mother's eyes.

"I *loved* that," she said. "You should record it."

"You think so?"

"Oh yes," she said. "It'll be a huge hit."

"Mother knows best," Big Mac said, "but I agree with her. That was fantastic, son. What else you got?"

He played for an hour, running through the old familiar Christmas songs and putting his own spin on each of them.

"Time to record a Christmas album, bro," Grant said. "Amazing."

"I'll give that some thought the next time I'm here long enough to record."

"When will that be?" Linda asked.

"March. We'll be home for a couple of months before the summer tour."

"I could never stand to miss summer on Gansett," Big Mac said. "Glad I don't have to go on tour."

"We're all glad about that, Dad," Evan said.

Big Mac was known for many things. Singing wasn't one of them. "On that note," Big Mac said, after tossing a few more logs on the fire, "I'm taking my lovely wife up to bed and keeping her there until sometime tomorrow after the day she's put in today."

"Thank you, Linda," Stephanie said, starting a round of quiet applause.

"You are most welcome," Linda said, taking a bow. "My day was made by having you all here." She blew air kisses to everyone as she left the room.

"No sex in the living room, boys," Big Mac said over his shoulder as he followed her.

"Said the guy who has *private* accommodations," Grant mumbled.

"You'll survive one night without," Stephanie said, crawling in next to him on one of the narrow air mattresses.

"*One* night without." Evan snorted. "Whatever."

"What can I say?" Stephanie smirked. "My husband is a stud."

Evan and Adam made gagging noises.

"That's right, baby." Grant pulled the sleeping bag over them and put his arm around her. "Turn over," he whispered.

STEPHANIE TURNED to face her husband. "What?" she whispered.

"I wanted to see you."

"You saw me all day."

"Not enough." He slid his hand down her back and tucked her in tighter against him, arranging them so her leg was between his. "That's better. Now kiss me."

She gave him a chaste kiss.

He squeezed her ass. "Not good enough."

"That's all you're getting tonight. Go to sleep."

"How am I supposed to sleep in this condition?" he asked, pushing his erection against her belly.

"Tell him to stand down."

"He doesn't listen to me."

Stephanie began to laugh and couldn't stop.

"Are you two having sex over there?" Evan asked.

"Wouldn't you like to know," Grant said.

"If he's doing it, I want to do it, too," Evan said.

"Not happening," Grace replied.

"Everyone's having sex but us," Adam said. "It's not fair."

"This is like the sleepover straight from hell," Abby said, laughing.

"You guys," Stephanie said softly. "I just want you to know that being part of this family is… Well, it's the best thing. The very best thing."

Grant hugged her tightly and kissed her softly. "You make us better."

"I don't know about that…"

"I do."

"I agree with him," Evan said. "And you know how rare that is."

"Same," Adam said. "You certainly make *him* better."

"Whatever," Grant said. "I was pretty good to begin with."

"She definitely makes you better," Abby said, sparking a wave of laughter. As his ex-girlfriend, she ought to know.

"Well played, my love," Adam said, laughing.

"Gracie, you could make *me* better if you just—" Evan's words were muffled by his wife kissing him. "Yes, just like that only *more*."

"Mom!" Grant said. "Evan's having sex!"

"Shut up," Stephanie said. "No one is having sex."

"I am," Adam said.

"No, you're not," Abby replied.

"I hate this sleepover," Adam said. "It's no fun. If we were home, we could have sex."

"No, we couldn't because it's freezing at home, and there's no way I'm getting naked when it's freezing."

"I could get you naked."

"No, you couldn't."

"Could."

"Couldn't."

"Oh my God," Evan said. "Shut the fuck up, will you?"

"Did someone say fuck?" Grant asked.

Grace began to laugh. She laughed so hard she went silent.

"Your laughter is highly inappropriate," Evan said indignantly. "My boner doesn't find any of this funny."

Grace snorted. "I can't," she said, gasping for air. "I can't take any more. Just shut up. All of you."

Meanwhile upstairs...

"NOT IN YOUR FATHER'S HOUSE," Quinn said as Mallory kissed his chest, moving lower.

"He won't know."

"Yes, he will. He's incredibly perceptive."

Mallory laughed softly. "He's at the other end of the hall."

"He's under the same roof, and he's a big dude."

"You're a big dude." She wrapped her hand around his hard cock to make her point.

Groaning, he said "*Mallory…*"

"Yes, dear?"

"Don't."

She stared at him, hoping her shock registered. He never said no to her. Ever. "You're serious. You really don't want to?"

"I believe you're holding *ample* proof that I *want* to."

She giggled at his use of the word *ample*. "So what's the problem?"

"It's disrespectful for me to fuck you in your father's house."

"No, it isn't."

"I'd like to ask him to be sure."

"Stop it. You're not going to ask him. And P.S. I'm almost forty years old. I can fuck my fiancé, as you so elegantly put it, anytime I want to."

"Under normal circumstances, your fiancé would completely agree, but with your six-foot-something father down the hall and in possession of two working legs, I'm going to take a pass."

Mallory positioned herself—naked—on top of him, sliding back and forth over his cock until he whimpered. That's when she knew she had him.

"If he guts me with that big fishing knife of his, you'll have only yourself to blame."

"I'll take the risk." She sunk down on him, and shivered from the impact the way she always did. "*There* we go."

Quinn put his hands behind his head and gazed up at her with amusement. "Go ahead and have your fun."

"Thank you, I will. I'm feeling rather fertile today. Must be all the little ones. Maybe this will be the night. Wouldn't that be something?"

"Yeah, babe. It would be. Hopefully, the father of this child you want will live to raise him or her with you."

"Stop it. My dad loves you as much as I do. He wants me to be happy."

"Are you? Happy that is?"

Mallory stopped moving and stared down at him. "How can you ask me that? You know how happy I am with you."

"Just making sure."

Mallory leaned in to kiss him. "Living and working with you is the most fun I've ever had."

"Me, too. I love everything about it—and you."

"Good, then prove it." She swiveled her hips, drawing a sharp gasp of pleasure from him.

He moved so quickly, she never saw it coming. One minute she was on top of him and the next she was pinned to the bed with him on top and in charge.

Gotcha, she thought, smiling as she wrapped her arms and legs around him, thrilled to let him take the lead.

"Are you happy now that you got to have Christmas with your family?" Joe whispered to Janey. He had her spread out under him, her body soft and pliant as he throbbed inside her.

"So happy. But this is the best part of the day—time alone with you at the end of it."

"Couldn't agree more."

They were in the room that'd been hers growing up. "I've never had sex in this bed."

"Never?"

"Nope."

"I can't believe you and what's his name never snuck up here, not that I want to think about you doing *this* with *him*." Joe gave an extra push of his hips to make his point.

"I had parents and four older brothers. There was no way we could pull that off."

"Well, I'm glad to be first for something."

"You may as well have been first for everything. I barely remember what it was like to be with him. You're the only one who matters."

"Good answer, babe."

Vivienne let out a squeak from her makeshift crib next to them.

Joe froze even as he throbbed with desire for his sexy wife. He dropped his head to Janey's chest and took a deep breath, fighting for control.

She ran her fingers through his hair.

He thought she was soothing him until she clamped down on his cock, nearly making him come.

"*Stop*," he said through gritted teeth.

"Don't wanna," she whispered, her lips brushing against his ear giving him goose bumps.

"You're going to wake her up before we get to finish." That had happened far too often lately.

"Then you'd better get moving." She pinched his butt to make her point.

She made him crazy, especially when they had to be quiet. Well, she made him crazy much of the time, if he was being honest.

He moved with her until they both gasped with satisfaction that ripped through him the way it always did when he made love to his wife. How was it possible that it just got better all the time? He'd waited so long for a chance to love her, and now every day with her made that long wait worth it.

"Love you love you, Janey Cantrell," he whispered, recalling when he'd told her he wanted her to *love him love him*—and not as an extra brother.

"Love you love you, too, Joseph. Merry Christmas."

"And a very happy New Year."

BLAINE HAD his hands full of Tiffany's spectacular ass, but she'd forbidden him to collect on the spanking she owed him until they were in the privacy of their own home and couldn't be overheard.

"This ass is so mine when we get home tomorrow."

"Yes, dear," she said, smiling up at him.

"Do I need to be concerned about how much pleasure you take in disobeying me?"

"You take just as much pleasure from setting me straight."

"Yes, I do," he said, nuzzling her neck.

"Did you stop by your mother's earlier?"

"Yep, everyone was there."

"We'll see them tomorrow."

"Your ass might be too sore to go out."

"Haha, no way. I'm not afraid of you."

"Good," he said kissing her. "Earlier, I was remembering that long awful winter I spent thinking about you and wishing I could be with you. I don't care what we're doing as long as we're doing it together."

"Speaking of doing it…" She raised her hips suggestively. "You wanna?"

"Um, yeah, I wanna, but we're not gonna."

"Why not?"

"Because, you were very, very naughty today, defying your police chief husband, and you need to be made to pay the price."

"I thought the price was the spanking."

"Hell no, that's not the price. You enjoy that too much."

Tiffany laughed. "Yes, I do. But may I point out that *you* enjoy *this*," she said, rubbing her belly against his hard cock, "so maybe you could make a little exception since it's Christmas."

"I suppose I could allow it this one time."

"You are just *too* good to me."

AFTER FEEDING BABY MAC, Maddie conked out while the baby remained wide awake. Mac sat up in bed, holding the little guy who had brought them so much joy since his arrival.

He grasped handfuls of Mac's chest hair and pulled so hard his daddy winced.

"Ouch, buddy." Mac no sooner disentangled the little fists than they had grabbed another handful.

Taking the baby with him, he got up to find the T-shirt he'd discarded earlier and put it on. "Much better."

Baby Mac reached for the hair on Mac's head and pulled. "Yep, you're a McCarthy boy. We start the hair pulling at a young age around here." He could remember wild wrestling matches with his brothers that included hair pulling and various other dirty tricks.

"Let me tell you a bedtime story about a guy who thought he had his life set up just the way he wanted it until he knocked a gorgeous woman off her bike—totally by accident, of course. And that accident turned out to be the best thing to ever happen to him. You know who was on that bike, buddy? That's right. Your mommy. She had terrible boo-boos, and Daddy moved in to take care of her and your brother and he never left. Well, except for a short time after Daddy did something stupid and Mommy got mad at him. Luckily for him—and for you—she decided to forgive him for that and many other stupid things he's done since then."

Mac stood the baby up on his chubby legs and let him bounce around, hoping to tire him out.

"Your mommy is the best mommy ever. She loves you and me and Thomas and Hailey and she takes such good care of us. When you grow up, I hope you find someone just like your mommy. Watch for gorgeous girls on bikes. They're the best."

"What're you telling him?" Maddie mumbled.

"The best bedtime story ever."

"Is it working?"

"Um, nope. He's wide awake."

"You want me to take a turn with him so you can sleep?"

"Nah. We're good. Right, buddy?"

"Mmmmaaammmm."

"You hear that? He almost said mama! Remember how I taught Thomas? Time to start your training, buddy. You should always say mama first. Happy mom, happy life."

"It's supposed to be happy *wife*, happy life," Maddie said.

"I'll teach him that one later. I've got so much to teach you, pal."

"Oh dear God," Maddie muttered.

Mac laughed at her predictable comment. "Let me tell you the rest of the best bedtime story ever… So your mommy, she fell madly in love with me…"

"BEST CHRISTMAS YET," Big Mac said to Linda, who was cuddled up to him in bed. He'd left the door open so he could hear the goings on downstairs, which had been highly entertaining.

"By far. Having everyone sleeping under our roof again is like old times."

"There were a lot fewer of them back then."

"When we bought this hunk of junk house, you said you wanted to fill it with kids. I'd say you more than succeeded."

"*We* succeeded. What a family."

"And how about Ned? Has there ever been a better friend?"

"Not that I've ever had."

"Me either. Maybe we should make the blizzard party an annual tradition."

"I like that idea."

"I wonder how many more people we'll have next year."

"What do you know Voodoo Mama?"

"I predict Grace, Stephanie and Mallory will have babies in the next year, and maybe Adam and Abby will get their miracle, too."

"God, I hope so. They'd be such great parents."

"They'll get there. One way or another."

"So we may be looking at close to thirty for next year's blizzard party?"

"Could be. Who knows if Mac and Maddie are done."

"At least Janey and Joe are, thank goodness." He couldn't bear to think of Janey giving birth to Vivienne *on the ferry*. What a day *that* had been.

"Yes, thank goodness indeed."

"Here's to another year on Gansett Island," he said, kissing her.

"I can't wait to see what happens."

Thank you for taking the ferry for a special holiday visit to Gansett Island. I hope you enjoyed spending Christmas with the McCarthy family. More to come from our favorite island in 2018! I can't thank you enough for all your support of my books in 2017. I'm excited about what's ahead in the New Year!

When you finish the novella, join the reader group to discuss the story.

So I'm settling in for a long winter's nap before the new year. Merry Christmas to all and to all a GOOD NIGHT! Have you read all of this year's books? What are you most looking forward to next year?

A very special thank you to my amazing team who made it possible for me to get this novella out to you on Christmas Day: Julie Cupp, Lisa Cafferty, Holly Sullivan, Isabel Sullivan and beta-reader-in-chief Anne Woodall.

From my home to yours, Merry Christmas and Happy New Year to you and your family!

xoxo

Marie

Check out *Yours After Dark*, Finn and Chloe's story, available now. Turn the page to read Chapter 1!

YOURS AFTER DARK

Chapter 1

"What in the name of *hell* is on your head?"

Arriving to work slightly hungover and in bad need of coffee, Finn McCarthy ignored the question from his brother, Riley. Finn had forgotten to buy coffee—again—and had gone without this morning. Living alone sucked. Before his dad and Riley moved out, one of them had bought the coffee. Now he had to do it, and he never remembered it until he woke up late and realized he'd forgotten. Again.

Riley wasn't giving up. "Hello?"

"What is what?" Finn choked back a yawn and tried to remember if he'd brushed his teeth before he left the house. He had, hadn't he?

Riley stepped closer to him, boasting the freshly fucked look that had made Finn want to stab him more than once in the months since his brother moved in with Nikki. "*That*." Riley pointed to the top of Finn's head. "What is *that*?"

Finn had no idea what he was talking about until he reached up and encountered the lump of hair he'd secured with a rubber band to keep it out of his face.

Their cousin Shane joined them. "It's a man bun, and it looks ridiculous."

Riley, that asshole, busted up laughing. "What the hell is a man bun?"

"That." Shane pointed to Finn's head. "Is a man bun. They're all the rage."

Riley couldn't stop laughing. He laughed so hard, he howled, while Finn prayed that his cousin Mac would bring coffee the way he did most days.

Thankfully, Mac walked into the Wayfarer a minute later with his business partner, Luke Harris, right behind him. And was that a tray of coffee Mac was carrying? *Yes!* "What's so funny?"

"Finn has a man bun," Shane said.

"And it looks ridiculous," Riley added.

Finn stole one of the coffees and took a big sip. *Ahhh*, pure bliss. "There's nowhere to get it cut out here."

"Go see Chloe at the Curl Up and Dye," Mac said.

"I don't get my hair cut in *salons*," Finn said disdainfully. "I go to barber shops, and there isn't one on this island."

"The way I see it," Riley said, "if it's a choice between a man bun or a salon, I'm choosing the salon every time."

"The way I see it," Finn said, "no one asked you."

"Wait till Dad, Uncle Mac and Uncle Frank see the man bun." Riley started laughing again. "I gotta get a picture so we can show them in case they miss it." The bastard whipped his phone out and had the picture before Finn could react or turn away. That picture would haunt him for the rest of his life.

Maybe the guys were right—a salon was preferable to putting up with this bullshit. His hair had gotten so long, it was either restrain it or wear a hat to keep it out of his face. Hats annoyed him when he was working, so he'd grabbed a rubber band to contain it without a thought to what it might look like. Apparently, that had been a mistake.

Today, they were finishing up the shingling on the exterior of the Wayfarer, which was due to open in a couple of weeks. They were on track to meet the aggressive deadline Mac had set for the project and had turned the interior over to Nikki, the general manager. She and the team she'd hired over the last few months would be loading in furniture this week, setting up hotel rooms and the dining room, hanging wall art and making finishing touches ahead of the grand opening on Memorial Day weekend.

On Saturday of that weekend, the Wayfarer would host its first major event—the wedding reception of Shane and his fiancée, Katie Lawry. They'd joked that they were the guinea pigs to test out whether the McCarthy family's latest Gansett Island business venture was ready for prime time. The day after the wedding, Finn's famous cousin Evan McCarthy would headline the outdoor stage at the grand opening to the public.

So far, the Wayfarer was a huge hit, with Nikki reporting that the hotel was sold out for the summer and ten other weddings were already booked. That was what they wanted to hear. Each family member had a stake in the business—some bigger than others—but everyone had put something into his uncle Big Mac's latest venture so they could all be owners. Finn was proud of the work they'd done to bring the old place back to life and even prouder of being part of something the family had done together.

Before going outside to get to work, Finn slathered sunscreen all over his face, neck and arms, gathered his nail gun and a ladder and followed the others to the scaffolding that was set up on the north side of the huge building they'd spent the winter renovating. They'd done a damned good job, if he said so himself.

With the end in sight, Finn was making plans to move to the mainland after almost two years on Gansett Island. It'd been fun to hang with the family for a couple of years, to see his father and brother fall in love with women Finn liked and respected and to be part of Mac's construction company. But it was time to get back to his real life, and that wasn't going to happen on a tiny island located off the southern coast of mainland Rhode Island.

He looked forward to skiing in the winter, driving the vintage Mustang he kept garaged at home and spending time with the friends he'd left behind. Not to mention taking his career to the next level with the large construction company he'd worked for in Stamford, Connecticut. There, he'd put his degree in civil engineering to good use. Here, he was banging nails. Not that he didn't enjoy the work, but he hadn't spent four excruciating years in college to end up a glorified carpenter.

Missy—or *Melissa* as she preferred to be called these days—his on-again-off-again girlfriend at home, was threatening to come fetch him if he wasn't home by June, and he would save her the trip to Gansett by heading home right after the grand opening. After going round and round in his mind about how he felt about her during the time he'd been gone, he was actually looking forward to seeing her. Despite the tumultuous aspects of their five-year relationship, they'd had a lot of fun together, most of the time anyway. Since they'd been broken up during the time he was gone, he'd indulged in a few one-night stands here and there, but nothing of any consequence.

It was definitely time to go home and figure out whether they had what it took to go the distance together. His dad and Riley said absolutely not. They'd never liked Missy for him, but Finn was determined to make up his own mind about her after seeing what remained after the long time apart.

He would miss his brother, father, aunt, uncles and cousins, and he would really miss working with Riley, Mac, Shane and Luke. He'd miss the family gatherings, the fishing trips Big Mac liked to organize and the time with his favorite men in the world. He'd miss Riley's girl-friend, Nikki, whom he called Nicholas while she called him Finnbar. The three of them had spent a lot of time together over the winter, and she'd become a good friend to him.

He liked being able to regularly see his cousins Janey and Laura and their kids, as well as Mac's brood and now Adam's little guy, Liam, too. Mac's wife, Maddie, was expecting another baby, and he'd heard rumblings that his cousin Grant's wife, Stephanie, might be pregnant, too. In addition, his cousin Mallory and her fiancé, Quinn, were talking about tying the knot at some point this summer.

Life on Gansett was rarely boring with the McCarthy family and their friends around to keep things interesting. It wasn't like Finn was dying to get out of there, especially with the summer coming. That was the best time of year to be on the island. But he'd promised himself over the winter that once the Wayfarer was finished, he'd make a move.

The Wayfarer was almost done, and the lease at the house was up at the end of the month. It seemed like the universe was conspiring to tell him it was time to get back to reality.

Nikki had offered him the garage apartment at Eastward Look, her family's home, if he wanted it. He was tempted to stay for the summer, but that would only prolong the inevitable.

No, he was going home at the end of the month. Tonight, he'd text his old boss in Stamford to let him know he'd be available in June, and he'd touch base with Missy, too. As he applied the nail gun to a row of shingles, he felt a sense of calm come over him. For so many months, the stay-or-go tug-of-war had raged in his mind while his family had pressured him to stay with them. He'd be the only member of the McCarthy family not living on Gansett, and while it was tempting to give in to the pressure from his family, he had goals and aspirations that couldn't be achieved on the island.

Someday, he'd like to own his own company the way Mac did. Finn considered self-employment the holy grail, accountable to no one but yourself and your employees. Mac worked his ass off, but it seemed nice to be the boss. Finn thought he would like that—someday in the far-off future that would be much farther off if he stayed here than it would be if he went home to Connecticut.

The workday dragged. Shingling was boring, monotonous work that gave him too much time to think. He wanted out of his own thoughts for a while. "What're you guys doing tonight?" he asked Riley as they helped the others clean up and shut down for the day.

"Not sure yet. Nik might be working late again."

"I want to go out."

"I'd be up for that. What do you feel like doing?"

"Drinking, raising hell, the usual."

Riley smiled. "That's your usual. Not mine anymore."

"Oh, shut up. You're not married yet."

"Nope, but I'd like to be. Sooner rather than later."

Finn stopped and took a closer look at his brother. "You're serious."

"Dead serious. In fact, I was going to ask if you'd help me pick out a ring."

"Wow. This is huge." While Finn was thrilled for his brother and Nikki, he couldn't ignore the nagging ache that came with losing his best friend. As soon as he had that thought, he felt stupid. Riley was getting married, not dying, for Christ's sake.

"You okay?" Riley gave him an odd look that had Finn pulling himself together.

"I'm happy for you, Ri. Nicholas is a great girl."

"I love her."

The stark simplicity of his brother's statement stayed with Finn on the ride home. Riley had promised to text him after he caught up with Nikki about the plans for the evening. *I love her.* He puzzled over his brother's heartfelt words while showering, and then while drinking a beer and eating his favorite after-work snack of corn chips and Cheez Whiz. *I love her.*

What must it be like to be so certain?

Had he ever said that about any woman, even Missy? Nope, and he wasn't sure whether what he'd felt for Missy was love or lust or some weird combination of the two. One thing he knew for certain—he hadn't had with her what Riley had with Nikki. The realization made him uneasy as he ran fingers through his unruly mop of hair, recalling that he'd planned to get a haircut.

He searched for the Curl Up and Dye salon's number on his phone and put through a call.

A female voice answered. "Curl Up and Dye."

"Hi there. What time do you close tonight?"

"Seven."

"Can you take a walk-in?"

"If you get here soon."

"I'll be right over."

"What's your name?"

"Finn McCarthy."

"Got it. See you soon."

He downed the rest of the beer and put the Cheez Whiz in the fridge next to the beer that was the only other thing in there. The meager contents of his fridge were further proof that he needed to get a life.

Since the salon was in town, he decided to walk rather than drive. As the season started to pick up steam with Gansett Island Race Week underway, parking in town could be hard to come by. A block from the salon, he noticed the dark purple paint and the sign with the catchy name painted in gold leaf. Two smiling, laughing women were leaving as he reached the door, and he held it for them.

One of them gave him the once-over as she went by. "Thank you."

"My pleasure." She was old enough to be his mother.

Inside the salon, the first thing he noticed was the rich scent of shampoo and the décor that consisted of golden wood floors, black leather chairs, chrome accents and mirrors all over the place.

"I'll be right out." The same distinctive voice he'd spoken to on the phone.

"Take your time." Finn looked around at the glass shelves of products that promised shine, body, vibrancy and a variety of other things he never gave much thought to.

"You don't need that."

Finn looked up from the bottle he was studying to find the sexiest woman he'd ever laid eyes on looking at him in amusement. Shoulder-length dark hair streaked with dark purple, ears pierced multiple times each, her left arm boasting a colorful sleeve tattoo, a sparkling diamond stud in her nose and violet eyes that riveted him. He'd never seen eyes that color before. She wore a black sleeveless top over black skinny jeans that clung to curves that made his mouth go dry.

"You must be Finn?"

"Ah, yeah. That's me." He put the bottle on the shelf and managed to knock two others to the floor. As he bent to retrieve them, his head connected with hers in a painful smack that made him see stars.

Fucking hell, that hurt! When he looked up, he found her rubbing the side of her head.

"Ow."

"Sorry about that." He picked up the bottles and returned them to the shelf.

"You've got a hard head." Her face flushed when she realized the double meaning behind her words.

A surge of heat to his groin caught him by surprise. It'd been so long since any woman had interested him, and he'd nearly given this one a concussion. "May I please request a do-over of the last minute?" He held out his hand. "I'm Finn McCarthy."

She eyed his hand before she reached out to take it. "Chloe Dennis."

The brush of her skin against his made his entire system go haywire. What the hell was that about? Stunned and unnerved by his reaction to her, he quickly retrieved his hand. "Do you have time for a quick haircut?"

"Sure, but with all that hair, it's not going to be quick."

"I can come back another time."

"No, it's fine." She gestured to one of three black chairs positioned in front of a row of mirrors. "Have a seat."

Finn headed for the chair she pointed to and sat, feeling out of sorts and off his game after the head bump. He wasn't usually so clumsy or awkward around women, but he'd rarely encountered one like Chloe.

Goddess was the word that came to mind. She projected a cool, aloof aura of self-confidence, which he found incredibly sexy. He stared at her in the mirror as she approached the chair, and when she ran her fingers through his hair, he felt her touch in every corner of his body. Even the bottoms of his feet tingled with awareness.

Holy crap.

"What're you thinking?"

He didn't dare answer that question.

"Short or on the longer side?"

God, she was talking about his hair, and his imagination had run away with him.

"Um, short enough that it's not in my face at work, but not super short."

"What do you do for work?"

"Construction for my cousin Mac."

"Ahh, gotcha. He's insane. In the best way, of course."

Finn laughed. "That he is. He keeps us well entertained." Finn would miss the older cousin he'd always looked up to. The ten years between them had all but disappeared in the time Finn had lived on Gansett Island. These days, Mac treated him more like a peer than a pesky baby cousin. Finn had learned a lot from Mac, both professionally and personally.

"You McCarthy men sure were blessed with great hair."

Watching her run her fingers through his hair was one of the most erotic things Finn had ever experienced.

"I cut your dad, your uncles, your cousins. You guys could be shampoo models."

Finn cleared a huge lump from his throat. "You think so?"

She met his gaze in the mirror. "I really do."

Was it his imagination or did she look at him much longer than necessary? No, definitely not his imagination. He shifted in the seat, hoping she wouldn't notice his embarrassing reaction to her. The movement startled her, and she looked away.

Nothing like this had *ever* happened in a barber shop.

Yours After Dark is available in print from *Amazon.com* and other online retailers, or you can purchase a signed copy from Marie's store at *shop.marieforce.com*.

OTHER BOOKS BY MARIE FORCE

Contemporary Romances

The Gansett Island Series

Book 1: Maid for Love *(Mac & Maddie)*

Book 2: Fool for Love *(Joe & Janey)*

Book 3: Ready for Love *(Luke & Sydney)*

Book 4: Falling for Love *(Grant & Stephanie)*

Book 5: Hoping for Love *(Evan & Grace)*

Book 6: Season for Love *(Owen & Laura)*

Book 7: Longing for Love *(Blaine & Tiffany)*

Book 8: Waiting for Love *(Adam & Abby)*

Book 9: Time for Love *(David & Daisy)*

Book 10: Meant for Love *(Jenny & Alex)*

Book 10.5: Chance for Love, *A Gansett Island Novella (Jared & Lizzie)*

Book 11: Gansett After Dark *(Owen & Laura)*

Book 12: Kisses After Dark *(Shane & Katie)*

Book 13: Love After Dark *(Paul & Hope)*

Book 14: Celebration After Dark *(Big Mac & Linda)*

Book 15: Desire After Dark *(Slim & Erin)*

Book 16: Light After Dark *(Mallory & Quinn)*

Book 17: Victoria & Shannon (Episode 1)

Book 18: Kevin & Chelsea (Episode 2)

A Gansett Island Christmas Novella

Book 19: Mine After Dark *(Riley & Nikki)*

Book 20: Yours After Dark *(Finn & Chloe)*

Book 21: Trouble After Dark *(Deacon & Julia) (Coming Soon!)*

The Green Mountain Series

Book 1: All You Need Is Love *(Will & Cameron)*

Book 2: I Want to Hold Your Hand *(Nolan & Hannah)*

Book 3: I Saw Her Standing There *(Colton & Lucy)*

Book 4: And I Love Her *(Hunter & Megan)*

Novella: You'll Be Mine *(Will & Cam's Wedding)*

Book 5: It's Only Love *(Gavin & Ella)*

Book 6: Ain't She Sweet *(Tyler & Charlotte)*

The Butler Vermont Series

(Continuation of the Green Mountain Series)

Book 1: Every Little Thing *(Grayson & Emma)*

Book 2: Can't Buy Me Love *(Mary & Patrick)*

Book 3: Here Comes the Sun *(Wade & Mia)*

Book 4: Till There Was You *(Lucas) (Coming Soon!)*

The Treading Water Series

Book 1: Treading Water *(Jack & Andi)*

Book 2: Marking Time *(Clare & Aidan)*

Book 3: Starting Over *(Brandon & Daphne)*

Book 4: Coming Home *(Reid & Kate)*

Historical Romances

The Gilded Series

Book 1: Duchess by Deception

Book 2: Deceived by Desire *(Coming Soon!)*

Single Titles

Five Years Gone

One Year Home *(Coming Soon!)*

Sex Machine

Sex God

Georgia on My Mind

True North

The Fall

Everyone Loves a Hero

Love at First Flight

Line of Scrimmage

Erotic Romance

The Erotic Quantum Series

Book 1: Virtuous (*Flynn & Natalie*)

Book 2: Valorous (*Flynn & Natalie*)

Book 3: Victorious (*Flynn & Natalie*)

Book 4: Rapturous (*Addie & Hayden*)

Book 5: Ravenous (*Jasper & Ellie*)

Book 6: Delirious (*Kristian & Aileen*)

Book 7: Outrageous (*Emmett & Leah*)

Book 8: Famous (*Marlowe*) (*Coming Soon!*)

Romantic Suspense

The Fatal Series

One Night With You, *A Fatal Series Prequel Novella*

Book 1: Fatal Affair

Book 2: Fatal Justice

Book 3: Fatal Consequences

Book 3.5: Fatal Destiny, *the Wedding Novella*

Book 4: Fatal Flaw

Book 5: Fatal Deception

Book 6: Fatal Mistake

Book 7: Fatal Jeopardy

Book 8: Fatal Scandal

Book 9: Fatal Frenzy

Book 10: Fatal Identity

Book 11: Fatal Threat

Book 12: Fatal Chaos

Book 13: Fatal Invasion

Book 14: Fatal Reckoning

Book 15: Fatal Accusation *(Coming Soon!)*

Single Title

The Wreck

ABOUT THE AUTHOR

Marie Force is the *New York Times* bestselling author of contemporary romance, including the indie-published Gansett Island Series and the Fatal Series from Harlequin Books. In addition, she is the author of the Butler, Vermont Series, the Green Mountain Series and the erotic romance Quantum Series.
Duchess By Deception is the first in her new historical romance Gilded Series, that will continue with *Deceived By Desire* in September 2019.

Her books have sold more than 7.5 million copies worldwide, have been translated into more than a dozen languages and have appeared on the *New York Times* bestseller list 29 times. She is also a *USA Today* and *Wall Street Journal* bestseller, a Speigel bestseller in Germany, a frequent speaker and publishing workshop presenter as well as a publisher through her Jack's House Publishing romance imprint. She is a three-time nominee for the Romance Writers of America's RITA® award for romance fiction.

Her goals in life are simple—to finish raising two happy, healthy, productive young adults, to keep writing books for as long as she possibly can and to never be on a flight that makes the news.

Join Marie's mailing list on her website at marieforce.com for news about new books and upcoming appearances in your area. Follow her on Facebook at www.Facebook.com/MarieForceAuthor, on Twitter @marieforce and on Instagram at www.instagram.-com/marieforceauthor/. Contact Marie at marie@marieforce.com.